T0146554

Footsteps

The Numerous Battles of
Survival Bonding Childhood Friends
Throughout New York City's Frenzied 1970s

FRANK JOHN AITA

authorHOUSE®

AuthorHouse™
1663 Liberty Drive
Bloomington, IN 47403
www.authorhouse.com
Phone: 1 (800) 839-8640

Published by AuthorHouse 05/08/2017

ISBN: 978-1-5246-7143-3 (sc)
ISBN: 978-1-5246-7141-9 (hc)
ISBN: 978-1-5246-7142-6 (e)

Library of Congress Control Number: 2017902110

Print information available on the last page.

Contents

Preface

1978

Yes, there are two paths you can go by,
But in the long run there's
Still time to change the road you're on.
And it makes me wonder.
—"Stairway to Heaven" performed by Led Zeppelin

Frank, write what you know.
—James Feely

"Father, it's been about five years since my last confession." The young penitent blessed himself then continued. "I ..." Examining the tight surroundings of the wooden confessional box, the remorseful teen experienced for the first time in his seventeen years the precise meaning of claustrophobia. "Sorry, Father, it's been awhile."

The priest understood the young man's angst. *The boy has a heavy heart, and he would like to cleanse for Christmas—guilt ridden, guilt driven.* From the teen's voice and what he could guess of his size through the confessional screen, the priest figured the penitent was about seventeen years old, no more than eighteen. *Two days before Christmas, the boy wants a clean conscience for the holiday, like so many others tonight—the usual quick fix for the seasonal Catholics.*

"Continue, son. Please go on." The priest yawned wearily as he watched the teen nervously tug on a silver chain hung around his neck. The priest's thoughts shamelessly drifted to the short story *How the Grinch*

Stole Christmas, which he read to his niece the night before. *Sister put out a pre-Christmas dinner with plenty of—*

"I think … I know I must have broken every commandment … one way or another over the past few years, but it is the one—well, really two—brutal acts I did not stop. I could have. It's why I'm here tonight." Blowing into his wet, reddened hands, the penitent proceeded to wipe the dampness from his forehead. "I know I'm too late now; there's no way for me to fix either one. Or myself."

The priest's daydream of horseradish-smothered kielbasa followed by a cold beer vanished. He had not expected this revelation from the teen behind the screen. The Grinch and his Grinchy shenanigans would have to wait for a second reading; the young penitent present was the perplexed character in tonight's tale.

"Tell me, why would you say that?" the priest asked. With no response, the sustained silence filled the confessional booth. Fearing he might lose the penitent's readiness, the priest gave a nod. "Please, son, go on. You have come to God; let me be His ears." The priest waited a few moments for the teen to respond but only heard sniffles. Wondering whether the penitent was fighting a cold or beginning to cry, the priest gave a few encouraging words. "Please, son, I am here to guide you, to help you." Through the mesh screen, he watched the penitent's head bow. "You feel like giving up, as if your world is over, but remember why you held on this long." The sniveling stopped, and the priest sensed a sudden burst of confidence through the confessional screen as the teen raised his head.

"Why I held on so long? I don't know." The teen gently touched his chain from behind his neck, feeling for its security. "Father, I have dreams in grayness. I am with people of my past, but I am always alone. I watch everyone go on by me, but I'm stuck doing nothing with nothing." The penitent sighed heavily, not waiting for the priest's response. Standing from his kneeling position, the penitent blessed himself. "Why did I hold on so long? I don't know." He stood up quickly and escaped the confinement of the confessional booth, momentarily leaving his guilt behind.

Shocked at the lively response of the penitent, the priest staggered out of the confessional booth to stop the teen from … what? *God forgive me. What just happened?* Leaning forward, he tripped on his robe and stumbled into the next penitent, who was already entering the confessional cubicle. Knocking the older and stockier lady back into the side of a pew, the priest stopped to help his heavyset parishioner back to a standing position. "I am sorry, ma'am. Please wait here. I will return shortly." The priest's tone was short because of the time he lost thanks to the blocking fullback.

Looking at the fear and concern in her pastor's eyes, Miss Fullback, for once, had no word or complaints; she could only nod with assurance. Before adjusting her bonnet, she watched her priest half sprint out of his church. She sarcastically thought, *Is the Pope in town?* Miss Fullback adjusted her scarf and tight bra before kneeling down to pray. She placed her fat rear cheeks against the pew while her swollen knees rested on the kneeler. It was her half-assed way of kneeling. She then blessed herself and began to abolish her most recent sin. *Forgive me, Lord. I know the Pope is not really in town.*

He's gone, the priest thought. And as he opened the church's main doorway onto the street, he decided his hunch was correct. *The boy is gone. What did I say? What was his rush? Why did he come here in the first place?* Thinking, incorrectly, that the teen had escaped, the priest carefully stepped out onto the snow-packed entrance of the church. It was then that he recognized the teen penitent sprinting between two parked cars. "Young man! Wait, don't go!" Surprised to see the teen crossing the street only now, the priest tried one last time to corral the fugitive. "Son, wait. We need to talk!"

Without looking back, the teen hurried his footsteps to a jog. A block later, the penance seeker disappeared from the priest's sight and vanished into the shadows of a Brooklyn park.

The priest stood bewildered on the snow-covered entranceway to his church, not knowing what to do next. The northern wind of the winter evening awoke the pastor from his stupor. *How did I lose him, and where is he off to?* Recalling their short conversation word for word, he did not notice the fluctuating wind, only the tortured tone of the confused teen. *What commandments did he really break? What brutal acts did he not stop? Dreams of grayness? What is he going to do now?* The priest silently pondered the unanswered questions in the wintery cold.

After a few minutes standing in the cold, he remembered the dazed Miss Fullback inside the church; the priest did not have the energy to hear her confession just yet. *Something is wrong out here, but what?* Dumbfounded, he remained on the top step of his church's entryway with the glow of the streetlights illuminating the landscape. He watched the hurried people returning home in the early-evening flurries—moms and dads, friends and neighbors, all carrying gifts. The priest frowned to himself for a moment, recalling a line from last night's reading of *The Grinch*. *"Carrying their packages, boxes and bags …" Now, what rhymed with bags?* Combing the street, he became unsettled for a moment. *Something is off here, but what?*

The priest took two careful steps into the freshly fallen snow of his church's stoop. To his left was the gated area with the stone statues of the Blessed Mother tutoring three young children, all four enduring the snow with their endless expressions. To the right of the entrance, toward the bevy of holiday patrons, stood the manger. *Darn it, it's right in front of me, but where?* As with the Blessed Mary and her pupils, the manger and its inhabitants were blanketed with about an inch of fresh, virgin snow.

Distracted momentarily by the screams of children laughing as they tossed snowballs at one another, the priest watched with admiration. *The children are carefree and innocent.* He noticed a boy about eight years old with a green Jets hat slip and fall. He rose quickly and continued dodging the onslaught of snowballs. *Nothing else new going on out here. Time to finish up with Miss Fullback.* Before reentering the church to hear his next confession, he watched a snowball splatter against the head of Balthazar; it nearly decapitated the black king. "Boys, boys, it's over. Move on now."

Among giggles, one child shouted out to his friends. "Did you see that shot? I hit Spooky right in the nozzle." Additional laughter rose as the boys ran off in the same direction of the lost penitent.

The park is a popular location tonight. The priest began to shake the snow from his shoes as déjà vu struck. *"And the Grinch, with his Grinch-feet ice-cold in the snow. Stood puzzling and puzzling: How could it be so? It came without ribbons! It came without tags! It came without packages, boxes, or bags!"* Completing the missing verse, his wonder overtook his total oblivion.

The priest reasoned that it must have snowed for the past two hours, generating about an inch on the sidewalk, street, and so on. With the ruffians, shoppers, and traffic mushing most of the white powder, there would be few unsoiled places. Inside the gated area of the church would be one of them. *This is off. I have somehow overlooked something.* "With his Grinch-feet ice-cold in the snow ... ice-cold in the snow ..."

He followed the footprints of the teen exiting the church; the imprints did not lead directly outside the church's gate to the sidewalk. Instead, the steps of the teen took a detour to the right toward the church's manger. From his standpoint, the priest could see the back of the wooden manger and the snow-marred Balthazar with his companion kings holding treasured gifts. The penitent's footprints went somewhere to the front before leaving the church's gated entrance. *Those are his footprints, and they are fresh! What was the teen doing at the manger? Did he take something? Or stay for a quick prayer before I came outside?*

The priest carefully walked down the seven stone steps of the church to examine his manger. The ox, cow, and shepherd were all in place. A kneeling Mother Mary and a standing Saint Joseph were on either side of the makeshift cradle. Inside the baby's crib were the open arms of Jesus with His wide-eyed smile. The priest realized how unrealistic this scene would have been. As the snow began to bluster around the iconic plastic statuettes, an uncovered baby Jesus would surely freeze to death on a night like this.

All is in place; all is good. Before walking back to a patient Miss Fullback, the priest flipped on the nightlight inside the manger. He'd changed the bulb last week from a white light to a yellow one, creating the illusion of firelight casting its warm glow on the exposed Savior. *Let's see how it looks in its first snow. Will baby Jesus be cozier?* The new light did create a warmer hue, as he had deduced. *The baby is still exposed, but the light transmits a kinder atmosphere.*

The priest had assumed correctly; the penitent had stood before baby Jesus, as the footprints indicated. *He must have prayed for a second or two before running off.* The priest wiped some of the blowing snow from Jesus's forehead. Bending over to do so, he noticed a metallic reflection from the baby's chest. Slouching forward, he removed a silver chain from the baby's neck. Dangling from the bottom of the chain was a Christ-head charm.

The snow remained steady as the wind increased. The priest had to wipe the weather's moisture from his eyes. *There is something written on its back.* Feeling the inscription but unable to read it in the yellow light, the priest walked outside the gated area onto the sidewalk under a bright, white streetlight. Unaware of a new group of children tossing snow, the priest wiped the moisture away from his brow with his sleeve, uttering the single-word inscription out loud. "Donny."

Chapter 1

1973

We must learn to live together as brothers
or perish together as fools.
—Martin Luther King Jr.

The echoing bells of Saint Stanislaus Kostka Church began to ring for Sunday's ten o'clock morning mass. Last minute arrivals elevated their paces, eager not to be spotted arriving to mass late. The men sported three piece suits and smoked cigarettes, while the women showcased knee-length dresses with fancy polished footwear. In their haste, the sound of the lady's high heels clunking on the concrete sidewalk, resembled the pounding of thoroughbred race horses.

A portion of the steeplechase competing to hear the morning sermon raced through Winthrop Park in the northern end of Brooklyn, New York. Built on nine acres of land, the park was a stone's throw away from the Catholic church. In the park's center, the thirty-foot-tall Shelter Pavilion stood towering over its neighbor, a statue of the archangel Gabriel, which stood at the pavilion's gate. To the northwest of the messenger of God was the children's playground. Ball fields and grassy areas comprised the rest of the park. People from the northeastern end of the neighborhood used Winthrop to shorten their Sunday morning journeys to mass.

With the second week of October coming to an end, the brown leaves brought on by the coolness of autumn began to litter the pathways and grassy fields inside the eighty-year-old park. Kneeling on his right knee near the border of the southern meadow, a desperate Johnny pled his case.

"Tommy, you come around me from the right side. I'll fake you the handoff, but I'll follow you to the hole." Tommy and the other players inside the huddle nodded and murmured agreement with Johnny's play-calling. "But this time, Donny will fall behind me from the left side, and I'll flip him the ball." Looking at Bain for support, Johnny continued. "Donny, just keep running down the sidelines, and Bain will pull from his center position to be there in case this doesn't fool all of 'em." Johnny could see Bain smile behind his face mask.

"Wait a second. You gonna trust this little skid with the game?" a flabbergasted Tommy protested while shaking his head in disbelief. Tommy searched for support from his teammates but found none. In frustration, he then grabbed Donny's shirt. "You better not screw this up. I don't care where you are off to." Tommy spat on the dirt, waiting for the other players to disagree with Johnny. *This ain't gonna work,* he thought, *and they all know it, too.*

"Tommy, cut the shit." Johnny focused back on Bain. "Let them through to me; I'll take the hits." Johnny peered between Joey and Kevin to see how the defenders were placed. "You pull to where Donny will be running," Johnny reminded Bain, the team's best blocker. "Junior, he's the one you gotta watch out for. As for the rest of yous, find someone—anyone—and hit 'em."

Tommy offered heartening parting words to his wide-eyed, eleven-year-old teammate. "Donny, stop twiddling your fingers. You're getting the ball, you baby, and you better not screw this up."

"Don't listen to him. You can do it," Porky whispered encouragingly to his wavering teammate.

"Okay, hike on one. Break," Johnny yelled.

Then as the huddle broke, Donny ran to Johnny for a little guidance. Johnny whispered down at his younger protégé, giving him a wink and a smile. "Who's better than us?"

Hearing only *who's* and *better*, Donny recognize the phrase. "Nobody!" he shouted. Not wanting to let his team or Johnny down, Donny hurried to his position on the field. Lining up on the outside of the offensive line, Donny assumed the tight end position. On his right crouched Porky, with Shanty playing guard, and Bain at center position.

Bain wanted to beat the Huron Street Hogs, but more importantly, he craved another opportunity to crush their biggest and strongest opponent, Junior. For Bain, football was an individual sport. *Hey, we lost today, but I did good. Did you see how I knocked him on his ass?* Bain placed his right hand on the football as it lay on the torn grass. With his left hand on the dirt, Bain spied back to where Porky and Donny parted to their respective positions. *Look at his eyes. Donny is scared shitless.* Knowing he must hike the ball and run his ass off in the opposite direction as Johnny and the rest of the team to block anyone who may not be duped by Johnny's ploy, Bain gripped the pigskin tightly in anticipation. *Okay, Donny my boy, I got your back. No one will touch you, and you might even win the game for us after all.* Bain bent forward and stared downward, squeezing the football as he waited for Johnny to yell hike!

Donny rubbed his nervous hands together and gazed forward, waiting for the "hike on one" audible from his quarterback.

On the defensive side on the field, Junior, the heaviest and quickest player on either team, stood at the middle linebacker position for the Huron Street Hogs. He waited impatiently for the ball to be snapped. "Come on, Johnny, let's get it on already!" Junior shouted. Then he yelled commands to his defending line. "Watch the ball hog"—he pointed at Johnny with his dirty index finger—"and Fagan, watch the queer. Tommy is going deep; don't let him get a step on you." Fagan put his hand up to signify it was understood. *That's all they have, Johnny running or Johnny throwing to Tommy. Same shit, same results, Johnny-boy.* It was not until Junior saw Donny—*the little shit*—blowing into his hands, that he became concerned. *Normally that freak plays with his fingers never touching the ball. Why is he stretching out his hands?* Junior's cracked lips grinned, yielding a trickle of blood onto his chinstrap. *Johnny-boy, what are you trying to pull here?*

"Hike!" Between Bain's thighs, the football surged upward to Johnny's open palms. As planned, Tommy raced from the right side as Johnny faked him the handoff. The defensive line followed Tommy into an insignificant hole. Meanwhile, Donny scampered from the tight end position to behind Johnny and caught the backward pass perfectly. Starting from the left side of the field, Donny cradled the football while the offensive and defensive lines collided on the trick play. Donny sprinted uncontested up the field to the open right flank with his prized possession.

Seeing Donny turn back and run behind Johnny piqued Junior's curiosity. *That smart-ass Johnny-boy, depending on the scrawny crapper to do his dirty work.* Junior watched Donny catch the backward toss and race to the open field. *Well, this is where I knock you into tomorrow … and win.* Zeroing in on his mark, Junior ran with abandon to dislodge the football from the runner. *See ya!* Before Junior could make the crushing game-saving and game-ending tackle, a blur from the corner of his helmet introduced an unexpected guest. *Shit … Bain.* Too late to lower his shoulder pad for protection, Junior had one last thought before unconsciousness captured him. *Johnny-boy, you're good!*

Eating dirt lying face down on the ground, buried under the opposing team's defensive players, Johnny could hear Porky yelling jubilantly, followed by Kevin's outburst. Pushing the fallen bodies from both teams off of him, Johnny found his footing and watched Donny cross the goal line for the winning score. *Holy shit! I don't believe it. It really worked.* Johnny dashed down the field to join his reveling teammates. Santiago

"Shanty" and Kevin already had Donny on their shoulders shouting out a victory roar. *Perfect, perfect. I can't believe it worked!* Johnny caught up to Tommy and Joey. "See, what'd I tell yous." Johnny playfully pushed Tommy sideways. "That kid," a teary-eyed Johnny exclaimed, pointing at Donny, "is good!" Beaming, Johnny cried out up to Donny. "Hey, who's better than us?"

Donny's one-word ecstatic reply: "Nobody!"

Laughing with disbelief, Joey half jumped up to smack Donny's helmet playfully. Landing on his handicapped leg, Joey distanced himself from the usual sharpness of pain to celebrate in their victory. "Hey, you. We should always run ya." Limping badly, Joey continued to pump his fist in the air.

As the revel continued, a key player was missing from the celebration, Shanty noticed. "Bain!" Turning around toward midfield, he called a second time. "Come on, we did it!"

Bain stood over a dazed Junior, with Fagan, Dylan, and the remainder of the Huron Street Hogs standing nearby. With his helmet in his fist, Bain thrust his dirty knuckles at Fagan before jogging over to his partying teammates. "Hey, we did it!" Bain exclaimed loudly but with little emotion. "Donny, you shit, you owe me one." Bain chuckled and then jumped into the inner circle of his friends as they all carried an elated Donny off the field.

Ten minutes after freeing Donny from their shoulders, the winning Humboldt Street Hawks finished stripping off their equipment. Johnny was aware of the hit Bain delivered to Junior and knew the Huron Street Hogs did not take losing or being "put to the ground" lightly.

"What did they say to you?" Johnny asked as he watched Bain tie his torn white Converse All-Stars high-tops.

"Nothin' much." Without raising his head, Bain went on. "You know, same old shit with them." *They won't learn until we beat the crap out of 'em,* he thought to himself. "Besides, today is Donny's last; let's make the most of it."

Johnny shook his head in agreement.

Good way to change the subject. I think Johnny-boy bought it, Bain thought.

After the last-minute victory over the Huron Street Hogs, the winning Hawks, apart from Santiago, changed their clothes on a bench parallel to the football field. They were unaware and unconcerned of the dirty looks from the parishioners returning home after morning mass. Santiago was different. He had scruples, as Bain would say. He was not from Brooklyn.

~~~~~~~

Santiago had been born in Cuba in 1961. His mother had fled her island country with Santiago the following year to escape the incoming Castro regime. It had been a punishing decision for Santiago's parents to either divide their family—their two sons—in half or sacrifice their whole family as one. Neither choice was correct, but the possibility of freedom for one child tilted the torn parent's resolve. Santiago's father and lone brother were forced to live in Cuba under the communist rule. Santiago and his mother fled oppression to appreciate the liberties and opportunities of America, while Santiago's father and older brother endured a lifetime of tyranny.

As of his eleventh birthday, the only family or friend Santiago had ever known and trusted was his mother—that was, until he helped a fellow student in the boys' bathroom at school. Santiago did not think much of the incident at the time, but had meant a lot to a certain schoolmate. Santiago had simply kept his mouth instinctively shut and refused to report what had happened to the toilet bowl. Bain was suspected, but

Santiago heard his mother's repeated warnings from the old country. "Never tell on another, Santiago. Son, mind your business and move on. You may regret words, son, but never your silence."

Santiago was one of only four "spics" in Bain's classroom. Cuban descent was a bit more exotic than a Puerto Rican, but he was still a "spic." Surviving the rule of a dictatorship held no merit and inspired no trust of the fleeing refugee. Santiago, pegged a *refugee*, sustained his muteness to the outside world and believed in no one, until Bain demolished the toilet bowl.

For his loyalty, Santiago was given the nickname of *Shanty* and gained Bain's absolute protection. You mess with Shanty, and you were messing with Bain. The classroom bullying subsided. Bain let Shanty be a part of his inner circle. Shortly afterward, he and Johnny began to call on Shanty to play ball with the gang. Although the biggest and, most likely, the strongest, Shanty lacked the hand-eye coordination to be a good athlete because of his early childhood isolation. His shyness and lifelong desire to fit in was quickly replaced with good humor and the tolerance of others, be they friend or foe. Shanty enjoyed the pranks of his newfound friends while holding on to the scruples his mother had driven into him. For when it was time to change out of muddied football clothes in a public park, Shanty, unlike his exposed teammates, hid behind an old oak tree for privacy.

Wiping his brow with one hand, Shanty put the other onto the oak tree for support. *What's that smell?* Shanty searched around the tree with one shoelace untied. *Oh man, my lace almost landed in that.* Looking down, he saw the cause of the unpleasant aroma—dog shit. "Hey guys, look how disgusting this is," he called out, pointing behind the tree as he scampered closer to the bench area. "I'm changing here. That shit is way too sickening."

Kevin and Joey, the first to arrive, both giggled and then quickly took a few steps backward. Tommy, the slowest to change clothing, was still shirtless. He investigated what was so funny. "That's not dog shit; its human!"

"Human?"

"Human what?"

"Shit, asshole. Human shit!" Tommy replied. Picking up a nearby stick, he took a stab at the fecal matter.

Porky joined in the chorus of laughter while watching Tommy impale the human residue.

"Porky, what are you sniggering about? We could have lost today because you suck." Elevating the human shit on his stick, Tommy playfully waged the fecal harpoon in the direction of his nemesis. Donny, Johnny, and Bain now joined in on the ruckus. "Just watch yourself, or I'll make you eat this," Tommy boastfully warned Porky while carefully waving the contaminated stick. A couple in their mid-forties dressed in their Sunday best, followed by their two daughters, scurried to the opposite side of the pathway to sidestep the "Tommy Show."

"Hey, you dropped a few passes yourself," Porky egged Tommy on. *The best defense is a good offense,* he thought.

"Oh yeah?" Without warning or intention, the human mother lode slid off the stick Tommy waved, hitting Porky's right thigh.

"Holy shit!" Tommy exclaimed, shocked. Not knowing what to say or do next, Tommy tossed the shitty stick into the grass.

"Ha-ha. Oh man, Porky's got homeless cooties," Bain wailed. Soon Kevin and Joey joined in.

Only one person was in more shock than Tommy, that being Porky. Standing with his arms out and mouth wide open, Porky had no words.

He only conceded to the humiliation. *Revenge, sacrifice, and respect,* he thought. *Wrong sequence. Revenge will have to be second.* No longer hearing the laughter of his friends or observing the wince on Tommy's face, Porky bent downward. Tommy, not understanding Porky's ploy, could only stare blankly. With his right index finger and thumb, Porky, to the horror of the spectators, picked up the human turd. Tommy, still in wonder, could only watch, unable to connect quickly enough to anticipate Porky's next nasty step. *Sacrifice, revenge, respect.* Cocking his arm back, Porky realized he was unsure how to throw his cootie missile. *As a football or baseball?*

Oh shit! Tommy didn't plan to find out how Porky will throw the human shit. He blindly spun about-face. Bumping into an old lady as she walked her dog, Tommy stumbled sideways into the wooden bench. The old lady fell back a step, using her dog's tugging leash for balance. Mumbling something in Polish to the dog, the shocked Pole side-stepped the commotion and hauled her ass away.

The delay caused by the old lady's unintentional interference was all the time Porky required to get his throw on target. *No football or baseball toss; the turd is shaped like neither. It is more like a rocket. Darts anyone?* Taking aim as if shooting for a bull's eye, Porky focused and then pointed the human shit. *Thump.* Too young to play for the local bar dart league, Porky was gratified merely hitting Tommy's bare left shoulder. *Not a bull's eye, but I do get points for that shot, don't I?"*

That wasn't the shit. Please God! That wasn't human shit … that wasn't … Porky you are dead! Tommy stopped running and clenched his fists to pound Porky. "You're dead!"

Johnny and Shanty quickly jumped in between a screaming Tommy and the nonchalant, grinning Porky. Johnny motioned to the others for some assistance. Donny, Joey, and Kevin grabbed Porky by his arms and lead him out onto the middle of the football field. Bain worked his way around the clutter of the helmets and pads to squeeze Tommy's arm, careful not to be near the "cootie shoulder."

"No way, man, he's dead," Tommy shouted, shaking his head. "He threw shit on me, man."

With a smirk, Bain added, "Human shit." Tommy gave Bain a frozen look. "Come on. I'm only playing." Bain turned to Johnny. "We gotta book." He grabbed Tommy's right shoulder. "This is the shitless shoulder, right?" Tommy nods, missing Bain's sarcasm. "Go home and wash it. Then we gotta get going."

Johnny nodded. "It's Donny's last day. Enough of this shit already." Johnny waved to Porky to come over. Johnny's focus went back to Tommy. "You did start it; now end it."

Slowing his breathing, Tommy began to protest.

"Damn it, Tommy, it's not about you today," Johnny pleaded.

Tommy saw Donny standing off to the side by himself holding the game-winning football. *Soon he'll be all alone. Porky, I'll get you later.* Tommy agreed by shaking his head. "Okay, Johnny. You guys can let go of me now."

"Swear to God." Bain demanded. "This is over now."

"Yeah … yeah, I swear." Tommy sniffled, his face hot with anger.

"Come on, guys." Johnny yelled for Porky to shake hands with Tommy.

Porky walked back to the shit-tossing ring and gave a little smile, happy the incident was ending. *Sacrifice, revenge, respect. All three complete.*

"Only for Donny, 'cause any other day I'd kill you," Tommy said. *I'm not done with you yet, asshole.*

"Okay, let's get a move on."

Porky put his hand out to shake Tommy's. Without thought, Tommy extended his own hand and then stopped himself. "That's his throwing hand! No way, guys. He's disgusting." Everyone laughed, as all were in agreement about Porky's personal hygiene.

~~~~~~~

Tommy and Johnny's families were considered middle class, as their parents owned individual homes on Humboldt Street, a tree-lined block around the corner from Winthrop Park and one block north of Saint Stanislaus Kostka Church. The homes built on the one-way street were constructed at the turn of the twentieth century. The two-family brownstones, all attached to one another, each contained a stoop to the second floor and a gated space below. The "areaway," as it was known, was protected by a half-foot iron fence in front of the empty forty-square-foot space. Facing any of the homes, to the left rear of each areaway is a door leading to the basement apartment. Two below-ground-level windows reflected the shadows of the shared chained trash cans stationed inside. Rallying on the top five steps of Tommy's stoop was this Sunday's winning football team, all waiting for their friend to scrub off human shit.

"Man, what a game today," Kevin repeated for the tenth time. "I think once Junior gets outta the coma and comes to, he's gonna be pissed they lost."

"Screw that! He knew what happened; he laid there playing dumb," chimed in Joey.

Shanty sat on the top step of the stoop. He tossed the football to a heedless Johnny. Johnny saw the blurred pass in his peripheral vision, but he could only duck the football.

"Hey, man, what you doin'?"

"You looked like Porky trying to catch the ball," Bain said with a chuckle. He picked up the football laying at Johnny's foot and whipped it in the direction of Shanty. Then in a low, serious tone, he asked, "John, what's up?"

Johnny shrugged his shoulders. "Well, for one"—he motioned for Bain to follow him away from the others on the stoop, particularly Donny—"where is Nicole? She was supposed to be here by now." Johnny watched Kevin toss Shanty the football, narrowly missing Donny's head. "The store is open at noon, and I wanted to give it to him before we left."

"What else?" Bain said, blowing off Johnny's concern for Nicole and her whereabouts.

"Tonight, I know, is gonna be shitty."

Bain nodded in agreement.

"And what was goin' on with Fagan and them before?"

Bain took the bottom of his dirty, white T-shirt and wiped away the sweat below his two eye sockets. Bain answered both of Johnny's questions. "The girls will be here by five after, I'll bet you." Bain pointed to the church clock; it was 11:45 a.m. "Fagan, Junior, the brothers, and the rest of them are and always will be a bunch wise-asses."

"Yeah, yeah, but still, they're getting worse."

Pushing Johnny toward a parked car, Bain announced. "Guys! Donny had the winning score, but let's not forget Johnny here called that play!" Everyone resonated in agreement. Johnny's face turned red, and for the moment, he forgot his second question.

Wanting to remove the attention from himself, Johnny thrust off of the car quickly and clapped his hands over Bain's head. "Look, I'm open."

Kevin riffled the football in the direction of the slapping sound. Kevin's arm was strong, but his accuracy was an issue, as the football arrived belt high. To Johnny's surprise, Bain sidestepped the missile, leaving Johnny open to a direct hit to his crotch.

"Ooh, you suck! My balls!" Laughing in pain, Johnny bowed over. "My balls. Oh, you shit. You asshole." Bain patted his friend on the back, picked up the ball from Johnny's feet, and then tossed it to Donny.

"You should take credit a little better."

〜〜〜〜〜〜

Inside of her right palm, Nicole held the Christ-head charm. Handing it back to the jeweler, she shook her head in dissatisfaction. "This won't do." Taking a deep breath, Nicole looked over to her friend for additional support, but Gina was admiring her new red boots. "Gina! Yo, help me out here."

Gina liked the way her heal rose up inside the shiny leather boot. Twisting her ankle from side to side, Gina was positive her ass would complement the tightness of her legs. "Let me see it." Taking the charm from Nicole, Gina blew through her red-lipsticked lips onto the front of the Christ-head. Wiping off the moisture of her breath with the tissue stationed on the glass counter, Gina shrugged both shoulders. "Well, the face is good." She then flipped the charm to its backside to read the engraving. "Oh yeah, this is a shitty job." Checking out the jeweler for the first time, Gina figured the lady was about fifty. She was a tad overweight but sported an expensive hairdo along with a pricier manicure. Her dress was too tight, and she wore a perfume that smelled like it was obtained from some crematory pyre. *Lady, don't shit on us*, Gina thought.

Unhappy to be working on a Sunday and very displeased to be serving these two callous young teens, the jeweler pled her case diplomatically.

"There is nothing wrong with this." She reached her hand out for Gina to return the charm. "I wrote what you asked for," she said, turning the charm front to back and then back again.

Gina looked down to her new boots one last time before talking. *I love this color red,* she thought, *it matches my lips.* "Here, this is the problem," she said, taking the Christ head from the jeweler and turning it back to the inscription. "See, this is what my friend was complaining about." Gina smiled over at Nicole. *I'm getting there, Nicky. I'm getting there.* "It says *D* and then *onny.* You have to connect it all together. It's one word." Harshly, the jeweler grabbed the charm from Gina and thumped her high-heeled shoes to the back room. Gina whispered to Nicole. "You see the size of that lady? Those poor heels." Gina then returned her attention to her own red-leather boots.

Nicole huffed out air. She could only shake her head in disbelief.

"Vroom, vroom. Aw, this ain't goin' nowhere." Turning the fire engine's steering wheel from left to right and then back, Billy cannot increase the truck's movement. "This sucks."

"Hey, watch your mouth. If you don't, I will," Nicole said as she stepped out of the jewelry store carrying a small white bag. Gina giggled behind her. Without turning around, Nicole uttered her position. "Don't encourage the brat."

"Get me out! Angie, get me out," Billy said.

Angela straightened up from leaning against a parked car and stealthily walked across the sidewalk to the children's fire engine ride where the whining Billy sat strapped inside. With upstretched arms, Billy smiled. He then glanced over to his older sister but whispered to Angela. "Thanks."

Angela unbuckled the four-year-old before placing him onto the pavement. "There you go." She knelt down to be eye level with the young boy. "What happened? You didn't like the ride, Billy?"

Billy shook his head and ran to his sister. Placing his hand into her closed fist, he looked to see what she was gripping. "What you got there?" Nicole jerked her wrist away from her nosy brother. Billy lost interest. *It's not cool … too small for me.* He ran quickly back to Angela, placing his hand into her warm, tender palm. "Aw, that ride sucks. It is a baby one."

Giving her brother the evil eye, Nicole offered the youngster some advice. "It's not what you say that matters; it is how you say it."

Billy didn't understand his sister's scolding, so he turned his head into the side of Angela's waist for defense. *I wish I had a brother. Yeah, Bain would be a good one.*

Out of Billy's earshot, Gina softly whispered to Nicole. "He's a bit of a wise-ass because he takes after you." When she received no response from Nicole, Gina realized she may have crossed her friend and her swift temper. She quickly changed the subject to the boys and Manhattan. "The guys must be done playing. I know they want to give this before going off to the city."

Angela felt Billy's hand loosen, so she gave the small child a playful little squeeze. Billy gave Angela a quizzical stare. Angela returned the puzzled look with a smile, and then she asked Nicole to see the newly purchased charm.

"Wow, it's nice … and holy?" Turning the Christ-head around, she read the one-word inscription. "Nice. Who's idea was it to get this for him?" Before anyone could answer, Angela continued, "It's so unlike those guys."

With a laugh, Gina ran from Nicole's right side to her left and stood next to Angela. "Angie, you may be new to this party, but they are all so immature, starting with Tommy and Kevin." Gina took the charm from Angela and checked the inscription on the back closely before returning it.

With a chuckle, Angela nodded her head in agreement. "But still, how did they come up with this?" She placed the charm back into its box and then into the white bag, handing it over to Nicole. "Was it you?"

Nicole shook her head. "Nope, it was all Johnny." Then with an exaggerated sigh, she added, "There's a limited vision with Johnny. I can only hope they all mature."

"I'll second that!" Gina laughed and gave her ass a little rehearsal wiggle. *I want them to notice these new red boots, or better yet, notice me in them.*

～～～～～～

"Hey, cootie boy, it's about time." Joey jumped off the stoop before Tommy could throw a cheap punch at him. Stealing the football from an unassuming Donny, Joey motioned for Shanty to go deep. "Broadway Joe has a man open down field, but wait, here comes Deacon Jones." Joey dodged the cootie boy and tossed the ball to Shanty.

"Let's get moving. We'll see the girls later." Johnny was referencing the surprise gift they all had bought Donny. "We have but one last day with our star running back." He messed up Donny's hair with his right hand and then faked a stomach shot to his friend's belly.

Donny overreacted to the playful gimmick.

"Come on, kid, you can't still fall for that," Johnny said. Donny smiled back, but his eyes painted a horrific picture. Johnny dismissed for the moment the distress in his friend's expression. *He knows I would never hit him. Why would Donny be so afraid?*

Not finding her friends or the boys in the park, Tori walked her newly purchased puppy to Humboldt Street, hoping to be around when Donny received his going-away present. Seeing Shanty and Joey playing catch with a football in the street, as well as the others on Tommy's stoop, Tori sighed with comfort.

"Yo, Tori, where are they? It's almost twelve thirty, and we gotta get goin'." Bain bent down to pet her Shih Tzu's head. "Come here, pooch." He vigorously scratched the dog's chest, trying to create an aggressive reaction.

"Hey, easy with her," Tori chided Bain, pulling the dog chain back. "Her name is Bella, and don't be so rough."

"Just toughening the pooch up a bit." Bain bent down and petted Bella gently. "Well, where are they?"

"They'll be here. Maybe the store opened up late. It is Sunday." Tori used a free hand to brush her long, black hair away from her forehead. "Here, Bain, take her for a sec. I've got something to show yous." She handed Bella's chain off and then reached inside her shoulder bag. "Look, a camera, my mom's Polaroid."

Bain was amazed at the sight before him—not of the instant camera but of the rare instance of Tori smiling.

"Good idea, right?" Tori said.

Joey and a freshly showered Tommy came over to Tori and Bain and the rest of the guys followed. "Cool, take a picture of this." Joey held the football above his head as if to throw.

Interrupting Joey's Joe Namath moment, Kevin yelled out the obvious, pointing to the end of the block. "They're here!"

Bain punched Kevin's shoulder at half strength, but it was nevertheless enough to hurt. "What's the matter with you? You're screaming in my damn ear." Kevin bumped into Porky before quietly rubbing his bruised shoulder.

"Okay, easy everyone," Johnny called out to Bain. Shifting the subject to Donny, Johnny requested no further distractions. "Nicky, thanks."

Smiling proudly, Nicole extended her right arm toward Johnny, handing him the white bag. Feeling her warm skin on his dirty knuckles, Johnny awkwardly jerked his arm back, almost dropping the present.

"Donny! Yo, Donny, over here." Donny remained on the stoop with young Billy and Shanty.

"Like this, Billy." Donny put his palm out for Billy to slap. "Give me five." Billy slapped Donny's opened hand enthusiastically. "Now on the dark side." Donny turned his hand over, exposing the dorsal surface. "Ouch! You are one strong kid." Shaking his hand in exaggerated agony, Donny playfully knuckled Billy's chin before running toward Johnny.

Bain was now holding the small box while Johnny punted the empty white bag into the street. "Everyone come here," he said. Shanty and Angela were the last two to enter the expanding circle; Billy had already squeezed through. "Donny, this is from everyone here." He nodded toward Nicole and Gina. "All the girls, too."

Donny stood next to Shanty as Bella sniffed his leg. Twirling his dancing fingers around one another in a nervous waltz, Donny could not voice a word.

It was Billy who disrupted the awkward silence. "Look, Bella's going wee, wee." He pointed to Tommy's left sneaker, where Bella squatted in the urinating stance.

18

"What the …" Tommy recoiled his marked sneaker. "Yuck! Tori, come on!" Stamping his foot on the sidewalk and creating a splattering sound, Tommy continued to curse and complain. "Uh, I gotta take another shower."

Johnny stopped himself from laughing long enough to quiet everyone else down. "Wait we're goin' now. Tommy, just change your sneakers. But first, Donny, open up the box."

Donny had ample time to compose himself after the show of unforeseen generosity from his friends. "Well, thanks everybody." Taking the gift from Bain, Donny removed the lid of the small box. He marveled at the silver Christ-head inside resting peacefully on soft, white cotton. "I … I … it's neat." Picking it up by the chain, Donny placed the charm in his palm.

"Turn it over," directed Nicole. Gina agreed.

Donny did and silently mouthed his name. Everyone remained silent, unsure what to say or do next. It was Donny's murmurs to himself that squashed the hush of the group. "Things are not so scary"—Donny paused for a moment and then raised his voice, addressing the numb audience—"when you guys are around."

"Hey, look, you're making Gina cry." Bain mockingly said. Slapping Donny's back, Bain went on. "Well, kid, put it on." Everyone agreed.

Donny had a hard time unhooking the chain with his nail-bitten fingertips. Angela gently took the chain from Donny and fastened the charm around his mud-spattered neck. "There you go."

Checking the clip behind his neck, Donny reassured himself of the chain's connection. "Do I wear it inside my shirt or leave it out?" Donny ran his finger along the crown of Christ.

"Best to wear it under your shirt, especially when you ride the train," Nicole reasoned. Angela stepped back and let the others review the charm before Donny could stow it beneath his shirt.

"Johnny, I'll be right back. Just need to clean this off." Tommy's anger and humiliation disappeared the moment he ran back to his house to change footwear.

While Tommy broke his promise not to shower a second time within twenty minutes, Donny, Billy, and Kevin played in the gated areaway with Bella.

"She likes to lick my fingers," Billy said. He quickly switched hands as Bella continued to lick. "I'm like the Flash!" Billy cried out, tricking Bella into kissing the air.

"Billy, you can be Superman or Batman but not the Flash," Donny said. He sat on the bottom step of the stoop, and Billy and Kevin joined him. "I'll tell you why."

"But the Flash is really, really fast," Billy said, trying to defend his superhero.

Porky jumped down into the gated area, startling the pooch. "Come on, Donny, I heard this from you before, and I still don't get it."

"That's because you're an ass," Kevin chimed in.

Billy giggled at the curse word *ass.*

"See, Billy, Batman is real because he has a utility belt with all those primo gadgets."

Billy interrupted, "Robin. Batman has Robin."

"Yes, he has Robin too."

"How you gonna make Superman real?" Kevin asked sarcastically, which Billy did not like.

"Donny knows." Billy attempted to punch Kevin's thigh but was easily stopped by Kevin's quicker hand.

"Look, Billy, I'm the Flash!" Kevin bolted into the gated area and motioned for Shanty to toss the football. "Shant, I'm open!"

"Don't listen to Kevin; he likes to tease," Porky said, attempting to shelter the youngster.

Donny went on. "Superman came from a planet where everyone was strong because of the gravity on his planet always pulling them down."

"What's gravity?"

"It's like astronauts walking on the moon. You see them bounce up and down because there is so little gravity. If there were people living on the moon, we would be supermen to them." Looking at a confused Billy, Donny shrugged his shoulders and tried to continue. "You dig?" Billy nodded, although Donny knew he'd lost him.

"It's about time!" yelled Kevin from the street when Tommy came out from his second shower of the morning. Kevin, Joey, and Shanty were tossing the football, playing monkey-in-the-middle with Shanty being the monkey. Bain and Johnny were still talking with the girls.

Not having enough time to explain superheroes, Donny had to finish his stint with Billy. "Someday I'll explain about the Flash." Donny had another thought before they left for their trip to Central Park. "Billy if you want the Flash to be true, we can do that, but let's believe in what is true."

Billy didn't understand Donny now, but later he would do his best to remember those words. *Believe in what is true.*

"Come on, Donny, let's book already," hollered Kevin.

"Wait … stop a second," Nicole shouted. "Before everybody runs out, get on the stoop for a picture." While the moans and gripes from the boys echoed in the early afternoon fall day, internally, all were keen to have eternal fame on film.

"Donny sits in the middle," Johnny barked out. "Kev, chuck him the football."

Everyone squeezed together on the upper half of the steps as Tori gave her camera to Billy and explained the simple device. "Get everyone in, and then press this."

Billy's first attempt was a throwaway, but his second shot was on target. He smiled proudly at Tori's praise, but he was disappointed that the older boys were rushing off to the subway on their way to Manhattan's Central Park. "I wish I could go. This sucks."

"Shhhh. Don't let Big Sis hear you say that," Tori warned Billy. Tori then held the snapshot above her head while waving it to speed its development. After two minutes of wagging, Tori smiled a second time. She then passed the finished photograph to Angela and Gina.

"Donny looks so happy," Angela noted.

Gina took the picture from Angela and shared it with Nicole. "We all do."

In two months, the picture of the dozen children crammed onto a Brooklyn stoop would be a keepsake for a nameless runaway living a thousand miles away.

Chapter 2

1978

…But now old friends are acting strange. They shake
their heads, they say I've changed. But something's
lost, but something's gained in living every day…
—"Both Sides Now" performed by Judy Collins

Chicken. Porky zipped up his parka for the last time. *One more step and
I'll be in. Tonight, I get my colors … and respect.* "Ma, I'm going out. I'll
see you tomorrow."

Calling from her bedroom in their three-room railroad apartment,
Porky's mother had other plans. "Whoa … wait a sec!" Mother ran
down the narrow hallway and entered the kitchen where Porky stood.
"Paulie, come with me to your grandmother's tonight. She has your
Christmas gift, and she never sees you anymore." Mother sat down at
the two-seat kitchen table to put her galoshes on. "Please, Paul, I never
see you either." She placed a plastic bag inside her boot to make it easier
to slide her sock-covered foot inside. "It's like I don't know you anymore,
and the kids you run around with these days I can't stand." *Boom.* She
stamped her boot to the ground, securing her foot's snugness.

"Ma, I gotta go." Porky, spotting his mother's displeasure, wanted to
end the repetitive conversation immediately. "We're goin' to grandma's
tomorrow … for Christmas Eve." Hearing his mother sigh, Porky had
a change of heart for an instant but thought, *I can't punk out now.
I'll never get respect, and I'll always be a chicken.* "We'll be down in
Dylan's basement playing cards and listening to music." Tugging at his

shirtsleeve inside his parka to pull it up to his wrist, Porky went on. "I'll be back early. I'll treat you; we'll go to The Greeks for a bacon-and-egg roll before goin' to Grandma's."

"Oh, Paulie, I just want the best for you." She stood up and adjusted her own winter wardrobe. "The choices you make now will be with you forever. I cannot follow you around; you are a young adult, making adult decisions."

"Ma, I gotta go."

"Wait, one last thing." After placing her hat on her head and then reaching inside her pockets for a pair of worn, black leather gloves, Porky's mother stared into her son's eyes. "You are all I have. Your father is, well … long gone, and your grandmother is very short on time." She touched her son's cheek with the back of her ungloved hand. "It's you and me, kid. Mama loves you … and will protect her cub." Taking a second scarf from her coat pocket, she placed it around Porky's neck. "It's cold outside. Wear this for me."

Not wanting to disappoint his mother anymore tonight, Porky grunted but didn't argue. "I love you too." As he raced out the door past the other apartments in the six-family building, Porky yelled his parting words to his worried mother. "Bacon and eggs at The Greeks tomorrow!"

⁓⁓⁓⁓⁓⁓

Johnny twisted off the cap of a newly bought Tango bottle. Normally, beer would do, but tonight he wanted to get wasted swiftly. *Getting stoned is pleasure for pain.* Johnny took a small gulp, enough for his taste buds to identify the orange socializing with the vodka. The second guzzle warmed his gut, and the third eased his pain.

The dwindling snow became a wind-blown dusting, forming a harsher wintry evening. It was "righto" for now, as Johnny stood beside a wood-burning garbage can in the park. Alongside were two of his cronies;

they were also absorbing the heat from the can. Tommy tossed a glance toward Johnny.

"What, Johnny, right to the hard stuff tonight?" Bain said in an offhand manner, his Marlboro cigarette bopping between his lips.

Ignoring Bain's inquiry, Johnny had his own question. "Where is everybody?" Not acknowledging Tommy's presence, Johnny went on. "I thought yous were hangin' out at Tori's house ... before tomorrow."

Chucking three pieces of wood from a broken park bench into the fire, Tommy grunted with exaggerated grief for attention. "Hey, this is the third time for me. If you guys wanna stay warm, your gonna have to break your own benches." Tommy tightened up the zipper on his coat with an ungloved hand. Taking a beer from a brown bag on the ground, he turned to Bain. "I'm done. When Angela gets back, we're goin' to Tori's."

"Yeah, we are all leavin'." Taking his cigarette out of his mouth, Bain responded to Johnny's previous statement. "Whaddaya mean by 'yous were hangin' out at Tori's?' You're goin' too." Bain's tone was one of a command not of submission.

Johnny took a fifth and then sixth swig of his Tango before waving off Bain from across the burning fire can. Being slighted by anyone was an unusual experience for Bain. Being the largest and strongest of the crowd meant you didn't have to take shit from anyone. It was an attitude Bain learned as an early teen, never having experienced a sober father. Bain's pop died of alcoholism before his fourteenth birthday, leaving Bain, his two-year-younger brother Kevin, and their widowed mother to slug though life without a genuine breadwinner.

His mom worked forty-five hours a week in a textile factory for pennies above minimum wage. On weekends, when she wasn't cleaning apartments, she was trying her best to raise her two sons and steer Bain and Kevin away from the antics of the neighborhood. But as her boys became young men, her vision of either one being any different from her late husband all but vanished.

Bain originally cherished the idea of having no abusive father to call upon. *Dad is a no-good bum. He don't work, and he drinks Mom's little money away,* he used to think. But by his fifteenth birthday, a year and a half after his father's defeat by the bottle, Bain had dropped out of high school to load and unload furniture. *It's the first time we've had a man of the house around here.* Through his deceased father's contacts, Bain was able to find employment with a neighborhood moving company. Failure was never an option, Bain labored intensely while blending in with the older workers, mostly drunks like his father. He cultivated a good reputation as a go-getter, a hustler. Never one to miss work or dog it on the job, Bain's status grew within the ranks of the company, as did his muscle out in the streets.

Kevin, always the baby, hated his brother at times for being so responsible. *It's like I gotta follow his lead or something.* Kevin resisted mostly and acted like a clown, a goofball. It was Kevin's way to dream of and hold on to a lost childhood. Kevin's identity was hidden behind a castle's curtain wall, showcasing only the jester for all to be amused with. Unable to be Bain, Kevin chose an opposing position: laughter instead of intimidation. It was cute when he was a child, but the tide of reality began its sobering rinse when Kevin entered his mid-teens.

Having achieved his bulk by lugging old refrigerators up and down spiraling stairways for the past two years, Bain projected a tough-guy image and at times could be a cruel tormenter. This contrasted with his internal disposition of reliability and trustworthiness. No one knew this better than Johnny, as the two were friends because of circumstances. Living in a different city or neighborhood or on a different street, Bain and Johnny most likely would have been archenemies. The luck or misfortune of each boy's location had bonded the two misguided children and made them lifelong friends.

Johnny was moody tonight and was still fixated on Tommy's negative attitude. *Scuzz,* Johnny thought. *Maybe less of the stained bench and more of the real wood for the damn fire.*

The paint on the wood of the park bench began to intensify the flames. The odor from the chemical cocktail endured inside the shifting smoke, hitting Johnny's face. Disgusted more with Tommy as a so-called friend than with the smoke, Johnny griped to the pyromaniac. "Tommy, there's gonna be no benches left this summer. Use branches."

Laughing, Tommy opened his arms wide and smiled, reminding Johnny of the baby Jesus in the manger. *Tommy's no Christ ... but a baby? Yeah. Oh yeah.*

"Dream on. Look around you; there's only snow on the shitty ground. Besides, you're using the fire, and like I said, I'm done." Tommy clapped his hands together and then took a beer out of a brown bag below the destroyed bench.

"Knock it off, guys." Realizing Tommy was ready to protest, Bain continued. "Johnny." Bain motioned for Johnny to be by his side. Johnny spat into the darkness and followed Bain's command. "What gives?" Johnny took another slug of his Tango. Bain noticed about a quarter of the drink was already gone. "Johnny, come over here." Bain walked Johnny away from the fire and Tommy.

Anticipating Bain's grumbling, Johnny spoke first. "I'm not going tonight. I'm pretty tired." Before Bain could protest, Johnny continued, "I know where to be tomorrow. I'll be there. Call for me at eight o'clock."

"Hey, you gotta get this bug out of your ass with Tommy, Angela, and even Donny." A snapping sound made Bain lose eye contact with Johnny for a second. It was Tommy tearing the seat off of a second park bench for his fire. *Dumb-ass. I thought you were done.* Returning his focus back to Johnny, he said, "If you don't get over what happened, you're never gonna be bangin' for things yet to come."

"What the hell, you ..." Johnny was unable to find the correct word to call Bain after this sudden philosophical lecture. Johnny slugged another drink from his bottle.

Bain, with an unlit cigarette in his mouth, jingled his left pocket searching for matches. "I feel sorry for you."

Johnny resented Bain's statement almost enough to smash his Tango bottle across his friend's face. "You don't get to feel sorry for me. Nobody does."

There was a hoot from western entrance of the park. As his eyes adjusted from the light of the fire to the darkness surrounding the park entrance, Johnny recognized Joey alongside a crony. Johnny could only assume the clown, with his head in a paper bag, would be Kevin. Johnny tried not to smile as the others around their makeshift campfire began to laugh. Johnny couldn't see Kevin's face, but he recognized him by his walk and dark-blue pea coat. What had created the sudden laughter was Kevin's guise: he was mimicking "The Unknown Comic."

Kevin's brown grocery bag exhibited slanted, Chinese-shaped cutouts for eyes with three oval tears tumbling down the left cheek. It had no nose and had an exaggerated smile for a mouth.

Kevin came up to Bain without saying a word and stood next to him alongside the burning garbage can. "Hey, if you get too close, you may burn your head," Bain said. He was still pissed at Johnny and did not want to encourage the stupidity of Kevin. Everyone else was in on the joke and joined in the hysterics.

"You should have seen Kevin; he was making out with Gina with the bag on his head," hooted Joey. "At first he cut his eyes like a chink, but he couldn't see good. He was banging into people, garbage cans, and all." As laughter continued, Kevin said nothing, warming his hands near the fire.

"Well, they still look like chinky eyes to me," Tommy added.

Bain interrupted the chuckling. "Kevin, you're such a ditz. Now get away from me." Bain playfully pushed his brother away from the heat inside the can. Kevin said nothing but gave the okay sign with his hand. On his return to the enthusiasm of the inner circle, Kevin reached into his pocket pulled out a half-smoked joint, placing it into the smiling mouth of the bag before lighting it. The laughter continued until Shanty, Nicole, and Angela entered the glow of the fire.

~~~~~~~

The Inkies were seven attached brick apartment buildings located two Brooklyn streets north of Winthrop Park. Each structure was comprised of ten units, ranging from three to four rooms with a bathroom. A fire escape running from the second to the fifth floor was mounted on the street side of each building. In the summer, parents would sit on the fire escapes to drink beer and watch their children play on the streets below. During the winter months, folks would leave beer for the evening outside their windows for chilling.

Two brothers now stood below a beer bag dripping from the second floor of an Inkies fire escape waiting impatiently in the cold for their Madd Tuff recruit to emerge. Bouncing on one foot for warmth and then switching to the other, the younger brother grumbled out loud.

"Where the hell is he?" Hogan blew into his hands and began to hop simultaneously on both feet.

"Stop crying like a girl. He's coming." Brodie was cold too. Their winter wear was for display, not for warmth. The Madd Tuff attire included a dungaree jacket in the gang's colors, a black, hooded sweatshirt, and a white T-shirt. The insignia on their jacket's backs showed the words *Madd Tuff* in black above an upside-down red cross. The jackets were cool, tough, and gang looking but were unfortunately, with frigid temperatures zeroing out tonight, impractical. Not wanting his younger sibling to screw anything up, Brodie changed the subject. "I think you should figure shit out after New Year's."

Hogan eyed the beer bag upon the second floor of the fire escape. "Hey, put your hands out. I can reach the ladder with some help."

"Forget that shit. We are to get Porky only." Shaking his head in disbelief, Brodie went on. "You know what would happen if we screwed this up?"

Hogan shivered and nodded his head up and down. "Yeah."

"What I was saying was, you gotta get back to school in January. You are too young to drop out." Brodie peered through the front door's cracked glass window. Now he showed his own anxiety. "Porky, where the hell are you?" Brodie complained to himself.

"You dropped out at sixteen; so can I."

"Yeah, and look at me now." Ashamed of his own words, Brodie went on, "You are better than this, better than me." Brodie stopped for a second, not wanting pity or to display any weakness to his younger sibling. "Look what we're doing tonight and afterward. This will not end well. It never does." Brody hated himself for exhibiting humility, but what other means did he have?

Through the shadows of the night, Hogan saw fear in his brother's eyes and for the first time thought Brodie regretted the life they were living. Before he could honestly speak his concerns, the front door opened wide enough to bump Hogan's right shoulder.

"Hey, watch it, asshole. You could have knocked me down the stoop."

"Sorry, just want to get it over with." Porky squeezed between the brothers and trotted down the icy brick steps. "Are you guys coming?" He wanted to book before his mother left the building. Porky knew she would not be happy with his company.

"Hey, you're late, and now we have to rush?" Walking down the steps with more caution than Porky, Brodie smiled. "I never seen anyone so gung-ho to play chicken."

Hogan went down the steps with the same recklessness Porky had shown and quickly paid the price on his second step. Hogan did his best imitation of a punter as his right foot kicked forward, but his left foot would be of no help. Falling onto his ass, Hogan could only yell. "Shit!" He rose up carefully and slowly as his brother laughed. "What, you never fell before?" Rubbing his frozen ass, Hogan turned to Porky. "Chicken tonight, and then you're one of us." Grabbing Porky's parka coat for support, Hogan gave his brother a wide smile.

Brodie couldn't smile back; he could only frown at Hogan and Porky. *This is wrong, for Hogan, this poor kid, and me.* "Yeah, let's initiate the chicken out of the Pork."

Chapter 3

1973

A nickel ain't worth a dime anymore.
—Yogi Berra

Wherever you go, go with all your heart.
—Confucius.

"Is that it?" Johnny took Porky's last two dimes before handing them over to Shanty.

"Wait, I have this too." Porky pulled a one-dollar bill from his rear pocket to everyone's delight, except Tommy's.

"What, you holding out on us?" Tommy, still sore from the human shit incident earlier in the day, went to smack Porky's head.

"Tommy, come on. Stop it already," complained Joey. Bain was ready to intercede if words would not stop Tommy.

Shanty counted the bills first and then handed them over to Johnny. "Nine bucks." Then he separated the quarters, dimes, nickels, and pennies before counting them. "Another $3.38. That makes … $12.38, plus the three subway tokens." Getting up off the sidewalk, Shanty put all the coins in his front right pocket, and then Johnny handed back the nine one-dollar bills.

"We can walk up another block and catch the GG train on Norman Avenue. With two tokens we can all fit through" directed Johnny.

"No way, man, that's too far. Let's just run through and cash the tokens in later," Bain said, looking at the others for support.

Hearing the murmurs of agreement with Bain, Johnny disagreed with the second plan. "The crappy Giants are playing home today. There's still cops by the toll booths. Let's just walk one more block and squeeze through." Johnny held his hand out to Shanty for the tokens. "We have three tokens left. We'll only use two of 'em."

The Norman Avenue subway station was an unmanned entrance to the GG train. You entered the station through two caged, revolving metal doors big enough to transit a large adult. The turnstile could not go backward and would stop after one half rotation. Two thinner adults could push against one another for a free ride, and for children, three was doable.

"Donny, Tommy, Bain, and Kevin, go together. Me, Shanty, Joey, and Porky will go next," Johnny directed.

Bain entered first, taking Kevin and pushing him down to the ground.

"Hey, you're squishing me," Kevin said in a muffled voice.

"Donny, come here, up on my shoulders." Picking him up, Bain nudged Donny between the metal door and his right shoulder. "Tommy, come in." Without much ado, Tommy leaned into Bain. "Okay, give me another little guy." No one moved. Bain yelled out to Joey. "Come on!"

Shanty placed the token in as Johnny helped the turnstile rotate around. With a few moans and some cursing from within the pile, the squeaky gate rotated toward the train platform. With Kevin on the ground, baby steps were all the boys could manage without stepping on him. Donny had to duck the metal ridge above before they all tumbled to the train platform. The five established a new world record, or at least they could get the boys a job jamming themselves into a clown car.

"It would be funny if a cop were on the other side waiting for yous," yelled out Porky.

In the mist of bodies, Tommy yelled back, "Shut up, asshole."

With the first five through, it was a piece of cake for the remaining three to join them on the waiting platform.

"See, Donny my boy, that's how you beat the system and break the record." Bain clapped his hands for the football. Kevin tossed it over. "Who are the crappy Giants playing today anyway?"

On the subway platform, the spirits of the traveling friends were high. It was ten minutes before one o'clock on Sunday afternoon. Killing time waiting for the train, Kevin, Tommy, and Donny were playing *salugee* with Shanty. *Salugee* was another name Brooklyn kids had for keep-away or monkey-in-the-middle. Shanty may have been the tallest, but he possessed little agility. He was no match for his quicker and shorter tormentors. Beyond the hustle of Shanty and his extreme attempts to not be *salugeed* for too long, Bain and Johnny stood to the side talking while Joey listened in.

"Any plans once we get there?" Bain asked.

Johnny shrugged his shoulders as he watched Shanty tip the football but be unable to recover it.

"I guess just getting out of Brooklyn will have to do then."

Joey was about to say something when the football landed on the tracks below.

"Shit, you suck, Shant. You're supposed to catch the damn ball, not knock it down there," Tommy yelled out.

Everyone stood on the platform edge staring at the football. "I'll get it. Just help me back up," Donny said. He took three steps toward the edge of the platform and glimpsed into the tunnel. Seeing a dim light from a distant train, Donny touched his new gold Christ head for luck. "It's safe. I'll get it. The train is a stop away."

"No way, man, I got it," Johnny declared as Bain grabbed his arm.

"Johnny, let Donny get it." With a shocked stare from Johnny, Bain went on. "It will be quicker lifting him back onto the platform than you."

With defiance, Johnny snapped back. "I can just hop back up here myself."

"Somebody better go before the train crushes the damn ball," Kevin interjected.

"Or somebody," added Joey.

Donny squatted down before jumping the three feet to the gravel below. "Here goes." Once on the tracks, Donny, peered into the tunnel at the approaching train. The light doubled in size. Walking to the football, Donny had a deadly premonition. "Here, catch." Tossing the football to Shanty, Donny asked for a penny to place on the tracks.

"Donny just get over here; the train is coming," Johnny snapped. He shot a nervous glance into the tunnel and surveyed the bigger and brighter train headlight approaching, as did the others on the platform.

"You got that penny?"

"Hey, you shit, get over here now," Tommy barked out.

Johnny was ready to jump down to grab the small teaser when he heard Shanty yell out.

"Donny, here's a penny for the track." Shanty almost fumbled the penny to the floor but thankfully recovered it, unlike the football in the *salugee* game earlier. "Here you go." He placed it in Donny's small hand.

The gang was startled when the train horn blared before entering the glow of the station. Taking his sweet-ass time, Donny gently placed the penny onto the track and then strolled toward his screaming friends. Bain and Tommy grabbed each of Donny's forearms. Without saying a word, the boys pulled Donny onto the platform, seconds before the screeching train arrived.

"Hey, you shit, what the hell is the matter with you?" cried out Bain. "That was so dumb. You could have gotten killed."

Johnny joined in. "Donny, why so reckless?"

Donny only smiled back. "I wanted a flattened penny before I go."

<p style="text-align:center">~~~~~~~</p>

"Nicky, Neeeeckeey, I have to make wee-wee." Billy came running to his older sister holding his crotch. "I gotta go bad." Billy began to jump up and down around his sister.

Turning her attention away from her girlfriends, Nicole tugged Billy by his forearm to a tree not more than thirty feet from the playground. *It's wonderful being a guy; just whip it out and go, anywhere you please,* she thought. She unzipped his pants and reached into her brother's underwear to pull out his boyhood while giving firm orders. "Now go."

Breathing heavily from playing, little Billy had a plumbing dilemma. "I can't go. The girls are looking at me." Billy began to cry.

Hearing this, the newly arrived Tori laughed and then poked Gina to look the other way. Angela had already walked to the end of their playground bench.

"See, no one cares. Now go, or you're going home," a frustrated Nicole grumbled.

Following a few sniffles, Billy was able to let loose. A straight path of urine hit the old oak, splashing a small portion of piss onto Nicole's sleeveless arm. *Great, Billy boy, what I need now is only your absence!*

"Look, I made the mark of Zorro!" Billy admires his piss art.

Billy had only managed a seven before his bladder was drained. *That's no Z!* Nicole thought. Without wanting an argument and needing to return to her friends, Nicole agreed. "That's a heck of a *Z*, Billy." After zipping up her sibling's pants, Nicole returned to the girls on the bench and to the discussion of Donny's chaotic situation.

"His mother is a mess. God only knows where and what happened to Linda." Tori placed her finger into Bella's mouth, removing a fallen leaf. "Stop eating crap." Responding to her dog's sad eyes, Tori then smiled and petted the animal.

"It's Lorna, not Linda," Nicole corrected Tori. "Besides, wherever she is, she's better off."

Angela sat quietly and listened to the girls speak. *Linda—no, Lorna— now Donny. What's going on in that household?* "I don't know. Will Donny be better off?"

Gina placed a tissue between her red lips to remove the excess lipstick before addressing Angela.

"Yes and no." Gina placed the powder puff into her Maybelline compact mirror before continuing. "Donny's mother is a drunk. She's with a different live-in boyfriend every other week."

Tori joined in. "She's nasty." She picked up Bella and set her on her lap and then spoke directly to Angela. "You weren't around when Donny was—how can I say it—on his own."

"I was getting to that," interjected Gina. "Donny, his sister Lorna, who was about sixteen or so, and their mother moved to the Inkies less than two years ago."

An impatient Nicole shot in. "Yeah, yeah. We all know. Donny's mother brought home some spic, and when he was finished with the mother, he went after the daughter."

"Lorna was being raped?" a shocked and disgusted Angela asked.

"Raped. And Donny was abused." Tori continued to pet Bella. "But it wasn't the spic boyfriend. It was that dirty Irish guy, remember? He had that red hair and scruffy beard."

Nicole yelled over at Billy to stop throwing rocks at the pigeons. "It doesn't matter which guy. Either way…"

"What do you mean abused?" Angela demanded, she no longer wanted to hear about Lorna but about Donny.

Gina took over the storytelling. "He never went to school. When he did, he'd get picked on. He was always dirty."

"You never knew why his eyes were always blackened—if he needed sleep, if his face was just dirty, or if he had been beaten," Nicole added.

"Most likely all three," Tori interjected. She put Bella back to the ground. "It wasn't until Brodie and Hogan tormented Donny that morning that things changed."

Angela tossed an errant kickball toward Billy's way and then came closer to Tori. "What morning?"

39

It was Nicole who took command of the story. "Two years ago, Johnny and Tommy were on their way to school. Neither knew or had heard of Donny."

~ ~ ~ ~ ~ ~ ~ ~

"John Riggins? I never heard of him," Johnny complained to Tommy. "They should have drafted Archie Manning instead."

"It doesn't work that way. You have to follow the draft in order. Besides, Broadway Joe will be around for at least another ten to fifteen years before the Jets need to draft a quarterback." Tommy kicked an empty soda can into the gutter and then waved to Bain from across the street.

"Yeah, his best years are yet to come," Johnny agreed. "Bain, what's up with your phonics and math books? You going to school today? And where's Kev?"

Shifting the two hardcover books under his right armpit, Bain popped a Bazooka Gum into his mouth. "Yeah, if I miss school again they're gonna leave me back." Bain brushed his dark-brown hair off of his brow and behind each ear. "In public school we get thirty sick days. I'm in the high twenties with still a couple of months left."

Above Bain's right eye was a butterfly stitch surrounded by a purplish welt. "My dad," Bain said, not waiting to be probed. "He came home drunk again last night, fell asleep in the hallway. Mom thought he was dead." He took a deep breath. "Kev was already in bed. He came out to help us drag him into the kitchen. It was then the bastard got up and started swingin'."

"What then?" an astounded Tommy asked.

"The usual, except Kevin got it worse than me this time. So he stayed home today." Bain wiped his left cheek as his two friends looked away.

40

Johnny needed to change the subject swiftly. "I wish I went to your school."

With Bain unable to talk, Tommy took the cue. "Why's that?"

"You get thirty vacation days!" Tommy let out a small laugh as Bain switched armpits for his hardcover schoolbooks.

Walking in silence, the three boys were nearing the street corner where Bain would have to cross to continue his journey to his school. Before splitting up to their respective destinations, the boys heard a commotion inside the alleyway of the last apartment building on the block. Bain sprinted toward the racket first, quickly followed by Tommy and Johnny. The scuffling sounds suddenly became screams.

The alleyway ended with a brick wall, as there were no first-floor windows or entrance doors. Where the second story windows began, empty clotheslines swung from one adjacent building to another. The darkened alley would remain in shadows until the noon sun revealed itself amid the four-storied buildings. The reek of urine blended in with spattered refuse hung in the air. Eight battered trashcans were scattered on one side of the brick wall, obstructing the view of the right corner. If not for the sense of sound rather than sight, Bain, Tommy, and Johnny would have not seen the ambush of a child.

Hogan's back was to the alley's entrance. He was twisting the arm of a boy of similar stature as his older brother began to choke their victim. "If you don't have money, you dig deep in daddy's wallet and get us some, or I'll kill you right here. Do you understand me?"

The nine-year-old prey could not speak, as no air remained in his esophagus while the choking marathon continued.

"Brodie, let go of him!" Bain nudged Tommy to the side so as to take the lead position. Brodie took a step back as Hogan let go of the target's arm. The mark began to cough as he leaned forward, spitting only air alongside a fallen trashcan.

"Mind your business, Bain." Motioning for Hogan to follow, Brodie decided to leave the battle and move far away from any confrontation with Bain, now or ever. Trying to save face with his younger brother, Brodie bumped shoulders with Tommy when they passed. "As for you, Tommy, you're dead when I see you."

On a normal day, Brodie and his brother would have made it through the three stunned boys with no further incident. Unluckily for Hogan, it was not an ordinary morning for Bain.

Reaching Brodie's side and the safety of the street with other school children, parents, crossing guards, and maybe a police officer, Hogan was relieved to leave the shadows of the darkened alleyway only to enter a much darker world.

〰〰〰〰〰〰〰〰

"And *whack!* Hogan went flying into a parked car, barely getting his hands up to protect his face," Nicole concluded, slapping the top of her forehead in exaggeration, to the delight of Gina and Tori. "Bain had never gotten so much use out of those text books." Nicole joined in the laughter.

A stunned Angela asked, "How can you all laugh?"

"I'll tell you," Gina said, waving off Nicole, who was about to respond. "What Bain, Johnny, and Tommy found was a nine-year-old with pissed pants, beaten, scared, and helpless. You might be new here Angie, but remember, we all live in a gutter. We are not all … how should I say it so you understand"—she tapped her chin as she thought—"seasoned."

Chapter 4

1978

A man loves his sweetheart the most,
his wife the best, but his mother the longest.
—Irish Proverb

If it doesn't feel right, don't do it … right? Porky was beginning to have second thoughts. "Now, once I do this, I'm in … no more stunts?" Porky directed his question to Brodie, the older of the two brothers. With no answer, the three teens sped across the street before a honking car. "You sure Junior and Fagan will know I did this?"

"Hey, if you are pussying out, just say so," an agitated Hogan grilled.

"Shut up, yous." Brodie banged the slush off of his boots as they stepped onto the icy sidewalk. Without looking up, Brodie heard a female voice.

"Hi, Pork." A shapely teen with her jeans tucked inside high, red-leather boots smiled. The young lady's long, dark hair bounced in the air, and her dark-red lipstick could be seen from a block away. She continued to march away toward Winthrop Park.

Hogan recognized the teen. It was Gina keeping warm somewhere inside that white, furry coat. "Hey, you slut, no one's talking to you!" Without missing a slippery step or turning around, Gina gave Hogan the New York salute. Embarrassed, Hogan tried to save face. "Don't you give me the finger. I'll kick your boyfriend's ass."

"Okay, shut the hell up already," Brodie said, pushing Hogan into Porky. "There's the bus stop, Pork." He grabbed Hogan's arm and pulled him into the flower shop doorway. "We will be right here. We can see the traffic light and you."

Porky blew into his frozen hands.

"Don't worry … do this, and we'll tell Junior. You'll be in," Brodie added. Stepping back, he eyed the oncoming traffic. "Last thing, Pork, don't chicken out, and you're in."

Without a word, Porky walked to the bus stop. *Mom, it's all right. I got this.* Moving his toes to remove the numbness of the wet and cold of the evening, Porky watched the B-48 bus turn onto Nassau Avenue and approach its next stop. *Three blocks away. I've never been so disappointed to see my bus arrive.* The light was still green. It would only work on the red light. *I don't—I won't wait for another bus. I'll be chicken! It is now or never. Mom, we are going out for breakfast tomorrow. Better yet, I'll meet you at Grandma's tonight.*

"Porky, it's changing," Hogan yelled nervously.

Yes, it is. Thank you, Hogie. You are one swell fellow. The bus stopped at the red light. Without saying a word, Porky watched passengers leave the bus from the side and front doors. When the last passenger exited, Porky quickly trotted from the curb to the street alongside the bus. The light remained red. *Here goes.*

Without contemplating it, Porky knelt down into the slush, not feeling or caring about the wetness of the street. He angled his skull in line with the rear tire of the bus and watched the traffic light. *Still red. Once it goes green, I pull out. A few more seconds and I'm in. I will be respected!* Wiggling his fingers to shake off the deadness of frostbite, Porky adjusted himself to prepare for his escape. *A piece of cake!* The light switched to green. *Ha, no problem. I hope you two pricks are taking notes over there.*

From inside the florist's doorway, the two brothers watched Porky pass his initiation. "I never thought he'd go this far. I really thought he'd chicken out," Brodie said, speaking more to himself than to Hogan. "He's in."

Thrusting his frozen hands onward, Porky thought of finally being accepted somewhere. The hum of the bus exhaust rang deep inside his ears, while the oxygen escaped Porky's lungs. He leveled his elbows into a push-up position but was dumbfounded and then horrified to find that his attempt failed. *Tung, tung, and tear. It's a sick joke. Who or what is holding on to me? Hogan? Brodie? Let go!* Porky could not grasp what pinched him to the street and the rear bus tire. *The scarf … it's tangled under the wheel.* Struggling desperately to escape, Porky could only feel the grip tightening. *Mom, we'll have breakfast together. I promise you … Yes, Mommy, we will. Oh, and thanks for the scarf. It really warms things up down here.* Full throttle of warm-heat-fire … total blackness.

~~~~~~~

"Look, let's split." From the orange glimmer from the fire, Bain could see the angst in Johnny's eyes. Out of hearing range of the others, Bain went on. "We can skip Tori's tonight and shoot some pool at the bowling alley instead." Bain tossed his cigarette over Kevin's paper bag head. Failing to get a laugh out of Johnny, Bain went on. "We'll catch up with everyone tomorrow morning. Look, I didn't mean I feel sorry for you, but you gotta get your fight back." Bain tried his best to reason quietly with his disturbed friend.

Angela placed her hand inside Tommy's pocket as the two were preparing to leave the park. "Tori said anytime after six. Whoever is coming, we are leaving now." While Angela spoke loudly enough over the fire for Bain to hear, she made no notice of Johnny.

Nicole walked between Bain and Johnny. "I told Gina I'd wait for her here." Nicole put her mittened hands above the fire. "What's his problem?" she inquired about Johnny as if he were not present.

"Nothing, I …" Bain was unsure of where Johnny's head was right now. "Yeah, I'll wait here with you for Gina, and we'll all go together."

Nicole gave Bain a slight grin and shot Johnny the stink eye. "Okay … thanks. Gina better get here soon; I'm getting cold." Nicole left Bain's side to talk with Angela and Tommy.

"Johnny-boy, we're all staying together tonight. It's important, all right?" Before Johnny could protest, a police car raced by parallel to the park, followed by an ambulance, a second police car, and a fire engine.

After departing from his two snow-covered friends, Billy knocked the snow off of his Jets hat. Though the cold began to freeze the moisture and sweat throughout his body, Billy felt the need for a hot chocolate before going home. Across the street from Winthrop Park entrance stood a small candy store. The one-step stoop led up to its glass-door entrance. Inside, two quarter pinball machines stood along the left wall. *Rocky* was Billy's favorite of the two, not because it was newer but because *The Six Million Dollar Man* machine tilted too easily. To the right, before the cash register were candies, chewing gum, rolling papers, and four different New York newspapers. Further down the counter behind the glass display were the eight different cigarette brands for sale. Laid on top of the cigarette arrangement were strategically placed baseball, football, *Star Wars*, *Partridge Family*, *Batman*, and other trading cards. Toward the rear of the store was Billy's favorite location, the comic book section. Here four display racks showcased many different genres of entertainment. *Spiderman*, *Superman*, *The Pink Panther*, *Looney Tunes*, *Sergeant Rock*, *The Archie's*, and many others were all on display. Billy would skim past the superheroes with a glance and concentrate on the more realistic comics of doom, such as *Weird Mysteries*, *Tower of Shadows*, *The House of Secrets*, and *The Haunt of Fear*. Above all four sections of the comic book display and out of reach of an eight-year-old like Billy were *Playboy* and *Penthouse*, the naked magazines.

"A hot chocolate," Billy said as he placed a quarter on the counter. Then he walked to the comic book section to wait for his toasty drink. *The Flash* comic stood out, triggering Billy's memory. *Donny, you were right. The Flash is bullshit.*

Three minutes later, Billy and his warm Styrofoam cup stepped into the frigid wind of the early evening. The street lights had been on now for at least a half hour, so Billy knew he was already late. Racing home would make little difference at this point; late was late.

Billy could see a bunch of teenagers standing around a burning trashcan in Winthrop Park. Knowing it was Nicole and her friends, Billy was prepared to toss a few snowballs over the park fence before hustling home. Ready to place his cup onto a snow-covered parked car, Billy notice two Madd Tuffs running his way.

With no time to yell for Bain or Johnny, Billy could only hide between two parked cars and hope not to be noticed. *Be calm, be calm … There's no time to be calm!* Standing in frozen slush, Billy watched Brodie and his younger brother, Hooky or something, zoom past. *They didn't see me!* He watched the brother's upside-down crosses disappear into the darkness of the street. *Man, I was lucky.* Sipping his hot chocolate, Billy decided not to toss any snowballs toward Nicole and the burning trashcan. Instead, Billy began his two-block trek home, continuing in the direction from which the brothers had fled. *I'm gonna be late. Mom will give me a break, for tomorrow's Christmas Eve.* Billy downed his cooling hot chocolate and then tossed the cup over the park fence. *She's making chocolate chip cookies now. I wonder what she got me for*—Siren's from a police car awoke Billy from his daydream of Christmas morning. This was followed by a police siren. *They're coming up this street.* Billy saw the first one stop on the street corner's edge; the second car pulled alongside a motionless bus. Additional sirens and more emergency vehicles had Billy thinking not of Christmas or being late but of the bus stop. *What happened?*

Father Jerry hurried out of the rectory after receiving a phone call from the volunteer ambulance service. With the recovered Christ-head and, of course, his vial of blessed olive oil in his pocket, father scampered out of his office with his coat open, en route to Winthrop Park. The sidewalk was empty, except for the boy with the green Jets hat. He too was going toward of the sirens and flashing non-Christmas lights.

Joey, Shanty, and Kevin departed the warmth of the fire to investigate the police and emergency vehicles on the park's northwestern end. Johnny waited one minute after the three hustled off to present his case. "Bain, I'll meet you on the corner. It seems like something big went down."

Bain flicked his cigarette into the diminishing trash can fire. "Tommy, toss me a beer."

Tommy bent down and stole a can from Joey's bag. "Catch." Returning his attention back to Nicole and Angela, Tommy complained, "Where the hell is Gina, already?"

"Okay, I'll see you there," Johnny said as he took another big swig of Tango, hoping his lie was not caught. He buried his half-empty bottle inside his army jacket. Without waiting for Bain's permission or objection, Johnny abandoned his alliance and walked to the northern end of the park. Before veering to the eastern exit of the playground and away from the commotion, Johnny could hear Bain yelling above the sirens.

"Individually, maybe! But as a group, no one is!"

Johnny made his move to the east, into the darkness and noiselessness and toward the peaceful portion of his spirit. *Yeah, Bain, who's better than us? Everybody, anybody …* Johnny began to jog for the subway, gripping his hidden bottle of Tango. *Central Park, Manhattan … When times were the best, we were all together. Then we all had to grow up quickly and then all fall apart inside this shitter.* Johnny almost slipped on the snow-covered ice as he ran from the park exit. *Tonight, all scores will be settled.*

⸝⸝⸝⸝⸝⸝⸝

Converse All-Star sneakers, black high tops with white laces. Billy stood in the closed-off street, heedless of the cold, the gathering onlookers, the emergency personal, or Father Jerry. *That boy put those sneakers on this morning … for the last time.* Lingering in a trancelike state, Billy could only wonder the obvious. *Who's that laying in the street?* Billy was brushed into another bystander as the crowd increased about the bus. *Those sneakers—how could he know … he would never untie them again?*

Billy had seen a dead person once before, but that was an old nun in a funeral home. *Everything was organized. We were prepared. The nun prepared too.* Billy was with his classmates then, and the only uncertainty was whether the nun would be wearing her habit in the coffin. She was. *This boy—teenager—is real. No time to ready him for the grievers. No time at all.*

"Billy, what are you doing out? Did mom send you here?" Nicole and Gina pushed their way between two gawkers. "Billy. Billy-boy, come on. I'm taking you home." Nicole grabbed her younger brother's ungloved hand and felt the cold seep through her own cotton glove. "Your hands! You're frozen. Let's go."

Bain, Tommy, Angela, and Kevin, his head still covered by a bag, joined in. "Get that stupid bag off of your head. You know, I almost got in trouble today because of you!" complained Gina.

Kevin, for the moment, listened to his part-time girlfriend and removed the paper bag from his head. The Unknown Comic look had created static electricity, causing Kevin's hair to stand straight up in spite of the cold wind. Gina could only smile. "You look like the Heat Miser." Gina went to Nicole and Billy. "You better get him home."

"Nic, I got him," Bain said. "Go to Tori's. After I drop Billy off, I'll get Johnny, and we'll meet you all there." Of course, Bain didn't know where the hell Johnny was at the moment. Before Nicole or anyone else could grumble, Shanty and Joey came panting up to Bain. Both boys appeared sick. "Well, what's the problem?"

"It's Porky." Joey pointed over the kneeling priest. "It's Porky … His mother is on her way now."

Gina and Angela gave out a cry, and the boys, along with Nicole, could only swear. As the shock began to subside, Billy had one final question before being taken to the safety of home. "Who's gonna take Porky's sneakers off tonight?"

Ice formed on Father Jerry's right hand from the slush in the street. His knees were not far behind. But frostbite would be the least of his problems tonight. He stepped aside for the lead police investigator. The father had only a few moments before the devastated mother would arrive. *I knew this kid, Paul, and his mother too. I recently buried her father* … Father Jerry stumbled as he walked away from the sheet-covered body and toward the worried onlookers. *Next up and batting cleanup … Paul.* Father Jerry put his immobilized hand inside his coat pocket while he walked into the crowd along the sidewalk. *Look at them, all looking to me for an answer. Well, you know what?* Opening and closing his numb right hand inside his pocket, Father Jerry stepped between two teenagers—one male, one female—and a smaller child. *Wait until Paul's mother arrives … Merry Christmas to all, and to all a good night!*

"Thanks, Bain, but I'll tell my mom. She's gonna be worried with all this goin' on. She also knows Porky." Nicole looked at Billy. "It's too much here. Mommy's gonna be worried. Let's get going."

Nice move, Big Sis. That kid should be nowhere near here, the priest thought. A sudden burst of wind came down from the stalled bus, bringing a dusting of snow onto the bystanders. A few flurries landed squarely in Father Jerry's eyes. Holding the Bible in his left hand, the priest clumsily removed his deadened right hand from deep down in his pocket to dry his brow. It stuck for a moment because of the numbness. Father Jerry jerked his hand from his pouch in an awkward motion. Escaping his pocket along with his hand came the shining silver charm.

The charm landed squarely on Gina's red boot. She bent down to politely hand the fleeing trinket back to the priest. With her gloved hand, Gina awkwardly untangled the silver chain before handing it over. *Nice chain. Looks like the one we gave Donny way back when.* Then the chain stopped spinning, it was Kevin who spoke.

"Gina, shit, that's Donny's chain."

Bain let go of Billy's elbow and walked up to the priest. "Hey, that's Donny's. How did you get that?"

Chapter 5

1973

We do not remember days; we remember moments.
—Cesare Pavese

The boys reached midtown Manhattan a few minutes past one. As they left the steps of the subway and its reek of urine, the rancid aroma was quickly replaced by the scent of charcoal. The smell of burning carbon was the first sense one recognized upon arriving in the most densely populated borough of New York. The food carts, or "roach coaches," were placed throughout Manhattan's sidewalks. The push carts warmed their hot dogs, knishes, shish kebabs, hamburgers, and pretzels with burning charcoal. It was game time for all the vendors ready for Sunday's business.

Additional merchants with non-food items for sale shared the walkways. Tables alongside the curbs displayed sunglasses, leather belts, wallets, pocketbooks, T-shirts, and amateur art. A person could walk for a mile missing most of these curbside vendors because of the world-famous structures—such as Radio City Music Hall, Macy's, the Plaza Hotel, the Empire State Building, Rockefeller Center, and FAO Schwarz—that surrounded them. As the hustle and bustle of the warm mid-autumn day began to increase, the boys touched the elite world of the rich, grasping how they could never be players in this inaccessible society and why they could only act out against it.

"Hey, asshole. Yo! Asshole!" Two young men crossing Fifth Avenue both turned around simultaneously to the delight of Tommy, Kevin, and

Joey. Unaware of the prank, the two men continued on their way to the opposite side of the street. "Hey, I'm two for two. Kev, it's your turn." Tommy pointed at an older couple ahead on the sidewalk.

"Tommy, can you stop the shit. You're gonna get your ass kicked," Johnny said. "Let's at least get to Central Park before you start up."

Tommy did not appreciate the scolding, and he mumbled something to Kevin. The two of them laughed. Walking to the curb, Tommy waited a second for the light to turn green so the traffic, mostly yellow cabs, could zoom by. One passed and then a second. On the third cab, Tommy slammed his foot down in front of the racing car. The cabbie hit his break, wrongly anticipating Tommy running into traffic. The screech, followed by the smell of burnt rubber, had everyone's immediate attention.

"Oh shit!" was all Bain could say as his friends stood in awe. "Come on, let's book."

The cabbie got out of his car as the blocked traffic behind the vehicle began to honk. In a heavy Bronx accent, the driver yelled out in a fury. "Get back here, you scum. I'll stick this boot up your ass!"

Bain responded before joining his fleeing friends. "You. Homo. So you like puttin' things up a boy's ass" before waiting for an answer, Bain followed his fleeing friends. "Hey, wait up!" After a block, Johnny and Tommy slowed to a trot, and the others followed their lead, enabling Bain to catch up. A bit winded, Bain instructed Tommy, "No more bullshit …"

"Yeah, let's have fun in the park first." Johnny agreed, as the others nodded. "Don't blow it for Donny. It's his last day here … for a while."

The boys continued their walk up Fifth Avenue with as little activity as possible. Joey, Porky, and Kevin were playing *salugee* with Shanty's Chap

Stick. Bain and Tommy argued about Joe Namath's knees as Johnny and Donny lagged behind.

"I don't even know these people." Donny bit on his bottom lip, waiting for Johnny's response.

"Are you worried about them?" was all Johnny could think to say.

"No ..." Donny could only chuckle lightly. "Things suck here at home, but I know what I have." After a few quiet seconds, Donny went on. "All my friends are here. I never had any ... anybody before."

Having had enough of Tommy's Namath and Jets Super Bowl predictions, Bain hindered back to Johnny's group. "That idiot thinks the Jets will be good next year when Broadway Joe is 100 percent." He put his hand up to holler out to Tommy. "The Jets won't win the Super Bowl for fifty years!" Tommy could only laugh off Bain's daring prediction.

"Bain, tell him"—Johnny motioned with his head toward Donny—"that he'll always be a part of us, no matter where he goes to live."

As they came up to the next intersection, a herd of cabs raced by on Fifty-Eighth Street. The *salugee* players were already on their way to Fifty-Ninth, but Johnny, Bain, and Donny had to wait for the light to change or else get smashed by a speeding taxi. Now while they stood fixed in place, was the perfect time for Bain to make his point. Sweeping his black hair across his brow, Bain looked into Donny's eyes. "You are not only part of the group, Donny; you are the group."

The traffic light had not changed yet, but there was a lessening in the flow of cars, so the three zigzagged across toward Fifty-Ninth Street. After a dark-green Ford Pinto narrowly hit Johnny, Bain, who was trailing behind, let out a lungy, a Brooklyn term for spitting a heavy snot. The phlegm is believed to originate from deep down in one's lung. Bain's lungy hit the car's rear window.

Standing unscratched on the desired sidewalk, Johnny commented on the incident. "That was more difficult than it should have been." Bain alone laughed.

Donny could only question his dilemma. "I don't want to go away. And what's that mean, 'I am the group'? That doesn't make sense."

"Donny, everybody likes you—the girls, the guys, even Tommy, for Pete's sake." Johnny glanced at Bain for assistance but received only a nod. *Thanks, Bain. You started this.* Johnny continued defending the truth of Bain's remark. "You are likable. You don't brag. You're quiet, but when you do talk, it's … knowing."

"I feel like you guys just feel sorry for me sometimes." Donny looked to his right across Fifth Avenue, not wanting Johnny or Bain to see his face.

Bain felt the conversation getting too heavy on Donny's last afternoon, so he had to end the topic. "You are our little shit. We save your ass because protecting Porky and Shanty isn't fun enough." Then with a little snicker, Bain finished up. "Remember, individually there might be someone better, but as a group, no one is." Bain jogged ahead, slapping his hands over his head for Kevin to toss the football.

"There it is, Donny," Johnny said.

Donny was unsure if Johnny was referring to the little heart-to-heart they'd just had or to the entrance of Central Park. In any case, Donny touched his Christ-head and was grateful for this sunny autumn afternoon with his closest allies.

The eight friends crossed over Fifty-Ninth Street to the Fifth Avenue entrance of the park. Joey asked out loud how old the park was, and Kevin wondered how were they able to place it in the middle of the biggest city in the world. Bain and Donny speculated about how big Central Park actually was. If the boys had not been strangers to their public library, they would have been amazed and schooled in a few facts about their chosen sanctuary.

The true beginning of Manhattan's Central Park came almost forty years before the park's construction was approved. It was the final defeat of Napoleon Bonaparte in 1815, which ensured a safe waterway across the Atlantic Ocean for a mass exodus of refugees. Many European and Chinese immigrants escaped tyranny, unemployment, and mistreatment in their homelands in order to pursue the American dream. In addition, the potato famine in Ireland led to a massive Irish migration during the 1840s. In the years between 1820 and 1855, New York City's population quadrupled in size. The city's population growth over this thirty-five-year span created an overpopulated city in need of accessible recreational space.

With little or no money remaining from their pilgrimages across the ocean, most immigrants had to settle in or near New York City. As the city's population grew, the uncluttered space diminished. The most popular place inside Manhattan where one could breathe a bit of fresh air with less noise pollution was the overcrowded church cemetery—not a desirable choice. To solve this dilemma, the New York legislature in 1853 decided to build a park in Manhattan to rival its European cousins.

The original 778-acre design would extend from 59th Street to 106th Street. A year later, the park was expanded with another 62 acres of city-owned land. The impending park's terrain was swampy, hilly, and rocky, with many fallen trees and shrubs. Clearing the land for an improved appearance would be a major undertaking. Land needed to be leveled and cleared, swamps emptied, pathways formed, and pedestrian bridges built. Before any reconstruction could begin, the generally poor inhabitants of the area had to go packing. Free Blacks and Irish and English settlers, if lucky, were given a small sum for their troubles. Families living on the future park were not the only displaced people.

Through eminent domain, two churches and a convent were also kicked off the newly prospected land.

After fifteen years of swamp draining, reservoir digging, and bridge, road, and pathway construction, Central Park was near completion. To transform the landscape, millions of cartloads of debris had been removed. Emulating European parks, many more plants and trees were planted throughout Central Park's countryside. The labor began before the Civil War and continued until well after it was over, using more dynamite to excavate the land than was used during the three-day Battle of Gettysburg.

Upon its completion in 1873, Central Park quickly became an escape for the people of New York. The transformation of the park continued over time. Roads became wider for the use of automobiles, an ice-skating rink was built, and many children's playgrounds were erected. The park sustains New York's first—and the nation's second—official zoo. There are restaurants, food wagons, bike and rowboat rentals, and horse carriage rides. Statues are constantly being added to honor figures such as Columbus, Shakespeare, the 107th Infantry, *Alice in Wonderland*, and Balto, the courageous Alaskan husky, all of which are on display throughout the park for adults and children alike to admire.

"Wow, look at all the horses." Joey pointed to a line of horse-drawn carriages parallel to the outside wall of Central Park. "I can smell them from here. Raunchy."

Donnie counted seventeen horse-drawn carriages waiting to pick up potential customers. Most could cart four passengers; a few had room for six, maybe eight if you squeezed. Two were coupes with an attached, fixed roof; the remaining carriages were landaus or convertibles, having their heads or hoods open. Each possessed a small battery-operated lantern on either side of the cab. Most of them were a reddish color, although there was one landau in white. The drivers or coachmen of the carriages brushed and fed their horses or peddled their merchandise to the passing public. It was all cash business, which would direct only a true New Yorker to haggle.

Shanty was their banker, not a negotiator. Being the one they trusted with their shared money, Shanty guarded their savings, but under no circumstance was he allowed to negotiate it.

Johnny turned to him. "Shanty, what do we have?"

Knowing what Johnny was asking, Shanty knew the answer, but he still dug deep into his pocket and opened the six bills and a handful of change.

"Eleven forty-four, but let me count it again." Shanty started to count the quarters first but stopped when Bain and the others jay-walked across Fifth Avenue toward the rear of the carriages.

A man in his forties stood in front of his horse-drawn landau flirting with potential riders. Wearing black pants and a matching vest with a white shirt, its long sleeves rolled up to his elbows, the coachman was ready for business. He rolled his black-velvet derby hat down his arm, enticing three teenaged girls before him. "Come … my Daisy will show you all the beauties of the park." Their only response was a girlish giggle as they escaped through the crowds up Fifth Avenue.

"Hey, mister, how 'bout you give my friend here a ride through the park?" Johnny pulled Donny toward the carriage. "It's his birthday today. How much?"

The middle-aged coachman observed the young ruffians. He'd seen plenty of wise-cracking punks before. *They'll bring bad attention here and kill off business.* "Okay, guys, move along to the front of the line if you're serious about a ride." The coachman watched the blond boy who asked about a price turn to his sidekick with dark hair and whisper something to him behind a raised hand.

"Look, mister, we have money," a short kid spoke out. He limped beside the birthday boy. "Your sign says ten bucks for twenty minutes." The disabled boy pointed to the posting on the side of the carriage.

"Yeah, and we have the money," spoke a second, taller, skinny, blondish boy.

"Sorry, guys, you have to go up front." It was not a problem to skip ahead, but the coachman wanted nothing to do with this crowd.

Tommy was quiet until he saw a man in a suite and a lady in a pretty yellow dress hop onto the white coupe that was stationed in the middle of the pack of carriages.

"Johnny, look at that crap." Tommy pointed to the happy, presumably rich couple adjusting their seats for a ride. With anger in his voice, Tommy confronted the coachman. "You're full of shit."

Bain began to join in the debate. "We saw you flirting with those three girls." He pointed into a crowd, although the girls were no longer in sight. "He's going on." Taking Donny by his soiled T-shirt, Bain pushed his friend toward the carriage.

The coachman had had enough. It was Sunday, and business would not be this good until Christmas season. *These punks are a pain and, most importantly, would be poor tippers.* "All right, kids, get away." The coachman walked closer to Bain and Donny. "You with the black hair, get yourself and your boyfriend outta here." The coachman assumed an air of power when he addressed Tommy. "Next time, smart ass, I'll straighten you out, 'cause your pop never did."

The other boys missed what happened next. They had already presumed defeat and began walking to the park entrance. A healthy wad of phlegm, a lungy, created at the bottom of Tommy's esophagus shot up at full speed, racing through his throat. Tommy leveled the clump with his tongue before shooting out with his gunslinger lips. Johnny could not believe his eyes or ears. Bain could, however, and he smiled.

Unaware of Tommy's method of got-you-last, known better as *revenge*, the coachman felt the front of his derby hat press back a speck followed by the ensuing spray. The stunned target did something he had not done since he was a small child growing up in Hell's Kitchen: he spat at someone, hitting Tommy's arm. Hearing the commotion behind them, Kevin was the first to turn back and support his friend. Porky, Donny, and Shanty quickly followed Kevin's trail.

"Shit!" Tommy wiped the spit off his arm with the bottom of his T-shirt. For the second time this day, he had to clean cooties off of his bare skin. *Can't shower now,* he thought. "Whoooth, mmmm, whooooth … Ha, take that." Tommy quickly moved away after spitting his second shot onto the nemesis's face.

The coachman was done talking and spitting, he reached into his cab and brought out a leather riding crop. Holding its silver-plated brass handle, the coachman took a wild swing at Tommy. "Come here you little faggot. Come on."

Bain calmly walked over to pull his friend back to keep him from getting whipped as the coachman took a second swipe. Again, he missed his intended mark but struck Bain on his left shoulder. Witnessing the coachman's pursuit of his friends, Porky didn't know what to do to the authority figure but spit. Unable to muster enough phlegm for a lungy, Porky searched the ground for anything to chuck.

"What the—Why the hell did you hit me?" Bain shouted. Without waiting for an answer, he went for the coachman's whip. Johnny followed Bain, knowing what would happen next.

The coachman, realizing that things had gone too far, retreated to his wagon. Taking his whip, he quickly directed Daisy to sprint in the opposite direction of traffic along Fifth Avenue, away from the park.

"He's making a U-turn right in the middle of Fifth," Shanty said to a stunned Donny. Then he pointed to Porky. "What is he doing?"

Porky hadn't found something to chuck, but he had found something to smear. His antics reminded Donny of a waiter—no, a bus boy—who was carting back a diner's plate and glasses. Like a bus boy, Porky was in a hurry but was very careful not to drop his pile. *Yeah, that's it. Porky's returning to the kitchen with a full load.*

Porky scooped good old Daisy's manure onto a discarded New York Post. Not wanting to duplicate Tommy's adventure with shit, Porky was sure-handed, maneuvering the cootie load onto the sports section of the Sunday newspaper. *I can't let the shit touch me twice on the same day. Tommy would be all over me, and I wouldn't blame him!*

The coachman maneuvered into a broken U-turn and directed Daisy in a straight path away from the chaos with a harried lash. Daisy, unfamiliar with being rushed, stalled for a moment, providing Bain with an opportunity. He rushed to the passenger side of the wagon and, to the surprise of the coachman, punched the lantern, knocking it back into the carriage door. Realizing the feeble attempt at knocking the light fixture off had failed, Bain saw he would need a second shot but at a different angle. Johnny, without hesitation or reasoning, hopped on the driver's side and ripped the second lantern off in one lucky swift stroke. The crack of the lamp leaving the coach alerted its driver.

"You bastard!" The coachman stopped whipping Daisy and took a swipe at the blond kid. After hitting his target's shoulder, the coachman realized a second hooligan was punching the passenger lantern. *Shit!* A subsequent, feeble strike missed the dark-haired kid and had no effect. Turning his attention back to the blond, the coachman hit his mark for the second time somewhere on his head. There was a grunt followed by a curse as the blond jumped off the wagon. At the same instant, his dark-haired friend released the wagon and leapt off. *Good riddance*, the coachman thought.

Continuing his way up Fifth Avenue, the coachman smirked to himself. *I showed those punks.* He brushed his hair back under his hat and then wiped sweat off of his forehead ... or was it spit? Disgusted, the coachman smirked. *Bastards. They'll get theirs someday ... someway.* "Come on, Daisy, we'll hit the other side of the park." Daisy enjoyed the stimulation of the chase but was relieved when routine was restored. *The two lamps are fixable; let's enjoy this beautiful afternoon.* "Good girl, Daisy, now let's make some money. We did show them." The coachman had to be positive to attract Sunday customers; he couldn't let the punks get the best of him.

Turning the corner from Fifth Avenue to Central Park South, the coachman felt a refreshing breeze in his face. He parked his carriage adjacent to the park and worked on the two broken lanterns as Daisy chowed her lunch. Then, as he smiled and sold his services to all would-be customers, the coachman was only rewarded with shocked stares or giggles. For the next three hours on this alluring Sunday afternoon, he didn't pick up one passenger. It was not until he turned his carriage around to return to Fifth Avenue when the breeze wafted the smell of shit toward him from the rear of the carriage. The coachman came to realize the damage that had been done to his business when he saw Daisy's shit smeared all over the back of his wagon. *Not giving a twenty-minute birthday ride ruined my day!*

"Johnny, holy shit. John, are you all right?" an alarmed Bain asked. Before going to Johnny's aide, Bain gave the fleeing coachman one last shout out. "Life is great, skuzz. Now get one!" He laughed, not at his attempt at humor but at the sight of the bolting carriage. "What did yous do to that thing?"

"It was me," declared a proud Porky to a chorus of laughter.

Johnny remained bent over, rubbing his head as his friends encircled him. The scene had Donny thinking of this morning's football game— Johnny calling a play from inside the huddle. "On two … who's better than us?"

"Here, let me see." Bain cautiously disentangled Johnny's muddled hair. "It's not bleeding or too deep, but it's a long mark."

"Let me see, let me see," whined Joey, and the others quickly joined in.

"Hey, hey, back the hell off. This is not a freak show. And you, Porky, with those shitty hands, you don't touch anyone," Bain ordered. Porky started to enlighten him about how it had been carried out but was shushed by the wave of Bain's hand. Everyone else backed off a few steps at Bain's command. Bain turned his attention to a too-quiet Johnny. "Are you good? Does it hurt a lot?"

Johnny spruced up his posture and traced the long cut along his scalp with his index finger. He wanted the attention off of him. *It's not about me. It's Donny's day. Could be Donny's last—last one with us, that is.* "So, Porky, are you done handling shit today?"

Chapter 6

1978

But I heard him exclaim
As he drove out of sight
Happy Christmas to all
And to all a good night.
—*'Twas the Night Before Christmas,*
by Clement Clarke Moore

"He'd go for you." Angela rewrapped her scarf across her face and stuffed the ends between her breasts. "You're only going to …" Sidestepping the location, Angela squeezed Tommy's forearm. "You're staying nearby." Tommy peeked into the doorway, waiting for Nicole, Gina, and Bain to emerge. Angela ignored Tommy's inattention. "Bain and Shanty are going all the way to Manhattan. It could be worse for you."

Tommy returned his attention to Angela. "Oh yeah, or I could just have a good time in a warm house."

Joey and Kevin stood at the bottom of Nicole's stoop, eagerly waiting for Tommy to finish his good-byes to Angela.

"Tommy, come on, we still have to get some beer," Joey called.

Kevin joined in the griping. "And it's ass-cold just standing here."

"Kev, why don't you put that bag back on your head if you're so cold?" Tommy snapped. He then turned to Angela and whispered. "After tonight, I'm done—no, we're done—with this shit."

"They're my friends," Angela protested. "They're yours too."

"Yeah, yeah," Tommy muttered.

Tommy, for once you're right. It is cold out here. I almost forgot about this thing, Kevin thought. He laughed to himself and then reached into his inner coat pocket to pull out his ignored paper bag mask. "Not so bad now." Kevin flattened the bag across his chest, before placing it on his head.

Joey resumed the conversation with Kevin as if the smiling paper bag were the norm. "Come on, come on. Let's go. I'm freezing." He bounced up and down. Then he saw Shanty crossing the street toward Nicole's stoop. "Hey, any luck at Johnny's?"

Besides Kevin with his makeshift headpiece, Shanty was the only male wearing a hat. Smiling broadly as if he had accomplished climbing Mount Everest, Shanty made exaggerated A-okay signs with both his hands before replying. "Johnny's not home, but I gave Terry Tori's number to have him call." Seeing the doubt in Joey's eyes that Johnny would actually call there, Shanty adjusted his original statement. "No matter what, Terry will call Tori if Johnny shows up." Shanty was excited about not messing up Bain's assignment. Now satisfied with his part of the mission, Shanty's smile increased almost to the size of that on Kevin's paper bag.

"Well, if anybody's gonna watch out for Johnny, its Terry." Joey reasoned.

~~~~~~

Tic, tic, tic, screeeech, tic, tic … The underground railroad car hummed its melody.

Johnny ultimately surrendered to the chaotic but metrical sound of metal thumping metal. The consumed quart of Tango would now join forces with the clattering sounds to deliver Johnny into a troublesome vision of the past. The images he would relive were of long ago—recollections Johnny had assumed buried by other, even ghastlier events. Johnny's pending dream, though, was only the leadoff hitter. The dream batting cleanup, with more smack and horror, was in the dugout swinging two bats; the predatory slugger would patiently wait to club later. For the moment, Johnny had to pitch to hitter number one. One demon at a time.

Screeeech, tic, tic …

<p style="text-align:center">~~~~~~~</p>

Johnny knelt down to eyeball his baby sister. "I'll let you do it, but the baby stays up front, not in back of the cow." Johnny handed his sister the crib first. "Here, put it here." Johnny showed the three-year-old the spot inside the manger. "Now you put everybody else around the crib but not anybody in front."

Placing the animals first, Theresa, nicknamed Terry, carefully arranged each figurine. When Terry finished her task, she sought her eight-year-old brother's approval.

"Good, Terry, that's great!" He then handed Terry the baby Jesus. "You get to put the baby in the crib now." Johnny pointed to the crib, and Terry nervously eased the Jesus ornament to bed. "Good job, Terry." Johnny had one last surprise for his sister. "You see this?" Johnny showed her a small round mirror. He'd found a lady's powdered blush outside in the street two days before. Johnny hadn't cared about the blush but had thought the mirror part of it was neat. Using his quarter-inch pocketknife, Johnny had been able to remove the glass without slicing his hand open. He hadn't known then what he would use the crystal for, but an idea struck him now.

"Terry, look at this." Johnny held his round mirror toward the living room ceiling lamp and reflected its light all around Terry's belly.

"Let me do, let me do. Pease!"

Johnny was happy teaching his sister new things but most of all prized her excitement. "Okay, but you gotta not run with it. It's glass."

Terry pointed the mirror to the ceiling and was unable at first to find its reflection. She started to laugh when a circle of light landed squarely on Johnny's forehead. Terry slowly moved the circle down Johnny's frame to the floor and then up the walls. Wiggling the image quickly, Terry screamed out. "It dancing!"

"Okay, Terry, give it back to me." With a little reluctance, Terry returned the glass. "Now where in the manger should we put it?"

"Where? Here." Terry's finger pointed to the right side of the manger where an ox lay. Johnny leaned the circle against the steer; it reflected the rear of a shepherd. Terry looked puzzled; she didn't like her choice.

Seeing his sister's distress, Johnny would now teach her. "Okay, okay … don't be mad."

Terry smiled; she liked being taught, and more importantly, she liked things looking right. "Where we put it?"

The living room had four doorways. There was the entrance to the apartment, the door to Johnny's room to the right, the door to their parents' bedroom to the left, and at the far end was the kitchen access. The couch lay against the one wall with no doorway, and between the entrance doorway and Johnny's room stood the Christmas tree.

The tree itself was a real one. "No fake trees here" his father often said. It stood less than four feet tall because "they charge so much for a tall live tree!" Being creative, Johnny's mother took Terry's toy chest and wrapped it in wrapping paper decorated with the dark-blue night sky with scattered stars of many sizes. On the top of the toy box she laid a blanket of cotton on which the stable was placed. The four-foot live tree was set up right behind.

"What else could this be?" Johnny asked.

Terry shrugged her pajama-clad shoulders. "A wheel!" Terry was happy to assume she had the right answer.

"No, but it could be one."

Johnny had baited his sister long enough. It was show time. Johnny removed the Three Wise Men and their camel from the cotton, as all the other figurines were placed inside the stable. With his open hand, Johnny flattened the raised cotton as best he could. He then moved the Three Wise Men and the camel further away from the entrance to the stable, reached in, and took out the shepherd and two grass-eating sheep. First placing the shepherd between the compressed cotton and the camel, Johnny laid the mirror face up on the level cotton coat.

"Now watch this," Johnny said as he carefully stood the two sheep on the uniform cotton with their heads facing their own reflections in the glass.

"Wow, Johnny, they see 'emselves."

Johnny could only laugh at how his sister grasped the gist of the mirror. "You're right. They can see themselves, but it's not a mirror no more."

Terry said nothing. She could only look at the sheep.

"It's water. The sheep are drinking water."

Terry understood immediately. It all clicked at once. *Oh yeah, water. Sheep are drinking water.*

"Come on, before Dad gets home you … we better get to bed." Mom was chattering on the phone when both children gave her a kiss goodnight. Johnny took one last look at the tree arrangement before departing for his room. Terry bent down to kiss one of the two water-drinking sheep before passing through her parents' bedroom to her own bed.

Johnny watched the blinking Christmas tree lights from his bedroom doorway. It was a peaceful sight. Soon Mom got off the phone, enhancing the quiet and stillness of the night. Just as sleep was about to take charge, the phone rang and then rang again. The front door opened in between rings and Dad yelled that he would answer the "damn phone."

"I got it." Mom replied. Then she picked up the phone and greeted the unforeseen caller. "Who? You want who?" Mom listened to the caller for only a few seconds before blowing her self-control. "You whore! Who the hell are you?" Not waiting for an answer, Mom ended the scandalizing phone call. "Drop dead and go to hell!"

Johnny heard his father speak but could not make out what he was saying. Johnny's mother continued to sob in between cursing her husband and the "whore" on the phone. Then there was a banging noise. *Was that Mom's hand slamming the table? She does that when she is mad,* Johnny thought. He was afraid to leave his bedroom, and he began to worry about Terry. *Stay in bed. Please stay in bed.* For the moment, she did. Johnny put his head under the blankets, not too sure he really wanted to hear what they were revealing. *What's a whore, anyway?* he wondered.

"Look, I love you. I ended it with her; that's why she called here."

"You are no good bastard. I gave myself to you!"

They are speaking louder and clearer now. That was the second time I heard the word "bastard." "Whore" cannot be good, and I know "bastard" is no better. Johnny heard movement in the kitchen. *Was that the chair or the table?*

"You're crazy. I'm outta here," Johnny's father yelled out. "Good-bye!"

"Go back to your whore. Leave me and the kids alone!" Mother's parting words as Dad was about to pass Johnny's doorway, "You're a loser!"

"Loser" is not good. I know that one.

A crash was followed by cracking and thudding sounds. The front door slammed shut, and Mother began to cry. Johnny uncovered his head. He could no longer see the Christmas tree light show from his bedroom. The living room was darkened but not void. Mom was somewhere in there; Johnny sensed her.

In the shadows of Johnny's room, on the floor, he saw a gold, spherical ornament roll to the foot of his dresser. *What did Daddy do?* Johnny waited a minute when he heard sobbing. *Mom's crying.* He jumped out of bed and flicked the living room light switch on.

"Get back to bed!" Mother's face was red and puffy from crying. It was the first thing Johnny noticed but not the last. Mom sat on the floor Indian style surrounded by broken Christmas ornaments, the string of darkened tree lights, tinsel, strung-up popcorn, the manger scene with its inhabitants scattered about, and the broken drinking mirror Terry had grasped so dearly. The tree itself had been flung into his parents' bedroom doorway, creating a forest view for Terry as she squinted through its broken branches.

Crying, Mother ranted about her son going to bed. She had this mess. Refusing to do so, Johnny began detaching the tree from the doorway. Before he'd dragged it a foot, Terry squeezed through between the tree and the doorway and came running to her mother. The two sat on the floor crying while Johnny adjusted Terry's toy box, taped the wrapping paper of the night sky back in place, and reset the manger scene, minus the drinking pool. He stood the trampled tree up on the torn cotton, salvaged the unbroken ornaments, and, with the help of Terry, placed them back on the remaining feasible branches. The broken balls, tinsel, and stringed popcorn mother picked-up. The vacuuming would have to wait till morning.

When most was cleaned, Father came home right on cue and said four words: "go to bed now." The two sobbing children did so without saying a word, although Terry began to cry louder. Mother walked her youngest to bed in a forceful manner. Johnny knew why mother would do such a thing—it pissed Daddy off. Terry was his baby girl, and Mother wanted her scrap of revenge.

Less than a minute had passed before their fighting resumed. Each parent was up for the knockout blow. Lying in bed Johnny could not confirm when exactly the knockout shot arrived, but when it did, the arena became quiet. Then panic rushed in.

"Oh my God, oh my God …" Good ole Dad began to pray. "Oh my God." Johnny had never once heard the old fellow plead so much. "I'm so sorry. Shit, I'm so sorry." Mom remained quiet. Johnny began to wish for his Father's death, or at least for the prize fighter to just disappear. "I'm so sorry," Dad kept repeating.

There was a few more minutes of whispers, and then Mom spoke clearly in a low, comforting tone. "It's all right. It will be all right."

Dang, no luck. The Ali versus Frazier fight was over and neither one would leave the ring. Terry and Johnny would have to stay around for the rematch.

"Here, let me fix it," Dad said.

Mom insisted all was good, but her voice told Johnny from two rooms away that it was not.

"Let me put a butterfly stitch or two on it," Johnny's Dad continued. "Hold it like this, and I will get them." A few seconds went by. "First we'll clean it."

Great, Mr. Fix It is now a doctor. Take her to the hospital! And what the hell is a butterfly stitch? Johnny put his pillow over his head. *That sounds cheap.*

Johnny stayed in bed the rest of the night. He continued to listen to the jesters in the kitchen. What was going on in there? He no longer cared; his worries were for Terry. Did she hear all of that?

When he got up for breakfast the next morning, Mother was in an insanely good mood. As Terry and Johnny ate Quisp cereal, Mom explained her blackened eye and her bandaged cheek. "It was an accident. I was vacuuming last night and tripped over the wire. You know, I was so tired. Anyway, I fell right on the butt of the cleaner."

The two stunned children said nothing but continued eating when Dad entered the kitchen. He asked Terry what she wanted for Christmas, and then he gave Mom a kiss. She gave him a cup of coffee. *All is good here in buffoon land,* Johnny thought. Terry put her spoon into her unfinished Quisp and began to cry. She realized it too. All was not so good.

"Terry, don't cry. You're a good girl. Santa will get you something special." Dad came over to kiss his daughter's cheek, but Terry turned away.

"Theresa, you give your daddy a kiss and tell him what you want," Mom said.

Mr. Fix It and Mrs. Enabler stood over their daughter to pressure her into a world that was in no way normal.

Terry would not accept Dad's morning kiss, but her crying did ease. Johnny figured it was because she was extremely tired with no fight inside. After a few deep breaths, Terry whispered to Johnny out of earshot of her parents, "I want sheep drink water again."

~~~~~~~

"I won't tell you again! Last stop. You gotta get off."

Johnny's foot fell forward, giving him the sensation of a misstep onto a sidewalk curb.

"Let's go."

Before the conductor kicked again, Johnny waved off the assault. "I'm up." Johnny's mouth was dry, reminiscent of the landscaped cotton where the sheep once drank. "Uh, what stop is this?" The train conductor fastened his top button and then pointed toward the underground platform. "Okay, I'm going." When Johnny stood up, he stumbled, grabbing the subway poll for balance. *I'm drunk.*

The conductor made way for Johnny to leave the subway car first. His voice softened as he offered some fatherly advice. "You better get on home, kid. Harlem ain't no place for whitey."

Johnny mumbled thanks and then went on his way to cross the platform. *I missed my stop. I slept right through it. What a drunken ass I am!* When the train exited the subway station, Johnny jumped off its platform onto the tracks, as Donny had once done to retrieve a fumbled football. Johnny crossed the tracks and managed to make his way up the three-foot platform for the train heading south to Central Park.

Chapter 7

1973

And they call it puppy love
Oh, I guess they'll never know
How a young heart really feels
And why I love her so...
—"Puppy Love" performed by Donny Osmond

"Look at those two girls." Bain perched near the top of an eroded rock. The boulder was one of many carried into Central Park ten thousand years before during the last ice age. "Shanty, I think she likes dark meat, 'cause she keeps lookin' up here." Below the boulder where the boys panted were two teenage girls lying belly up on a blanket.

"Na, they don't want spic mutton; they want the Polack sausage," chimed in Tommy. With his mouth, Tommy mimicked a fish out of water. "Joey, let me get another slug." As he put his hand out for Joey to pass along a can of Dr. Pepper, Tommy slyly swiped from Porky's hand a piece of his pretzel.

"Hey, you ate yours."

"Screw you. I'm not done with you yet." Tommy chewed the stolen bit of knot and promptly chugged his soda.

Donny disliked it when Tommy bullied people, especially Porky. "Tommy."

"What?" Tommy gulped the last of his soda and then burped. "What, what?"

"Porky never washed his hands, not after the horse shit or after touching the human shit neither." Donny saw Porky quickly look down at his hands.

Tommy could only wave off the obvious. "Smart ass, I took the piece your boyfriend hadn't touched." To the delight of Bain and everyone else, Tommy knew he had gotten zinged. "Yeah, yeah, yeah," was all he could mutter before returning everyone's attention back to the girls on the blanket. "How old do you think they are?"

Johnny, who had never taken his eyes off of their bodies, was quick to respond. "About sixteen, maybe older." Kevin and Joey nodded in agreement as they continued to eat their charcoal-heated pretzels. "I like the one with the blonde hair better. She sorta looks like Marcia Brady." Everyone on the rock agreed. "The other one could be Mary Ann from *Gilligan's Island.*" There were additional nods to these assertions. "But I wouldn't throw neither one out of bed. Who am I to do that?" The affirmations became laughter, although only Bain and Tommy truly understood the wise crack.

"What are you laughing at?" Tommy said, tossing a pebble at Porky. "You wouldn't know what to do with a girl in a bed."

To the left of the rock, shaded by an oak tree, Joey began to laugh about a different subject. Embarrassed about the information he had just entrusted his pal with, Kevin pushed Joey hard to the edge of the boulder.

"Hey, I almost fell off!" Looking downward fifteen feet to the ground, Joey added, "I can't help it. You're retarded." Then he snickered some more.

"Hey, what did he say?" asked Shanty, relieved it was not him uttering something stupid.

"Remember in the park this morning when Pork was chasing Tommy with shit?" There was a mumble from Tommy as everyone else agreed. "Well, that old Polish lady Tommy ran into, she had a dog." Joey started to laugh again before continuing. "She said something to her dog in Polish."

"So?"

"Kevin wanted to know if dogs understood Polish."

Bain gave his younger brother a soft jab and waited for the laughter to subside. "Yeah, Kev, dogs only understand English. It's the universal language of dog." The laughter continued until Tommy went back to harassing Porky.

"So, Porky, what would you do with a girl all night?"

"Oh yeah." A defiant Porky assumed he knew the answer. Making a circle with his thumb and middle finger on his right hand, Porky put his left index finger through the hole.

"Oh big deal. Everyone knows that." Tommy shot back. "How long does it stay in?"

Porky had heard the expressions *they slept together*, *they spent the night together*, and *all night long they did it* on more than one occasion. He didn't want to sound foolish, but he had to answer Tommy with what he assumed to be true.

"You put it in … and in the morning, you take it out." Porky looked over at Joey and Kevin for some reassurance. They only shrugged their shoulders in halfhearted agreement. Tommy was not so subtle.

"You're an asshole," Tommy shot back, then he continued to be brutal until Johnny interrupted the onslaught.

"Marcia Brady's takin' her shirt off." Johnny spoke louder than he had intended, but he was too excited to hold it in. Bain hushed Johnny as the boys were provided with their first strip show. Marcia Brady slowly unbuttoned her blue, round-collared shirt and exposed her white tube top held up only by two robust breasts for all to see.

"I think she heard you," Bain whispered to Johnny, "but I don't think she cares." Marcia Brady turned to the boys and gave them a smile before lying down on her blanket. "Please turn over … please," was all Bain could say.

Mary Ann from *Gilligan's Island* did them one better. Facing away from the boys, she removed her T-shirt, revealing her bare back. If she'd had a bra on, it was already disconnected. Mary Ann then laid stomach down, joining Marcia on their shared blanket. Both girls began to giggle as they cherished the warmth of the sun and the ogles from the adolescents up on the rocks.

When the boys had mounted the ancient boulder fifteen minutes before, they had spread out into smaller groups to eat their afternoon snacks, but as Marcia and Mary Ann began to striptease for the boys, the youngsters funneled their way to the narrow edge of the rock. The span of eight spectators decreased dramatically as they all rivaled for a better view.

"Maybe they'll kiss. Oh, please kiss," begged Bain. Johnny and Tommy agreed.

"Move over, homo. You're breathin' on me," Kevin said, offering a comeback to Joey's earlier Polish dog remark. "It's like you never saw a real boob before."

"Like you have," Joey countered.

"Guys, cut it out," demanded Bain. "They won't kiss if you two keep it up." He then grew impatient. "We can't see shit from here anyway." Bain thought for a second and then spoke to Johnny. "I got a great idea."

Johnny took his time answering Bain. "What?"

Bain's plan was simple enough. "Let's just go there and tell the girls the *truth*. We'll swear we think the blonde girl is Marcia Brady. Okay, that's a lie, but they won't know it. She'll be flattered and laugh. Then we can hang out on the blanket with them."

"Oh yeah, that sounds good," Tommy remarked sarcastically. "What, are we just gonna walk up to them and say that?"

"No, stupid." Bain took the last sip of his soda and then continued. "Kevin, can you reach them?" he asked. "You have the strongest arm of all of us."

"But he can't quarterback for shit," added Joey.

"He doesn't have to be too accurate; just stand up on the rock and throw the ball. Johnny and I will be between the girls and here. Kev, throw it a little bit over our heads. When the football stops bouncing in front of their blanket, Johnny and I will introduce ourselves, and we can all have a good look."

"Why do you and Johnny go? I'll go down with yous," Tommy protested.

"Because if it's too many of us down there, they might cover up," Bain explained. "The rest of yous, wait here till we call you down." Tossing his empty soda can, Bain spoke directly to his brother. "Kev, it will only work if you throw the football far enough, because if you can't reach us, there's no way for us to get to their blanket. Make sure you at least reach us."

Kevin smiled, it would be his time both to show he's a better quarterback than Johnny and to see his first live tit.

The girls relaxed unaware on their red-plaid blanket as Bain and Johnny climbed down the left side of the boulder. Once the two boys reached the grassy knoll, Johnny pushed Bain to the side of the rock and sprinted toward the direction of Marcia and Mary Ann. "Kevin ... look, I'm open!" Johnny shouted as he clapped his hands for the football.

Kevin stood on top of the boulder griping the pigskin tightly. "Hey Kev, there's chips on the ball," yelled out Shanty as he and the others followed Johnny and Bain down the rock. The term *chips* was Brooklyn slang for the financial responsibility one had when handling another's property.

"How much?" Kevin responded, knowing that never in Brooklyn's history had anyone ever paid a *chips* debt.

"Five bucks!"

"Yeah, ok!" Now it was back to business. *Don't worry, Johnny-boy, I see ya.* Kevin planted his feet firmly on the loose gravel, not wanting to slip after this lengthy toss. *The fall would surely break my neck.* Kevin heard his friends from below cheering and encouraging him on. *Keep running, Johnny. I'll show everyone here how great my arm is.* Kevin, with all his might, released the football high and far in the direction of Johnny.

Bain was trailing his conspirator by at least seven feet when the football glided directly above him. *Good throw, bro.* Bain admired the height and the perfect spiral of the ball overhead. *You really want to be quarterback. Too bad you can't hit the side of a barn ... but you do have a helluva rifle.*

Kevin quickly raised his arms in triumph to the cheers and praises beneath. *You want it deep, Johnny? You got it.* Regrettably, the hailing lasted not more than a couple of seconds before they all saw the football's endpoint.

From his perspective on the ground and lagging behind, all Bain saw was a perfectly thrown ball. From his position further up the grassy turf and closer to the landing of the flung pigskin, however, Johnny was able to estimate its crash site with sounder precision than Bain's. Stopping about eight or nine strides from Marcia and Mary Ann's blanket, Johnny could only watch the football sail over his head toward the unsuspecting sunbathers.

Oh, Shit! "Heads up!" was all Johnny could muster as he stopped fifteen feet from the plaid blanket.

Marcia relaxed on the overlay with her tube top half folded into itself, exposing additional skin to the sun and her salivating audience. Unfortunately, in Marcia's world, *heads up* meant nothing. She remained stationary until the football torpedoed into her left hip, narrowly missing her exposed ribs.

Unaware of the missile launched by Kevin, Mary Ann was lazing in a peaceful slumber, enjoying the sun and the soft breeze stirring through the trees. The sensation of having her spine visible created a feeling independence that Mary Ann enjoyed the most. *Look here, boys. Do you like what you all see? If your good and with a little luck, maybe I'll—* Suddenly she was thrust into reality by the nightmarish scream of her friend lying beside her.

Bain reached Johnny's side as the smack of leather slapping the skin of Marcia's hip echoed. It was promptly followed by the victim's loud shriek.

"Oh shit, oh shit," was all Johnny could muster as he lingered in shock.

Bain sprinted to the football, which rested on the blanket to Marcia's right side. Marcia continued to roll in agony when Bain knelt down on the grass and slowly reached over the blanket to fetch the ball. "Eh, sorry 'bout that one," he said. Then he smiled. "There's chips on the ball." Bain calmly but quickly jumped back to Johnny's location at the same moment the remaining gang arrived.

"You assholes!" Figuring out the football most likely had something to do with Marcia's pain, Mary Ann lashed out at the stunned boys before her. "You … idiots." Marcia stopped rolling and began to rub below her rib cage. "Are you okay? Is it your ribs?" Mary Ann saw a red welt grow on her friend's skin, infuriating her further at the youths. "Well? What are you looking at? Get the hell out of here!"

Marcia adjusted her tube top, which kept her knockers hidden, unlike Mary Ann's attire. When she sat up, she felt a bit dizzy, although the aching of her skin began to subside. "You heard her. Get the hell away!"

Unmindful of showcasing her own topless self, Mary Ann continued to curse out loud and directed her rage at the latest person to join in the spectacle. Joey had missed the original onslaught of Mary Ann's anger because of his limp but not her finale. "What are you staring at, you dumb-ass cripple!"

Tommy first giggled. Then he brought his friends out of their stupor and the teenage girls into a frenzy when he responded, "*He's* a cripple? How come that boob is pointing to the left and the other booby is drooping down? Your tits are the crippled ones here."

Mary Ann quickly covered herself with a corner of the blanket, knocking Marcia off onto the grass. Marcia grunted as the pain in her hip returned with full force. "Easy! My side is killing me."

Mary Ann had had enough embarrassment and torment at the hands of this curious, pesky brood. So she did what, as the boys each surmised, all teenage girls do when in a crisis: she yelled.

~~~~~~~

"What did she mean by *seasoned*?" Angela asked Tori of Gina's apparent put down. She eyed the intersection before crossing the street. "If she's saying I'm a snob or something, well, she don't know me." Angela was upset with the whole Donny situation but she was selfishly more distressed about her newly found friends' demeanors. "Look, if you all think that way of me ... so be it. I don't—" As they stepped onto the safety of the adjacent sidewalk simultaneously, Tori motioned with her eyebrows for Angela to enter the candy store first.

Once inside the store, the girls walked to the *Elton John Pinball Wizard* machine. One quarter got you two games with five balls each. Tori had no interest in the high score or in a free game; she was here to educate her sensitive friend.

"You are what you are. You have more than most of us. Everything is handed to you, but that's not always a bad thing."

Angela bit her bottom lip. There was no evidence of sarcasm in Tori's voice, so Angela listened.

"See where you come from, everything is black and white, yes or no. There is no gray area. Your life has a steady path ... a destination." Tori waved her right hand with the bravura of a cowboy releasing his rope to snare a bull. "Things in life don't work that way here. We do many wrongs to get a right; that's the norm."

Angela understood what Tori was saying but did not like it. Before she could speak, Tori confirmed it.

"We want a clear road to travel on too, but we don't have one. What we have is ... each other. Okay, I know that's corny. I should have said we just live for the day and react to it the best we can." With a sigh, Tori finished. "So, someday you will go away to college in some fancy city, like your sister. You will be far from here and back to your clear, black-and-white world. If by chance you ever do return, you'll be conceited and all high and mighty. You'll pretend like you don't even know us."

With tears in her eyes, Angela walked toward the back of the candy store to the comic book section. There she heard Tori order two ten-cent Lucy's and a nickel cherry water. Angela picked up *The Archie's* comic and inspected the cover. Archie was dancing it up with Veronica as the band played on in the background. *How short are her shorts? And the tits on this one …* Angela flashed a smile before reality hit her. *They hate me. Why am I even here?* Flipping through the comic, Angela regained her composure and was ready to head on home, *where it's safe, and black and white!*

Tori walked to the comic book stand holding her sixteen-ounce cup. "Hey, I don't know how I got so far off the subject, but what I started to say is this. You are what you are. We all like you. We can't all be the same, and besides, it's no fun that way."

Angela tossed the comic into the *Superman* pile and then amended her lob. *Everything has its correct spot. Black and white, all right.* Angela turned to leave the store, uncertain what to do next—go to the playground with her so-called friends and live life's full-color-gamut high wire or walk on home to the stability of the black and white.

"Wait up!" Tori's lidless nickel water was filled to the top. "I can't walk so fast without this shit spilling."

Angela stopped at the entrance of the park as Tori reached her. The two girls walked together while Tori went on about some gray issues in her life. To her left, Angela could see the playground through the bushes and scattered trees. Nicole had Bella's chain and was walking the dog back and forth between the bench and the monkey bars. Angela could only assume it was Gina who sat on the bench conversing with Nicole.

I can keep on walking and be done with them all. Clear-cut. No gray area here.

"I said, where are the kids that were just playing? Are you even listening to me?" Tori got on her tiptoes to give herself an additional inch. "I don't see anybody besides Nicky and … there's Gina."

What keeps me with them? What draws me to these girls who think I'm a snob, that I'm spoiled or privileged? Though, you are right, Tori. I am what I am; there is no changing me. The longing to be here? I don't know why, and I no longer care. "Tori, hey listen." *Be swift, be clear, and no backing down.*

"Oh shit, there are the kids." To the right of Angela, as Tori pointed out, was a crowd of encircled youngsters. Those closest to the center of the circle knelt. On the outer edge, the standing children leaned forward, not wanting to miss the lesson. Tori noted the pupils' studious behavior. "What are they all up to?" Tori wondered aloud to herself.

"I was saying …" Angela was forced to follow Tori to the right side of the playground so her adios conversation would and could continue. *Give me a second here. I don't want to talk around all these kids.* "As I was saying—"

A small, fat kid of about six years old sporting a crew cut and a red-striped shirt that he had grown out of long before today turned to quiet Angela's whispers. "Shhhhh. She's talkin'."

"All right, fatso. We want to hear too," was Tori's response. She was not going to be disciplined by a fat kid.

Angela shot Tori a look but was unable to make it stick. *Did I say my friends are crude too?* Angela watched Tori squeeze between the fat kid and a squatting red-headed girl. *What's the fuss about? Now I have to wait till this breaks up.*

Catching Angela's attention, as well as everyone else's, was the tutor in the center of the loop, a girl no more than seven or eight years old. The young tutor had the blondest hair Angela had ever seen. It was neatly tied back in a ponytail. She was wearing a white United States Navy outfit with clean, white Converse All-Star sneakers with dark-blue laces. The young tutor's face had a clear complexion but was smudged with a few colored chalk markings. Her blue eyes darted from child to child. Everyone here felt as if she were only talking to him or her. *Every child feels special,* Angela thought, and she bent forward to eavesdrop.

"It's very easy once you break it down." The young tutor reached into her rear pocket and showcased a thick, gray-colored piece of chalk. "Now watch. You can and will do this." Taking the chalk, the young tutor drew a large X. "See how easy? That's the hardest part, and you can do it," the young tutor said, repeating her encouraging phrase. "Now at the top part of the X, you draw parallel lines up a little and cap it with a triangle." She drew as she explained. "These two lines are parallel because they run along each other but never cross, and everyone here knows what a triangle is. There you go." Pulling a second piece of chalk from her pocket, the tutor continued. "It looks a little like a tall pencil. So we put dots in it to make it appear like light is leaving the windows. Now to the left and right sides of the X, we draw lines connecting the top part of the X to the bottom part." She spaced the lines differently on both sides. "See, these are buildings. Now, you put in a door for each enclosed space with added windows, and of course chimneys, too." After filling up her drawing, the young tutor was ready for her finishing touch. "Lastly, the bottom half of the X is the street. Here we put broken straight lines. These are the traffic lines."

"Wow, I want to do it!" was the most popular response from the young lads in attendance.

The young tutor tossed out her remaining chalk sticks to her audience before standing up.

"I want one. I want to draw it," several children called out.

The young tutor brushed the chalk from her knees and enlightened the kids. "Everyone will have a chance." She then walked to Tori, said hello, and asked for Bella. "I love that dog. She always gives me kisses."

"Bella is crazy about you, too." Tori moved away from the mob of young artists. "I have to say, you are such a wonderful teacher."

Angela joined in. "Sweetie, that was … just so good." Angela could not compliment this child enough, so she went with the obvious. "You will make a difference someday." The young tutor's cheeks turned red in embarrassment. Not wanting to put her on the spot, Angela moved away from the subject and asked a question. "What is your name? Mine is Angela."

The young tutor's hands were chalky, so she wiped her itchy left eye with her inner wrist before answering the question. "Hi, my name is Terry."

Tori interrupted. "Hey, Terry. We're over by the monkey bars." Tori nodded over to Gina and Nicole. "Just send Billy there when he's done here. Thanks."

Once out of earshot, Tori whispered to Angela. "You know who she is?" Angela somehow recognized the little girl but didn't know. "She's Johnny's little sister."

"Wow," was all Angela could mutter. She walked in silence with Tori toward the monkey bars. *It sorta makes sense—Johnny, the great big brother; Johnny the glue that holds them all together; Johnny the one orchestrating the Christ-head for his misfit friend, a gift with plenty of thought and consideration; Johnny the one they all turned to when things were not right, when their times turned to shades of gray. Johnny, what is about you … that keeps me near? Johnny …*

"Damn Angie, can't you hear me?"

"Oh, I'm sorry. I was thinking what a sweet girl Terry is."

"Yeah, very, but I'm sayin', what were you going to ask me before?"

Angela exchanged her escape-route question for one regarding something she was really curious about. "What is a Lucy? I heard you before in the candy store asking for two of them."

Tori laughed. Then she bent down to pet Bella. "Come here, baby. Mommy loves you." Bella jumped up Tori's knees as Nicole passed off the dog chain.

"What's so funny?" Nicole asked.

"It's not a Lucy, like *I Love Lucy*; it's a loosey, like a loose cigarette." Pulling the two she bought out of her top pocket, Tori flipped one to Nicole. She started to light the other for herself but then turned to Angela. "Unless you want it. I know Gina won't smoke." Gina waved her hand side to side in a negative demonstration. Angela too declined the cancer stick. "I figured." Tori placed the nickel water on the bench and then lit her cigarette.

Angela subconsciously side stepped the cigarette smoke and gazed at the area where the small children and their young tutor were. *Johnny, there are gray areas all around us, but you are not one.*

~~~~~~~

The boys ran until there was no breath left in them. Laughing and running at the same time had its way of extracting precious oxygen from one's lungs.

"That's it. I can't go anymore." Porky put up his right hand as if to wave a cab.

"Yeah, this is far enough," joined in Bain. "Screw them. Now they can see firsthand why Kev can never be our quarterback." Bain's joke created elicited sounds somewhere between coughing and laughter from the group.

"All right, we stop here, but not because Porky says so," chided Tommy. "And Kevin, you do suck!"

"Never mind that. Did you see their tits?" asked Joey. Everyone except for Shanty joined in to reminisce about the prized sight. "Donny, you'll never forget your first bouncy titties."

"It didn't go as planned, Bain, but I have to admit, it did work out pretty good." Tommy wiped the sweat off of his forehead with his T-shirt and then winked at Donny. "How's that for a going-away present?"

Before Donny could answer, there was a call from the distance. "Hey guys, over here." A shaken Shanty had continued fleeing from the scene and was further up a hill beyond where the boys had originally stopped. "The pond is right down here." Shanty pointed along the widened hill toward a view the boys were unable to see.

Johnny, shrugged his shoulders and spoke to Bain and Tommy. "It's getting late. Let's hang out by the water for a bit, then we gotta get goin'." The two friends nodded in a solemn agreement, all aware of the growing size of the afternoon shadows.

Time's running out for us, for Donny. Pick it up. Don't be a downer, Johnny thought. "Kev, look, I'm open." Johnny slapped his hands together as he raced up the hill waiting for that perfect pass. Bain quickly pushed Tommy to the side and hurried after Johnny to intercept the thrown football.

Chapter 8

1978

Strange days have found us,
Strange days have tracked us down.
They're going to destroy,
Our casual joys…
—"Strange Days" performed by The Doors

In the early part of the 1800s, the cemeteries of Manhattan began to fill to capacity because of a cholera epidemic. The Catholic Church of New York City decided to build a new cemetery outside the populous borough and continue burials across the East River in Queens.

The planning and construction of Calvary Cemetery overlapped the building of Central Park during the 1850s. The seventy-one acres of land purchased for the dead was located on the southern point of Queens, touching the northern peak of Brooklyn. Calvary Cemetery would continually expand, eventually reaching over three hundred and fifty acres of land, to accommodate the interments from influenza and tuberculosis outbreaks.

Many boulders besieged the land of the future cemetery. The builders decided to use these obstructions to create one of Calvary's charms. The encasing walls of the cemetery were constructed from the dormant stones. The hilly and sloped grounds demanded a stone barricade from three feet to as high as twenty feet tall. The entrance of Calvary Cemetery was deliberately constructed on the low ground that required only a short, four-foot wall so that all could view its sacred grounds and tombstones.

In time, teenagers would take advantage of the low wall to gain easy access to nighttime mischief. Ultimately, an eight-foot, picketed steel fence would be added, drilled into the cemetery's boulders, to discourage off-hours access. The defensive strategy worked against most but could not intimidate all delinquents.

Across from the one-hundred-twenty-year-old graveyard's gateway on the Greenpoint Avenue side of the cemetery remained a flower retailer, a tombstone display shop, two bars, four empty dirt lots, and two beaten-down single-family homes. Where the cemetery bent eastward, adjacent to its stone walls, ran the Long Island Expressway, better known as the LIE. The LIE followed the asymmetrical outline of the graveyard for a quarter mile before the grasslands curved south onto Laurel Hill Boulevard. The southern backdrop was similar to that of the eastern, except the highway running parallel was the Brooklyn Queens Expressway, or BQE. The cemetery's last twist heading west leads to Review Avenue. On Review is the continuation of junkyards, empty lots, and a lone active business—a stone quarry. Beyond the quarry, at the end of Review Avenue, one passed an abandon storefront before reaching Greenpoint Avenue.

The deserted storefront had been a thriving flower business throughout the 1940s and '50s, back in the time when families visited their deceased loved ones on a regular basis. By the late 1960s, families were continuing their visits but placing flowers on grave sites less frequently. With competition from the flower store on the busier Greenpoint Avenue, the Review Avenue shop could no longer remain in business. Soon after the last flower arrangement was sold to a World War I veteran's widow, Review Flowers closed its doors, and the owners left their second-floor living quarters in the spring of 1968. For ten-plus years, the only inhabitants of the building were rats, mice, squirrels, and stray cats—that was, until Dylan, one of the Madd Tuffs' scrubs, and a few glue-huffing lowlifes began to shelter themselves there from the world outside. They all got high off of the bagged, venomous industrial fumes "to dream." This lasted a couple of weeks before the sanctuary was taken over by the Madd Tuff gang itself after Dylan spoke of his whereabouts to Fagan. Dylan's glue-huffing buddies would have to find another hellhole to die in, because this shithole would now be run by Junior and his gang.

Two hours after Porky's startling death, Fagan stood by a window on the second floor of the shithole. Adjusting his droopy pants with an irritated motion, Fagan could no longer tolerate the whining of his fellow gang member. "You better stop crying like a freakin' baby." Fagan picked up his falling pants with his oversized belt. Then he pointed into Hogan's face. "If anybody's goin' down, it's you and him." Fagan gestured toward an upset Brodie.

"Screw off. We didn't do shit," Brodie shot back at Fagan. Then he spoke to his younger brother. "Come on, Hog, we're goin' home."

"Bullshit." Entering the barren room was Junior. He had his girlfriend, Kimba, on his arm. Fagan was about to explain the situation but was cut off by Junior's wave of the hand. "You two ain't goin' nowhere, at least not now." Brodie wanted to speak, but he knew it was Junior's pulpit for the moment. "What that asshole Porky did tonight is on him, and that's what we'll all stick with." Junior smiled at Kimba as she pulled back her dirty-blonde hair. "This will only make the Madd Tuffs more feared; guys are *dying* to get in. That'll be the word on the street."

Fagan whispered out loud. "And it's true."

"Right," agreed Junior. He returned his attention to the brothers. "This is why we have initiation. Some get in; others don't."

Brodie turned his attention to Fagan, pointing his own finger in Fagan's face. "Don't threaten him again, or I'll tear that finger off of your goddamn arm." Brodie bumped shoulders with Fagan as he passed him by. Fagan was about to say something, but Brodie had already left the room.

Hogan wanted to follow his brother but didn't want to seem like a pussy, so he remained in the front room, standing between the two sheet-covered windows.

Junior whispered something to Kimba, and she quickly left the room, following Brody's exit. Junior nodded for Fagan to walk with him to the far end of the candlelit room, leaving Hogan between the two windows. "Make it right with both of them. There's no need for us to fight each other." He then instructed Hogan, "Hogs, come here and get away from the windows too." Hogan hesitated. "Come on, cops ain't comin'. If they were, they would have been here by now."

"That's if they knew where we were," Hogan replied. He left the window as his brother entered the dimly lit room.

"Junior, we got a problem." Brody wiped his running nose with his exposed wrist. Before he could speak further, he was cut off by Fagan.

"Guys, we gotta stick together. We are all in … and Porky's an asshole for screwing himself up. It's on him not on any of us."

"Yeah, yeah," Brody replied before turning back to Junior. "It's Dylan. He's havin' a bad trip. I took the bag from his face. He's on the floor of the kitchen; he's trippin' out."

"Asshole," was all Junior could say before he was followed out of the room by Brodie and Hogan.

Kimba was not in the mood for any this drama tonight, so she sat on the lone piece of furniture in the room, the "make out couch," and lit her cigarette. Fagan didn't follow the other members to the kitchen area but remained by the street-facing front windows. Fagan's presence pissed Kimba off. *He's a creep. This is somehow all his fault.* Kimba climbed out the window facing the garage rooftop to enjoy her loosey in peace. Smelling the coldness of fresh snowflakes and the warmth of the cigarette, Kimba stared out into the desolate cemetery wondering what the hell she had done to be involved in such a mess.

⁓⁓⁓⁓⁓

The entranceway to the second-floor apartment opened onto its kitchen. The only remnants of the once-used refrigerator and oven were their yellow-stained outlines on the wall. The Formica counter top had been ripped from the cabinets and wedged between the wooden butcher's block in the center of the room and the closed bathroom door, strategically set to warn all not to enter. This was because the stoned glue-huffers had figured out early that one didn't want to have a bad dream while tripping. If Junior, Fagan, or any guest removed the blockade, the scent behind the door was enough to sicken one to sobriety.

What remained of the checkered, black-and-white linoleum flooring had barely withstood the test of time. Its corners curled upward, exposing the wood flooring beneath, and it buckled in the flooring's midpoints, creating the illusion of a tsunami approaching the main land.

The two windows in the rear of the kitchen faced the garbage-littered backyard. Broken bricks, bottles, a tire, a smashed television tube, a rolled-up rug, and many bags of assorted garbage were strewn about. The chain link fence once erected for security now lay twisted and mostly hidden by the overgrown shrubbery and the disposed refuse.

Beyond the cutting board and the reeking bathroom, an open passageway led to the living room, or parlor as it was known back in the 1950s. A sixteen-inch black-and-white Zenith television set once leaned against the wall across from a red Koehler sofa and matching chair. Now a discarded queen-size mattress adorned the parlor, its exposed springs twisting upward as if pursuing freedom. The floor was covered with beer cans, fast-food takeout bags, and other random garbage trailed into the chamber. The scent of the bathroom combined with the pong of the room with the archaic television was too much for any Madd Tuff to tolerate. The gang had to reside inside one of the two bedrooms.

Luckily, the door separating the living and sleeping areas remained functional. The first area past the doorway was the bigger of the two bedrooms. Here was the Madd Tuffs' sanctuary. Junior felt they needed one place where they could all congregate. It was essential that the location be free of garbage and stench; it should be an organizational setting resembling a room with resolve. Kimba explained to Junior what the missing elements were, along with what the requirements would be for such a locale. First, everything had to be chucked out—the second mattress, three full garbage bags, the worn rug, broken glass, and any other trash, all shoved out the kitchen window to the pigsty of the yard. Second, the walls and ceiling needed to be painted, the brighter the better. Fagan and Hogan stole four gallons of matte white paint from the local paint supplier; unknowingly, they pinched ceiling paint. The walls befell a dull finish. The plywood originally laid down as the subflooring had withstood the test of time and remained intact. The flooring would occasionally be swept clean by the newest member of the gang. In the center of the room stood a wooden table with a propane lantern bordered by six worn but sturdy wooden chairs. On the left side of the windowless room, there was a dresser full of propane tanks, candles, matches, three baseball bats, a four-foot industrial chain, a flashlight, a few looseys, and a hammer. On top of the bureau, two candles burned on either side of a JVC dual-tape boom box. The opposite wall remained empty for the moment. The matte coated walls dimmed the light from the lantern and candles, lending a coziness to the rally point.

The second and last bedroom in this apartment haven looked out onto the street below. This room was in a similar condition as the parlor, with garbage thrown throughout, but it was absent the torn mattress or any other castoff furnishings, besides the make out couch. No candles or lanterns were allowed here, since they did not want to draw attention to their hidden fortress. The darkness of the area was perfect for sexual activity but not much else. On the left side of room were two recently sheeted windows. Both windows faced Greenpoint Avenue, and if you stuck your head out of one and stretched to the left, you could see the Greenpoint Bridge connecting to Brooklyn. Extending your head in the reverse direction, you could see Calvary Cemetery.

On the right side of the room, there was one double window, which provided an entryway to the roof of the single-car garage. It was here that Kimba had questioned her sanity after having come out onto the roof to escape the lunacy inside. The roof operated as a stepping stone for the gang's bathroom. To eliminate any further odors in their future palace, the rule was that you simply stuck your dick over the edge—no pissing or shitting where you slept. As for the shitting, if you had to go, you'd have to find a bucket, use it once, and then toss into the yard.

The end wall of the apartment, which was the back wall of the bedroom, was where the last two covered windows looked out on Calvary Cemetery from the Review Avenue side. It was here, between the two rear windows, that Fagan pondered, staring out into the graveyard, and wished for a lucky break.

~~~~~~~

"It could be a lot … burrrp …" Joey wiped his mouth with the back of his jacket sleeve and then added with a chuckle, "Bain could've sent us to Manhattan."

Kevin nodded his bag-covered head in agreement. The Unknown Comic look still had some humor left.

"Yeah, right. No way was I goin' in the city … and Bain knew that. That's why he didn't ask me to go." Tommy looked over at Kevin's bagged head and shook his own. "Guys, I gotta take a piss. Give me a second." Tommy walked to edge of the Greenpoint Bridge guard rail and unzipped his pants, pointing his manhood out over the frozen creek below.

Joey and Kevin continued walking slowly down the second half of the bridge. The snow stopped, but the wind became stronger, icing everything, including their exposed limbs.

"Damn beer. I gotta keep switching it from hand to hand," complained Joey.

"Do you really think Johnny's here?" Kevin wiped his hidden running nose from outside the paper bag. "He's been different lately, like he never got over Angela or what happened way, way back after that night in Central Park …"

"He always blamed himself. No one else would ever, but Johnny's so freakin' stubborn. No wonder Angie left him." Joey's limp kept pace with Kevin. He turned around quickly to ensure Tommy remained out of earshot.

"Yeah, Bain says the same stuff about Johnny." Now it was Kevin's turn to look behind them. "Bain also said it was Johnny who dumped Angela. Even after what he did to her, she still wanted him." Then with a little chuckle from under the bagged head, he added, "That's what drives Tommy crazy."

"Hey, there it is," Tommy yelled from behind. He was referring to the dimly lit corner of Greenpoint and Review Avenues where Calvary Cemetery began. "He's here. If not, I'm done."

"It won't be for nothing if he's not," Joey chimed in. "We can still have a beer there before Christmas. This could be a new tradition."

"Like hell it—Hey man, what the …" Tommy watched Kevin walking and pissing simultaneously. "I hope the wind changes. Please, God, if you can hear me, blow it back on him." Tommy shook his head, cracked open a beer, and then spoke to Joey. "How many more do we have left?"

"Six. I told you two six packs wasn't enough."

"Cool." Tommy shrugged, not taking the bait from Joey's preaching. "We'll have one inside and one on the way home or before we hit another bodega."

Leaving the walkway of the Greenpoint Avenue Bridge, Tommy and Kevin were the first to reach the picket fence of Calvary Cemetery. Joey followed ten feet behind the two, as hobbling and peeing had a way of slowing a person down. "Hey, wait up. Someone might have to nudge me over the fence."

"The pickets are all iced up." Kevin muttered.

"Duhhhhh, of course, asshole." Tommy punched a hole in the snow and dirt between the steel poles. Then he grabbed the steel rod and hoisted himself above the three-foot stone foundation. He then slid his boot between two of the parallel bars. "See, it's easy … just follow me up." Tommy's attention went back to the top of the fence, where some eight-inch spikes glistened with snowy ice. "Put your hand in between and be careful of those." Tommy pointed to the spikes. With a slight slip of his second boot, Tommy adjusted his balance, muscled his way between the spikes, and jumped down into the fenced-in cemetery. With a whoosh sound, he landed in the snow. Then he took three steps back and clapped his hands for the bag of beer.

〜〜〜〜〜〜

Screw you … you bitch! Fagan sucked off the last of his cigarette before tossing it in the direction of Kimba and the rooftop-facing window. With his cigarette snuffed, the back bedroom returned to its grayish hue. The light originating from the street lamps outside, the sole light source in the room, barely strained through the murky bed sheets hung in the windows. *We're losing it. Porky's dead, Dylan is more trouble than he's worth, the brothers want out, Junior's girlfriend is trouble, and now … now we need something—anything—to get our mojo back.* Fagan listened to Junior and Brody try to wake Dylan from his faraway glue trip. *"The Sound of Silence"—great song. It's not Zep, but … Hello darkness, my old friend. I've come to talk with you again …* Fagan pulled out a sixteen-ounce Budweiser from his inside coat pocket, popped the lid, and sucked down half the can. *Everything is goin' to the shitter. Something has to give now, or we're done.* There was more commotion from two rooms behind him. *How about "The Sound of Crazy"? Hello darkness, I'm in pain. I am surrounded by the insane … Better yet, "The Sound of Hullabaloo"?* Fagan watched Kimba climb back through the window and leave to the second bedroom. *I should've locked the damn window; it would have been one problem solved.* Fagan listened to the commotion inside the kitchen through the closed door. Dylan wanted his glue bag back. *Great … just call it a night.* Fagan then experienced a peculiar impulse to peak outside the sheeted window.

"Holy shit! Junior! Yo, Junior, come here. Hurry!" Fagan open the mock drapes up for all to see clearly through the window.

"Hey, close that up. Someone could see us here," Brodie said. He was the first into the room, followed by Hogan and Junior. Kimba and a stumbling Dylan were ten seconds behind the first crusade of onlookers.

"Shhhhhh … look." Fagan's bent elbow pressed against the uncovered window as his index finger pointed across Review Street to the Calvary Cemetery side. "See, they came out on our turf, tonight of all nights." Fagan stood back so the others could witness the intruders. "They must've followed us to this area and are looking for us now."

"No, they ain't like that," Hogan butted in as he watched from the window. "Its Joey and Tommy … and Kevin. I saw him earlier with that stupid bag on his fat head. They aren't lookin' for any trouble."

"Shut up. You don't know shit," Fagan countered. He was delighted someone of Hogan's stature in the gang had spoken out first. Shutting him down quickly would put the others in tow. "Look"—Fagan backed off his offensive tone for the moment, trying to sound reasonable to the others—"we just have to see what they're doing here."

Junior nodded in agreement. "Yeah, let's go down there and figure this shit out."

Fagan smiled to himself. *This is exactly what we need to get our mojo back!* "Just in case, we'll take some backup," he said, referring to the bats and the chain."

The gang ran to the dresser to retrieve the weapons, while Kimba got the window view all to herself. The sheet used for a curtain fell back across the glass, so Kimba raised the cloth with her left hand and peered into the shadows.

Yes, that is Joey on the outside of the cemetery gate supporting Kevin, the fool with the bag on his head, his foot helping him over the spiked fence. Tommy is already in the cemetery standing in the snow, ready to catch The Unknown Comic if he falls face-, or should I say, bag-first to the ground. Kimba turned away from the window and marched past the chaotic and scrambling Madd Tuffs in the living room. She grabbed her coat, which was lying on the cutting board table inside the kitchen. She felt a sudden chill in the air. She was about to rid herself of the shithole and its squatters once and for all when she heard the rumbling of a ... *bus?*

Chapter 9

1973

Reflections in the waves spark my memory,
Some happy, some sad.
I think of childhood friends and the dreams we had.
—"Come Sail Away" performed by Styx

"Watch this one." Porky side-armed his rock into the shallow end of the pond. Following its first splash, the flat stone never emerged for a second plop.

"You suck. Look at this." Bain mimicked Porky's horizontal motion with his arm, and the thrown flat rock landed further out into the pond. He cheered as it skipped nine times on the surface. "That's how ya do it."

Joey's attempt went three and under, and the other friends had similar results. Bored, Tommy began to shot-put larger stones into the calm water by its shore, splashing anyone who attempted to beat Bain's nine-skip record.

"All right, all right. That's enough. I'm all wet, Tommy, you ass," complained Joey.

Porky joined Shanty and Donny under a Norway maple tree while their friends continued to skip small stones and lug boulders into one another's areas. Twenty feet from the controlled chaos, the three rested and chatted. Donny sat on a boulder with his torn sneakers dangling a couple of feet above the grass explaining his situation.

"Shanty, it could happen to you. If your mother dies and your whole family lives in Cuba, who'd take you in?" Receiving no answer, Donny went on. "Then the state has to." Donny ran his fingers through his Christ head's chain, appreciating its weight on his dirty and stained T-shirt. Shanty, unaware of his vulnerability until this moment, wiped many small beads of sweat from his forehead. Donny, sensing Shanty's sudden discomfort, quickly added, "Nothin's gonna happen to your mom … She's not a mess like mine."

Porky, for the minute, wasn't concerned with Shanty's imagined dilemma but with the facts presented by Donny's narrative. "So a family takes you in to live with 'em?"

Donny nodded.

"Do they have kids, too, or other foster ones?"

"What about school? Do you even have to go? When are you coming back?" interjected Shanty.

Donny could only shrug his shoulders and whisper, "I don't know." Taking a blade of grass and then darting it into the direction of the pond, Donny had one closing declaration. "I know one thing: I want to stay here. I don't want to go."

At that moment, Johnny walked to the underbrush of the maple and caught Donny's last statement of displeasure. Grasping everyone's anxiety, Johnny decided not to let their afternoon end on a sour note, or without a memorable mark. "Kevin, look, I'm open."

Kevin chucked one last flat stone, hoping to beat Bain's nine-skip record, before picking the football up off the grass and openhanded a long hurl to Johnny. Johnny sprinted from the cheerless shade of the tree and raced near the water's edge. Though he'd hoped Kevin's usually inaccurate arm would stay true to its fashion, Johnny was disappointed by the thrower's precision. In contrast to Kevin's earlier pass to a sunbather's hip, this time Johnny was able to catch the football running in stride before both hit the water's touch. *Timing is everything. For once I needed a shitty throw from ya!* Not able to pin this on Kevin, Johnny had to take the situation into his own hands—or foot. *Watch this guys. How long before Shanty yells out "chips"?* Johnny stopped running with the football and took a deep breath. Facing the pond, Johnny held the football and extended his hands while dropping the ball forward above his right foot with perfect punter's form. The football fell diagonally onto the navicular portion of his foot, better known as "the sweet spot." The football soared far, sacrificing height for distance, which was Johnny's desire. The shoreline friends stopped and observed the destiny of Shanty's football in disbelief.

Shanty's yell the instant the football splashed into the center of the pond did not surprise Johnny or any other child. "I said it before! Chips! That's five bucks!"

Before the circles on the pond surface could dissipate, Johnny trotted back to the maple tree without saying a word and sat beside Porky. Johnny hurriedly kicked off his sneakers, socks, and dungarees. Lastly, he tossed his shirt onto a low-hanging branch. Everyone gathered around Johnny, questioning his next move.

Bain asked first. "Are you goin' in?"

Johnny, in his underwear, feeling the coolness of the early-autumn afternoon, went to the pond's edge and touched the cold water with his foot. Wordlessly, Johnny dove into the shallow water head first. *To shake them up? To unify us? To give Donny and everyone else a lasting memory? To get the damn football? All the above. It's worth a shot.* Swimming into the deeper water, Johnny could hear laughter behind him. He knew the laughter was not directed at him but was created by his unexpected act. Johnny was about five feet from the floating football when he began to doggy paddle. Now without the sound of his own splashing and kicking, Johnny could take notice of the activity behind him.

Bain was following Johnny, trailed by Tommy and Shanty. Donny, Porky, and Joey were dog-paddling closer to the shore but remained determined to reach the deep end of the pond. Kevin, too afraid to swim, walked out into the water up to his neck, his arms raised high as if in a stick-up. *He's trying his best, as are the others, to present Donny with this fantastic send off.*

Johnny grabbed the football and tossed it as best he could to the dog paddlers. Joey grabbed the ball and tossed it over to Kevin closer to the shore. "Broadway Joe looking deep. A man is open!" Kevin threw it back to Johnny as the passing, catching, swimming, dunking, and laughter continued hysterically in the pond.

When the commotion in the water began to attract a small audience of onlookers, the boys in the pond decided the adventure and fun of the afternoon should come to a bittersweet end. The crowd and the racket would surely interest the police, so it was decided to leave the meadow on a high note, which had been Johnny's goal from the start.

Bent over laughing in two feet of water was Kevin. He remained there while his friends passed him by as they climbed ashore. "Oh shit, that was too funny," was all Kevin could muster.

Joey faked Kevin a hand off with the football and then tossed it to Shanty, who was running out of the pond. "Play action pass!" Joey yelled. The unexpected pass hit Shanty's right shoulder and then fell into the shallow water beneath. "Shanty, you suck." Then Joey went into his best Howard Cosell imitation. "Meami has da orrangeas, but Buffalo has da juuice!" At everyone's laughter, Joey went on. "Cuba has the seagarz, but Brooooklyn has the Shant!"

Tommy grabbed his dry T-shirt off of the tree branch and whipped Porky's bare back.

"Oh shit!" Porky yelled out, more shocked than hurt.

Bain got in the action, snapping his shirt at Johnny; then there was a retaliation from Joey. Donny, the only one who'd had his shirt on in the water, whipped his torn pants at Tommy and then Bain. All were joshing each other indiscriminately one way or another.

Standing up on the boulder where Donny had sat previously, doing his best to explain foster care, Johnny yelled, "King of the mountain!" Everyone quickly focused on him and succeed in knocking the king off of his throne. As the group piled on the king, Johnny could only shriek. "Uncle, uncle. I give!" To the delight of his challengers, Johnny had one additional declaration. "Guys, guys, who's better than us?"

In unison, the gang yelled, "No one!"

The boys looked at one another, as they all laughed and cheered their daring accomplishment in the water. It was the happiest moment of their lives. They would never again feel so independent and free from the real horrors to come. They had one another; individual faults and differences only cemented their friendship. Shortcomings were a part of life. If there was a heaven, all would agree it was now.

Johnny ran to the shore of the pond and picked up a flat stone, similar to the rocks the boys were side-arming into the water earlier. "Guys, everyone find a good rock." Johnny displayed his own. "When Donny comes back home, we'll come back here and toss these stones into the water together."

With electrified emotions, the gang searched the grounds for their temporary keepsakes. One by one, each child proudly exhibited his gem before burying it inside his pocket.

The cheerfulness and attachment each boy felt for one another delivered an uplifting surge of hope for all. The common thought of *Donny may be leaving us, but we will get through this together.* For about a minute, hope did arrive, but it quickly disappeared before all were even dressed.

Reality wantonly crushed the optimism of youth with its stranglehold on their foreseen adult lives. The cheerful aura of the group was socked by the realism of adulthood. Being muddied, wet, and cold could not squelch the joy in the air, unlike Shanty's next question.

~~~~~~

"Billy-boy, you are such a mess. Here, have some cherry water … before Nicky drinks it all on ya." Gina winked at Billy and then placed the sixteen-ounce drink into his chalk-covered hands.

"Thanks." Billy downed half the flavored water in one gulp. "Damn, that's good."

Nicole was about to reprimand her brother's fresh mouth when Angela interrupted. "Billy, what did you draw?"

Billy took a second swig of his drink and then spoke rousingly of drawing Batman, Superman, and The Flash. "But I had to tell Terry what Donny plained to me."

"Explained, Billy. *Ex*-plained," Nicole corrected.

"Flash can't be."

"Why's that?" Angela wanted to know. Nicole and Gina giggled, but Tori seemed interested too.

"Because The Flash would starve to death if he ran soooo fast, silly." Billy smiled at himself, proud to get all the wording and theory right.

"Well, I think all the superheroes are full of it."

Billy finished his drink before kicking the empty cup behind the bench into the bushes. "I'm tired and hungry. I wanna go home now," he whined.

Angela peered over the bushes and searched for Terry or any of the children who had shadowed her earlier. The section of the playground where the Manhattan skyline was drawn was now empty, as the pack of young pupils had scattered about. Angela's concern was for Terry, the child teacher. *Johnny lives across from Tommy a few blocks from here. I can catch her if I leave now.* "All right, I'll see you all across from the church at six tonight." After a few grunts of agreement, Angela finished, "Bye-bye."

Leaving the park as quickly as she could, Angela began to doubt that she would be able to catch up with Terry before the young girl reached home. *Please, please, I have to meet her ... know her ... know Johnny.* At the park's entryway, Angela worried that she may have somehow already passed Terry. Angela turned around and searched the other pathways and benches in case Terry's pace had slackened. *Nope, she had to leave.* After exiting the park and hurriedly fleeting the corner bar on Nassau Avenue, Angela paused in front of a six-family tenement. She was sure the young artisan would have had to pass by this building. She eyeballed the sidewalk on both sides of the street but saw no sign of Johnny's sister. *Where did she run off to?* Angela stood with her hands on her hips, upset that she was not quick enough to catch the young girl in the white sailor's outfit. Angela bit her lower lip in frustration and contemplated a return trip to the playground. Before moving her feet one way or the other, Angela identified an unpleasant, gamey scent. *Like at the zoo ... the inside a lion or gorilla cage.*

"Hey, jerk-off, what you standing in the way for? Move the hell over. You're blocking my door."

"Oh! Oh, sorry," was all a surprised Angela could mutter. She watched the older woman stumble up a step and into her building's vestibule. *What was her problem? There was plenty of room to get in.* The woman was in her late thirties, maybe forty, but could have been older. She wore a house dress, had her hair in random curlers, and wore beaten Whalebone Platform wide-heeled shoes. *What a mess. She's angry. No, she's an angry drunk.* Angela observed the irritated lady through the glass front door as the woman fumbled for the secondary hallway keys while balancing a brown bag, most likely of booze. Finally she found the keyhole and entered the hallway.

~~~~~~~

Damn radio. It's a piece of shit. Marian played with its dial, trying to arrange a vibrant sound from her transistor. Frank Sinatra was singing "My Little Valentine" through the clatter and static of her handheld tuner. *What's the use?* Frustrated with the jangle, Marian turned the dial down to the off position. *Sorry, Frankie, but you sounded like I feel: like shit.* With her beer still in its shopping bag, she tossed most of it inside her refrigerator. *But one of you will stay out with me.*

Marian popped open her beer can and scratched her itchy head. *These are coming out.* She removed the four mingled curlers and flipped them onto the small kitchen table. *What's the use?* Dragging out one of the two wooden chairs, Marian sat down and began to massage her foot with her left hand while she held her Budweiser in the right one.

Four pints of beer later, Marian felt light-headed but happy, for now. She checked out the clock on the oven; it was going on four. *He should be home soon.* Getting up from the kitchen table, Marian took a sharp left turn to the bathroom before plopping herself on the living room couch. *That's better.* She reached under the couch for her personal stash—a bottle of Windsor Canadian Whiskey. *Okay, okay, I promised I'd be good tonight. Just one. Yeah, one and done. My baby will be home soon. I need to hold him one last time. He's such a good boy, unlike his dad.* Marian slugged a two-shooter down. *Perfect ... and then I'll do my hair up nice, like it used to be.* Marian closed her eyes as the whiskey brought her a ray of sunshine. *Oh so warm.*

Fifteen minutes and three slugs of whiskey later, Marian's emotional roller coaster took a nose dive from euphoria to despair with a sudden turn toward gloom. When the incline slowed the ride as it rose up the lift, Marian's gloom built with anticipation and weakness. *Thump, thump, thump. Up I go!* Stopping momentarily at the top of the hill, Marian anticipated the last free fall, while her foremost character flaw patiently waited at the bottom beyond the ride's end. *Where's my boy? He's goddamn late again!* The cycle was complete when anger greeted her on the slope at the ride's end, replacing the coaster's break system with a green light for a second ride. *And around we go again!*

Two slugs later, Marian's head began to spin as she stayed lying on her couch. She stared at her torn wall paper and the peeling paint on the ceiling. *No amount of booze can doll this place up.* Her eyes stopped moving around because she became dizzy and did not want to get any sicker. Marian fixed her glare on the side wall where her couch was parked, and she placed her left foot on the floor. She'd once heard that when the room is spinning, you should always place a foot on the ground as you lie there. It gives you stability. *Well, the trick worked before. Why the hell not today?*

Two minutes later, the motion of the room decreased. Marian continued to stare at one spot as the shadows began to play tricks on her, or so she thought at first. *No, no, that's not a shadow figure. That's real.* Walking down the wall toward her space was a certified Puerto Rican cockroach. *La cucaracha, la cucaracha. Da na na na na na na. La cucaracha, la ...* With her right hand, Marian intentionally smacked the wall some six inches below her intruder. *Just need to scare it off.* The cockroach took the message and hurriedly retreated back up the wall. *I bet he's a scout and is going to warn his spic relatives. La cucaracha, la cucaracha. Da na na na na na na ...* With a little insane laugh, Marian picked up the bottle with her left hand and downed the last ounce and a half of whiskey. Before closing her eyes, Marian twisted her head and glanced over at the stove clock. *Twenty minutes to five. He was supposed to be home by four, damn it! He's as bad as Lorna. I can't—I won't—have another one like her. He'll learn.* Marian's fury was overridden by her drunkenness; she closed her eyes and fell asleep.

111

Less than ten minutes later, Marian was awoken by the whisper of her smiling son. He stood before her in the shadowy room holding a glass of ice water. Marian rubbed her eyes clear. The red, hooded "I Love New York" sweatshirt was something new.

"Here, Mommy … this will make you feel better."

~~~~~~~

"Donny, how come you kept your shirt on? It's all wet. We still gotta get home." Shanty asked this harmless question as he and the others put on dry shirts.

"Anybody lookin'?" Tommy asked no one. Then he quickly tossed his wet underwear onto Porky's exposed shoulders.

"Hey, what the …" Porky complained, but he knew Tommy was on to something. "Yeah, screw this." Porky tossed his wet shorts off in the direction of Tommy before putting on his dry pants. The others followed suit. No use having wet underwear with dry clothes. Donny, too, flung his underwear off into the bushes, but he still wore a wet T-shirt.

"Yo, Donny, you shoulda taken it off before goin' in," Kevin jawed about Donny's wet T-shirt, rolling with Shanty's question.

Bain gave his younger brother a stare and then nodded to a grimacing Johnny. Donny could only shrug his shoulders, hurrying to zip his pants. Bain, Johnny, and Tommy all knew why Donny's shirt stayed on, but it was Bain who acted upon the knowledge. "Well, we just have to get our football hero a dry shirt."

Kevin remained tenacious. "Yeah, but he shoulda taken it off."

Without warning, Bain's open hand rammed Kevin's forehead. Kevin's feet tangled as he fell back, falling to the ground and landing on his ass.

Shock and then pain passed over Kevin's face. "Hey ... what the hell?" Embarrassed, he decided it was time to save face. Kevin jumped up to go after his older and stronger brother.

"Woo, woooo, grab him." Johnny seized Kevin's arm and was joined by Joey in firmly guiding one sibling away from fighting another. Kevin continued to curse Bain as he was pushed further from the area. "Kev, stop it now!" Johnny shouted. He got into Kevin's face and was ready to hit him if needed be.

"Come on, you wanna go too?" Kevin shoved Johnny. Johnny swung and hit Kevin's cheek, knocking Kevin into Joey's arms. Shanty, Tommy, and Porky came in to separate the two bare-knuckled boxers.

The threats and cursing continued until Donny uttered two words that ended the dispute among brothers and best friends. "Hey ... guys." Standing upon the rock where Johnny had declared himself king of the hill not more than thirty minutes earlier, a shivering Donny removed his wet T-shirt. All could see the reason why the shirt needed to stay on.

"Holy shit," "What is that?" and "What happened?" were the most common responses from his pals. Donny said nothing but moved the Christ-head chain toward his right shoulder to give them a full, unobstructed view of his bare left chest.

A disturbing mark—a purplish red oval, or as Kevin saw it, an incinerated football from hell—covered Donny's left nipple. Located inside the oval football were brighter red markings. Kevin was about to ask what those were but wisely stayed quiet. It struck him at about the time it struck everyone else what they were and how the injury most likely occurred.

Teeth marks!

Without a word, Donny jumped off of the king-of-the-mountain boulder and began to put his wet T-shirt back on. Porky was the first but not last to remove his own dry shirt and hand it to the abused victim.

Kevin, who was in a daze, was the last friend to follow protocol. "Take mine, please. I … didn't know."

"Neither did I," added Shanty.

"Enough … Shanty, how much money do we have left in the pool?" asked Johnny. Then he spoke to Donny. "Put on any shirt. We're gonna take care of this."

"We have $3.85, but we need $2.80 to get home," Shanty figured.

"Look, there are a lot of carts selling shirts and shit all over the park. We'll work it out," Johnny replied. He then pulled Tommy to his side. "Just see what you can do."

Tommy smiled. He already had a plan figured out. "Okay, but I'll need two others. Everyone else, we'll meet you at the Fifth Avenue exit."

"Joey, me, and you, then," Johnny answered. "We'll catch up to the rest of you by FAO Schwarz." Johnny figured he and Tommy were the fastest runners, and Joey's handicap had a disturbing effect on strangers.

"Just like the horse ride went," a sarcastic Porky said.

"Shut up, asshole." Tommy threw a fake punch at Porky. "Lucky for you I'm busy, or I'd kick your ass now."

Donny began to protest but was cut off by Johnny. "Here, you take my shirt for now. We're getting you a new one." He pointed his index finger skyward. "Bain, see you at the toy store."

Bain, Porky, Donny, Shanty, and Kevin departed Central Park through the Fifth Avenue exit, as Johnny, Tommy, and Shanty ventured north toward the park's zoo section, where many late-day merchants continued to sell their goods. It was four o'clock, and an abundant number of people strolled about the park. No matter. Donny needed a shirt, and the boys would get him one despite the situation.

"Asshole," Bain said to Kevin as Shanty, Donny, and Porky continued to keep their eyes on their three friends inside the park. "Yeah, you."

Kevin stopped watching Tommy, Joey, and the shirtless Johnny to wave off his brother. "Listen, I had no idea about Donny. Neither did the others. Only you and Johnny did."

"And Tommy," Bain corrected.

"Whatever. But that was no reason to smack me. And Johnny should mind his own damn business once in a while."

Bain peered over the four-foot stone barrier erected over one hundred years before on Central Park's east side. Not surprisingly, Bain watched Tommy and Johnny haggle with a dupe as Joey wormed his way behind the shirt stand. "It's not about Johnny, and you know it." Bain looked for Donny, making sure he was out of earshot. "Donny's in deep shit, both at home and wherever he's gonna end up."

Kevin was quiet for a minute before uttering. "What can we do?"

"There may be something. Let's wait for the others; we can all talk about it on our way back to Brooklyn."

"Look, you stupid refugee, I can go up to $3.50 and not a penny more. I need a shirt." Shirtless Johnny reasoned.

The "refugee" Johnny referred to was a young man no more than twenty years old. The man spoke with a thick Haitian accent. He had an irregular mustache, and his hair was collar length and parted to the right side, reminding Johnny of a West Indian poor man's version of Ringo Starr. Ringo was tall and well-built but hunched forward, as if he were dealing a deck of cards constantly. *He must be working plenty of overtime at this slab peddling shitty stuff.*

An older lady behind the stand, Tommy and Johnny presumed, was Ringo's mother. She began to pile the sweatshirts back in their boxes. Already the concert T-shirts were put to rest for the night. *They're getting ready to close shop*, Tommy thought correctly, understanding that time was running out.

"Okay, okay, we ain't no tourists. How much are those concert shirts in the box?" Ringo pointed to his mother for assistance as Joey lingered, kicking the grass about fifteen feet behind the cartons. Ringo proudly unfolded the blue concert shirt and displayed the singer on the shirt's chest.

"It is five dollars, but we are closing, so I give it to you for three dollars and quarter, quarter, quarter." Ringo smiled at Tommy while Joey inched closer to the goods.

"What the hell does 'quarter, quarter' even mean?" a dumbfounded Tommy asked.

"And quarter. You missed one. He means it's $3.75," Johnny interjected. "And who wants an Elton John shirt anyways? I want the hooded sweatshirt for three bucks, quarter, and one—and only one—more quarter. Besides, Elton is a—"

"Now you boys go home, or I call the cops." The mother stopped packing the shirt boxes and walked around the table to face Tommy and Johnny. "Go on, get out of here." She pointed her finger in Tommy's face and then in Johnny's. During this planned commotion and distraction, Joey came up behind the stand and easily swiped a red hooded sweatshirt and for kicks swiped an Elton John T-shirt too. "Go, go now. I see a cop over there."

"Lady, that boy is your son?" Tommy asked as Johnny began to hurry away, knowing the shirt was taken and an insult was to follow. "Yeah, him." He pointed to the big Haitian.

The Haitian mother said nothing.

"I could tell." Tommy saw Joey leaving the park while Johnny waited within range. "You both sport the same mustache."

~~~~~~~

"Wow, thanks guys." The boys off to the right of FAO Schwarz on Fifty-Eighth Street surrounded Donny as he gave Johnny's shirt back and put on the stolen red, hooded "I Love New York" sweatshirt. "It has a zipper! Zippers are so much better."

"Good, champ. You'll be warm in that." Before Bain could explain his plan to everyone, he had a few words of advice for Donny. "Donny, you're gonna need that sweatshirt where we are off to."

Chapter 10

1978

These boots are made for walkin',
And that's just what they'll do.
One of these days these boots are gonna walk all over you ...
Are you ready boots? Start walkin'.
—"These Boots Are Made for Walkin"
performed by Nancy Sinatra

When logic and proportion have fallen slowly dead...
—"White Rabbit" performed by Jefferson Airplane

Clap. "Shit." *Clap.*

Ignoring the sound of clapping, Dylan twisted his ass for comfort. *Out there is cold ... yet so welcoming.* Dylan peered through the back window of the imaginary bus and saw nothing but the inviting softness of cotton. *Clouds ... they dip and rise. Or is that snow ... maybe snowy clouds?* Dylan glanced forward, trying to recognize the driver of the animated vehicle. *I know him ... I know ... Yo, man, when is the next stop? Vroom ... Off we go!*

"Dylan ... Dylan ..." a soft pretty voice called out. Dylan quickly rotated away from the bus driver and turned to the seat on his right. "Dylan, come on in. Can you hear me?"

Dylan could only nod to Kimba.

"Come on, Dylan ... take my hand."

Dylan put his hand forward and felt the warmness of Kimba's touch. *She's so pretty—the curly blonde hair, her raised cheekbones, her smile, and ... the fear on her face?*

"Dylan, come back with me. Please," Kimba pled.

Dylan twisted away from Kimba and gawked out his rear-seat window at the entertaining clouds. *I want to run through them.* Breathing heavily onto the glass window separating him from his vision, Dylan cleared the moisture buildup on the glass with his sleeve.

Clap, clap.

The fogginess remained. He wiped again. Dylan lost the view, so he stood up to leave the bumpy ride of the bus and connect with the beauty of the clouds and snow. *Vroom ... Off I go!*

"Dylan ... Dylan, where are you going?" Kimba held her smile, but her eyes reflected terror. "Stay here. Don't go out there." Kimba reached for his hand, but he opened the exit door. "It's a long fall."

Only one step off the bus, Kimmy. Whaddaya mean "long fall"?

"Last stop! Everyone off," a familiar voice yelled from the driver's seat. Dylan knew the voice and suddenly wanted out of the bus. "What is the hurry, Dylan?" the driver of the bus cried. "I'm a Madd Tuff now." Dylan put his right foot on the first step down to the exit, but there was nothing there, only air. Dylan needed to ask the driver where the step was.

"Porky?"

"Yeah, Dylan, it's me." Dylan could only see half of his friend's face, as the other half hid in the shadow of his scarf. "I tried to fit in, and I woulda, but Ma made me wear this." Porky lifted the scarf from his neck to showcase it. "It does keep me warm. It's very cold here where

I am." Porky stood up from his chauffeur's cushion and began to walk toward Dylan. "If you jump off now, we can be ghost riders forever."

Clap, clap.

"Who's better than us?" Porky put his hand out for Dylan to grasp. When he did, the scarf fell to the floor of the bus. Dylan could see what was left of Porky's crushed skull.

As fright hit, Dylan put his right foot out of the bus door. *Where's that step?* Dylan's foot peddled downward into a bottomless vortex. *The clouds have no surface; that's it.* The blast of icy air and blown snow began to awaken Dylan from this dreamy mayhem.

Clap, clap.

Dylan began to focus on reality when he heard Kimba's soft speech change to a high pitched scream.

"Move!" Junior knocked Kimba down as he grabbed hold of Dylan's collar. Junior and Dylan tumbled together to the kitchen floor narrowly missing the fallen Kimba. "He's in a glue dream. Clapping and speaking softly don't work," Junior scolded Kimba.

Dylan began to moan and complain about the cold outside. Kimba stood up but did not offer to assist Junior off the floor. "Well, excuse me. I'm no expert on your glue-huffing shit." Pulling her hair back off of her face, Kimba bolted from the room in disgust.

Hogan pushed a stunned Brodie to the side of the cutting-board table and nearly stepped on Dylan's chest. "What's going on?"

Brodie gestured to the fallen Dylan. "He was havin' a bad trip. He wanted to jump out the window. Kimba was trying to talk him back inside. He kept saying Porky's name … and saying how he wanted to join him."

"It's that damn glue," Junior correctly assessed.

"We have Tommy and the other two shitheads snooping around out there on our turf," Fagan spoke softly. He did not want to lose any mojo because of Dylan. "Let's get Dylan outside too; the cold air is what he needs now." Walking to the dresser, Fagan was followed by all the gang members. "How are you, Dylan? Any better?"

Dylan mumbled "Yeah" as Fagan opened the dresser draws.

"Let Dylan have the hammer."

"Asshole," Kimba spoke under her breath but loud enough for Fagan to hear. She watched them gather their arsenal before bolting to the street below. Kimba smiled, for it was the first time in a long time, that she was truly happy. *I have finally hit rock bottom. I can't go any lower. I'll finally start my climb.*

⌐⌐⌐⌐⌐⌐⌐

Tommy knew Johnny would not be here. It made no sense, and more importantly it was a waste of his time. Angela had asked him to go, and not wanting to look like a dick, Tommy had no other choice. *This is it, Angie. I'm done. We are both done after tonight.* Tommy stepped off the plowed road onto the curb and into the snow-covered pasture. The mausoleum with the modest Italian name *Aita* was the final landmark on the way to their dismal destination. The snow removal from the road had made their earlier walk slippery but bearable. Walking onto the snow-covered grass increased the difficulty level for their final steps.

"Wait … be quiet for a sec." Tommy's gestured with his right hand for them to stop.

Kevin began to giggle under his bagged head, but Joey was worried. He twisted around to survey the tombstones and their shadows behind them. *Nothing.* "Na, it's nothing."

122

Tommy agreed and then blew into his frozen hand and continued up the hill.

On either side of the searchers stood headstones of many sizes and designs. Most were cut with a smooth, finished, curved top; there were a few topped with stone crosses, and then there were Tommy's all-time favorites—the few gravestones with crying, winged angels. Spotted throughout the graveyard were mausoleums with family names, such as Aita, carved into the stone above their iron crypt doors. Tommy had been to the cemetery a few times in the snow but never at night. As the snow stopped and the clouds began to dissipate, the three-quarter moon began to shine its bluish-gray light on the snow-covered tombs and their surroundings. It was all like a mystic, dreamlike place beyond this world. Tommy guessed that the sensation of being there was similar to what the astronauts must have experienced as they first stepped on the moon.

In his haste to be the first to hopefully discover Johnny below the hill, Kevin slipped, falling into Tommy's right shoulder. "What the hell's the matter with you!" Shocked and a little scared, Tommy shouted louder than he intended. "Come on, Kev." Tommy composed himself and whispered. "Take the bag off and watch what the hell you're doin'."

Joey squinted down the hill and was the first to see the gravesite empty of Johnny or anyone else. "Johnny's not there. He never was. We would've seen footprints somewhere."

Kevin removed the bag from his head for a clearer view into the darkened shadows. "Yep … no Johnny." The cold air caused Kevin's eyes to water, but he continued to observe the backdrop. "Let's go. There's no one here."

Tommy agreed, but Joey was unconvinced that they were alone in the cemetery. "Wait … shhhhh."

"It's nothing. I thought I heard something before." Tommy's hands had warmed enough for a beer. "Joey, pass me one." After he caught the beer, the boys walked in silence until they reached the graveyard's road. Here they shook the loose snow off their boots and began the five-minute walk to the picket fence of the cemetery. "Crazy night."

"What?" asked Joey. "Out here?"

Kevin popped open his beer, using the brown paper bag to wipe off the spillage on his hand. "Tommy's talkin' about what happened to Porky."

"Yeah," Tommy replied. "We never got along. He always got under my skin"—he paused for a second—"but those scumbags killed him."

"Shhhhh … someone's here." Joey turned around and squinted at the outline of the Aita mausoleum. "You hear that?" The sound of metal hitting stone broke the silence of the night.

Clank, clank, clank.

"Well, faggot, us scumbags are here. Why don't you do something then?" Fagan asked as Junior and Hogan approached from the left of the entrance to the mausoleum and Brodie came from the right side. Standing in the doorway of the crypt directly below the *it* of *Aita* was Dylan. He was tapping the tomb's metal gate with a hammer.

<center>~~~~~~~</center>

While Johnny had slept through his Fifth Avenue train stop in Manhattan, Bain and Shanty did not. Unaware of Johnny's impending arrival, Bain and Shanty entered the city ahead of schedule. The first item on the agenda upon leaving the subway was to find a pay phone to contact the girls. There could be a chance Johnny had already been found, and then the two could turn around and go home.

The sidewalks of Manhattan were filled to capacity with Christmas shoppers and tourists. Yellow taxis dominated the motorways. It appeared to Shanty that everyone was in a rush to arrive somewhere else, unfortunately not enjoying the beauty around.

"Here's an empty booth … with the phone still attached," Bain sarcastically observed. He reached into his pocket and pulled out a quarter. Before placing the coin into the slot, Bain checked the ear and mouth pieces of the phone, searching for any crap intentionally or unintentionally left there.

"No, nothin' yet," Bain reported back to Shanty after hanging up the phone. "Angie just got off the phone with Terry. Terry is now nervous … but nothin'. First Porky and now this. Everything's goin' to the shitter tonight." Bain bent over and cupped his hands to protect a lit match from the wind. After lighting his cigarette, Bain sucked down hard and blew out smoke before speaking. "I'm worried, Shant."

Shanty's usual smiling face suddenly matched the somberness of Bain's. "He's there. I'm sure of it." Shanty's smile did not return as his own pessimism overtook him.

"Let's book," Bain said. And he and Shanty wormed their way through the crowds and traffic of Manhattan's last-minute Christmas rush. Once the two passed the enormous crowd entering Radio City Music Hall, the density of people decreased drastically enough that Bain and Shanty could walk side by side.

"Wow, the city is so packed tonight," Shanty said, trying to make small talk to ease his and Bain's apprehension. "I haven't been here … since that day."

Bain would have to recollect the painful past if he was to find Johnny tonight. *I know Johnny's coming here.* "Look, Shanty, at the carriage rides." Bain pointed to the line of horse-drawn carriages waiting for tourists outside the Central Park's entrance. "Remember Joey—or was that Porky—dumping horse shit on the back of the wagon? And Tommy getting into that lungy war with the stage coach driver?"

Waiting for the light to change before crossing over Fifth Avenue, Shanty joined in. "Or when you and Johnny started punching the carriage lamps?"

"Yeah, I do." Bain reached into his pants pocket to grip the Christ-head. *What's going on, Johnny?* The silver charm warmed Bain's palm but sent a chill throughout his being. *Something is terribly wrong tonight ... Maybe it always was with all of us.* Bain stuffed the medal back deep into his jeans. *Don't worry, Johnny, there are things we can't always fix ... but we can at least live with them.*

"Shanty we're here," Bain announced as the two cut between two stationed horse carriages onto the footsteps of Central Park. *Johnny, we are not leaving here without you.*

╱╱╱╱╱╱

Kimba climbed over the refuse scattered throughout the bottom floor of the storefront before leaving the shithole forever. *It is so over! I don't need Junior or any of the other losers! Or any guy for that matter.* Kimba took her cigarettes out and tossed them into the snow-covered street. *First things first: no dopes and no smokes.* Kimba smiled to herself. *There's a Caribbean song somewhere in that.* Despite a moment of humor, Kimba needed to do what was right, and she did so one block away at the bottom of the Greenpoint Avenue Bridge. Unlike Bain, Kimba didn't check the phone receiver for dangling shit; she placed it to her mouth and ear while dialing zero.

"My name is not important. There are five or six teenagers running through Calvary Cemetery. They're knocking over headstones and making a lot of noise." With a sly grin, Kimba added, "They could wake the dead!"

Kimba assured the operator of her sincerity and then hung up the phone. *That will at least minimize the damage tonight.* Kimba reached into her left coat pocket and pulled out her scarf, wrapping it around her upturned hood. *It's so cold, but it feels so good—the stench of losers no more.* Kimba took her crumpled gloves out of her right pocket and wiggled her fingers inside. *Merry Christmas to me!* Kimba was about a quarter of the way up the bridge when she heard a police siren. *Good. At least that's over with. Now the rest of them are on their own like me.* She grinned. Kimba continued her long trek in the wintery night, dreaming of a boy she once truly loved. *But my jealously and insecurities lost him ...* She stopped at the bridge's center and stared down to the frozen water below. *So peaceful, so dead.* Kimba heard the police siren cease. *Good riddance, Madd Tuffs!* She turned away from the bridge's frozen guardrail to continue her hike home. *Back to my family ... and on to my future.*

Chapter 11

1973

I was raised by a toothless, bearded hag.
I was schooled with a strap right across my back.
—"Jumpin' Jack Flash"
performed by The Rolling Stones

"So nobody's gonna be there?" Johnny shook his head in disbelief. Back in Brooklyn, the boys bunched together a block away from Donny's apartment. "Even if we do go, your mom will tell the cops about the place." Johnny looked around for his usual support team but received nothing. The chill from the afternoon swim had evaporated as sweat began to intensify on Johnny's forehead. Johnny ran the bottom of his dirty shirt across his face for a moment of relief. Then he spoke directly to Shanty. "You're telling me you of all people will go?"

Shanty nodded yes. "If you go."

"Come on, guys, the shit will hit the fan. They'll get us right away." Johnny rambled. "And Shanty or anyone, don't put this on me!"

Bain combed his greased hair back and then spoke to Johnny as the others listened. "I told ya, my uncle got his knee operated on, and he's not goin' up there to hunt or do anything in his cabin this fall." Then Bain spoke to Kevin. "Right, Kev? You heard mom." Kevin nodded. "He's staying in Brooklyn until the spring."

"What's he, a groundhog?" Johnny's attempt at a joke was met with silence.

It was Kevin's turn to support Bain's idea. "The guy has over a hundred acres of land, a pond, rifles, bow and arrows, and cans and cans of food. Whatever you want, he has."

Bain interrupted. "We can go by train tonight. All of us can 'borrow' any money we can from our houses. We'll hike over the mountain to his cabin, leave with a tent or two and supplies for a few days further in the woods, and then return after the cabin is checked. We'll stay at the cabin for as long as we can. When we come back home, it will be too late to have Donny sent away. Everybody will feel bad for the kid, and we'll look like heroes."

"Go, then." Johnny threw up his hands. "But I ain't goin'."

"You have to, or else they won't go." Bain referenced his audience. "Plus, it will work if you go. You'll make it better," pleaded Bain.

"You can't put it all on me. For once you guys take charge," Johnny shot back.

"Forget it. Johnny's right; it can't work. I gotta go home now. I'm already late. Thanks anyway, guys"—Donny touched his red, hooded sweatshirt—"for this, the chain ... and for everything." Donny walked a few feet and then turned to Johnny. "You were there from the start. You always knew what was best for us. Thanks again."

Johnny stood mesmerized. There were no words to offer his departing friend. He wanted to go and protect them all, but this time ...

Joey yelled out their team slogan. "Donny, who's better than us?"

Donny turned back and smiled. "Nobody!"

Turning the corner to say their own good-byes were Angela, Gina, Nicole, and Tori with Bella on her chain. "Donny! Donny, wait up!"

Tori yelled out as all the girls rushed to his side. "We waited and waited; we thought you'd be home earlier."

"We went for a swim," Donny explained.

"Wow … I like this shirt. Where did you get it?" Gina asked.

The boys filled them in on the adventures of their Manhattan trip. Donny mainly spoke, but each boy inserted some detail. The curious girls had questions, which only prolonged the grace period of Donny's curfew. Twenty minutes would pass before Donny said good-bye to his friends.

He silently walked up the creaky wooden steps to his apartment. The door to the kitchen was closed but unlocked. Donny could her his mother snoring. *She must be passed out on the couch already.* He kicked off his sneakers in the hallway and then entered. He rinsed a glass out in the sink and then reached to the rear of the freezer to retrieve two ice cubes to plop inside the crystal.

"Hi, Mom, I'm home." His mother kept snoring but did stir. Donny cleared his throat to subtly awaken her. "Here, Mommy … this will make you feel better."

⌁⌁⌁⌁⌁⌁

"Ma'am, my name tag is spelled wrong."

Disregarding the volunteer's statement, Nurse Joan, or NJ as she is known throughout the hospital, had a bigger issue. "What happened to the two other candy stripers?"

"They got up and left a couple of minutes ago," the lone survivor answered.

Nurse Joan sat behind an average-sized, uncluttered desk. Everything appeared to have its place. On the wall behind the organized bureau were neatly arranged family photos. *Nurse Joan likes her vacations on the beach,* thought the lone survivor. *She has two preteen girls and a husband. Swimmers ... She's about thirty-five, evidently happily ma—*

"I asked, which one are you?" Nurse Joan frowned for a second and then continued before the volunteer could respond. "If you are a dreamer and can't pay attention or follow rules, now is the time for you to leave too." Nurse Joan tapped her pencil on the desk waiting for a reply.

Wow, what a bitch! "My name is Nanci, but it's spelled with an *i* not a *y*. See, my name tag is spelled wrong." Nanci pointed at the white badge with the black lettering pinned to the right side of her chest.

"Okay, Nanci with an *i* not a *y*, you are to report to the night supervisor before your shift. If you are going to be late or absent, your super needs to know an hour before your shift begins. You cannot leave early unless you have your super's permission." Nurse Joan stopped tapping her pencil long enough to hand the volunteer a clip board full of names. "Your ward is full of old people who have very few visitors. That's where you come in. You are there to listen to them. If they don't talk, move on to the next. Some like games. If you play, make it short; win, lose, or tie and move to the next room. There are about twenty to visit, some days more or less.

"Less?" The volunteer did not understand the reality in the ward.

"Less ... yes, people do leave here suddenly." Nurse Joan took a deep breath and continued. "In the beginning, you will be nervous and overreact to their complaints. If you are unsure of anything, contact a nurse. In time, you will see them for what they are—lonely and dying. We call it the waiting room here; you call it what you like. Your skin will have to be thick. You'll be overwhelmed at times, but I can assure you, if you stick it out, it will be the most rewarding experience of your life, volunteering at Woodhull Hospital. Do you have any questions?

"Yes." Nanci looked to her badge. "When can I get my tag corrected?"

~~~~~~~

"Where the hell were you today?" Marian sat up from her sleeping position on the couch, knocking the ice water from Donny's grasp. "Now look what you done." Donny backed off and said nothing. "I asked you something. Where?"

"We were playin' ball, and it got late … I'm sorry." Donny tried to be cheerful. "But look at what my friends gave me as a goin' away gift." Donny proudly reached inside his new sweatshirt and carefully exposed the Christ-head to his mother. "Even the girls chipped in. And look." Turning it around, Donny showed Marian its inscription. "Pretty cool. My name." Donny cautiously waited for his jealous mother's response.

Uninterested for the moment in any charm, Marian wanted other questions answered, so she continued to interrogate her son. "So you played ball with your gift charm on all day? Where'd you get that sweatshirt? It's also new. Did you and your friends steal that too?" Marian sat up and rubbed her temples, the head pounding began. "I told you to be home before five. You're late, and you're lying to me too. Now tell me where you were, where the chain and shirt came from." Marian adjusted her curled hair but understood that her ugliness extended externally also. "We know your friends are no good; that's why I'm sending you away." Both knew Marian finished with a lie.

Donny normally would have walked away from the argument, especially with his mother in a fiery stupor, but talking shit about his friends on this day was a bit too much. "Mom, they are my friends; they'd do anything for me …" Frustrated, Donny added, "and you don't." *Dangerous, very dangerous. Let it go.* "Don't lie, neither. You're sending me away because you're a drunk." Donny touched his Christ-head, searching for something to help him.

Slap! Across Donny's face went Marian's hand. "You little thief and liar, it's your fault. Everything is." Getting up from the couch, Marian took a second swing at Donny, hitting his left shoulder while bending her wrist on the attack. "What are you doing with those whores? Why are they giving you anything?" Donny backed up banging into the television set. "That Joe and John and the rest of your homo fag friends, all no good." Marian's wrist began to hurt and swell from her shot to Donny's shoulder. *Strap time. Oh yeah! This will hurt me more than you son.* Adding insult to injury, Marian commanded her son. "Donny, get the strap. I'll make a man outta you yet. Your father never could."

Donny did not budge from the television, too afraid to move and regretting the decision to challenge his mother. "Ma … please don't. I'm sorry." Tears welled in Donny's eyes and ran quickly down his dirty cheeks.

Marian's eyes glazed over, moving from rage to compassion, which gave Donny an instant of hope. Unfortunately, the mood changed quickly, since as usual, alcohol and anger trumped all. Donny recognized the familiar situation, so he covered his previously bitten chest with his hands.

Marian got into Donny's face to taunt her scared son. Donny could only whimper and plead for all of this to end. "Go get the strap!" Donny shook in fear, unable to retrieve Mommy's weapon of choice.

Misreading her son's predicament, Marian found her Padrino Whalebone shoe beside the couch. *This will do.* Needing something else to pummel him with beside her fist, Marian began to batter Donny's hand-covered chest. As Donny squirmed, he fell to the floor in a fetal position. Marian, frustrated at not landing a direct blow to the chest, altered her strategy and went for her son's head.

"Mommy, please stop. You're hurting me. Mommy ... please." Only Marian's exhaustion, not Donny's begging, slowed her beating down to one last shot. Her shame and internal disgust demanded a knockout punch.

The heel of Marian's shoe connected with Donny's exposed temple. The gamey scent Angela had recognized earlier surrounding Marian now receded from Donny's awareness. The tingling sensation started at his toes and immediately skyrocketed throughout his body, ending in his scalp. As fast as the tingle started, it was replaced with numbness and then blackness.

All down here has gone slow, real slow ... Mommy, I'm right here. Can't you hear me? Don't cry, Ma ... The Christmas tree lights are awesome ... Johnny, it's not your fault ... Nurse, I like Tom Sawyer ... Gina, Angela, smile ... Tommy's funny, but leave Porky alone ... Don't you feel me squeezing you back Johnny? ... Don't cry. I'm okay ... Everything is so slow ... I'm with you all. Don't leave me ... please. It's cold ... I don't want to be alone ... Lorna, you've come for me?

Marian sat on the floor with her fading son lying across her lap. She remained, rubbing Donny's bulging temple while sobbing his name. When the police arrived ten minutes later, Marian revealed the thoughtful gift her son had received, the Christ-head. With no resistance, she was handcuffed and arrested for assaulting a minor.

Comatose, Donny lay silently in a siren-blaring ambulance racing its way to Brooklyn's Woodhull Hospital.

~~~~~~~

Nanci stood outside the hospital waiting for her bus to arrive, happy her first day of volunteering was finished. Nurse Joan had dismissed her a few minutes early for no apparent reason. *That chick's got her shit together, but why break a strict rule like that on my first night?* Nanci

135

peered up Graham Avenue, searching for the bus that would take her home. *The seemingly cool Nurse Joan lost it at the end, though. She scared? What happened?* The bus turned onto Graham Avenue, heading to Nanci's stop. *About time!* The bus pulled up along the curb. Nanci politely let an older couple board first but bounded on before a wobbly man could. *He's a drunk. Back of the line, fellow.* Nanci sat two seats from the bus driver and thought of the old people in her ward who would never ride a bus again.

The drunk fellow passed her and hobbled to the nearest available seat. Nanci observed his actions. *Dad always said trust no one.* Nanci held on to her pocketbook a bit tighter. Nanci remained suspicious of the man until she spied a metal leg brace connected to his right boot. *He's not drunk at all. He was in the hospital for therapy or something.* Her stomach turned for a second, but she quickly recovered. *Better safe than sorry.* Nanci relaxed and thought of her hospital departure and Nurse Joan's loss of composure. Nanci opened her eyes to see what street the bus had turned onto. *Five more blocks.* She closed her eyes one more time. *I was wrong once tonight about the guy sitting across from me but not twice. That chick looked scared!*

Chapter 12

1978

Love is but a song to sing.
Fear's the way we die.
You can make the mountains ring
Or make the angels cry.
—"Get Together" performed by The Youngbloods

Every city in the world always has a gang, a street
gang, or the so-called outcasts
—Jimi Hendrix

A friend is one who has the same enemies as you have.
—Abraham Lincoln

"We aren't lookin' for any trouble," Joey appealed. Reaching into his coat pockets, Joey felt two beer cans. *Shit, I should've bought bottles!*

Kevin tried a different strategy. "Did you see Johnny and Bain come in yet? They should be here by now." Kevin's lie was too obvious.

Tommy in his rashness could not control his mouth any longer. *A jab now will be remembered forever.* Smiling at Fagan, Tommy pressed, "Fag? And how does it feel to be a killer?"

Without warning, Dylan did what any street tough would recommend you don't do; if you have a weapon or any advantage, don't lose it to the enemy. But Dylan threw his hammer, missing Tommy's head by six feet. The tool landed harmlessly on the icy road beside Kevin's foot.

Before Kevin could pick the weapon up off of the ice, Dylan raced toward Tommy. "I'll kill you!" Dylan's glue high created a feeling of invincibility beyond natural wisdom. Dylan stumbled onto the snow-covered grass, falling a few inches off the plowed roadway. "Uhhhh … shit."

"Stay down, egghead." Kevin could throw a football further than any other kid in the neighborhood with little accuracy, but fortunately his kicking ability, which had the same muster as his arm, had a bulls eye aim. "Take that, you glue head!" Kevin buried his foot into the fallen Dylan's rib cage, hoping to break each one. Before Kevin could get a second punt off, this time at Dylan's head, an industrial chain, swung by Fagan, hit Kevin's own rib cage. "Damn …" Kevin was able to reach out to grab the irons and stop an additional strike. Kevin collapsed sideways toward Tommy and Junior.

Junior pushed the teetering Kevin into the swing punch of Brodie, which drove him back and into Hogan's headlock. With his free hand, Hogan began to pummel Kevin's face and ribs. Kevin, in an awkward position, was unable to use his hands in combat. He was only able only to protect his face or to keep the chain away from his attacker. Kevin choose his looks.

Joey went punch for punch with Dylan, although at this point of the rumble, Joey understood he needed to do more to help Kevin. Reaching into his coat pocket, Joey hurled a beer can at Fagan's head. Fagan ducked but was too slow to totally miss the collision of the canister. On impact, the can dented and sprayed beer into Fagan's face, delaying him from swinging the chain at a defenseless Kevin.

"Shit … that's sirens!" yelled Junior as he put his hands down from bashing Tommy.

Hogan let Kevin out of the headlock. "We gotta go. Brodie … guys, let's get out of here."

Dylan stumbled in circles, unaware that the fighting was over with the arrival of the police. With a feeble swing at Kevin, Dylan missed badly only to complain about his side hurting.

Junior grabbed Dylan's arm and hustled him to the route of the picket fence down the hill. "Dylan, no more shit. We gotta go now." Junior continued to hold on to Dylan while the two bands of rivals took flight together as brothers.

Tommy, Joey, and Hogan were the first to reach the fence, followed by Brodie, Fagan, and Kevin. Junior and Dylan arrived at the edge of the cemetery after Tommy and Hogan had already scaled the picket fence. Joey and Brodie carefully squeezed between the spikes of the fencing just as they heard the whistle of a police officer.

"They're on foot," Fagan surmised.

"The front gate's probably locked," added Junior. "They must've come through the caretaker's house." Then Junior pushed Dylan toward the fence. "Come on." Cupping his two hands together to form a step, Junior encouraged Dylan to plod on. Dylan's iced right boot stepped up on Junior's bare hands and was blasted upward. "Hold on to my shoulder with one hand; use your other on the fence."

Dylan's hand slipped on the frozen spike, but he was able to regain control and maneuver his balance before jumping to safety on the other side of the fence. Landing with a plop onto the snow, Dylan wobbled but was able to contain his footing. Junior, Brodie, and Kevin quickly followed, leaving Joey hunched and hobbled inside the cemetery.

The two gangs outside the cemetery could see two police flashlights near the Aita mausoleum searching through the crypt. Kevin and Tommy encouraged the injured Joey to get a move on. Joey could barely raise his hand, but he told his friends to flee.

"Hell no. We ain't leavin' nobody for the pigs," Junior said. Then he spoke to Fagan. "Help me back over. These two are too beaten up to help." With a wink at Tommy, Junior scaled the fence.

Joey, unsurprisingly backed off when Junior landed before him. From the other side of the fence, Kevin hollered that it was okay over the raging of police whistles.

"Here … climb on." Junior scuttled on all fours, transforming his back into a launch pad for Joey. "Hurry they're coming." Joey could only grunt in pain as he slowly climbed aboard. Tommy and Hogan put their hands through the fence to help stabilize Joey's balance. Once he was raised between the spikes, Fagan, with the help of Brodie, guided Joey rapidly, hurling him to the safety of the street.

"Get back here, you hooligans!" one officer yelled. He then fell to the exact location where Dylan had nosedived earlier. "Bastards … Mick, wait up. I twisted something." The fallen officer called his partner over for help, giving the fugitives a few additional seconds.

Joey got up off the snow-covered sidewalk slowly. "Thanks." Gently touching his crippled leg, Joey concluded nothing was broken. "Just sore. Hogan, next time …"

"That's it for now. We're even." Junior signaled to Fagan and the other Madd Tuffs. "Let's get back. More cops are coming, I'm sure." With one hand around Dylan's right elbow, Junior began to walk his crew to their hidden sanctuary. When all were about twenty feet from Kevin, Tommy, and Joey, Junior bellowed back. "Stay off our turf, or you're all dead next time!"

"Screw you … you spic Polack!" shouted Tommy.

"Enough of them. We gotta figure out where to go. We can't go back over the bridge into Brooklyn. That's where the cops are gonna come from," Joey reckoned.

Tommy protested. "They're going that way. Why don't we?" He started to follow in the footprints of the Madd Tuffs.

"Wait," Joey spoke softly. "They said to stay off their turf. They ain't goin' over the bridge, anyway. They're staying nearby."

"Shitheads must have place close by," Kevin added while rubbing his bruised ribs, "a hideout or something."

Tommy's agitation was apparent when he spoke. "What they hell are we gonna do now? Go hide? How 'bout climb back into the cemetery with the other stiffs? I'm frozen."

Joey interrupted, "Let's go up to Hunters Point Avenue then over to Pulaski Bridge back into Brooklyn.

"Oh yeah, that's a plan," Tommy said sarcastically. "That's a two-hour walk or more. We ain't never gonna make it back tonight." Then he softened. "What about you two? How you gonna walk all night?"

Kevin saw one police officer approaching the fence as the second one remained, barking orders from the ground "We have no choice." Kevin motioned to the rushing patrolman inside the cemetery. "This one is pissed. Let's go."

Tommy turned up his collar and mumbled a complaint about the cold, before assisting Joey's first few steps. Once Joey got control over his own balance, Tommy released his grip, letting Joey fend for himself. As the three fugitives hurried into the cold, dark night, Tommy had one word to yell in his continued frustration of the evening. "Johnny!"

~~~~~~~

Tori and her mother shared a two-room apartment on the Brooklyn side of the Brooklyn-Queens border. Tori lived a significant distance from all of her friends, making the trek to Winthrop Park and the bowling alley a pain in the ass. Nevertheless, the distance provided a barrier from the daily shenanigans of the neighborhood. No parent or guardian could ever rat Tori out. No one knew exactly where she came from or who she actually was. *Just another wise-ass. Wait until we find her parents!* Tori heard many accounts of her friends getting in trouble because of a truth or rumor. It didn't matter. Once someone was labeled as a troublemaker, it was easy to convict. Tori appreciated her invisibility; she never had to dance her way out of any trouble at home. Her mother never heard or witnessed any problems with her only child. She greatly trusted Tori, as well as her girlfriends. When her mother would travel to Atlantic City with this boyfriend or to a resort for vacation with that boyfriend, Tori could be relied on at home with her likeable friends. Tonight, Tori expanded the trusted girlfriend party to include a few select trusted boyfriends.

"That was Bain. They're in Manhattan and about to enter Central Park. They're goin' to check out a few spots and then call back." Tori sat down on her couch, which would later be opened to serve as a bed. "What a waste of a night. The guys could have been here all along, but Johnny had to screw this all up."

Nicole agreed about Johnny's selfish attitude. "And tomorrow morning, the hell with him. We'll go straight from here as planned." Nicole lit a cigarette.

Gina relaxed on a sleeping bag perched against the love seat with one hand rubbing her foot and the other rubbing Bella's belly. "This dog loves me soooo much."

"You spoil her, that's all." Tori lit a joint and passed by Gina, handing it to Nicole. "Now let's get this party started."

Before Nicole could agree, Angela returned from the bathroom in her pajamas. "We're trashing Johnny, and rightfully so, but what about Porky? Don't anyone care about him? I bet his blood is still in the street."

"Blood? I bet his brains are still there too." Nicole's joke echoed in the silence that met it.

Angela continued, "What about tomorrow? When will this dark cloud of the past be past us?"

"What is your problem, Miss Goodie-Two-Shoes?" Gina pushed Bella off of her lap and then patted the dog hair off of her thighs. "You know we're all part of it, forget what happen to Donny for a moment, and Porky too. You did a number on Johnny. Maybe that's the reason he's the way he is now."

"Yeah, and why all the guys are out looking for him tonight," added Nicole.

"My boyfriend is one them too," Gina poured on.

"Well, so is mine," responded an upset Angela.

"It must be nice being beautiful and having just so many guys to worry about," finished Nicole.

Angela could handle one of the witches from her crowd but not two or more. Upset, she stormed out of the living room into the bathroom, shutting its door, not knowing what to say or do next.

Tori broke up the silence around her couch. Ignoring the fact that Angela was distressed, Tori spoke of herself. "Funny, I don't have a guy out there or anywhere for that matter to fret about. But I'll say this"—she accepted the joint from Nicole—"guys are a handful, all of them. But what choice do we really have?" Tori took a long hard toke and passed it back to Nicole. "Nobody's leaving here until tomorrow morning, and we're all going together." After a few silent seconds, Tori went on. "We need each other now more than ever. Look how the boys responded."

Angela stepped out of the bathroom sheepishly. "I'm sorry I acted like a baby, but sometimes you guys can be so crude."

Gina laughed, and she was quickly joined by Tori and Nicole. "You are so dramatic. You're gonna need a lot tougher skin to get by in this world," Gina reasoned.

Angela sat beside Gina on the floor and put a couch pillow under her knees. "Maybe there's a reason why I'm the way I am."

"What a big baby?" Nicole scolded.

Angela puffed out some air before stating her case. "I'll tell you what happened between Johnny and me. I hope it stays in this room, but if it doesn't, it doesn't. I know you all heard things." Angela asked Tori for a vodka and lemonade. Tori teasingly bowed her head and then fetched Angela's request.

"Wow this is something," an amazed Nicole exclaimed. "How long has it been? I thought you gave this up, chick."

"Pass it here." Angela motioned for the roach clip for the joint. "I swore I'd never do this, but I need to get through tonight just like everyone else."

Gina looked around and laughed. "I'm not gonna let this prima donna out do me." Gina ran into the kitchen and mixed herself a drink too. "And when you get that next joint going, I'm gonna need a hit too."

Tori winked at a stunned Nicole. "Newbies. Their first drink and smoke in a year."

Nicole had to remind herself to close her mouth. She wet her lips and then spoke. "Watching you two get high and drunk is story enough for me."

"Wait, wait, I want to be comfy. Let's all put on our pj's on first." Gina jumped up, and Nicole and Tori followed.

Chapter 13

1973

If you aren't going all the way,
Why go at all?
—Joe Namath

I can't believe Thanksgiving is next week. Nanci led with an ace of hearts. Mr. Baden laughed and then trumped her card with a three of spades. "I don't get this game," she said. "You box me in all the time." Nanci frowned for a moment but quickly fashioned her broad smile the patients and staff had fallen for.

"Oh, Nanci, you let me win again," Mr. Baden responded. "You know, if you had been around when I was a kid …"

Nanci folded up the playing cards before offering Mr. Baden a cup of water. "Now, you be nice." Nanci patted the patient's hand. "I have to leave you. Mrs. Mikulka has to finish her tales of bootlegging in the 1920s." Nanci walked over to the blinds and closed them. "I know you like it dark in the evening." Nanci rolled the empty food tray away from Mr. Baden's bed. "Good night. I'll be right next door if you need me."

Mr. Baden waved Nanci over to the side of his bed. With his right hand, he clutched Nanci's wrist. "You're either a terrible liar or a bad card player, but it doesn't matter. Someday soon, you will make a difference. Always follow your heart, Nanci with an *i*."

Nanci patted Mr. Baden's wrist. "Why are you saying things like that?" Nanci laughed. "You're not going anywhere. You'll be here kicking my ass in spades on Monday." Then she gave him her trademark smile. "I really try to beat you," she fibbed, "but you're too good. And stop being so darn gloomy. No one likes negative vibes."

Mr. Baden laughed. "You are crude and to the point, and you cheat to lose. But my dear, thank you." Mr. Baden wanted to go on, but he resisted, not wanting to keep his candy striper girl all to himself.

Nanci walked out of Mr. Baden's room never knowing when it would really be the last time they play spades together.

"Nanci. Nanci!" Nurse Joan appeared from nowhere. "Why is it you never listen when I call you?" Nurse Joan looked tired and a bit antsier than normal. "Wait here." Nurse Joan turned away from Nanci and marched to the nurse's station. After uttering orders to the two nurses behind the counter, Nurse Joan rubbed her forehead and spoke more softly to Nanci. "Tonight is my last. I'll be on vacation for two weeks, Thanksgiving week and the one after."

Nanci nodded. *She's always emerging from nowhere, like Lurch from the Addam's Family.* "You rang?"

"The patients and the staff like your … enthusiasm." Nurse Joan pointed toward the counter area. "They are the specialists. You continue to obey them, remember that. But keep the patients comfortable—and happy." Nurse Joan led Nanci to the end of the hall. "Things have calmed a tiny bit around him." Nurse Joan pointed to room 18. "The news in New York is always changing, mostly for the worse, so this story is no longer the lead. But remember, it's still ongoing." Nurse Joan peeked into room 18 and she signaled for Nanci to do the same. "See all the flowers strangers from our city and around the country sent in?" Nanci nodded a second time. "Well, the flowers are dying, and not many new ones are coming in these days. The janitor has been instructed to remove the dead ones, but I need someone who cares in charge of leaving the boy … something pleasing." Nurse Joan sadly shook her head. "He's yesterday's news out there, but in here, we are to make his stay as pleasant as possible." Nurse Joan half-closed the door of room 18.

Nanci knew from her six weeks of working at Woodhull Hospital never to interrupt Nurse Joan, out of respect and, of course, a touch of fear. *I guess she's done yapping.* "So, I'm allowed to go in there?" Nanci pointed to the closed door. Nurse Joan rolled her eyes and nodded yes. "I'm in charge of the flower arrangements and all?"

Nurse Joan stared at Nanci for a few seconds before talking. "Nanci, I may be a bit hard on you, but I am sure you can do this … without screwing up."

Thanks for the show of confidence … Lurch!

~~~~~~~

"You're breathing on me. Get away, you faggot!" Tommy yelled at Porky. "Damn, now you made me tilt it." Tommy kicked the pinball machine's leg, knocking the game into the back wall of the candy store.

"Hey, kid, you break that leg, I break yours," the storekeeper bellowed from behind the counter.

"Yeah, yeah," Tommy answered back. Then he ordered a hot chocolate and sat down with Bain, Johnny, and Shanty in the comic book section of the candy store.

"It's been almost two months and over a month since we last tried. I say we try again," Bain reasoned. "At least send one of the girls in to see him. Girls have a way of getting through people."

"Or getting things done," chimed in Shanty.

"What are you, a women's libber or something? Next you're gonna say they can go fly into space or, God forbid, be president," Tommy shot in.

"Okay, okay. We're getting off the subject. It's not even in the news no more," Johnny began. "'Marian the Mauler,' 'Mommy Meat-Eater,' 'Hell for the Heeler'—those headlines are done, and so is everyone's curiosity." Johnny leaned forward, speaking his next sentence softly. "Thanksgiving is now over. People may not be on guard after a long holiday weekend."

Bain took a sip of his chocolate drink and then quizzed Johnny. "What do we do, then?"

"Let's just go there tomorrow—everyone, girls and all. The hospital might still be in a daze. If not, we can figure it out one way or another. We'll wing it."

"Yeah, shit happens when you put it out there," Bain agreed. *Wing it. Why the hell not?*

~~~~~~~

Nanci stood at the bus stop waiting for her ride. She was sad Thanksgiving break was over but eager to start her second week of work in the hospital with no Nurse Joan. *The other nurses like me, and I can see they dislike her.* It was four o'clock and already getting dark and too cold for Nanci's liking. *Where's that bus already?* An old man walking with a cane smiled at Nanci as he joined her in the wait. *Poor guy has to ride a bus at his age and in his condition.* Nanci thought of Mr. Baden lying in bed and wondered how lonely he was for Thanksgiving. *I should have went to the hospital over the weekend and visited them all. Darn it ... Well, I won't miss Christmas. I'll be there.*

Ten minutes later, Nanci sat looking out the side window of the Woodhull Hospital-bound bus. Normally she would do her homework on the ride to work, but today was the first day back at school, and the teachers still appeared to be on holiday break. *Everyone has been so sluggish today. Must be from too much turkey and that boring football!*

148

Nanci peered out the side window of her bus and saw a man placing an evergreen against a ten-foot-high wooden stand. *Is that guy setting up Christmas trees already?* Nanci was a bit shocked but pleasantly surprised by the sight. *Why not this early? Christmas is the best time of year; make it as long as possible.* Nanci closed her eyes for a second, imagining the scent of a live tree. She was quickly removed from her daydream by a thudding noise from behind. Turning around to investigate, Nanci saw four, no five, male youths clutching a section of the outside fender of the bus. *They're hitching. The two on the ends appeared to have it easier, holding the inside of the rear window, but what are the three in the middle holding on to?* Nanci was about to warn the bus driver of the hooligans' misbehavior when four young girls and a Spanish-looking fellow paid their way onto the bus. Nanci suspected the two groups were traveling together. Waiting for the situation to play out, Nanci witnessed the driver leave his seat to deal with the tomfoolery himself.

"Hey, guys, you wanna get killed? Come on, now, get off!" After some laughter and a few protests, the five boys presented their bus passes, and each placed a nickel into the toll taker. "You're willing to get killed for a nickel?" Shaking his head in disbelief, the driver sat down onto his cushioned seat and closed the bus door.

"Yeah, Porky, I told you it was a bad idea."

Nanci observed a blondish Polish boy, shoving this Porky kid to an empty seat alongside her as the other pals raced to the rear of the bus.

Nanci closed her eyes. Forgetting the Christmas tree stand outside or the foolishness of the ruffians nearby, she concentrated on her continued responsibilities in room 18. *"You will have help from the janitor if you need it. Make the room nice, but don't forget to keep up your other visits too. You can do this."* Nurse Joan was right. *Last week I got rid of all the dying or dead plants and flowers. This week I gotta add something nice. That poor boy deserves something special.* Nanci tried her best not to let the conversations between the scolded hitchhikers, the four girls, and the Spanish boy interrupt her thoughts. With no success seeking solitude, Nanci listened in on the onslaught of wisecracking, teasing, and immature boasting inside the bus.

"Nicky, like this." The short, shapely Italian girl removed her lipstick case from inside her white pocketbook. After covering her lips with the red rouge, the Italian girl kissed a tissue paper. "See, you don't want to overdo it."

"Yeah, 'cause you'll look like a clown," one of the boys yelled out from the rear of the bus to the laughter of the others.

"Bain, you're such an ass." The Italian girl handed the lipstick to a younger version of Gloria from *All in the Family*. "These dopes won't get in, but if we look at least sixteen, we'll have a chance."

"That color is too much for me. I'll have to try something else," Gloria said.

"Like a mask!" someone roared from the back seats.

"STP!" a third girl shouted. "STP."

If Nanci had to describe what character this girl resembled by a stretch of her own imagination, it would have to be Lily from *The Munsters*. Lily was tall and skinny and had long, dark, straight hair, white Irish skin, and dark eyes. *I have a Lurch at work and now a Lily on my bus. Since I'm on creepy characters, who do I know from Dark Shadows?*

"STP yourself," the one named Bain yelled back.

"That's made up. It don't mean anything," added his friend, another blond boy. This one had some bulk—less than Bain but more than the others.

"Yeah, yeah, yeah. STP," the Italian girl hollered. She then gave Gloria a second case. "Here, this one is a gloss." The Italian girl opened her bag and let the fourth, quiet girl pick through the makeup.

The reserved girl did not remind Nanci of anyone. The girl had long, brown hair and big lips, though not as large as the Italian girl's. There was something Eastern Mediterranean about her. Turkish? Syrian? Nanci was unsure of the girl's origin but was fascinated by her attractiveness.

"Let's go in there maturely and see," the girl said, putting her hands up. "If we walk in like we belong, then maybe there'll be no problem."

"Donny has nobody but us," the Italian girl said, peering into her makeup mirror. "To get to see him, we'll need an in."

The bigger blond boy left the ruckus of the rear of the bus, squeezed in between the Italian girl and the quiet Spanish boy, and sat directly across from Nanci. "Gina, do you have a plan?" The boy brushed his hair off of his face as Bain walked over to join in the conversation. "Bain, what you think? Go through the front desk and hope for the best?"

"I guess, but we did try that before," the dark-haired Bain doubted. "Maybe if two of the girls walk right past security and not ask like we tried before …"

Gloria joined in. "But things have calmed down since then. The news isn't about Donny in a coma." Lily and the Mediterranean girl agreed. "That's what we'll try first—the girls in smaller groups. If we get past, then you guys can try. Right now, we have nothing else."

Nanci could no longer hold her tongue. She shot out, "There is something else you—we—can do together, and I'll help everyone see … your friend Donny."

~~~~~~~

151

One week after Nanci had gushed aloud on a Brooklyn bus to a gang of youths, Nurse Joan closed the door of her Eldorado and walked across the parking lot to Woodhull Hospital's main entrance. *Believe it or not, it feels good to be here … to get structure back, get my game on.* Her body felt sore from snorkeling, hiking, and dancing, as well as the lack of sleep over the past ten days. *Like they say, you need a vacation after your vacation.* Nurse Joan's flight from the Caribbean had been delayed in San Juan, which brought her to New York eight hours later than planned. Arriving at Kennedy Airport after midnight, she was tempted to call in for an additional vacation day but decided she had been away long enough. *Tough it out. Tonight I'll have a glass of red wine after picking up my vacation pictures and …*

"Joan!" It was Nurse Ellen from first shift. "Welcome back."

Ellen and Nurse Joan had graduated together twelve years before from Rockland County Community College. After completing school, Nurse Joan had married and started her family immediately, while Ellen had begun her career. After eight years of being a stay-at-home mom to two daughters, Nurse Joan had decided to put her education to work when her ex-schoolmate Ellen contacted her about a nursing job in Brooklyn. Needing to have her own identity and purpose in the world, Nurse Joan immediately said yes. After two years working hard on day shifts and many sacrifices, Nurse Joan had taken the second-shift supervisor's position as soon as it came available. She had Ellen to thank for kicking off her career, but Nurse Joan had always known she would someday follow her dream outside the household.

"How was your vacation?"

Nurse Joan gave her friend a quick smile and thanked her for the greeting. "Like they say, too short." Nurse Joan got immediately to business. "We got home late last night, and there were no American papers on the island. Anything new here?"

Ellen understood the meaning of the question. "Joan … I don't know if it's a good thing or a bad thing, but the news has moved on. As for Donny's condition, unfortunately nothing has changed." Ellen then put a big smile on. "But that candy striper you put in charge … wow!"

Nurse Joan had missed the overexcitement of her friend. "Yes, Nanci does work hard, although at times she's overzealous in her endeavors."

Ellen grinned. "Joanie … the other changes, too. Her methods are so unlike yours, but they work."

Ellen said her good-byes and ran off to the bus stop, leaving Nurse Joan to wonder, *What the hell did Nanci do now?*

Chapter 14

1978

When my fist clenches, crack it open
Before I use it and lose my cool.
When I smile, tell me some bad news
Before I laugh and act like a fool.
—"Behind Blue Eyes"
Performed by The Who

On his return to the Central Park subway station, Johnny would not make the same mistake of falling asleep on a moving subway car again. Although there were plenty of open seats now, Johnny stood and held on to a handrail. When the train jumped forward during an electrical short, Johnny jolted sideways toward one of the empty seats. *Drunk ... and alone. Merry Christmas to me!* Johnny watched the station signs hurry past the windows. *One Hundred Twenty-Fifth Street.* Knowing Central Park began at 110th Street, Johnny figured he would walk a few blocks and sober a little before reaching his final destination. As the train pulled into the 116th Street station, Johnny exited the underground ride.

The cold night air felt refreshing. It was the sensation Johnny was seeking. Taking his first step away from the tunnel and into East Harlem, Johnny noticed the brownstones' Christmas light show. Most buildings displayed their illuminations in the windows, across stoop railings, weaving through iron fences, or hanging down and around their buildings. Johnny could hear Christmas carolers singing "Silent Night" from across the street. *Man, the blacks up here love their—*

"Hey, mister. A-okay ... my candy?" A short, stocky fellow who appeared to be a man surprised Johnny from between two parked cars. He wore a dark, hooded sweatshirt under his coat, worn-out jeans, and unlaced boots. The intruder's face was hidden inside the extended hood, reminding Johnny of the Grimm Reaper. The Grimm Reaper had a slight limp favoring the left leg and had his right, shivering black hand out pleading for a ... fix?

Johnny knew the street name for *cocaine: candy. He must think I have coke or something.* Without a response, Johnny removed his warming hands from his coat pockets, expecting a confrontation. *Where did he come from? I must be so freakin' drunk to miss his approach.* Knowing not to look directly into the potential mugger's eyes, Johnny straightened out his posture and proceeded to the end of the block where the street came upon increased activity.

"I'm talkin' to ya, A-okay." The Grimm Reaper began to walk alongside on Johnny's left, parallel to the parked cars. With his humble but persistent voice, the Reaper appeared kind of threatening to Johnny. "Give me some candy. I'm cold and A-okay hungry, and I worked for it." Putting his shaking hand out for anything Johnny might offer, the Reaper's face remained hidden inside the hooded sweatshirt. "A-okay."

Johnny was aware of his own height advantage and was sure he was stronger than the drugged-up Reaper, but he was curious if his foe had a concealed weapon. *What kind of shit is he smoking? A-okay?* The Reaper slipped on the iced concrete sidewalk and leaned into Johnny in an awkward stumble. The voices of children singing "Holy infant so tender and mild" in the background rang hollow in Johnny's ears. Mistaking the slip of the Reaper for an attack, Johnny became defensive quickly. The drunkenness evaporated from Johnny's body while rage made its best *Kool-Aid Man* smashing entrance.

The first time that he heard Johnny's voice, the Reaper was struck with fear.

"You little bastard!" Johnny shouted, and with much of the despair and hopelessness filling his troubled treasure chest of emotions, he directed his deep-down fury at the smaller prey.

"Sleep in heavenly peace ..."

Johnny grabbed the Reaper's neck, tossing his body between two parked cars onto the frozen street. The shoveled snow absorbed most of the impact, but the Reaper's head bounced off of the ice. Johnny quickly fell onto his prey to switch from a defense to offense. Johnny did release his cold grip, however, when he heard the *Reaper* gasp for air. *Don't need to kill him ... just hurt him a little.* Johnny began to punch his pinned target. With both of his knees crushing the Reaper's shoulders, Johnny continued his barrage of shots to the head of the flightless victim. *Where is your game now?* The Reaper barely could cover his hidden face from the onslaught. *Had enough, you shit?* Johnny became winded. He decided he was safe and that the beatdown should end. Stopping the carnage, Johnny stood up over the choking and crying target. The Reaper rolled to his side and continued to cough and cry, as he did, the hoodie came off.

Even in the shadows, Johnny could see how young the Grimm Reaper actually was. *Twelve? eleven?* Johnny's stomach began to warm and then turn downside up. *Oh shit, what am I doing?* "Hey, dude ... I didn't ..." Johnny offered his coat sleeve for the Reaper's bloodied face. "I'm sorry, I thought ... you were someone else," Johnny lied.

"Don't hit me no more, A-okay? Please mister ... we sing for candy ... A-okay." The Reaper coughed hard into Johnny's face, but he had two hands forward in a feeble defense. "We get candy when we sing, A-okay?" the Reaper repeated. The beaten youngster's dread quickly became trust when Johnny helped him to his feet. "Sometimes we get cake or, A-okay, money too." Then with a frown, the hooded one finished. "Sometimes we get nothing, but Miss Crystal says that's A-okay."

Or a beating. Did Miss Crystal say that was A-okay too? Johnny guided the Reaper to the sidewalk. "What's your name? Mine's John." Johnny looked up the street toward 116th. "Is that group of singers Miss Crystal and all your singing pals?" Johnny knew the answer and wanted to dump this kid before anyone found out what had gone down here moments before. *Miss Crystal, how did you misplace one of your retards?*

"My name is Malcolm." Wiping snot and blood from his nose, Malcolm finished "A-okay?"

"Well, Malc, I have to run, but here is my last seven bucks." Handing the simpleton a five and two ones, Johnny patted Malcolm's shoulder and sidestepped to the curb toward 115th street. "Malc, go ahead." He pointed to the small mob of carolers surrounding Miss Crystal. "Your friends will be missing you."

"Wait, John!" Johnny stopped for a second. "A-okay, do I put this money in our carol pool?" Malcolm held the seven dollars toward Johnny.

Johnny needed to go but was fascinated by the young boy's appreciation and honesty. "Give them the two ones. You hide the five. It's yours, A-okay?"

"Thanks, John, you a good guy! A-okay."

Johnny, checked his coat pocket for the rock he'd removed earlier from his bedroom shelf. *I could have lost it just now ... I gotta be less careless.* He pushed the stone deeper into its hole and reflected on where he'd originally found it. *What I wouldn't do to be there with everyone again.*

Johnny hustled with tears in his eyes to the corner of Fifth Avenue and then turned onto 115th Street. *You're a good guy! Who's better than us?* Without acknowledging the Christmas spirit of his surroundings, Johnny remained focused on his final destination of the night. *The pond, it's where it all began ... where it all will end.* Johnny stepped into Central Park's northern end at 110th Street and Fifth Avenue minutes before Bain and Shanty exited the southernmost exit some fifty blocks south.

<center>~~~~~~~</center>

Terry stared at her self-portrait with disgust. *I look crazy, or better yet, like some insane clown.* She sat on her bed surrounded by disorganization. Terry's easel was placed squarely in the center of her small, twelve-by-ten room. Behind the tripod stood Terry's dresser, safeguarding her art supplies and whatever clothing could neatly fit inside. The remaining tools of her trade and attire were scattered on a small desk to her right or on the dresser top. Surrounding the lone window, as they had all of her Christmas's of the past, multicolored lights split their flashing array between the cold streets of Brooklyn and Terry's sanctuary. Directly across from her window, where the easel partially blocked the light show, Terry's silver-metal bed frame rested. Clear of all foreign objects except her bedding, it was vital for Terry's oasis to harbor a white, fleece blanket and three fluffy pillows.

What am I missing here? Details. Johnny always said details push good to greatness. Terry jumped off of her bed and switched the Christmas lights off in her window. *No different.* She put them back on and moved her easel to face out of her bedroom doorway. Standing in the family room ten feet further away from her sketch than she had moments before, Terry still could not see what was wrong. *My smile is off. When I show teeth, I look like a vampire. No teeth, and I'm pissy looking. And now with my smile, I'm a crazy-looking clown.* With her arms folded, Terry stubbornly continued to stare at her portrait.

"Theresa, we're going across the street to the Warren's. You want to go?" asked Terry's father. "I'm sure their boys will be there."

Pains in the ass! "No thanks. I want to work on this and watch Rudolph and Charlie Brown tonight," Terry lied. *I'm waiting to hear where your*

159

son is and how he's doing. If you weren't half drunk, you might have noticed Johnny's turmoil lately.

Mom patted Terry's shoulder and commented on how well the painting was fashioned. *It's not a painting, and what does fashion have to do with it?* "Yes, Mom, I know the Warren's number by heart. I'll be all right."

Watching her mom and dad stumble out into the hallway, Terry bolted the front door. She looked at the manger below the tree and the sheep grazing about and thought of what Johnny had told her recently. Johnny hadn't wanted to go in to details—*details again*—but she had wanted to know what led up to the night the Christmas tree was tossed and why Mommy had received a permanent facial scar.

"Well, … if you really want to know, it had nothing to do with Dad not loving Mom." Johnny had said. "He does love her, in a crazy way. That scar on her face is there because Dad got caught cheating, and he was embarrassed and ashamed about it. He does care for Mom. Look at them now. They're always together. Always. They're into each other maybe too much for a normal couple, but that's what works for them."

"What's normal anyway? Oh, forget that. Why did dad cheat at all?" she'd asked.

"You ever hear of a midlife crisis?"

"Yeah, that's when you want a new car, buy a boat, or get a girlfriend … right?"

"Right, but do you know why? Why people do it?"

"No."

"Because it is your last able stage in life before old age strikes. Your last chance to have fun or regret not trying to have it. You see, there's something hidden deep down in all of us. At some point you gotta act on it or pass before it's gone forever. If you didn't adventure out because of guilt before, then when midlife crisis comes, it's a now or never dilemma."

"So Dad began to feel old and desperate too?"

"Sort of. He wasn't in any rush to get there ... or to miss out on something he must have always wanted to have."

"A girlfriend? Dad wanted someone different from Mom?"

"Yep. Guilt has a way to keep the young in line, and regret ... well, finishes the old."

"Yeah, Johnny, I think I got it."

"One last thing, Terry," Johnny had added. "Nobody's family is perfect ... nobody's."

Terry had had enough of Mom and Dad's flawed memories. She was only concerned for the whereabouts of her brother. She retreated to Johnny's empty room, praying the phone would ring, or better yet, Johnny would stroll through the front door.

Despite the fact that his room had the same square footage as her own, Johnny's bedroom had a spacious flow. There was no easel in its center, nor were there paints, brushes, sketches, tape, rulers, wipes, schoolbooks, hairbrushes, lip gloss, mirrors, or clothing, clean or dirty. Johnny's room had none of that. His items were few. If one component was moved or went missing, Johnny would surely know. Johnny's bed, dresser, and desk were in the same locations as Terry's. His window was between the dresser and desk, as was Terry's, but Johnny's view was of the yard, unlike his sister's view of the street.

When Johnny was ten years old, he had begun to paint and build Aurora plastic models. Almost every Saturday throughout the fall and winter of 1971, Johnny and Tommy would walk to the Jack's Hobby Shop to buy figurines such as Godzilla, The Wolf Man, King Kong, the Creature from the Black Lagoon, the Forgotten Prisoner, and Dr. Jekyll as Mr. Hyde. During the model-building year, Johnny would explain to Terry why it was important to put blood inside the mouth of The Mummy but just as important to scuff up the dragging foot of Frankenstein. Every piece was part of the story, and to ignore something so little would lower the quality of work. Then good becomes only … okay. Terry had learned this lesson well and held a high standard in her own paintings.

Terry sat on Johnny's bed and stared at the shelf her father had built for Johnny's models. *He surely built that shelf before the cheating. Did he know his midlife crisis was coming, or does it hit you all at once?* Terry wondered. *Like he hit Mom.* Terry did not want to focus on anything but the here and now. She went to Johnny's window and plugged in the Christmas lights. Then she laid down on Johnny's made bed and stared at the monsters dancing in the flickering green, red, blue, and yellow lights. *I'm missing something. First my portrait is off, and now something is wrong here. What's missing now? Something in Johnny's room, but what?* Terry watched The Wolf Man's shadows bounce off his chest, creating an illusion of breathing. Then she concentrated on the Forgotten Prisoner. He too began to take in air, as did all the others if she put her mind to it.

Terry's eyes wandered to the end of the shelf where the breathing models ended and Johnny's championed possessions were exhibited. Terry's favorite was the framed picture of the two of them at the Bronx Zoo. She and Johnny sat inside a howdah, the seat on top of an elephant. Terry was only three years old and terrified when they boarded the animal ride. She'd held on to her brother's arm for dear life, but it was Johnny making fun of the chair's name that eased all her fears. *Howdah … howdah … how dah doin'?* Terry and Johnny's laughter was caught in the snapshot, and she would never forget the five-minute ride or the name of the elephant chair … *howdah.* Thankfully, unlike the three-dimensional monster models, the snapshot did not breathe, although their two-dimensional chuckling would survive forever. In between the Phantom of the Opera and the giggling siblings was the foul ball Johnny had seized at a New York Mets game. Terry had never understood the fuss behind getting the ball but knew how important it was to Johnny.

"John Milner, 'The Hammer,' hit it. Good thing the Mets suck, because no one else was there to chase it but me and Bain," he'd told her. Johnny had let Terry hold the ball for a bit, then quickly put it on his shelf for safe keeping. She'd never touched it again but was always reminded of its existence because of the ball's placement beside the elephant ride picture.

Terry closed her eyes for a few minutes and let the flashing lights bounce off of her closed eyelids. *The ball, why is it different tonight? Details ... details.* Terry's mind, out of exasperation, went back to her portrait. *Shit, I got it!* She realized what she'd missed: *details! The smile isn't the smile by itself; it's the whole face. My eyes need to be closed just a bit. Too wide open makes me crazy looking. It's not my smile that's off; it's that I need my eyes to add to my smile! Details ... the eight slices of a pizza make the whole pie complete.* Before Terry could touch up her personal sketching, the second and most important solution came to mind. She jumped out of the bed and knelt onto Johnny's desk, facing the shelf where the ball sat. *I knew it. I just knew it.* The shelf itself had a fine layer of dust, but the layer ended in an erratic way around The Hammer's foul ball. To be sure, Terry ran her fingers along the shelf, and sure enough, it was clear of dust in the area around the ball. *Shit. For years, the ball has rested high up on the rock from that pond in Central Park.* Terry moved her head back to examine the photo with the ball placed down to its side. *Yep, it is definitely lower than normal. The rock was here without fail, and now it's missing. Johnny took it out tonight ... to the pond.* Terry jumped down from Johnny's desk and ran to the kitchen phone. She dialed Tori's number.

~~~~~~

"How's your ribs?" An antsy Joey slowed his pace for Kevin to walk beside him. Tommy remained a few strides ahead.

"Hurts, but I'm more cold than anything." Kevin answered. For the first time since the mini-brawl inside the cemetery, Kevin caught sight of Joey's swelling left eye. "Damn, Fagan got you good." When Joey did not respond about his increasing purple knot, Kevin finished, "When you went to help me ... thanks."

"Looks like that bar across the street is open," Tommy yelled out to Joey and Kevin. "I need a beer, and we can call the girls too." Tommy would not admit to being cold and tired, but that was fine with the two lagging behind. Tommy ran ahead, crossing the desolate street without watching for traffic. Once on the bar side of the street, Tommy lit a cigarette and waited for Kevin and Joey to join him. Tommy did not want to enter a strange place so far from home alone. "Come on, guys!" As the two cautiously stepped or limped over the ice in his direction, Tommy looked around and wondered, *What the hell am I doing here?*

Here was the Hunter's Point section of Queens, about a mile northwest of Calvary Cemetery, where the boys search for Johnny had officially ended. Tommy's hand shook as he smoked and watched a cat—*no, it's a rat*—mull around in garbage. *It's all abandoned here,* Tommy thought, but his observation was not entirely correct. The bar was open, and two blocks further, on the corner of Eleventh Avenue, where the boys would turn left and head south to Brooklyn, a pizzeria showcased flashing, neon lights. *Good, more life up that way.*

"What's the rush man?" Kevin tossed his empty beer can into whatever animal lurched in the shadows of trash. He nearly hit the creature, chasing it out into the street. Tommy's guess of a rat was correct. "Broadway Joe hits an open Eddie Bell!" Kevin pumped his fist up, practically knocking the bag off of his head. "Shit, that hurts." Kevin leaned forward and carefully elbowed his ribs for comfort.

"Come on, guys. I'm freezin'," Tommy finally admitted.

The boys walked into a typical old man's bar. On the right, a jukebox stood with a table and two chairs on either side of it. Down further in the corner, there was a darkened phone booth. On the opposite wall, a long, mahogany bar faced eight worn and torn red bar stools. On the wall behind the wooden alcoholic serving stage, a raised mirror with glass shelving showcased no-more-than-half-filled bottles of vodka, whiskey, and gin. A line of Christmas lights blinked randomly behind these liquor bottles. At the end of the bar, a closed doorway led to the bathroom, with handwritten words declared to be "For Customers Only."

In the center of the lonesome bar, stood a man of about seventy years old, bald, short, and surprisingly stocky for his age. He wore unpolished black shoes, dark dress pants, and a wrinkled, collared, button-down white shirt. Ties, here, were not required.

Kevin walked in first, his brown bag stuffed into his coat pocket for the time being. Joey had to remind Kevin moments before to take it off. "You don't want them to think it's a stickup or something." Joey and Tommy squeezed through the door together to escape the cold.

The temperature inside the bar was in the low sixties—cold for a home but plenty warm for the three sloggers as they sat down and ordered a beer each.

"You and you, okay … but you got ID?" the bartender asked Joey.

"Dah … aaa"

Tommy shot out, "Just give him a glass of milk."

Joey shot Tommy the stink eye. He then limped to the phone booth to call Tori's apartment to ask about Johnny. Without a word, the bartender placed two six-ounce glasses of beer in front of Kevin and Tommy. Kevin downed his. Tommy held his glass to the flickering lights behind the bar and complained that it was dirty and that the beer was flat.

"You don't like it, pay and get out," the bartender shot back.

Tommy held his nose in a dramatic fashion with his elbow pointing to the tin ceiling and closed his eyes to drink his beer. In one gulp, his beer vanished. Tommy playfully slammed the glass down on the bar coaster and asked for another.

"That's two dollars, if you want more. Watch it," the bartender ordered.

"Yeah, yeah." *Merry Christmas to you too!* Tommy thought. He put a five on the bar and asked for quarters. *First time tonight I feel good.*

Kevin saw the change in Tommy's mood and was quick to question it. "I know we're getting closer to Tori's, but we still haven't found Johnny."

Tommy swallowed another six ounces of flat beer and then wiped his mouth and unzipped his coat. Tommy had no answer but to shrug his shoulders.

Joey hobbled out of the phone booth with no news of Johnny. "Nicky said the only calls coming in were from Terry."

"Did you tell them what happened?" Kevin asked.

"Only that the cops chased us out of the cemetery. Nothin' about the Madd Tuffs." Joey subconsciously touched his swelling left eye. "I said we'd be over in an hour." Joey rubbed his bad leg next. The cold and the walking had increased his shredded-nerve pain.

Tommy got up from the barstool and walked three feet back to the jukebox. "What a rip-off. For a quarter you only get three songs?"

The bartender said not a word but aimlessly wiped down the far end of the bar.

"Let's see … "Runaway," "Teen Angel," "Travelin' Man," and "Downtown." These records haven't been changed in years," Tommy complained, but he kept reading the record labels. "Here we go." Tommy placed a quarter into the jukebox and picked his first song. "Perfect one for tonight."

Shelley Fabares began singing her signature track, "Johnny Angel." Tommy kicked off into a slow, overplayed dance with an invisible partner, singing behind Shelley's voice, *"He's got something I can't resist, but he doesn't even know that I exist."*

"Hey, no dancing here!" the bartender yelled from across the room.

"Yeah, Tommy, what's your problem?" Joey did not want to hear the answer, so he turned to Kevin. "Are you ready? Let's get out of this dump."

"One more beer and a piss." Kevin saw the frustration on his friend's face. "Two minutes. It's cold out, and we still have an hour walk."

Tommy plumped on his stool at the bar.

"How I tingle when he passes by."

Tommy raised his hands and swerved onto his bar stool. "Hey, mister bartender, can I dance in my seat?" Tommy did not wait for an answer but turned his attention to Joey. "Relax, kid, there's another song I want to hear before I go Johnny-searching." As Shelley's voice faded off the jukebox, an all too familiar harmony rang in.

"Oh, you are such a faggot," Joey declared.

"Wait … this is the best part." Tommy held up his hand for Joey to be patient. "I was kicked around when I was born," he sang. Tommy watched Kevin leave for the bathroom as Joey continued to massage his leg. "He's a baby. Now down his beer …"

Without a word, Joey chugged the full glass of beer and placed it on the coaster. "Better than milk, but you, you are the fag." Joey then burped while Tommy laughed.

Kevin walked out of the bathroom as Tommy finished the first verse of disco's trademark song. "Ah, ah, ah, ah, stayin' alive, stayin' alive …" Tommy shoved his index and middle fingers deep down his throat, imitating a person trying to vomit. Thrusting too deep, he actually began to puke and then cough. Tommy spat phlegm and beer onto the bar.

The seventy-year-old bartender had had enough. He reached below the bar and raised a baseball bat. In unison, the three boys cursed out loud and then raced onto the snow-covered sidewalk.

Chapter 15

1973

I need someone to love me the whole day through.
Ah, one look in my eyes,
and you can tell that's true...
—"Old Man" performed by Neil Young

How was your vacation? Welcome back. It looks great. They really did a wonderful job. Nurse Joan, it works. It's so not like you, but it is exceptional. Genius! Candy striper Nanci and those kids ...

Nurse Joan had been away from work for less than two weeks. She could not comprehend what had gone on without her. Curiosity and wonderment tore at Nurse Joan's mental well-being, tormenting her spirit as she raced to room 18. *What happened in the past week and a half? Everyone in the hospital has something to say ... something about Nanci, room 18, and the kids? What kids?* Nurse Joan did not clock in or remove her opened duster jacket—*no time for that shit*—but went straight to the focal point of the hospital's staff.

Nurse Joan stopped at room 14 to compose herself. She did not like surprises. From the time she was a child through this upcoming Christmas, Joan would hunt the house for her future presents. She could guess what was inside by the presents' shapes. If that didn't work, then she would shake the gift and, in some extreme cases, tear some of the wrapping paper for a quick peek. *One has to be sure ... and in control.* She took a deep breath before walking two rooms further. *It's like* Let's Make a Deal. *No, Monty, not door number 16. No, not door 20.*

Yes, the middle door. That's the grand prize. What's behind door number 18? A caddy?

The first sense Nurse Joan had that something was not right behind door number 18 was the scent of pines. This smell was succeeded by sight.

"Hello, Nurse Joan. How was your vacation?" Candy striper Nanci stood behind Mr. Baden's wheelchair. "Mr. Baden needs to go back to his room for dinner."

Mr. Baden turned around and nodded for Nanci to move along. Nanci maneuvered the wheelchair around Nurse Joan, through the doorway, and to the patient's room at the end of the hallway. It was now that Nurse Joan was fully able to recognize the transformation of room 18.

Donny, his bed, and the medical devices were all in place. Donny's facial bruises had improved; the swelling and purplish-yellow color had disappeared. The bed sheets covered Donny to his chest, with his left arm exposed to receive an intravenous needle. All this was the same as when Nurse Joan skipped off to the Caribbean. But as for candy striper Nanci's refurbishment, the eight or nine vases that had contained mostly dying flowers were now reduced to two bearing fresh hydrangeas. The above-ground el train outside room 18's windows was now hidden by curtains in two different Christmas designs. The one cushioned bedside chair had been joined by five others, and another four chairs surrounded a small, circular card table stationed between the windows and Donny's bed. The coatrack that had once stood in the furthest corner of the room to the left of the windows had been replaced by a manger on a cotton-covered footstool below the source of Nurse Joan's first sense alert: a Christmas tree.

The tree itself was not Nurse Joan's style, first because it was alive. Nurse Joan never appreciated the mess of falling needles, the watering, or the uneven way nature grew its branches, since the placement of her decorations had to be consistent year after year. Then of course there was the tree disposal. *If you want the scent of pines, get a candle.*

With all the rearranging of furniture and the addition of holiday curtains, the tree, the manger, board games, cards, hydrangeas, and the scent of pine needles, it took Nurse Joan a moment to focus on and be mystified by the starry eyes of a group of speechless children, one in particular. A boy stood at the foot of Donny's bed. He was about twelve years old and was wearing a shirt with a picture of Elton John ironed onto its front. Elton's name was printed across his portrait, in which he wore a white suite and hat and was staring forward. But the image had obvious additions. In marker, an *F* had been added before and *son* after the end of his full name, and the word *sucks* was scribbled on poor old Elton's fedora. *"Felton Johnson,"* Nurse Joan read to herself. *"And he sucks too. Candy striper Nanci, what did you do when I was away?*

Nurse Joan silently walked around the Felton Johnson fan to take Donny's medical chart. She quickly glimpsed at his stats and then put the clipboard under her left arm. Nurse Joan raised her right hand for all not to move as she swiftly ran out of the room after her candy striper.

Nanci could not stop giggling. The chuckling came from deep inside her belly, not from laughter but from nervousness. "Oh, Mr. Baden, did you see Nurse Joan's face? She was pissed. She's pissed. I'm done. I …" Nanci wheeled her patient to his bedside and pressed her right foot down on the chair's brake. "I don't know what I did." Nanci's foot slipped; then she stepped down harder, nearly knocking Mr. Baden out of the chair and onto the floor. "Oops!"

"Hey, Nan! Please don't get all crazy on me now, especially with those kids in there." Mr. Baden put his hand up. "Don't let her get to you for what you did."

Nurse Joan stood in Mr. Baden's doorway. "The orderly will help you back in bed, unless you want to have your dinner in your chair tonight."

"In my chair." Mr. Baden wanted to defend Nanci, but Nurse Joan had already nodded for Nanci's departure from the door entrance.

"Holy shit." Tommy got up from the card table and walked to the doorway to sneak a peek after Nurse Joan's exit. "Oh shit, there they go to the nurses' lounge." Tommy stepped back into room 18, bumping into Shanty and Porky. "Homos, back the hell off." Shanty went to the cushioned couch beside Donny's bed, but Porky stood his ground, staring Tommy down. "Mooove!" Tommy took his hand and palmed Porky's face against the wall.

"Bain, stop him." Nicole yelled from one of the chairs. "We're all gonna get kicked out of here." The girls agreed with Nicole. Tommy, thwarted, shuffled back to the card table to finish *Monopoly* with Johnny, Angela, and Joey.

"Tommy!" Gina, sitting in her cushioned chair, looked over Donny's laid out body. Once she had received Tommy's and everyone else's attention, Gina planted her right fist at her throat and then swiftly pushed it out toward her target. "Stronzo!" Gina eased up in her chair and went back to reading *Cosmopolitan*. She spoke into her magazine. "We all have to stay quiet and let them figure it out."

Before rolling the dice, Johnny waved for everyone's attention. "Everybody calm down. We didn't do anything wrong. We followed their rules." Johnny put his two fingers on his ship and counted to eight, landing on the box "Go Directly to Jail." "Shit!"

"Candy striper Nanci stuck her neck out for all of us, too," Angela added. "We don't want her in any trouble."

Kevin stated the obvious. "That gal's gettin' her ass chewed out now. She's gonna lose her job or worse."

Tori pulled back her long, black hair and said what they all feared. "We're out." Out of crossness she finished. "That Nurse J, you can tell is such a bitch. But I do think she liked Joey's shirt."

"Amen to that! To her being a bitch, of course. As for Joey's shirt, eh." Gina placed her stamp of approval on Tori's assessment and then added with a glimmer of hope, "Put the radio back on. We need some Christmas music."

<center>~~~~~~</center>

The nurse's lounge where Nanci was ordered to was not much larger than a janitor's closet. The windowless room, contained one rectangular table placed against its left wall with four chairs, and a phone on top. Across the room, a small table held a coffee machine and a toaster oven. Below the cooking appliances, a small refrigerator was stationed. Leaning against the back wall, a couch was set down for quick naps when shifts were added and working hours became marathons. On the two sides of the sofa were three open lockers for the nurses and candy stripers to share.

Nurse Joan closed the door of the deserted room and gestured with her right elbow for Nanci to sit on the couch. The candy striper did not feel secure and chose a chair nearest the exit door.

"You got me. Nanci, what were you thinking?" Nurse Joan stood over her volunteer and waited for a reply. Receiving no answer, Nurse Joan rubbed her tanned forehead and went on. "I figured you had more sense. I can't reverse this, not now." Nurse Joan pulled up a chair next to candy striper Nanci's but was unable to sit. Taking a deep breath with her hand on her hips, Nurse Joan gawked at the drop ceiling, not knowing what to say or do next.

Candy striper Nanci had a brief moment to explain how things had gone from the children's first visit to the point where it became a sort of

173

commune. *Is that the word I'm looking for?* "Nurse Joan, it started on the bus. They wanted to see him. I … they didn't realize I could help them. I listened to all of them. They're friends and good kids, but they are hurting. Once you get to know them, you'll see they're … good. You'll like them. All are different but very supportive, in their own ways. The staff likes them, too, and the seniors love them." Nanci began tearing up but refused to cry in front of her nemesis. "All they want is to support a friend in trouble. They're lost and hurting."

Nurse Joan was heedless of Nanci's ramblings about a bus, friends, staff, seniors, good kids hurting. The one word that broke her out of a self-induced spell was the word *lost*. *Yes, they are lost, but just wait, my little naïve candy striper girl. The situation will only worsen, and who will be holding the bag? It is happening already. Donny's health is declining rapidly.* Now was the time to open candy striper Nanci's eyes to the ominous circumstances awaiting that little boy in bed as well as his "lost" friends.

"Nanci." Nurse Joan elevated her right hand so as not to be interrupted and pulled from under her armpit the clipboard she'd looted from Donny's bed. "Let me get right down to it. Donny's vital signs are deteriorating, his blood pressure is weakening every day, his heart is slowing, and the medications that are pumped into that little body will keep increasing until he …"

"What are you saying?" Nanci's eyelids were open wide, exposing the whites below and above her pupils. She was struggling her best to keep tears from escaping out and down. "No, no you haven't been here. You don't know. The kids … they're all friends. They're pulling for him. He's gonna get better. I know it. They all know it." Tearful, Nanci remained in her seat defiantly glaring up at her nemesis. While her tears built up uncontrollably inside her exploding head, Nanci's helplessness and vulnerability was exposed. She dreamt of some kind of compassionate talk from Nurse Joan, but there was nothing but negativity. *Nemesis has no hope!*

Candy striper Nanci's eyes, swollen with fluids, reminded Nurse Joan of an old Bugs Bunny cartoon in which Witch Hazel was about to slice wisecracking Bugs's head off with an axe. As the tied-up Bugs Bunny sat and waited for the inevitable strike, tears pleading for mercy welled in his wide-open eyes too. "Nanci, it is what it is." *Gotta be firm. This is the unfortunate world I'm in. We all are. And it's called life, dear.* "Nanci … get up please. Now come here." In an instant of humanity, Nurse Joan put her arms out for a hushed hug. Candy striper Nanci let out a whimper when she rose and hurriedly buried her head in Nurse Joan's shoulder. "It's okay, Nanci …" Not wanting to bring up the inevitable at this point, Nurse Joan could only soothe her candy striper's spirits and sidestep the subject. "You are in charge of that group. If there are no complaints in the ward, they can stay, but only during visiting hours." Candy striper Nanci mumbled an agreement, and then Nurse Joan finished. "But I want all their names and home phone numbers, just in case there is a problem." Again, Nanci agreed. Nurse Joan had to remain the authority figure, not a friend, so she released Nanci from her embrace.

Nanci sensed the change in Nurse Joan's position. *She doesn't think Donny will live. Well she's wrong! She's pacifying me.* Nanci wiped her eyes and rubbed her small pug nose, not embarrassed any longer of her own crying. Once she composed herself, Nanci needed to get the last word in. "I don't care what that chalkboard—I mean, clipboard—says. It's so wrong, and you are too." *Don't worry I'll get their names and numbers, but now, please don't say another word to me!*

Nanci marched out of the room, leaving Nurse Joan alone holding her thin, wooden slat. *Oh, Nanci, you are such a wishful dreamer. For the sake of Donny, the kids, and yourself, I hope to God you are correct.* Nurse Joan rubbed her sunburned forehead a second time and walked silently out of the lounge to begin her nightly rounds.

~~~~~~~

175

For the next two weeks, Donny's health continued to fail. The ward's undertaking was to create a comfortable setting for room 18's fading patient. To prevent bed sores from developing, the nursing staff bestowed Donny with extra bathing, along with plenty of moisturizing cream. Donny's undergarments were changed every four hours, and his bedding was changed each morning. Nurse Joan allowed the Christmas tree and window lights to remain on all night. Tori's radio, too, would play softly the seasonal songs. If one could block out the monitors and life supporting instruments attached to Donny, one could welcome the Christmas spirit of the room. There was little left for the caretakers to do but pray for a Christmas miracle.

The children continued to visit their friend on Tuesday and Thursday nights. On Sundays, the boys would change the radio station from Christmas music to the dreadful Jets and Giants games. Sitting around playing Monopoly, Battle Ship or Hearts, the boys argued about the upcoming football playoffs and who would win the Super Bowl. Most had the Dolphins with Larry Czonka, Bob Griese, Mercury Morris, and the No Name Defense winning it all. Only Johnny and Joey put their stake on the Dallas Cowboys with Roger "The Dodger" Staubach, Bobby "The Fastest Human" Hayes, Bob Lilly, and the Doomsday Defense winning the Super Bowl. Everyone agreed that if Joe Namath could only stay healthy one more year, the Jets would win it all.

Nurse Joan had seemed to daydream the previous fourteen days away. She'd volunteered extra hours nursing Donny's sores at night, leaving her understanding husband to tend to their two preteen daughters' swimming schedules, the house duties, and of course, the last-minute Christmas shopping.

Nurse Joan would shiver when comparing Donny to her own two girls. *How can a mother do that? That boy will not die alone.* She didn't know how to cope with the inevitable. She could only keep it deep inside, to herself, and do what she could. Unfortunately, the staff, the elderly patients, Nanci, and especially the lost children wrongly judged

Nurse Joan's heartache as her being a "snobbish bitch." Once, Tommy remarked, "If NJ's head were any further up her ass, she'd disappear." Porky got a slap in the head when he questioned that analogy.

Nanci remained the ward's smiling face. She volunteered extra hours, splitting her time between the old folks and the group of believers in room 18. Nanci became friendly with all the girls but became especially close with Gina and Angela, recognizing them as the two with the most heart. As for the boys, Nanci enjoyed their company, as they treated her as one of the girls. In contrast, the boys bullied each other and made certain to push—no, shove—the envelope as far as they could when possible. *Maybe to hide their own pains and uncertainties?* Still, Nanci could not grasp that style in a relationship. *Here they are, though, comforting a friend in trouble.* Nanci could feel the goodness of the boys, which was most important.

Just as Nanci was wrong about the boys' true sense of each other, she was also mistaken about Nurse Joan being a bitch and her nemesis. For Nanci's whole life, she'd heard from her dad, "Your heart leads your noggin, for good or bad. It is not always up or down. Sometimes, little girl, you have to look at the whole horizon." It took Nanci forgetting to secure a clipboard six days before Christmas for her noggin to finally catch up to the whole horizon.

⸝⸝⸝⸝⸝⸝⸝

"Here, go get me a pack of Marlboros"—Bain's father slapped a dollar bill on the kitchen table—"and another one of these." He picked up an empty beer can and motioned to the refrigerator. "I want change on that bill, too."

Bain was sitting across the four-chair kitchen table on a tepid radiator facing his father. Adjusting his buns for expanding warmth, Bain pushed his dark hair off his face, grunting back, "Hell noooo." Bain got up and walked to his and Kevin's bedroom, the fourth and final room of their railroad apartment.

"Mom home yet?' Kevin asked. He was laid across their shared bed tossing a torn football up to the ceiling. Bain shook his head no. "Damn, she's been workin' a lot."

"Yeah, that bum in there does shit around here." Bain intercepted the descending ball. "I wish Mom would just leave him already … or better yet, let him leave us."

"Yeah… what was he just yelling about?" Before Bain could answer, Kevin clapped his hands for the football. "Forget it. It's always the same shit." Kevin took the football and reassumed lofting the ball upward. "What's everybody doing tonight?"

"No hospital. I guess the park, for starters … It's cold. Probably the bowling alley later. I'm sure the girls will be there."

"Johnny coming here soon?"

Bain bounced onto the bed, making Kevin bobble but gain control of the falling football. "No, he's going … out somewhere. I think he said something about school. Not sure now."

Kevin used the football as a pillow while he lay back into the bed's headboard. "Strange … Johnny's different lately. He's just not the same anymore."

Johnny got off the bus a block from Woodhull Hospital. *Odd, coming here alone.* Johnny sprinted across the street to the main entrance of the hospital. Strolling through the lobby, Johnny was relieved to see the security guard at the elevator entrance. *Doughboy … but he hates it when Tommy calls him that.* "Hi, Doug, what's up?"

Pulling up his plummeting security pants, Doughboy's shirt began to spill over the thin, black-leather belt. "Hey, boy, it's only five. You kids can't go up until six. You know the rules."

The man, in his mid-thirties, was the prototypical tormenting security guard of every boy and girl's imagination. *A wannabe cop. He surely lives with his mom. Fat. Smelly. If he has friends, they're losers like him, and know-it-all bullies. Like Gina and Tori said, he's a pervert too!*

Doughboy detested the direct orders he'd received from the administration to admit these kids up the elevators with no room passes. *But they're only allowed up during visiting hours. Having power and authority now over this wisecracking punk will be very enjoyable, although it'll only last an hour at best. I'll make the most of it.*

"If you don't leave the premises, I'm gonna call for backup." Doughboy put his hand out as if to stop traffic. "Stop! It's only 5:05 p.m. You got another hour."

Well, I tried to be nice. I even called Doughboy by the name on his name tag. Johnny walked up to the guard's hand and nearly touched it with his nose. "Okay, okay …" *You don't have to be such a fat pussy about it.* Johnny took two steps back to allow a hospital worker pushing an empty gurney into the elevator. Johnny then reached into his pocket and took out three one-dollar bills. "This is all I have."

"I don't take bribes. I'm gonna call for backup."

What's up with this backup shit? They pay you, asshole. Do your job without backup, Doughboy. "No, it's not a bribe at all. It's a challenge." Doughboy seemed interested, Johnny knew the type. *We have this fish, and it's a fat one.* "This is how we play. If I win, I go up early, and if you win, you can keep my three bucks and I don't go up at all tonight."

Doughboy liked games, as Johnny had correctly reckoned. The elevator opened, and two nurses sidestepped Doughboy and walked out. "You're just killing time until it's six." Doughboy smiled.

"No, no, this is how it goes," Johnny pleaded. "If I say something that is true, then you gotta let me go up the elevator. If I say something that's a lie, then I have to leave the hospital for the night and you get the three dollars."

"Wait, you wise-ass ... all you have to say is a true statement? That's easy enough. Of course you'll win." Doughboy had had enough. "Go get lost before I call for—"

"Hold on, there's more." *If I hear 'call for backup' one more time ...* "What if I say something that puts you in a corner with no solution ... no yes or no answer?" Johnny rubbed his hands together as if rolling the dice for snake eyes. "Whaddaya say? If I can't trap you in the puzzle, you win."

"No tricks. You have to put me in a paradox then." Doughboy's smile decreased in size. He did not trust this *wise-ass* but had to know the endgame.

"Yeah." *Yes, a paradox. I wanted to keep it simple for you. I didn't think you'd know the word, fatso.* Johnny spotted his right pinky out, and Doughboy did the same. "On three." The two closed the bet once both pinkies jerked severely apart from one another—the Brooklyn method of sealing a bet.

"Go ahead, smarty. What you got?"

"You won't let me go up the elevator." Johnny smiled and waited for the dumb-ass fatso fish to respond.

"You're damn right I won't. Now give me the three bucks and get out of the hospital." Doughboy put his hand out for the money. "If you don't,

I won't let you up there for the rest of the week or next week either." Doughboy reached for his radio.

"Oh no! We pinky bet, and you lost." Johnny took a step forward as the elevator doors opened, letting out two cleaning ladies, who walked around Johnny.

A nervous look appeared on Doughboys face. "What are you talkin' about?"

"I said you won't let me up the elevator. That's … what did you call it? Right, a paradox." Johnny began to walk around the stupefied security guard.

"Hold on a second." Doughboy remained lost in thought, as Johnny pressed the elevator's up button.

"See, I said you would *not* let me up the elevator, so if you do let me up, then what I said is a lie. So you can't let me go up."

"Yeah, yeah." Doughboy had only ventured into part one of the riddle.

"But if you don't let me up, then what I said is a true statement, because I said you wouldn't let me on the elevator. That means you gotta let me go, because that makes my statement true." The doors of the elevator opened as Doughboy stood rubbing his forehead. Johnny stepped inside the shaft and slapped his stupefied opponent's back. "Sorry 'bout that one … Doughboy." As the doors closed, Johnny could here Doug the Doughboy swearing.

~~~~~~~

"There are sad, happy, and just miserable people." Mrs. McMail motioned for her half-filled plastic cup of water. Candy striper Nanci quickly reached over the nightstand and handed it to her philosopher patient. "At a funeral, a mourner would be classified as one of the three 99 percent of the time."

"Wait … wait a second, I don't get it." Candy striper Nanci did not like the direction their intimate conversation was going.

Mrs. McMail had a difficult time adjusting her pillow against its headboard, unlike Kevin had seconds before with his torn football. Candy striper Nanci raced to her bedside, gently guiding Mrs. McMail's right shoulder forward and placing the pillow lower for better back support. "How's that?"

Mrs. McMail nodded. Then she began to explain her funeral-audience theory. "Sadness at a funeral is obvious—for the dead, the living, and for yourself. Normal."

Candy striper Nanci nodded and wondered where the funeral theory would be going.

"Being happy inside yourself at the funeral parlor is not always a bad thing. It could be, but understand, the world has always been wicked with wicked people. So, if the son of a bitch lying in that coffin was a wicked man or woman, a mourner does have the right to be happy."

Nanci rubbed her arms, unsure what would define a miserable person. Mrs. McMail coughed lightly and motioned for another cup of water. Nanci refilled it to the max.

"Oops! Be careful; it's full." Nanci placed it under her patient's lips for her to take a small swig.

"Nanci … thanks." Mrs. McMail continued, "Miserable people are in a category all by themselves, and they carry their misery with them throughout the day, day in and day out."

"I'm a bit lost."

Mrs. McMail coughed three or four times before her caretaker handed her two tissues. "Thanks, Nanci." Mrs. McMail wiped her mouth and then spoke in a lower tone. "Miserable people are just miserable; they are happiest in others misery. As for the funeral, miserables don't care for the dead. No, no. They want to see the sorrow on the faces of the loved ones; that is their joy."

"I can't believe people can be so simply categorized like that." Candy striper Nanci smiled halfheartedly. "How would you even know it to be that way?" She stuttered her final question.

"Here, let me simplify it a bit." Mrs. McMail tried to cough, but no air escaped her lungs. "Please ..." She motioned for the cup of water candy striper Nanci now held. After wetting her lips, the dying patient continued. "Remember this forever, for you will always know who a real friend is. When you speak of a tragic moment in your life, any kind of hardship, your friend will listen intensely and will never interrupt. They want all the juicy details and want to give you a slap on the back of support."

Candy striper Nanci nodded in agreement.

"But the same so-called friend"—Mrs. McMail successfully coughed— "will barely listen to your joyous event, and will do so with little interest and judgmental responses. It's called jealousy."

Candy striper Nanci put her hands to her mouth in shock but had to agree. Mrs. McMail might be on to something here.

"I am an old lady. I once had a family. I ... you see, Nanci, I started out like most everyone, but life has a way of beating you up." Mrs. McMail produced a halfhearted smile. "You're sweet. Never let life change who you are." The old lady put her hand onto Nanci's arm. "Do not let life beat you up."

Mrs. McMail sighed. Before she could comfort her any further, candy striper Nanci caught a glimpse of Johnny walking past the room's open doorway. Nanci got up quickly and spied down the hall. *That's Johnny all right.* Nanci looked at her watch. *Only 5:10 p.m. Why is he here alone and so early?* She watched Johnny confidently pass the nurses station without incident and stroll toward the end of the hall to room 18.

Chapter 16

1978

True friends stab you in the front.
—Oscar Wilde

The sound of a trumpet clamored in the north from the bowl-shaped horizon. As Bain and Shanty carefully stepped deeper into the sloping, snow-covered landscape, the sound of the bugle disappeared, as did the hope of finding Johnny in Manhattan. Bain stood alone on the water's edge at Central Park's biggest pond. The snow had stopped, but the night sky was overcast. The reflection of the city's bright skyline from the cumulus billow lent an eerie grayness to the treetops and open areas, such as the frozen pond. The icy snow on the ground glistened on all sides of the walkway lamps. Everything else hid its features in the silhouette of the night.

"Do you see him anywhere?"

Shanty stayed twenty feet behind Bain in the blackened outline of the extended stone bridge. "No, but maybe he hasn't gotten here yet ... or maybe he left already." Shanty, avoiding the potential danger of the snow-covered pond, waited in the shadows for Bain's next course of action.

Bain turned from the blueish-gray of the pond to speak to his friend directly. Barely recognizable in the darker hue, Bain answered Shanty's two remarks. "Yes and no." Bain walked up a hill to the abutment section of the bridge where Shanty bounced on the snow to keep from freezing. "Look around where you can. The only footprints are our own."

Shanty obediently surveyed the grounds; it took a few seconds for his eyes to adjust to the outline of the terrain. Then he asked, "Should we wait?"

Bain tried to light a cigarette, but his matches were damp. "Damn it." Flinging the remaining matches into the air, Bain reckoned, "No, let's get to a phone and call Tori's. Maybe I'm wrong; maybe Johnny's not coming here at all." With a slight slap on Shanty's back, Bain, in his own way, apologized to his friend. "I dragged you out here tonight. I'm cold too." To demonstrate the bone-chilling effect of the night, Bain blew into his hands. "I'll get you a beer for the ride home." Bain took two steps toward the walkway, before Shanty spoke out.

"Bain … if it weren't for you and Johnny, especially you, I would still be holed up in my room, too afraid to do anything." Shanty sauntered to Bain's side. It was now his turn to pat a bud's back. In a sheepish voice, he ended with, "I'd be lost too."

"Aw, you're still a pussy." When the two friends reached the summit of the hill, they heard for the second time from the panhandler bugler, trying his best to blow out "Have Yourself a Merry Little Christmas."

<center>~~~~~~</center>

"Did you see that guy? That old fart looked like he really could swing that bat." Tommy stopped running to find his two lagging friends. "Hey, what's the matter?" He saw Kevin bent over with Joey's hand on his back. "Joey, is he okay?" Tommy ran hard for ten feet and then stopped suddenly so his feet could "ski" the remaining five. Unable to time his skiing correctly, the off-balance Tommy crashed into Kevin's hip.

"Hey, what the hell is the matter with you?" Joey shoved Tommy off of Kevin's shoulder.

A defiant Tommy charged back. "Easy, shit head, I didn't mean to bump into your boyfriend."

Kevin continued to stare down at the snow, but he was able to raise his arm up and gesture for them to stop, halting both friends from exchanging blows.

Joey had had enough from Tommy tonight and many other nights. *Is it him giving a damn about Johnny or taking advantage of Angela that's bothering me? Or better yet, him ordering me a shitty cup of milk in that old man's bar?* Yes, Joey had had enough. Being three inches shorter and twenty pounds lighter, Joey had to have the first and hopefully the last shot, a knockout punch. With Tommy bent over to match Kevin's disposition, Joey pulled his intended target by the forearm.

"Let go, man. What's your probl—" Tommy straightened himself up to meet the unforeseen assault.

Without explanation, Joey tightened his fist and clouted Tommy's jaw. Tommy stumbled away from Kevin and initially outstretched his hands to calm his combatant. Regrettably for Joey, hotter heads prevailed. Tommy soared past Kevin and wrapped his hands around Joey's neck, beginning to strangle his foe. To Tommy's shock, Joey's neck was warm and a bit boney. *Or is that still muscle in there? Where is that darn neck bone … vertebrae?* Tommy firmly pressed onward. *Who's he to sucker punch me after all I did for him and everyone else?* Tommy watched Joey's eyes stare back at him in anger as a scream echoed from behind. Joey tried his best to push away Tommy's arms but was too weak to budge his stronger and puffing rival.

Kevin's initial reaction was hampered because of his own bodily pain, his drunkenness, and the nerve-racking night, but once reality struck, there was no delay. Letting go of his bruised left ribs, Kevin yelled out before head-butting Tommy's hip. All three boys tumbled into the plowed snow embankment on the sidewalk's edge. The gagging Joey took the brunt of the fall, with Tommy and Kevin bouncing off of his body. Kevin tumbled off of the snow pile and rolled over to the street, embracing his side. Tommy's left knee was entrenched into the snow, but he was able to balance himself with his two hands, one on his left thigh the other near Joey's half-buried head. Rising to his feet carefully, Tommy recovered from the anger and shock. He offered his hand for Joey to take hold of.

Coughing hard, Joey could only shake Tommy's gesture off with a wave of his hand. Rolling over to his side, Joey spit up phlegm and continued to hack away.

"What the hell is the matter with you, asshole. You could've killed him." Kevin knelt down in the pile of fresh plowed snow beside Joey. It was his turn to aid a friend.

Tommy stood over the two wounded, wondering what to say or do next. *The best defense is a good offense.* "He started it. He sucker-punched me for no reason. Next time he'll remember, and I don't know what the hell your problem is anyway." The only response was the slowing of Joey's hacking.

After a minute of Joey recovering from the lack of oxygen, he was able to spit out two words to Tommy. "It's you."

"Me?" Tommy answered back, flabbergasted. "Me? If it wasn't for me, you wouldn't even be here. You were a loser when I found ya."

Kevin shot up and got chest to chest with Tommy. "You're makin' this worse. You know, sometimes you can be an ass. Not everybody feels about things like you do."

"But … shit." Tommy did an about-face and realized he was on the wrong side of everything tonight … maybe every other night too. He knelt down to a teary-eyed Joey. *There are some things you never say to a hurt friend.* "I'm sorry. I got carried away, and I shouldn't've." Common sense and decency punched Tommy's jaw harder than Kevin or Joey ever could have. "You know, Joey, I was there with you from the get-go. When it mattered most, I kept my mouth shut about everything."

Tommy corrected himself. "So did Johnny, Bain, and of course you." Tommy motioned at Kevin. "I didn't mean anything about you being a ... loser." Tommy was aware calling a friend a loser hurt more than any choke hold ever could. "We always protected one another."

Joey nodded as if to say everything was okay. Kevin felt the tension dissipate and figured it was time to bring some joy on this pre-Christmas Eve night. Reaching into his pocket, Kevin pulled out his wrinkled paper bag and placed it on his head. Joey let out a small giggle while Tommy, for the first time all night, released a genuine Tommy laugh.

"I still say you cheated at pin-the-tail-on-the-donkey that afternoon. That big Polack nose pushed your blindfold above your cheek, and you were peeking. I know it," the Unknown Comic declared in reference to Joey's long-ago birthday party.

Joey cleared his throat and then joined in on teasing Tommy. "Yeah, there was no way you could've nailed that pin so close."

"Who's better than me?" Tommy responded.

"You mean *us*," Joey corrected.

"Yeah ... who's better than us!" Kevin yelled.

Tommy put his hand out for Joey to grab hold of. "Nobody's better." Tommy patted Joey's back as the three crossed the street toward a neon pizza-place sign five blocks away. "You guys hungry? My treat."

"Your treat? That's a first," Kevin stated.

"You are right, though. I did cheat that day, but not to get the pin on the donkey's ass so perfectly. I had to be off a little bit. I really did try to win the volleyball game though."

"Wait, what did you mean before about keeping your mouths shut?" Joey challenged Tommy.

"I remember, Joey, your leg got hurt when we were playing volleyball with the balloon."

"I had to take a leak." Kevin chimed in through the paper-bag smile. "But when I went, there was …"

Joey crossed the darkened street first. Tommy and Kevin followed. "What you mean?" Joey nervously asked.

~~~~~~~

It was the beginning of March on a Saturday morning, seven years earlier. Tommy and Johnny were returning from the hobby shop with their new Aurora plastic models. The boys would buy identical monsters each week and, after completing them, would compare them to see which one seemed more realistic. To Johnny's surprise, Tommy was able to keep pace in the monster-model challenges.

The two ten-year-old boys, to save time reaching home, cut through Winthrop Park clutching their Godzilla models in hand. Johnny was enjoying the smell of the air, and both were excited that fifth grade was nearing its end.

"Let's play some baseball today. We can play against Sutton Street," Johnny reckoned.

"Junior's team? I can't … not today. My grandma's friend from work, the one she cleans houses with … well, that lady's son is havin' a birthday party today. The kid has no friends, and Grandma asked me if I would go. You know, so the birthday boy won't be alone." Spotting a pigeon about five feet ahead picking on a piece of stale bread, Tommy, with one big snort, shot a weighted lungy at the cooing bird. "Shit!"

Missing his target, Tommy lightheartedly kicked at the pigeon, scaring the flying rat, which soared away.

"So he has nobody going to his own party? No friends at all? It's baseball season now … Who is this kid, anyway?" Johnny needed facts as to why Tommy would not be playing ball.

Tommy shrugged his shoulders and then began to explain. "My grandma says he has no friends, no dad either. It's just him and his mom." Tommy shifted Godzilla from his right armpit to his left. "He's sorta a cripple too."

"Sorta a cripple? What's that mean? He in a wheelchair?"

"No, no. Not that bad. He got hurt when he was small. He fell on a glass jar, which tore up nerves in one of his legs."

Johnny's first thought was of the Jerry Lewis Telethon. The talent on the show was mostly boring but was ambushed by the touching segments with kids on crutches and in wheelchairs trying their best to cross a stage for money donations. "Can I go? It would be better, I guess, to have more than you there." Tommy nodded yes. "Where does he live, and how old is he?"

Tommy let out a sigh of relief. At least he wouldn't be going alone. "In the Inkies. I bet Donny knows him; he lives in the same building." Tommy added, "He's gonna be nine." Tommy saw three more pigeons about thirty feet away in the open ball field, but they were too far to spit at, so he picked up a stone. "Watch this. You throw this about five feet above their heads. When they see you throw they'll take off right into it the flying rock."

"Wait, don't do that …" Johnny did not want to seem like a pussy, but he also didn't want to see a bird killed. "We're playing ball there after the party, and I ain't movin' a dead bird off of third base." Tommy bought the lie and tossed his rock halfway to third, scaring but not hurting the fleeing birds. Satisfied with Tommy's reaction, Johnny had additional questions. "How crippled is he, and what's his name?"

"I think he can walk and maybe run, but one of his legs turns in. He trips over it once in a while, but my grandma says once you know him, you never notice the tripping." Tommy playfully punched Johnny's left shoulder, nearly knocking Godzilla to the pathway. "Maybe now you'll have somebody you're faster than."

"I don't care what you say. You might be—I say *might* be—the only one faster than me, but nobody has a better arm." Johnny punched Tommy back and then flexed his right bicep, showing off his quarterback arm. "Broadway Joe Willie Namath ... Who's better than me?"

In unison both friends yelled out. "Nobody!"

"Thanks for going with me. Is that Bain over there?" Tommy saw Bain on the playground with his little brother and yelled for him. "Yo, Bain! Over here!" Bain grabbed Kevin, and both ran up to Tommy and Johnny. "You guys want to go to a birthday party today?"

Twenty minutes later, Tommy, Johnny, Bain, and an excited Kevin stood on the stoop of one of the four Inkies apartment buildings. Tommy and Johnny were eager to get in and out, unlike the brothers, who would never miss a chance for a free meal. "You sure we can all go?" Johnny asked Tommy.

"We'll find out soon enough." The four boys stepped into the vestibule with Tommy in the lead.

Bain tugged his younger brother's shirt and warned him. "Kev, you listen to me ... whatever happens with me and my friends stays between us. You dig?"

Seven-year-old Kevin smiled and shook his head yes.

The hallway to the birthday party was lit by a single dim, yellow light. The walls were covered in copper tiles pressed with square designs with triangles in their centers. The ceiling held a light bulb, but it was long burned out. The color of the ceiling might have been white at one time but was now a dark-tan hue from smoke and time. The stairs were carpetless, with rotted wood and a few scattered nails extending and curling upward toward the lightless sky. It was as if they were venomous flowers of some hideous darkened underworld.

Bain and Kevin saw little difference between this place and their own living conditions; unfortunately, it reminded the brothers of home. Tommy could not keep his mouth shut and blurted out. "Come on, we're gettin' out of this shithole."

Johnny put his hand out to stop the party pooper from leaving. "Hey, we ain't ditchin'." Before Johnny could finish scolding Tommy, the apartment door at the end of the hallway opened. Standing at the threshold, a young boy smiled and asked the partygoers inside. The four boys said nothing but followed the limping child to his party.

Once inside, Tommy could not believe how big this kid's pad was, at least the front room. The area had so much space in it. You could easily play knee football and have plenty of room to accommodate spectators. In its center was a folding table with a birthday-party cloth covering it. There were eight wooden chairs surrounding it, with balloons tied to each seat. To the right of the table was a couch with a dresser beside it. This wall had no windows or doorways, but a tailless donkey was taped to the peeling paint. On the left side of the room were two windows separated by a dust-gathering potted snake plant. Outside the two windows, which fronted the street, Tommy could see the railing of a fire escape. There was a curtain-covered doorway straight across the room. Tommy reckoned that it led to the rest of the pad.

The boy led the group to the table and offered everyone sodas. He said his mom would bring out miniature hotdogs and afterward a chocolate cake. The five boys waited in silence until a man entered through the curtain doorway from the other half of the house and exited the room without a word.

Kevin broke the silence. "What's your name? Was that your daddy?"

The birthday child replied. "Joey ... No."

With a gaze full of loathing at the departing stranger, Joey's mother came out of the back room and welcomed the gang with ice pops. Fifteen minutes later, the memory of the suspicious man from behind the curtain was forgotten by the boys. They played balloon volleyball in the sparse living room. Then the hot dogs were served and devoured. Pin-the-tail-on-the-donkey was next on the agenda. Tommy easily won but was accused of peaking from under his blindfold. The incident became so heated that Kevin began to cry until Tommy gave him the prize, a pack of baseball cards.

After the chocolate cake was eaten, it was time for a rematch of balloon volleyball. The boys went at it hard and pushed each other across the floor. It was crucial not to let the balloon touch the surface, or the other team gained a point. Losing was not an option, as Joey found out quickly.

Johnny's shoulder unintentionally rammed into Joey's nerve-damaged leg. The birthday boy let out a scream but was given no sympathy as the game's competitiveness went on. Joey shrugged the pain off as best he could. Another ten minutes passed before Tommy mistimed his shot, letting Bain spike the balloon down for the final point and the win.

"Oh, you suck!" Johnny yelled at his teammate. "What the hell? How'd you miss it?" Tommy turned red and was upset at his flop. Johnny got the cue and turned his attention to Joey. "Sorry 'bout crushing that leg." Johnny pointed to Joey's turned-in leg. "Is it okay now? Can you play ball with it?"

Now it was Joey's turn to flush red. "I don't really know … My mom says if I play and get hurt not to cry about it." Joey subconsciously rubbed the injured leg softly. "I want to play … and I won't cry."

"Bain, I have to make wee-wee." Kevin stood up holding his crotch. Before Bain could answer his younger brother, Kevin ran off into the kitchen area behind the curtain doorway.

Tommy had drunk too much soda also. He waved off Bain. "I got him. I gotta go too."

Joey stumbled to his feet. "Wait, not that door!" It was too late, as the two boys searching for a toilet removed the curtain and ran inside.

⸜⸜⸜⸜⸜⸜

"I knew something was wrong when I went through those curtains," Tommy said shyly. "I didn't know then or anytime after what Kevin might've seen, but I turned him around as quick as I could when you came running in." Tommy's face became red but not from the cold. "Joey, I never said a word to Johnny, Bain, or anybody." Tommy stopped to take a deep breath. "Kevin, did we ever bring it up?" Kevin's paper-bag-covered head shook no. "There was no reason to …"

Joey stopped hobbling and rubbed his sore leg. "All the years we've hung out, none of yous ever put me down because of my screwed-up leg. Everyone treated me like everyone else, no better or worse, which I wanted. But the thing that was most important to me was the way everyone kept quiet about me having a shared bathroom in the hallway and sleeping in a one-room apartment, and most of all about my mother when she did … her thing to pay the bills."

"We all seem to be moving on with our lives sooner rather than later, but back then, we were one," Tommy reasoned. "Everybody had shit goin' on—at home, in school, or on the streets. As a group, we hung tight. No reason now to think it was different then."

"You're right I shouldn't've went after your neck. But I don't know why you have such a hard-on for Johnny." Joey cupped his hands, protecting the half-smoked joint from blowing out as he lit it.

"Johnny's different now. He's not the same. But because of our history, I'll do whatever to find him and get him back." Tommy put his hand out for the lit joint, Joey shook his hand instead. Tommy laughed and then playfully pushed Joey. "Okay, we're even. Now pass that here."

Kevin stayed on the worrisome subject of Johnny. He wiped his running nose from inside the bag before ending the previous conversation with "Maybe we all have changed and moved on, but Johnny stayed the same, living in the past."

⸝⸝⸝⸝⸝⸝

Blushing, Shanty called for Bain to spy on the open magazine he held. "She's only two years older than me." Shanty flipped the page. "She likes to—"

"Hey, kid, I don't need those pages stuck together," The clerk behind the counter yelled for the embarrassed Shanty to put the *Playboy* monthly back on its shelf.

Bain walked around the convenience store with a bag of chips, wondering what to do next. He was certain Johnny was in Manhattan someplace but didn't know where the hell to find him. *One last call to Tori's. Maybe he's at the cemetery with Tommy, or better yet, home.* Bain was at Shanty's side when the guy behind the counter continued to complain. "Easy, dude, my friend's never seen such a hairy pussy before." Bain snooped over Shanty's shoulder. "Or such big knockers." Bain then offered his friend the open bag of chips. Shanty reached inside and took a mouthful. "Shant, we'll get change and call Tori's before leavin' the city. I don't know what else to do."

"You two go now, or I call police," the dot-head Indian threatened.

Bain cut in. "In a second. Chill out." Then his attention returned to Shanty. "You need a beer for the ride home?" Shanty shook his head no, but Bain thought better and grabbed him one anyway. *It won't go to waste.* On their way to the counter, Bain tossed the half-eaten bag of chips back on the shelf and took a full chip bag off, to the wonder of Shanty.

"What're you doin'? We ate half that bag."

Bain smiled. "I ain't paying for a half bag of chips."

Shanty jumped up a couple of inches. "I shoulda pissed in the park. I have to go before we hit the train."

"It's all right. I'll go again too." Bain dug into his pocket.

Bain paid for the beers and the full bag of chips. Then he had one last matter for the cashier. "Where's your bathroom?"

The response of the cashier was too quick for Bain. "We don't have one."

Cold, wet, and worried, Bain had had enough. "Then where the hell do you go?" Bain popped his beer can open and swallowed most of it before throwing it at the man behind the counter, splattering suds all over the cashier's chest. "The beers on me!"

Chapter 17

1973

Told you once about your friends and neighbors.
They were always seeking, but they'll never find it.
It's alright. Yes, it's alright.
—"It's Alright" performed by Black Sabbath

Dream as if you'll live forever.
Live as if you'll die today.
—James Dean

The door to Donny's hospital room was open as usual. Johnny was satisfied with the conditions inside; they did not change just because it wasn't visiting hours. The ceiling light was off, but the little lamp on the night table was on. Johnny walked to the Christmas tree and plugged in its lights. Then he checked the water in the stand; it was full. *Glad someone here is doing their job.* The room was quiet and peaceful. Johnny sat in the empty chair between Donny's bed and the night table. *I don't think I've ever sat on this chair. No wonder Gina parks her fat ass here all the time; the cushion is so comfortable.*

From Gina's chair, Johnny studied the profile of his dying friend. *Your eyes are always closed, but are you thinking? Do you know I'm even here?* Johnny heard rumblings from the nurse's station, *an emergency ... another beat down of a child, or worse yet, a beat down of ... of what? What can be worse?* After rubbing his forehead, Johnny accidentally bumped his elbow hard into the nightstand. *Damn it. That shit hurts.*

The drawer to the night table slid open almost six inches. Johnny's stinging elbow was about to close the compartment when he noticed the upright flap of a soft-cover book. Curious, he removed the paperback and read its cover. *The Adventures of Tom Sawyer.* Johnny had read the novel in the fifth grade. He opened the novel up where the page was turned in and read the first paragraph to himself. *Yep, I remember this part. Tom and Becky were lost in that cave.* Johnny closed the publication and wondered to himself, *Who's reading this book? Nobody I know ... it must have been here before Donny was wheeled to this room.* Johnny placed the book next to Donny's pillow, trying to create a normal setting. Sadly, a sickening impression struck Johnny. *Maybe the kid lying here died before Tom and Becky got out of the cave.*

Johnny tried to distance himself from further morbid thoughts. *That's not why I came here alone. I'm here to ... to what?* Johnny stared at his friend as the lights from the Christmas tree played tricks with Donny's silhouette. *Oh, Donny, I should've listened to Bain and the others. I was too worried for myself. I hated always making the decisions. I was jealous, too. I would've run away to the cabin if it had been my idea. I needed a bit more convincing. For your sake, I should have just said yes.* Johnny moved Gina's chair closer to Donny's side. Resting his head on the bed sheet, Johnny continued to contemplate with closed eyes. *Everything has been on me from the get-go. I didn't make the right choice that day. I made one mistake, and now look at you.* Johnny put his hand out to hold on to Donny's cool wrist. Johnny's words escaped his thoughts as he began to whisper, "Donny, please wake up. I'll never let anything ever happen to you again." Johnny began to whimper and started to pray. "God, it's my fault. I was being the pigheaded asshole. I made it about me ... I always have." Johnny squeezed Donny's wrist, hoping it would somehow shake his friend to life. Getting no response, Johnny held on to Donny's hand and prayed for a miracle. *Please, God, it's Christmas time. Punish me if you want meat. You need a piece of meat? Then beat on me ... Please, God, it's Christmas. Punish me if you want meat. Please, God, it's ...* An exhausted Johnny fell into a dream while holding Donny's hand.

"Nanci!" Nurse Joan stormed the hall in search of her candy striper. "Nanci! Has anybody seen her?"

Candy striper Nanci stuck her head out of Mrs. McMail's room, bumping into Nurse Joan. "I was finishing up with …"

"What's the matter with you? I was calling you the whole time," was the welcome from her boss. "Nanci, go get the list of names and numbers of the kids. There's a problem with one of them, and he's here alone. I thought you said no one comes in Wednesday nights. Plus, he's here before visiting hours begin. How did that kid get in here?"

Nanci blew her nose into a tissue and wiped her watery eyes with a second. "What problem? The kid you mean is Johnny."

"How'd you know it was him?" Nanci began to explain but was cut off. "Never mind." Nurse Joan began to bite her upper lip. Nanci was familiar with the rage building up. "I knew this would happen, having them all here in the end would be a problem."

Nanci's eyes began to water for the second time in ten minutes. "You're a witch. Why must you insist there will be an end? You don't believe in miracles. This isn't the end, and you should stop being so negative. Donny's not gonna die."

Nurse Joan stopped biting her lip long enough to respond. "Honestly, I was praying the kids would stop coming here until … until this was all over. I am not a witch, and I do believe in miracles." Frustrated, Nurse Joan could only bark out an order. "Now Nanci, get me that list."

Yeah, witch. Or was it "bitch"? Either one fits! Before fetching the phone list for her nemesis, Nanci gave Mrs. McMail a hurried good-bye. "I'm sorry. I have to take care of something, but we can talk more … after dinner."

Running to her locker, Nanci did not wait to hear about Mrs. McMail's three types of people any longer. *She's a downer too. What the hell is going on around here tonight?*

Candy striper Nanci hustled in the opposite direction of room 18 to the nurse's lounge. *Shit ... I hope that list is still there. What if a cleaning lady threw it out? I didn't think the telephone numbers were so important back when I took them. Why the hell didn't Nurse Nemesis take care of it if it was so*—Nanci nearly knocked over Nurse Ellen when she barged into the lounge. Excusing herself, Nanci raced to the locker and reached for the top of its metal frame. *Yuck ... nothing but dust ... Here it is. Thank God! God is good, good is God!* Nanci took the clipboard with the names and numbers and walked calmly to the nurse's workstation. "Here, can you pass this along to Nurse Joan when she returns. I believe she is looking for this."

Nanci swiftly walked to room 18 to see what the whole stink was about. The room was quiet while the Christmas tree lights flashed. Johnny sat slanted over Donny's bed. One of Johnny's hands was cupping his forehead while the other held Donny's wrist. *He's asleep, that's all. Johnny's worn out.* Nanci tiptoed to Gina's unofficial chair, picked up a soft-cover version of *Tom Sawyer* off the floor, and put it on the night table. Mistakenly believing the book belonged to Johnny, Nanci wondered to herself why he'd brought it here. She heard him sniffle but thought, *Best to let the guest rest.* Nanci was powerless to giggle at her little rhyme because of the sudden shock of Nurse Nemesis calling to her.

"Nanci ... oh, Nanci." Nurse Nemesis motioned for her candy striper to join her in the hallway. Nanci saw Nurse Joan bite her lower lip. She knew something else was wrong. "Did you read this? Did you take the time to finish the job correctly?"

Nanci began to speak but decided it would be best to let Nurse Joan vent.

"Look, this one says Joey, last name Namath. Here's Gina, last name Lollobrigida. This one is so obvious: Johnny Unitas. Come on, Nanci." Nurse Joan tossed the clipboard onto the nurses' counter.

Nanci's face turned red. She began to feel hot and a bit dizzy. She did not finish the job or do it correctly, as Nurse Joan had asked. Nanci had been thrilled at the time the children could stay, and she trusted them to do her right. *But no!* "I … I messed up. I'm sorry. I don't know anything about baseball players."

"They are football players and actresses, but we—"

Nanci picked the clipboard from the desk. Then she interrupted her reprimand. "Here, what about this name? This one could be legit." Nanci pointed to the second from last.

Nurse Joan took the board and quietly read the name. "Maybe … All right, call, and make sure this Johnny does not leave on his own." For the first of two times during this night, candy striper Nanci sincerely heard the warmth in her nemesis's voice.

~~~~~~~

"Joey, you're not limping anymore," Johnny cried out. It was awesome seeing his friend no longer disabled.

"Limping?" Joey asked. "Johnny, here everything is magical, of course." Joey ran with great speed to the open field where a football was being tossed between joyous friends.

"Magical, yeah, but where are we?" Johnny yelled out, but Joey was too worried about running and catching a football. Johnny observed the area where Joey sped off to. It was a mystical but welcoming setting. On the ball field stood Bain and Tommy, choosing sides for their football team. Kevin, Shanty, Porky, and Donny, now joined by Joey, all begged to be picked first.

The ball field was stationed in an open pasture covered with the greenest of green grass. The trees surrounding the players were the tallest and fullest Johnny had ever seen. To the right was a pond with two rowboats attached to a wooden dock. Johnny saw fishing poles and oars off to the side under a tree. On his left stood a log cabin. It had a gigantic porch with wooden chairs, a table, two hammocks, and a dart board off the end. In front of the cabin, a stone fireplace was set for nighttime barn fires and marshmallow toasting.

"Johnny, come on. I picked you first!" yelled Tommy.

Johnny hustled down to the open meadow and was greeted by everyone. Bain playfully pushed Johnny into Shanty. "Didn't I tell you my uncle's place is so cool?" Johnny could only smile. He'd never been happier. "Who's better than us?"

In unison, the gang responded. Bain then lightheartedly pulled Donny from behind Shanty and Porky.

"In this magical place, no one ever gets hurt or bitten or beaten with the heel of a shoe. No one dies." Bain's face became sullen. "If you would've only listened to us, Johnny."

Johnny's merriment vanished instantly and was replaced by grief. "Donny ... I didn't know ... I ..."

Donny smiled. "You always looked out for me ... us." Donny scratched his shoulder through his torn, dirty shirt. "You let me score that winning touchdown that morning. You trusted me. All of yous always made me feel like part of the team."

Bain butted in. "No! Donny ... you are the team." Bain let everyone agree and then finished with "Come on, let's get the game started. It's late."

"Wait! Bain, don't say *late*," Johnny shouted out. He needed more time here. There was never enough time. "Donny, you ..." The sky became gray. The shadows of the tall trees darkened the football players. "I messed up. Please, let me get it right this time." Johnny began to cry.

Porky, Shanty, and Tommy disappeared together. "Wait, Tommy, we have to play this game." Johnny pleaded. Kevin went next. Bain said good-bye before vanishing.

"Look, Johnny, no brace on my leg, and I'm so fast here. And see how high I can jump?" After his second leap, Joey faded in midair.

Donny bounced the football from one hand to the other. "You know I have to go now too. I don't want to go. I'd want to stay here with my friends." Donny's face became bruised and swollen as the surroundings darkened. "Johnny, you said you'd visit me at my foster family's house. You promised, but now it's too late. You can't go where I'm going."

"No, let me ... I can fix this." Johnny went to grab Donny, but his arms passed through the air. "Please God let me have another chance. God, please no ... Donny, don't go."

"Sorry, Johnny, I must go ... 'cause the game clock is running out for me." Donny's usual smile faded. "Don't cry, Johnny. Please don't cry. Who's better than us, Johnny ... who?"

Donny's figure became an outline. "Nobody! ... Don't go, come back with me Donny. We can do it all over again. Don't we ever get a do-over?" Johnny became angry and suddenly reached out for Donny's wrist. This time was different. There was no more waving at the wind; instead Johnny caught a cold, very cold layer of flesh. *Donny's?* "Come with me. I'll make sure nothin' happens to you this time. Donny ... grab a hold of my hand. Follow me out of here, just like in football. You run behind me, and I'll block. I will take the hit. You can score the winning touchdown again ... just grab my arm ..."

A warm palm touched Johnny's clenched fist. *Donny?* Johnny wiped his eyes, raised his sweaty head from Donny's hospital bed, and looked at the person lightly tapping his skin. Johnny could only mutter. "You gotta be kiddin' me. You gave candy striper Nanci your real telephone number?"

~~~~~~

Fifteen minutes later, Johnny and Angela stood outside Woodhull Hospital waiting for the early-evening bus to arrive. Johnny stared up at the street lights, watching the illuminated snow flurries twirling in the wind. *I wanted time here alone. There was no reason to call in the cavalry.* He walked to the curb, praying for the bus to turn their corner. *No such luck.*

The sidewalk bustled with rush-hour patrons. Angela wondered if anyone had noticed her or Johnny. *Probably not. They all have a place to go, someone home waiting for them ...* A chill trampled through her body. It was not from the weather. Angela trudged to where Johnny stood. *It's now or most likely never.* "Johnny, don't be upset with me." In spite of the cold, Johnny's coat remained unzipped, with his wool Mets hat emerging from his back pocket. *He's lost and embarrassed.* A strong wind pushed against Angela's spine, nearly knocking her into Johnny's chest. "Whoa!" Angela did her best to stay unyielding, but her vulnerability became apparent. She bundled up her fleece coat and its fur collar. Conveniently, Angela had forgotten her hat as she left the house in haste after the phone call from candy striper Nanci. "I'm cold. Can I borrow that hat you're not using?"

"Sure." Johnny faked tossing it before handing the Mets cap to Angela. "I'm not mad at you. I don't know why they dragged you out here, that's all."

Angela adjusted the blue hat over her ears. "I get earaches when it's cold." Angela wiped her nose with her gloved hand and then pondered.

"It's not seven yet. If you want, we can walk home. I don't have to be in until eight."

Johnny, for the moment, forgot about being caught crying, about the dream of Bain's uncle's cabin, the disappearing friends, or Donny. *Now is for the living…* "Yes, Bain, me, and Tommy walked here last Saturday in forty-five minutes, and we took our time too."

Good, he's talking. "First, let's zip you and get your collar up. I'm cold looking at you." Angela situated each glove under her armpit so her freed fingers could work on securing Johnny's framework. "You gotta get a scarf and gloves." Angela winked and then added, "Maybe you need a second hat too."

Johnny laughed. *She's beautiful … her smile, her windblown hair, her scent, even her forehead. Everything is so perfect with her.* Johnny gazed at Angela's beaming brown eyes as she turned up his coat collar. Johnny always thought Angela was a pretty girl, but so were so many others. *Angela is beautiful on the inside, too. Why did it take me so long to see it?* Johnny did not know. *Details, details. How did I miss all of these details?* Johnny knew his sister Terry would mock him now for missing all the details.

"Johnny, I asked if that's warm enough now?" Angela did not wait for an answer. She rewrapped her scarf, adjusted the Mets hat one more time, and then slid her arm into Johnny's. "Come on, we have a long walk home."

Johnny did feel the warmth descending from his previous exposed chest. "Yeah … it's warm."

Angela playfully tugged on Johnny's arm. "Well, you can't be warm yet. I just bundled you up." Angela giggled and put her head onto Johnny's shoulder. "I'm warming up too."

The recent dreamy episodes of tingling release during his sleep, Johnny for the first time became vigilant of this new phenomenon. While the pulsating blood acted on his sexual desire, Johnny simply became embarrassed. *Does she know? Can she see it?* Johnny tried to walk off his rigid third leg, but Little Johnny would not cooperate. It was tightly packed in his underwear and rubbing against Johnny's jeans. There was little he could do to stop the onslaught. "Angela, why did you come here tonight? And don't tell me it's because yours was the only correct number they had." *Get my mind off of her head on my shoulders, the warmth of her cheek, the scent of her body ...*

Angela was quiet for a block and a half, Johnny, who remained walking with a trio of legs, began to wonder if she'd heard him at all. "You're a good guy."

"And?" *Thank you, Angela, now keep talking.* "Okay, but why?"

Angela slowed her footsteps, and the two stopped at the tail end of a sidewalk Christmas tree display. The scent of fir was thick and pleasing to the two. "You're a good guy." Angela then removed her arm from Johnny's and bit into her left glove before placing her bare hand into Johnny's pocket. "My hand is cold. Can I warm it with yours?"

Shit! Little Johnny had died down a bit, but now ... boom! His two legs welcomed back the slumping middle friend immediately. Johnny was helpless. *Angela, oh Angela.* Johnny slightly pushed Angela into a staged, six-foot balsam fir and torpedoed into her mouth. He didn't know exactly how this all worked, but his intentions were honest. Angela became the raider. She took the lead and opened her mouth, allowing Johnny to find her tongue. The two stood inside the pines and branches of a for-sale Christmas tree until Angela puckered her lips inside Johnny's mouth, letting him know the kiss, for now, was over.

"Come on, Johnny-boy. I gotta be home by eight," Angela teased, securing her hand deep inside Johnny's palm.

For the next five blocks, the two were lost in their own thoughts. There was an isolated comment on the obvious Christmas decorations, but neither spoke about anything of any weight till Johnny spotted dog shit off the curb. He gently guided himself between the shit and Angela.

Once underneath the darkened Brooklyn Queens Expressway overpass, Johnny had enough nerve to kiss Angela again. He used the same approach as he had inside the Christmas tree displays. Johnny leaned into Angela and moved her slightly to a metal post beam for the second kiss. Angela giggled to herself, already anticipating Johnny's move.

Their second make-out session lasted longer, as both eased the pressure of their tongues and began to enjoy the closeness a kiss could bring. Angela, for the second time, stopped the smooching with her own newly found move. She puckered her lips inside of Johnny's mouth, letting him know the extravaganza was kaput for the moment. Johnny followed Angela's lead and pulled himself back, letting their lips part. No words were passed, as the two shared the same consensus: *practice makes perfect.*

Five minutes after eight, Johnny stood with Angela on her stoop. Johnny wanted to kiss her one last time but was too nervous because of their location. Instead, he thanked her for getting him and, of course, for the walk home.

"You took *me* home, and almost on time too." Angela laughed. Johnny gazed into Angela's rosy cheeks, wind-tossed hair, dark-brown eyes, and beautiful red-lipsticked lips. "What's the matter? You all right?"

Johnny rubbed his forehead as he faced Angela's slush-covered boots. "I was a bit screwed up at the hospital. It was nice waking up with you at my side." Johnny wanted to tell her more but was lost for words. *What did I just say? I sound like an idiot …*

"Johnny you're a nice guy. I always thought that about you. After tonight, I'm sure of it." Angela tossed her head to her left shoulder, letting Johnny's cap fall into her open hand. "Here you go, and thanks for letting me wear it. You kept me warm all evening." Angela leaned into Johnny and pushed him into the stoop's metal railing, pinning him. Angela applied Johnny's own move on him, and she finished their time with a quick kiss on his lips.

Johnny said nothing but watched Angela bolt through her doorway and up the hallway stairs. *She's fast ... and beautiful, inside and out.* Johnny held his hat and took a whiff of it before placing it on his head. *She smells so good, too. What's her shampoo ... Breck?* Johnny carelessly scampered down the stoop's icy steps. *Nothing can hurt me tonight, or tomorrow neither.* Walking home with ebullience, Johnny mimicked kissing Angela by fluttering his tongue inside his closed mouth. *I can't wait to see her again.* Johnny turned the corner of Angela's street and continued his journey home, captivated. *Angela must feel the same way. She must. She was there for me when I thought I needed no one.* Johnny felt the cold of the night for the first time. He wiped his frosty nose with his palm. *She's always shy, even with the other girls. Something changed within her.* Johnny passed by Tommy's house. He looked up to his friend's lit bedroom window. *What do I tell my friends? Will Angela say something to her big-mouth girlfriends?* Johnny crossed the icy street to his own house. *I can't worry about it now. Tomorrow I'll get Angela to the side, and we'll talk. Maybe make out again. She likes me. Angela's my girlfriend ... Do we keep it a secret? Angela, what are you thinking now? Are you as happy as me?*

Johnny stopped inside the hallway, kicking off his frozen boots. When he entered the living room, Terry was lying across the couch watching a Christmas show. Barely looking up from the television set, Terry had a startling question. "Who did you make out with tonight?" Mortified, Johnny asked what she meant. "It's the smile on your face. But what really gave you away"—Terry sat up on the couch—"was the lipstick around your mouth. Details, Johnny, details."

Johnny quickly wiped his mouth and then ran into the bathroom to erase all evidence. While he was inside, Terry knocked on the door, teasing him but earnestly wanting to know who this lucky girl was. Johnny needed to confide in someone, so it might as well be his younger sister. Before he could say anything, Johnny needed to calm his nerves. The last thing he wanted was to appear hopelessly in love. *Not this quick, not too soon.*

"Okay, Terry give me a minute. I'll be right out."

Sitting back on the couch, Terry told her brother that their mom and dad were still at the Warrens but would be home by nine. "So make it quick." Terry could hear the excitement in Johnny's voice and could not wait any longer for the details. Johnny wisely kept the story short and neat for his sister, making her pinky swear to keep her silence. Terry naturally obliged, as she would never have betrayed her brother's trust.

The two stayed up watching *A Charlie Brown Christmas.* Terry questioned what Snoopy fighting the Red Barron in the sky had to do with Christmas. Johnny agreed with his sister but laughed at the idea of a dog dogfighting. Terry understood the gist and joined her brother in laughter.

Little did either know, though, that before lunch the following day, Johnny's happiness would take a U-turn to heartache. As for kissing Angela for a fourth time, that would not happen another year and a half. Johnny would be stoned and drunk, while Angela would be second-guessing what the hell happen to the nice guy she'd originally fallen in love with.

~~~~~~

The same moment Johnny was inhaling the scent of his wool Mets hat, candy striper Nanci was realizing that she'd left the clipboard containing the kids phone numbers on the table inside the nurse's lounge. She knew it would be safe there, but Nanci did not want anyone reading the false names. *Joe Namath. Gina Lollobrigida. What was the other one, Johnny Ulysses? Whatever. I don't need them teasing me. Besides, I hate football.* She made a go-around in the lobby and went for the elevators.

"The candy striper gal is back. Did you forget something?" Doughboy Doug goaded.

Normally she would have smiled and gone on her way, but tonight Nanci would not play victim to a bully. "You know, the younger girls complain about you all the time. I'm sure if we all went together and ratted you out, you'd lose your shitty job. Or better yet, I could get my dad to come down here and kick your ass all over the parking lot. Which one works best for you ... Doug?" Having an Irish, connected father did have obvious benefits. Not waiting for a reply, Nanci boarded the elevator, never to hear a peep out of Doughboy again.

After retrieving the list, Nanci instinctively peered down the hall to room 18. As usual, the door was open, and the Christmas lights remained flashing. But it was evident from the glow that the night table's lamp was still on. Before investigating, Nanci checked the nurses' attendance board. *Nurse Joan has clocked out. She must have passed me on my way up the elevator. Good, I've had enough of her shit tonight anyway.* Nanci smiled at one of the nurses behind her post before heading to Donny's room.

Before entering, Nanci listened intently. *Aunt Polly, Injun Joe, Becky, Huck, and of course Tom. I know those names, and they ain't football players.* Nanci stood silently as Nurse Joan, sitting in Gina's chair, continued reading Tom Sawyer out loud to her lifeless patient. Listening to Nurse Joan's soft voice caused Nanci to become disoriented. *Who is this lady reading? What is she still doing here?* Nanci felt like a spectator at a Broadway show. *No, that wouldn't be right. Those are actors on the stage; this is real. Nurse Joan has a hidden heart. She's hurting like everyone else around here.* Nanci began to understand her mentor. *She was only protecting the kids … and me.* Nanci's eyes started to moisten. *I was so wrong about her. She cares; she always has. But why keep it so secret? Not to lead us to false hope?* Nurse Joan kept on reading. *She's trying her best to make Donny's last hours normal, softly reading Donny a bedtime story.* Nanci shifted her quivering right hand. *Please, God, let him hear her loving voice. Donny deserves to die in peace.* Nanci, for the first time, admitted to herself Donny's terminal fate. *Tom Sawyer is every ten-year-old boy's adventure.*

Nanci stepped back into the corridor. It was time to go home. *I was only fooling myself. This whole time I was wrong. There's nothing anyone can do now, no Christmas miracle.* Nanci ran for the elevator with her clipboard in hand, yearning for her mother's invulnerability. *I can't. I can't do this anymore.* Nanci stormed out of the main entrance lobby, past Doughboy, and into the chilled parking lot. With the luck of the Irish, Nanci's bus pulled up the moment she reached the curb. Her tears were frozen when she entered the shuttle, Nanci was fine with that. The small ice knobs radiated a magnificent sense of life to her rosy cheeks. *It's good to be cold, to feel. It's good being alive.* Nanci settled in the back of the bus and tore up the list of names she held. She squeezed the papers into the slit of the bus's rear window and let them fall onto the obscure street below.

↗↗↗↗↗↗

Shit, it's eleven o'clock. Nurse Joan arrived at her rural home, which was located forty minutes north of Brooklyn, a far cry from New York City's largest borough. *It was so hard leaving tonight.* She'd felt an eerie chill watching Johnny cry. *The end will come soon for that poor child. Sorry, Nanci, there will be no Christmas miracle.*

Nurse Joan surveyed her center-hall colonial home before setting foot on its porch. The front door's porch light was on. The single-color Christmas lights wrapped around the porch's white railing were shining with dark-blue brightness. Joan had explained the setup to her husband during the previous Thanksgiving. "Simple and clean. We don't need ten different colors flashing out front."

Buddy began to bark. Nurse Joan hurried into her house and let the pooch greet her with licks and sniffs. "Easy, baby, you're gonna wake everybody up." Buddy kept jumping on Nurse Joan until she gave the critter a treat. "Now Momma needs to check on your sisters and then take a hot shower." Buddy knew the routine and followed Nurse Joan up the stairs to the girls' room. Despite having two additional spare bedrooms, the "Irish twins" insisted sharing one room. With puberty around the corner for her eldest and her second only a year and two months behind, Nurse Joan figured a four-bedroom home may soon come in handy. *For now, though, don't shake the boat. All is happy; all is good. Soon simple and clean will no longer apply here, and neither will law and order.* Nurse Joan cringed at the idea of having two teenaged daughters but figured, *So far so good.*

Nurse Joan bent down to give her eldest a kiss goodnight. Before she could do the same to her youngest, she covered the child's exposed, muscular leg with the blanket. Her daughters' determination and success on the grade school swim team was a pleasant surprise, and she took pride in it. *They are such great children—smart; funny; pretty, of course; and surprisingly athletic.* She smiled to herself, knowing the girls were only successful in sports because they were driven. *If given the chance, I could have been an athlete, as could their father … but we grew up in a different time and place. In Brooklyn, there are few ball fields and even less encouragement.* Nurse Joan sighed, thinking of Donny and his bed sores. *Were the children in room 18 ever encouraged? Enough, Joanie … get on with your night. You're home; separate it all now!* She regained control long enough to give both girls a kiss goodnight. *They are getting big so fast. I must concentrate more on my own family after all this is done … What's done? Donny's demise?*

She walked backward out of the girl's bedroom, watching both sleep peacefully. While Nurse Joan's eyes adjusted to the darkened room, she focused her attention on the corner wall display. *Soon the posters of David Cassidy, The Monkey's, and The Jackson Five will be replaced.* She bit her top lip slightly. *Yes, I'll be here when the posters change, when my girls change ... Life waits for nobody.* Nurse Joan took her last step backward and nearly tripped over Buddy. "Oh, sorry, Bud. All right, now get to bed." Buddy wagged his short tail and jumped into his younger sister's bunk. "Good boy. Now get to sleep."

After getting out of shower and towel-drying her wet hair, Nurse Joan continued her drill before bed. Taking baby oil from the medicine cabinet, she began to rub it into her dry skin. *The cold outside and the hot water inside does not help.* Massaging her breasts, Nurse Joan experienced soreness in both, followed by a slight pinch to her temple. *Darn it, I'm definitely not giving in to a headache tonight.* She put the oil away and then took three aspirins. *Fifteen minutes is all I need. I'll be as good as new.*

Nurse Joan quietly stepped into her bedroom, where her husband was sleeping soundlessly. *He's such a good guy. He works so hard, and works even harder here at home when I'm gone.* She thought again of her daughters growing up too quickly before pulling out her wrinkled tank top and tangled pajama pants. She decided the undies could wait inside the drawer tonight. *Headache is not forming, actually disappearing.* She slipped slightly putting her leg through the leg of her flannel pants when the seam touched her in an erotic zone. *Sore breasts, headache ... now horniness.* Nurse Joan let out a faint sigh. *Ovulating? How did I miss it?* She watched her husband sleeping and thought of her two beautiful Irish twins slumbering with the pooch down the hall. *I have wonderful husband, two great kids, a beautiful home, a career, and of course, Buddy.* Nurse Joan giggled to herself, surprised at her oncoming mischievous thought. *Life starts tomorrow morning with decisions made tonight.* Nurse Joan tossed her sleepwear to the corner of the bedroom, walked briskly to the closet, and pulled out her Valentine's outfit. *Yes, red lingerie should do.* She crawled into bed next to her husband. Nurse Joan needed to forget Donny, candy striper Nanci, Johnny, and the rest of the world, at least for one night. Tonight would be about her own needs and family. *Dear, get ready for a midnight ride.* Nurse Joan reached down to her husband's midsection, while rubbing her swollen, sore breasts against his bare back. She then bit his shoulder slightly before getting down to work. *I'll start tonight with the Joanie special!*

Chapter 18

1978

And I guess I never told you
I'm so happy that you're mine.
Little things I should have said and done
I just never took the time
—"Always on My Mind"
performed by Willie Nelson

Bain dialed the pay phone at the foot of the Fifth Avenue subway steps. Minutes before, he and Shanty had fled from the beer-soaked lunatic merchant. *He's gotta piss somewhere ... don't lie to me about it. Not tonight!* Frustrated at getting no results and wishing for a miracle, Bain decided to call the girls before heading back to Brooklyn. *Just in case something has changed. Maybe Johnny's already at Tori's.* Bain let Shanty know the phone was ringing. *I'll let them know to cross off Central Park, 'cause Johnny ain't here.*

Shanty was no longer cold. The sprint through the Christmas crowds and the rush from Bain's antics did warm things up a bit. Shanty's heart continued to thump while he surveyed the area they'd both ran from. He was grateful to see nothing new emerging from the nightly organized chaos on the streets. *No beer-drenched store owner with a police posse slicing through the twilight.* Relaxed a smidgen, Shanty watched his friend talk inside the phone booth but couldn't come up with exactly what was going down. There was something going on, since the conversation was clearly longer than if it had just been a yes or no on Johnny's whereabouts.

Shanty's thoughts drifted off to the first time he'd met Johnny. Bain had brought him to the candy store where Johnny and Tommy were playing pinball. Tommy had tilted his machine and cursed the game, but Johnny had coolly continued to play his. After winning a free turn, Johnny passed it to some little kid in the store. Shanty thought that was so neat. *Bain saved my ass at school that day and then introduced me to his friends, who were good-natured and normal.* Shanty again checked down the street to see if they were being pursued. *Can't tell with so many people out, but all looks good. If not, I feel sorry for anyone chasing us. At this point, Bain will destroy any disruptions.* Shanty blew into his hands, glad he was not a smoker and was not drinking that second can of beer. *Johnny would always suggest we do something, and everyone would follow, whether it was to play football or take a train ride to Manhattan. He wasn't bossy or anything, but it always seemed like the right thing to do—like what we all wanted to do. Johnny always knew best.* Bain juggled his beer as he hung up the phone and lit a cigarette before telling Shanty the next course of action. *Johnny was always the brains and Bain the muscle. Everyone understood that. Were they the mother and father none of us had? Maybe, but more importantly, it worked. It was how it always worked. We were happy, and it was how everything was formed ... until Johnny's fatal decision. Since then, the world has never been the same. We all grew and adjusted, but Johnny couldn't. And now we're here ...*

"Terry thinks Johnny's coming here to the pond. I thought so too." Bain flicked his cigarette out into the street. "Terry says he took that rock we all swiped that afternoon. She told Tori he's got to be here or on his way."

"Do you want to go back one more time?" Shanty guessed. "The girls hear from Tommy yet?"

"Yeah, and no." Bain took a slug of beer. "We'll check the pond again, but there's been nothing from Tommy lately." Bain wiggled his belt buckle. "I still gotta take that piss." Shanty agreed, and the two trekked back to Central Park.

~~~~~~

"So you're saying that you kissed Johnny that night and not again for almost a year and a half?" a stunned Gina questioned.

Nicole was second to interrogate. "I don't believe it. How old were yous, twelve?"

Tori swallowed her drink and added, "He went out with Nicky that first summer. You weren't around much." Tori smiled slyly. "Me and Johnny swapped spit a few times between you two." She pointed at Nicole and Angela.

Nicole questioned Angela. "Johnny never said anything about you, but then why would he?"

A bit embarrassed but defiant, Angela went on. "It was only three kisses, maybe four, that night … but then everything went to the shitter real fast." Angela got up to get a glass of water, as her throat had become extremely dry. "You want me to go on? Because the four kisses are only the beginning."

"Wow … somebody's testy. Am I the only one Johnny didn't have?" Gina brushed Bella off of her lap and then threw her hands outward, as if being crucified.

"Oh, stop being so darn dramatic. Johnny ain't that good," Nicole shot back.

Gina scurried to the bathroom while jokingly fussing about why she'd never had Johnny.

"I told ya, he wasn't that good!" Nicole finished.

Angela waited for the teasing and laughter to end before she continued telling her history with Johnny. "First of all, he was good. He's still a good guy, just a bit lost."

"Oh, he's lost all right," Nicole added.

Gina covered her lap with a blanket and then clapped her hands for Bella to join her on the couch. "Still not fair I missed out on the fun with him," she said in one last jab.

Angela put her hands up for all to relax and then proceeded. "Right after everything went down, Johnny wasn't interested in anything. You all remember, no one was doing anything back then. Even when it got warm out that spring, no one had any motivation to do a thing. I tried to talk to Johnny many times when I had the chance, but it was like he didn't even know me, never mind our night together. He was hurting, but so was I, and I saw no reason to feel that way. I did nothing wrong. By the end of school that June, I had given up chasing him."

"Yeah, that spring was plenty dull. No one talked much or did anything. But the summer was a real party," chimed in Tori.

"I didn't think of it like that," Angela added.

Nicole shot in. "Didn't think of what?"

Angela rubbed the back of her neck and then confessed, "I didn't realize how everyone was hurting all the same way. I was selfish when it came to Johnny. I thought it was all about me then. I didn't see the whole picture of where everyone was at. Remember, I was still pretty new to your group and not as attached as the rest of yous." Angela sighed. "I gave up on Johnny and went to spend the summer at my cousin's house out in Long Island."

Nicole lit a cigarette and reached for an ash tray. "So you skipped town because Johnny-boy didn't want to look at you anymore."

"Some of that's true," Angela answered meekly. "I was drained and needed to figure things out."

"Wait!" Gina said to Nicole. "Don't beat on Angie about skipping out on everyone, because others left town too. Maybe they didn't leave physically, but they left by staying here in Brooklyn … drinking and getting high." Gina nodded at Tori. "Like she said, that summer was a party. Everybody checked out one way or another."

"Thanks." Angela half-smiled at Gina. "And if it weren't for you, I wouldn't have the second half of the story to tell you all." Angela adjusted her ass while sitting on the rug, bending her knees to a few inches below her chin. Angela began part two of her story with Johnny in a low voice, bordering on an apologetic tone.

"I heard about Johnny going out with Kimba … and some of the other shit going on in the neighborhood." Angela put her hand up to quiet Tori. "I didn't mean anything by that. We all moved on …"

"Yeah, what were we supposed to do?" Nicole demanded. "So we smoked pot, drank, and made out with Johnny … big deal. He wasn't that good."

"Oooooh, somebody sounds a bit jealous for Johnny-boy," Gina taunted.

"It's all right." Angela went on. "When I came back home in September, all I wanted to do was concentrate on school, or at least that's what I told myself." Angela sighed. "Gina was the only one to call me from time to time. Of course, when I ran into any of you, you all were cool with me, always saying 'We gotta get together' and so on. I'd lie and say yeah, knowing it would never happen. That was until … until the anniversary of … was coming up. It was a week before Christmas, and Gina called me and told me what the plan was."

"You asked me if everyone would be there," Gina interjected. "When I told you yes, you said of course you'd go. I was a bit shocked how easily you agreed to come. Why did you?"

Angela let go of her knees and stretched her legs outward. "I missed everyone, Johnny too, of course. For the past year, I'd only kidded myself that I didn't need anyone anymore. I felt like an outcast. With the anniversary or whatever you want to call it coming, I was aching to be back." Angela wiped her nose with her wrist.

"That first Christmas Eve, I remember how quiet everyone was. Nobody knew what to do there," Tori said.

Nicole snuffed out her cigarette and chuckled. "Not until Tommy broke the ice by pouring the beer."

"Then Kevin lit that pack of firecrackers off. It had to be a first at the cemetery," added Tori, and all the girls joined in the laughter. "It's been a tradition since."

Angela became serious. "Everybody had changed drastically, but then in a strange way, you didn't. I know I'm not making sense now, but I was afraid back then. I wondered how everyone, Johnny especially, saw me." Angela took a deep breath. "I wanted to be the same person, but being the same, I guess wouldn't have fit anymore."

"Funny, you seemed the same to me … but so did everyone else," Gina recalled.

"No … no, I understand what you're saying," Tori jumped in the exchange. "That one year did make a big difference. We weren't kids anymore …"

Nicole interrupted. "Tell that to the boys. They still haven't grown up." The girls laughed in agreement. "Remember STP?"

When the giggling ended, Tori pressed on with her theory. "There's something missing when you get older." Tori tried her best to explain. "When we were younger, everything was out in the open. We didn't need encouragement to vent or express ourselves." Tori took a swig of her drink. "Now look at us." She toasted her inner circle of friends. "We need shit like this to be honest. Angela's letting loose tonight, and why is that?"

Angela nodded in agreement. "True, this does help"—she nodded toward her drink between her legs—"but it's more than this. Even with this, we're more private or protective of where we are and what's really inside us."

"Angie, when you started hanging out with us again, I did feel you were different, only because we'd all grown up from the previous year," Nicole confessed. "I was unsure how to read you, whether you'd changed as we did." Nicole did not wait for a response. "I could only imagine how you saw the rest of us. You must have had a lot to deal with at once."

Gina wanted to hear Angela's story, so she directed their attention back to the storyteller. "And then there was Johnny. Go on, Angie. I get the feeling there's plenty more before you finish."

"I was nervous being around you all, and very confused. Johnny, I'd heard, was still going with Kimba. Thank God she didn't go that Christmas Eve morning, but even so … Like Tori just said, everyone needed their fix to open up," Angela recalled. "You two were smoking cigs regularly." Angela motioned toward Tori and Nicole. "The boys were drinking beer, being louder and more obnoxious than normal … and we were all supposed to be grieving."

"We were grieving. It was how everyone dealt with it," Nicole corrected.

Angela decided not to debate Nicole. It would take her away from her story. "I decided I'd done the right thing going. I wanted to be there with everyone. I was hurting too, but I figured it would be best not to be around Johnny." Angela sighed. "I could not fathom him with another girl."

"You still love him," Gina blurted out. "This whole time you never stopped loving him." It was not a question but a statement.

Angela was surprised the two-and-a-half mixed drinks she'd consumed did not affect her balance. She swirled her cup and asked Tori to tighten it up with vodka. "I'll always have feelings for Johnny, but it would be impossible for the two of us to ever be together again." Angela thanked Tori for the refill and then pressed on. "I'll explain why in a few, but let me go back a bit." Angela took a bigger gulp before recounting her time with Johnny. "After leaving everyone that morning, my intent was to hole up at home … forever, or at least until summer came around again so I could go back to Long Island." Angela brightened up. "But Gina, my pal who kept tabs on me all along, called a week before Saint Paddy's Day and invited me to a party."

"Oh, you said yes right away." Gina triumphantly smiled.

"I did. I was only fooling myself by thinking I could stay away from everyone, especially Johnny, forever. After the long winter, I needed to be out. I missed everyone. Yous scared me, but … I was glad Gina called." Angela held her cup up and smiled at Gina. "When I got to Tommy's basement, everyone seemed to be in a great party mood. Kevin had that big green hat, Joey was wearing some glittery vest, Gina, of course, had her green boots, and everyone else had some kind of Irish paraphernalia on. The music was loud, and there was smoke and the scent of beer and booze in the air. I quickly scanned the room for Johnny. I saw him back at the beer cooler, but there was no Kimba. Was she in the bathroom? I didn't know until I saw Bain push the closed door open and walk in. Yes!" Angela laughed. "They had to be broken up. She wasn't around at Christmas, and she's wasn't there that night either."

Nicole complained. "Why the hell didn't you ask anybody. I mean, jeez, they broke up way before Christmas."

"You're right." Angela agreed. "I should have been more straight forward, but I was … I don't know … I was embarrassed. I didn't want to seem desperate, and no one knew Johnny and I had even been together." Angela went silent for a second. She let her vodka do its job. "I often wondered if that walk from the hospital ever really happened. I had no confidence and didn't want to look like a fool if he rejected me a second time."

"Okay, we get it," Nicole finished.

Tori piped in, "Whaddaya mean a second time? When was the first?"

Angela would not take Nicole's bait but instead answered Tori's questions. "After the wake … you know, the night before the funeral … but that's not really important now. Anyway, back to the party. I saw Johnny turn from the cooler. I saw his face. He seemed … lost. I wanted or needed to comfort him in the worst way, but I was afraid of him, for him. He was no longer Johnny, or that's what I thought. But then I looked into his eyes, and he gave me that boyish smile. It was like we were kissing between the pine trees all over again. Our separation of the past year and a half had vanished. My heart skipped a beat. I couldn't wait to touch his skin." Angela sighed once again.

"You know, you're crazy," Nicole said, eliciting laughter from Tori.

Gina thought otherwise. "She was in love."

Angela frowned. "That was, until I was near him." With no concern for what her friends thought, Angela spoke of her dilemma. "Be careful for what you wish for." Angela took a small sip of her stronger Vodka mix. "Johnny took me to the back room, the make out room. He didn't want to talk, reminisce, find out how the hell I was doing—nothing but get his tongue down my throat and grab me all over. It was disgusting. He was drunk, high, and disgusting. I left in tears, swearing I was completely done with him."

"Drum roll please." Gina giggled. "Cause we all know you two were a hot couple for a while at least. How did that happen?"

"Yes, we were for a while." Angela smirked. "The following Saturday when I got home from work, Johnny was standing on my stoop with that puppy of his."

Tori injected, "Cuddles!"

"Yes, it was Cuddles," Angela verified. "He told me he'd won it at a poker game. He claimed the dog was half shepherd and half wolf. He said the puppy needed training and asked if I would help him. I could have cried. I hated him so much, but Johnny was charming when he wasn't stoned. Before I knew it, we were on our way to Winthrop Park." Angela pushed her hair from her brow before speaking. "He took me inside the fenced around the statue of the angel Gabriel. Once there, he took Cuddles' chain off and let the dog romp around the sculpture. Johnny explained that smart dogs could be off of a leash. Dumb ones had to stay on one. He then apologized for trying to make me into something I was not. He was sorry for being drunk and a fool at the Saint Pat's party. He was nervous and didn't know how else to act around me. If he hadn't been so sincere, I'd swear that bastard was putting some of the blame on me." Angela giggled, and the other girls joined in. "I couldn't speak. I only watched Cuddles scamper through the uncut grass. Johnny took my hand in his own, as I once had done to him. He suggested we sit on the angel's stone base. I still hated him, but I was intrigued by what he was up to. So, I sat beside him. Johnny then took out a small black box and handed it to me. He said it was long overdue, again apologizing."

"Let me guess, let me guess," Nicole interrupted. "He bribed you with the ankle bracelet."

"Yes, the ankle bracelet. Maybe it started out as a bribe." Angela unconsciously rubbed her heel before stopping at her bare ankle.

"Johnny, with his enormously fat fingers—or as I used to tease him, his mozzarella fingers—fumbled with the bracelet's link as he put it around my lower calf. When it slid down to my ankle, I looked at the date inscribed alongside of our names. It was the date of our first kiss."

"Oh, I'm gonna cry," Tori teased. Then she steered off of the subject matter. "Is it true guys with, as you call it, enormously fat mozzarella fingers, have matching ..." She pointed between her legs. "This thing?"

"Of course they do," Gina chimed in. "Why do you think Italians have the fattest fingers and are the best lovers?"

"You're only saying that because you're Italian," Nicole protested.

"No, think about it for a sec. Why would one accessory be big and thick and another be twiggy and short?" Gina cracked up.

The two Irish friends, Tori and Nicole, challenged Gina's anatomy lesson. Nicole then puckered at Gina. "Well, then, with that reasoning, girls with big lips up here have bigger lips down there." Nicole pointed to Gina's luscious mouth.

To everyone's surprise, Gina agreed. "You're right. Irish gals don't need any big lips down there or up here on da face. Your men are skinny and short. You only proved my point." Gina leaned back onto the couch laughing.

"Aw, you're drunk," was Nicole's only defense.

Tori rubbed her chin, wondering out loud, "Gina could be right. Why do you think Irish guys are always fighting? Because they are angry they have small ones." The three girlfriends joined Gina in the laughter.

When the hysterics quieted, Angela put her hand up. "Where was I?"

"Johnny's fat mozzarella fingers," Gina reminded her. "You can have the piano-finger guys." Gina stuck her tongue at Nicole.

"After forgiving Johnny, as you all know, we became very serious." Angela became solemn.

Tori unlocked the living room window and tossed her spent cigarette out onto the fire escape. A strong wind nearly boomeranged the cigarette back onto her sweater. "It's cold out there. Does anyone want to walk Bella with me?"

A moan from Nicole was followed by Gina's answer, "Sure, I will. She's been keeping my lap warm all night"—Gina petted the pooch—"but first I want to hear the rest of Angela's story about Johnny and their break-up."

"Yeah, and your black eye, too." Nicole circled her own left eye socket and then nodded at Angela.

A sullen-faced Angela grinned. "And my black eye." Angela stood up. With her feet planted firmly, she twisted her back side to side, relieving her tight lower-back muscles. "Johnny was troubled with guilt from the past, more so than any one of the other boys. It wasn't his fault what happened, but I could understand in a way why he felt the way he did. I tried my best to convince him, but he was … too dark about it all." Angela put her arms straight up and then swiftly slapped her thighs. "Johnny did stop smoking pot and drank less, especially when it was just me and him."

Angela sat back onto the carpet, took one of the pillows from the couch, and placed it between her bent knees for stability. "I was very attracted to him and wanted to be totally his. I know he's a guy and always horny, but Johnny didn't push me to do anything like that … not after the Saint Pat's party. It became frustrating at times, because I wanted him. I was definitely ready. Then on a Friday night at the bowling alley, we were sitting at a table listening to the jukebox while the guys played pool. In came Junior with my old buddy Kimba on his arm."

"I remember that. You were so pissed!" Tori said.

"I was because I watched Johnny's eyes when she came in. I knew he was still attracted to her. He wanted her."

"You felt he didn't want you?" Gina chimed in.

Angela nodded. "I wished he wanted me like that, but … I don't know. Maybe I was too rough on him from the get-go, or maybe he just liked getting stoned. But when that skank came in, I knew he wanted that." An upset Angela became silent.

Gina tapped Angela's side. "Bella, over here. She needs some loving." Bella obediently listened to the simple command and trotted to Angela's hip. "Johnny cared for you a lot and did not want to make the same mistake a second time," Gina reasoned.

"I thought the same thing," Angela concurred. "I decided that night that things between Johnny and I would change. I'd make sure of it." Angela frowned. "I should have left things alone." Angela sipped her drink and then spoke somberly. "Johnny's instincts were right. We weren't ready."

"Why, did he tire of you afterward?" Nicole asked, not waiting for the sex details.

"He didn't. It was the opposite. We became very close. I loved him, and I know he felt the same."

"Then what happened? How did it end? Why the scratch marks on him and your black eye?" Nicole wanted to know.

Gina shot Nicole the stink eye. "What are you, stupid or something?" Gina turned her attention to Angela. "You don't have to say what happened next."

"I'm this far. I might as well finish," Angela dismissed her friend's petition. "I only wish it were the few scratches and the black eye you keep asking about, Nic." Angela gave a short smile. "It's all in the past now, though. I was late, and I'm never late. I was pregnant; I knew it. We both got careless. For two fifteen year olds, it was amazing it didn't happen sooner." Angela spoke quickly. "When I told Johnny my fears, he brushed them off in a casual way. He said things would work out; they always did. But I could hear and see the panic in him." Angela slowed her voice. "I wanted to protect Johnny the best I could. After everything else, after everything he and the boys and everyone else here went through, I decided to take care of the decision-making by myself without the support of my lover."

Tori appeared puzzled, matching Gina's and Nicole's gaze. After a few seconds, Tori asked what everyone else was wondering. "How the hell did you do that?"

"Remember the week Johnny and all the guys were going away to the camp upstate for inner city kids?" The girls recalled. "I was with Johnny at the bus stop waiting for them to depart. He didn't want to go or leave me, but I insisted he not miss this trip. I needed him to go, for his sake and my own. I convinced Johnny my period would come once the pressure was off of me, most likely with him a hundred miles away. I promised him so. So I watched him board the bus and waved him good-bye." Angela took a deep breath. "Then I turned the corner, and there he was."

"Who?" asked Nicole and Tori.

"Fagan … I know everyone hates on all the Madd Tuffs, but I did make out with him one night. But that's a whole other story." At the shock and

230

disdain of her audience, Angela could only giggle. "All right, all right. I know he's disgusting … and short." Angela laughed harder. "His pants are always falling down."

"And he's Irish too." Gina raised her pinky finger up to the ceiling, while everyone cried out in hysteria.

When the giggling and teasing ended, Angela continued. "I asked Fagan if he had anything on him. I knew they all dealt." Angela finished her drink. "He stuck his finger into the cellophane of his cigarette box and carefully pulled two small paper squares out of it. Fagan explained it was a double blotter, and it was important not to touch the center yellow droplets, because that would partially remove the potency of the LSD trip."

"You did acid?" a disbelieving Gina called out.

"Fagan couldn't believe it either, but for him, a sale is a sale," Angela answered. "I was afraid to take it by myself, so I called Kimba. I told her I was in trouble … I needed help."

Gina and Tori interjected together, "What about us?"

"What, we ain't good enough for you?" added Nicole.

Angela stared into the pillow on her lap. "I was embarrassed … Kimba and I had been close once. And please, nobody take this wrong, but I knew I could trust her."

Nicole finished, "Oh yeah, we won't take that the wrong way."

Angela let Nicole's sarcasm slide. "Kimba and I cut my square hit of acid at ten in the morning. I had already called off of work. I wouldn't be missed until dinner time that night, and then I'd could call home and say I was staying at one of your houses for the evening."

"Yeah, use us now," a rejected Nicole responded.

"Shhhhh …" Gina was still amazed. "What did you two do all day?"

"We laughed a lot; I remember that. Then we walked to the cemetery and read the names off of the tombstones until the afternoon, but at some point, I got scared when the angels would not stop flapping their wings and would not shut the hell up. Later on, we were down at the piers, watching the ships go by. Sometime that evening we ate at the bowling alley before going to Kimba's to listen to records. By then I'd started to tire, so Kimba took me home. She saved my ass once we got there, explaining to my mother that I'd gotten sick at work so she'd walked me home and that I just needed to sleep for the night, which I did."

Nicole quizzed Angela. "But why did you take the acid?"

Sitting motionless, Angela answered, "I wanted to make Johnny's decision for him. He didn't need any additional guilt. I took the LSD to hurt the baby—physically, mentally, both. It didn't matter anymore. The abortion would have to happen then. There would be no choice about it … the baby was already dead to me. Johnny need not worry."

Gina spoke only one word. "Shit."

"Yeah, shit." Angela nodded. "When I first saw Johnny the night of his return from the camping trip, I noticed how eased up he appeared. His hair had gotten blonder, his skin was tanned, and his old smile was back. He was rested and happy. My first thought that was Johnny must have misunderstood what I told him before he left. Did he think I wasn't pregnant? Did I not tell him that?"

"You did say maybe you weren't," Nicole suggested.

Angela waved her suggestion off. "It was about being pregnant now … and about not being pregnant anymore."

"What are you talking about?" a disorientated Tori wondered. Nicole and Gina were lost too.

Angela enlightened her audience. "Johnny and I met inside the empty schoolyard that night. Johnny went on about what a great time they'd all had—the boating, swimming, archery, and so on. I began to get pissed because he didn't ask about my condition. When I finally had a second to jump in, I told him I was indeed pregnant."

Tori lit a joint, and before passing it to Nicole, she asked. "What did he say?"

"He said he'd thought about it all week and that everything would work out. We both had families to back us, we loved each other, and we were always going to be together and have children anyway. This was just getting a jump on life. He continued with, how could we have been so selfish to even consider killing our baby?" Angela laughed. "He swore it was a boy. Johnny said the baby would be blond like him but would have my brown eyes and my nose. Our boy would be an athlete. He said he would never make the same mistakes raising the baby that his parents had made with him. He finished by saying the baby boy or girl would be loved and that we would know all would be right once we held him. Everything would work out." Angela rubbed below her right eye and then asked Nicole for the joint. "I was devastated, hurt. Then I felt betrayed and pissed off. Where the hell was this Johnny before he'd gone away? He had been nervous, scared, unsure … then he comes back like the man I needed him to be before. He should have held me and told me we would be okay." Angela bit her lip but would not cry, not now. "I told him time was running out and that the abortion would happen with or without him. I was going for it the next morning. Before he could protest, I told him I'd dropped acid the week before and that the baby ain't got a chance, so now we move on."

Gina muttered, "Ouch …"

"Now it was Johnny's turn to feel devastated, hurt, and betrayed. He was sullen, adding how it was the end of the two of us. There would be no way he'd stay with me. He could never look me in the eyes again." Angela rubbed her eyes with her index and middle finger. "I was hurt and got angry at Johnny for his disgust at me. I saw only blackness, and then it turned to fury. I needed to hurt him physically. With my right hand, I went to slap Johnny's face. He wasn't expecting the attack but still managed to pull his head back slightly. I guess it made things worse. My fingernails caught Johnny's cheek, leaving long gashes in its tracks."

"That explains Johnny's marks," Nicole surmised. "But what about you?"

Angela smiled weakly. "I got mine right after. Johnny took a swipe at my face, but to his surprise, I did not pull back. I wanted the shot. I wanted plenty more, too. I wanted to be numb; I needed the blackness."

Nicole connected. "The black eye."

"Yes, my black eye." Angela sniffled but would not cry. "Johnny was shocked at my defenseless posture. He didn't hit me a second time, although he wanted to. He only looked down. He couldn't look me in the eyes or face." Angela blankly gazed into her open hands. "I reached out and placed his hand in mine as I had first done at Donny's hospital bed. Johnny's hand shook because he was scared, ashamed, hurt—all of them. He silently held me. Our heads were buried in each other's necks. We didn't want to face one another. He cried. I cried. We clutched each other for as long as we could, knowing once we let go, our life together and whatever future we'd dreamed of would be over ..." Angela was quiet for a second. "We were done. Johnny loved me but hated me. I screwed everything up."

"Angie, you can't really think like that—you know, the guilt part. You did what you had to do," Gina reasoned. "Most any fifteen-year-old would have done the same. Shit, look how many adults have them."

Tori joined in. "Think of all the girls out there who had sex without being careful and didn't become pregnant. I'm sure many of them would have had an abortion too. So in reality, all of us are as guilty as you."

Angela frowned. "I can only speak for me and Johnny." Angela finished her vodka drink and then stood up and gazed out to the frozen fire escape. "Johnny met me the next morning on my stoop. He said nothing. We rode the train together in silence to the clinic's Manhattan office. In a crazy way, I felt happy. The weight of being pregnant would soon be over. Once I got into the, I guess you can call it, operating room, the whole procedure only took a few seconds. My body felt no different from before, but my mind was relieved. In a sick way, I was at peace." Angela turned away from the glare of the window to face her friends. "When I walked into the waiting room, Johnny put his head up and gave me that boyish smile of his. For a split second I thought we would be okay, but ... Johnny asked if I was all right. It was his first and last words to me that day. Once we got to Brooklyn, he returned me to my stoop without a word. Johnny then jogged off to ... I have no idea." Angela began to tear up. "It was not supposed to end like that. It wasn't."

Chapter 19

1973

If you love life, don't waste time,
For time is what life is made up for.
—Bruce Lee

"Hey, lover-boy," Terry called in reference to Johnny's make-out session with Angela the night before, "Bain and Kevin are coming up the street." She then playfully swiped Johnny's elbow with the morning newspaper.

"Shhhh, stop it. No need for everyone to know." Johnny's face reddened as he pleaded, but he allowed his little sister to poke fun. *She's a bit jealous, that's all.*

Terry, rooted in a silly mood, giggled as she pointed to the window. "I saw them coming after getting Dad's paper." She retreated to the kitchen and passed the newspaper off to good old dad before returning to menace Johnny a bit more.

"They're early," Johnny mumbled to himself. "I wonder what's up."

Terry's smile disappeared quickly when she saw the sad looks on their faces and put that together with their early arrival. "Johnny, let them up. Something is wrong." *Details, Johnny. It's all about the details …*

Johnny ran to the front window and yelled down from the second story." Guys, come on up."

Kevin did the answering. "You better come out now. Joey and Shanty are coming." In a bone-chilling addition, Kevin ended, "It's all over."

From somewhere inside the kitchen, Johnny could hear his father's voice holler out. "The paper is saying your friend didn't make it!"

~~~~~~~

Three hours later, Nurse Joan observed the family photos of a chubby and worried man sitting across from her. Normally she would listen intensely and question the many angles of a business transaction, especially one concerned with something so intimate, but for the moment, Nurse Joan would have to take a pass on reality. The photos in his office would be her distraction. She daydreamed of the happier times depicted in the chubby fellow's still prints as his comforting voice narrated the inevitable.

"Joanie, will one day be good?" Her husband squeezed her cold hand and then leaned over and whispered in her ear, "Baby, hang in there. We're almost done." He then spoke to the chubby fellow across the desk. "Yes, one day. Tomorrow's Sunday, and Monday will be the ..."

Nurse Joan did not want to hear any additional details, so she went on examining the photographs inside their frames. *For a chubby guy, he has a pretty hot wife—and good looking kids, to boot. Two boys and a girl, it appears. He's got that hot wife because of his money!* As Nurse Joan snooped deeper into the pictures, she saw the obvious and became embarrassed. She spied into the goodness of the chubby man's heart. Each frame presented smiling and cheerful family members in some far away local. *Fancy expensive resort? No, not at all.* A dirt hut, not a five-star hotel. A beaten-down soccer field, not the New York Jets fifty-yard line. Hammocks hung from dirty posts, not plush beds with clean linens. All the while, Chubby's family was surrounded by needy but happy underprivileged children. *Chubby's family knows all the good they have … and rather spend on exotic vacation time, they all enjoy helping others as they help themselves.*

"So how much?" her husband asked.

Nurse Joan knew this annoyed tone from her husband. *He's supportive of me, but my dear does have his limits. My man will do anything I ask, but please, Mr. Chubby, no more talk of this or that. Get on with the totals.*

With a little laugh, the chubby man behind the oak desk waved off the question and turned his attention to Nurse Joan. "I see you admiring our latest vacation." Not waiting for an answer, Mr. Chubby spoke further. "We used to come home from holidays with great memories of fun and pleasurable times but with an emptiness, a big void."

"So why go there, then?" asked Nurse Joan. "Why the void?" She was glad to sidestep for a second the reason the three adults were bargaining at this man's desk.

Mr. Chubby spoke seriously. "Two years ago our void was filled." The man behind the desk rubbed his second chin and grinned. "I was fortunate enough not to miss a Sunday sermon pertaining to a Franciscan monk who was starting the SOS Children Village in a poverty-stricken area in El Salvador. Long story short, they needed volunteers … so we went as a family." The smile left Mr. Chubby's face and was replaced with an earnest stare. "Having my children—actually, all of us—search our inner selves made this vacation and the one after the most rewarding, fulfilling trips ever." Mr. Chubby's smile returned when he held up a photograph of his wife holding an infant. "From kindness comes … true grit."

Nurse Joan nodded, but her husband wanted the numbers immediately, not bullshit. "Very nice, but how about this?" He sat back and circled his arms above his head.

"You're right, sir. Sorry for the delay. Now we get down to business," the chubby fellow agreed.

"Yes, business. How much with everything?"

Mr. Chubby's smile disappeared. "I know your wife was enamored with some of the photos; her mind was not with us totally. But you, I thought you were listening." Before Nurse Joan's husband could defend himself, Mr. Chubby put up his hand to halt any words. "You see, I, as a business man, have certain edicts I must follow, but as a human being, I have only my conscience. In this situation, they coincide. I don't take a penny to bury a child."

Nurse Joan's heart swelled as she began to cry.

～～～～～～

"Look at this fag tie." Tommy took hold of Porky's clip-on necktie and yanked it downward. Then he tossed it into the gutter. "That's better. I ain't goin' in there with this loser lookin' like that."

Porky put up with Tommy's bullying most of the time, but once in a while he could and would not. That was definitely the case most recently. Being called a loser was beyond any rank out. It was personal. Without warning, Porky swung his fist and hit Tommy's throat. He wanted to pummel his antagonist's jaw, but this would have to do.

"You little"—Tommy coughed—"shit!" Tommy finished swearing before easily knocking Porky to the sidewalk and surging to his assailant's chest.

Johnny stood on the doorstep of the funeral home thinking of Angela. He felt guilty hardly thinking of Donny, but he needed a reprieve, even for a minute. *The girls will be here soon with Angela. Everything will be better once I see her, hear her voice, smell her shampoo, maybe touch her skin, kiss her mouth …* Johnny was adjusting his own necktie when the roar of a fight ten feet to his left began. Without waiting to see who was in the middle, Johnny plunged into the center of the fight to separate the two contenders.

"Let them go!" Bain yelled from behind Johnny. "Let 'em finish." Bain pulled Johnny's collar with one hand while the other hand pushed him into Shanty. "Let 'em fight it out! This is overdue."

"Bullshit" was all Johnny could muster as he rammed into Bain, trying to get back in the middle of the mix. *Touch me again, and I'll knock you out!* Anticipating Bain's whack, Johnny clenched his own fist, ready to strike his ally.

Bain understood Johnny's temperament, but even so, he reached for his friend's neck.

"Whoa, hold on everybody!" A lady with a three-button, black, wool coat squeezed between Joey and Kevin, colliding with Johnny. Bain quickly pulled back his arm and buried his hand inside his coat pocket. Tommy pressed Porky's head with his knee before getting up. Porky swore but went silent as the lady put her hand out to help. "Now, what's going on here. What's the matter with everybody? Better yet, no more of this fighting." She took a deep breath before her familiar voice continued. "I know everyone is hurting, but that's no reason to take it out on one another. Do you think your friend inside would like all of this?"

Johnny, Bain, Joey, Kevin, Shanty, Tommy, and Porky encircled the women with their mouths agape. They could not immediately recognize her. What was throwing all of them of the obvious? Was it her endless dark-brown hair? The lengthy coat with the high heels giving her a statuesque figure? The makeup of a movie star? It was all of the above. She knew them, but who the hell was she?

"Nanci. Candy striper Nanci!" Gina yelled from across the street. She was trailed by Tori, Nicole, and Angela. All four girls wore dark coats, hats, scarfs, and gloves. Tori and Nicole sported black dress pants, while Angela and Gina wore long skirts. "What's goin' on?" Gina inquired.

Nanci threw back her head to let her hair fall back to her shoulders. "Nothing," Nanci lied. "I surprised the boys … that's all."

Immediately, the boys found fault with themselves—not because of the fighting between Tommy and Porky or the impending battle between Johnny and Bain, but because of how not one of them recognized candy striper Nanci. Kevin was the first to speak.

"Shit, Nanci, I didn't know that was you." The other boys understood Kevin's assessment of Nanci's off-work appearance. "Your hair is always tied up in your cap, and …"

"And she's always dressed in a white-and-red outfit," Nicole concurred.

Gina finished it off. "Plus no makeup or … I love those shoes." Gina gave Nanci a hug hello. "I can hardly reach up to you now." The shorter girl laughed.

Angela, Tori, and Nicole also embraced the candy striper as the red-faced boys adjusted their clothing. Johnny took a peek in Angela's direction, but her back was turned toward the funeral home's front entrance. He took a step toward her, wanting to enter together, but was slapped in the back of the head. "Hey, what the …"

"Easy there, Johnny-boy." Bain playfully put up his fists. Then pointed with his thumb toward Nanci and Angela. "She's hot."

"What?" Johnny wanted to bash Bain's face inside out. *How dare he talk about my girl like that.*

Misreading Johnny's rage, Bain could only laugh. "What, you don't think the candy striper is hot?"

"Uh … no, my head isn't here," Johnny explained.

"Well, what do you think?"

"Yeah, yeah. She's hot. Come on, let's catch up to everybody. It'll be better going in all together."

Johnny, Bain, and a worried Kevin were the last three to enter the lobby of the funeral home. The girls, Nanci, and the rest of the gang stood in a semicircle waiting for the group to be one. The sight of everyone in this position triggered Johnny's memory of the dreadful morning when Gina show Donny's Christ-head charm to everyone on Tommy's stoop. *We weren't dressed up in our best then. We didn't have candy striper Nanci then, neither, but we did have Donny.* Johnny rubbed his eyes and then tried to halt the onrushing septic sight. *Maybe we can gather around Donny's coffin and call a play for him, like the good old days. Bain, you block. I'll pitch the ball back, and Tommy, you make believe you got the ball though … Candy striper Nanci could take the picture after Donny scores the winning touchdown. Nanci, take the camera and press this button … everybody smile. Donny, come on, you gotta smile. It's your nightmare too.*

Unintentionally, Johnny was the first to step into the funeral reception room, getting smacked with the scent of roses, lilies, and other fragrant florals. To his right, an unknown, chubby fellow dressed in a dark suit pointed to a small book sitting on a pedestal. "Here, son, sign in. Then …" The chubby fellow pointed to the front of the room.

As Johnny became accustomed to the scent of the room, he noticed the soft melody playing through the four speakers surrounding the quarters. Johnny took the pen attached to a small chain, noticing as he did so that he was the second name behind a Mr. and Mrs. So-and-So, a name he was not familiar with. As he wrote his own name and address, Johnny wondered if anybody would write *Broadway Joe* or *Willie Mays* down. *Nah, not today. This is Donny lying here; he would know if we lied.* Johnny felt a nudge on his elbow and turned around.

"Hurry … you're holding everybody up." Angela smiled warmly and then whispered, "Johnny, please know I'm here with you." Before a stunned Johnny could speak, Angela spoke a bit louder. "I miss you."

As Angela signed the guest book, Johnny silently walked past nine rows of empty chairs. In the tenth sat Nurse Joan with her husband and their two daughters. It was not too hard to recognize the four. Nurse Joan's charcoal-black hair remained in her hospital-mode bun. Although her daughters had their mom's coloring, their hair dangled beyond shoulder length. Their dad, a muscular guy, held his wife's knee and whispered into the older daughter's ear.

Johnny's attention focused on the "guest of honor." Donny's hair was cut short and combed to the side. *He looks so young … like a little boy.* Johnny walked past Nurse Joan's family and knelt on the small kneeler alongside the coffin. *His face is so pale.* Johnny put his hands together to pray, but he couldn't remember any prayer to recite. *Donny, do you know what I'm thinking? I am so sorry. No one, especially not you, deserved this.* Johnny felt a soft poke. *Angela.* He unmindfully moved over to make room on the coffin's kneeler. *Donny, you can't be dead. You cannot. I know this is not a dream, but it's not happening. It's not.*

Angela leaned over to murmur in Johnny's ear. "Come on. It'll be all right." The two got up and let Bain and Kevin say their respects. Angela gave Nurse Joan a big hug and was introduced to her family. Johnny stood silently until Bain guided him to the rear of the room, trailed by Kevin. As the others knelt before Donny and paid respects, they all followed Bain and Johnny to the back row of seats. Candy striper Nanci remained up front sitting alongside Nurse Joan.

Neither the boys nor the girls knew what to do next. Both groups kept silent until the chubby fellow stepped in front of Donny's coffin. He said a few nice things he'd heard of Donny but admitted he had not known him directly. He then asked if anyone who had known Donny would like to stand and say a few kind words.

The room became alarmingly silent. No one dared move, too afraid of being asked to speak. The chubby fellow reassured Donny's audience. "Come now, we are all here as friends. There is surely someone willing to speak of Donny."

Johnny heard whispering to his right. Tori was in Nicole's ear. *What's she saying?* A second passed before Nicole nodded, and both girls rose to their feet, placing their gloves, hats, and coats on their seats. Walking to the chubby fellow's right, Tori and Nicole smiled shyly. In a low voice that was nevertheless heard by all, the chubby fellow thanked the two girls for stepping up and encouraged them to say whatever they would like about Donny.

Tori opened. "The first time I met Donny was when Porky and Kevin brought him to the schoolyard. He was so quiet. He hardly spoke to the guys, never mind to us girls. But once you knew him and he began to know and trust you … well, he didn't have a mean bone inside." Tori wiped her right eye before a tear could find her cheek. Nicole patted her friend's back and then spoke.

"Tori, it's okay." Nicole faced Donny's still body before turning to the small group. "A lot of kids will always try to be bigger than they are, but never Donny. Whenever he was around my younger brother, Donny would always shower Billy with attention." Nicole fell silent for a moment regaining her composure. "For example, Donny would take the time out to explain why Batman could be real but The Flash could not." Nicole's nervous giggle led to the laughter of the group. "To this day, I wish someone could explain that one to me …"

"Very good, young ladies. I am sure your dear friend appreciates your words." The chubby fellow grinned. "Anyone else?"

Kevin, Porky, and Joey surged to the coffin's edge, nearly knocking over a chair in the process. All three had their coats unfastened, with Porky the lone speaker without a tie.

Joey began. "Donny, you were such a good friend, and …"

Porky did his best to help Joey. "Yes, a good friend. You always stuck up for me when I needed you most."

Kevin's mouth was agape, but no words were able to escape. *But it's for Donny. It's for Donny. It's for …* "Donny." Kevin turned around, speaking softly to his dead friend. "Who's better than us?"

"Well, thank you, young men. Sometimes a phrase can say more than a whole story." The chubby fellow patted Kevin's right shoulder as all three boys raced back to their seats. "Very good. Who will be next?"

Angela and Gina were next to talk. Gina said things similar to what had already been spoken of Donny. When it was Angela's turn to speak, though, she offered a contrasting narrative. "When I first starting hanging out with everyone and met Donny, I didn't understand what the whole fuss was about. He seemed like everyone else." Angela reached back and ran her hand along the coffin a few inches from Donny's shoulder. "I was so wrong." Angela rubbed her red nose. "I didn't know where he came from or what he had to put up with. He never pitied himself. Donny was so grateful for the attention his friends gave him and never let the hell he came from define who he was." Angela coughed. "I know I'm rambling, but Donny, you touched all of us more than you'll ever know. I want to thank you for that." Angela put her head down and followed Gina to her seat.

Before the chubby fellow could speak again, candy striper Nanci took the floor. Even from the rear of the room, where Johnny and the others sat, all could see her mascara was smudged from recent tears. Nanci's nose was pink and leaked mucus. She wiped it halfheartedly with a tissue and then began to address Donny and his brethren. "I didn't know Donny when he was brought into the hospital, but I met him through his friends. There were many stories told, happy and sad, of triumphs and failures, victories and defeats, and struggles ... always with friends. The outcomes mattered little; it was always about the story ..." Nanci blew her nose into her wet, snotty tissue. "Donny won't be with us any longer, but his story will last with all of us forever." Nanci stopped to catch her breath, then she twisted back to gaze at Donny. "In your short life, you made us all cherish our own."

Nurse Joan got up. She hugged Nanci tightly and murmured, "Nanci with an *i*, that was beautiful, dear." Nanci sat down beside her old nemesis, crying into her wet, snotty tissue. A few moments passed before Johnny reached the coffin's edge.

When speaking to an audience, speak to one person, the one who makes you feel at ease. Johnny scanned the room and found Angela's eyes. She smiled meekly. Johnny felt at ease, but he continued searching for someone of authority and courage. *That's what I need now. Bain? No. Shanty? Uh-uh. Porky, Kev, and Tommy? No, no, and more no. The other girls? Nope. How about candy striper Nanci? Naw, she's still crying. Nurse Joan? Yes, Nurse Joan. She's been a thorn up our ass from the get-go, but she's always been steady ... stern.*

Johnny removed his coat, holding it between his left forearm and hip. *When did it get so hot in here?* Johnny backed up till his waist nearly touched Donny's coffin, providing himself with additional space between himself and the mini audience, still unsure of what to say or where to begin. Johnny glanced away from Nurse Joan for a moment to peek at her oldest daughter. *She's almost Donny's age—well dressed, certainly schooled, well fed, and, most important ... well loved. How can two kids of the same age be so different? Donny had none of those things going for him. Now this little girl lives, and Donny is ... well, dead.*

"I didn't believe in Donny." Johnny could hear one of the girls in the rear of the room moan, and then a shushing sound followed. "Until I got to know him." Johnny spoke to Nurse Joan but loud enough for the whole room to hear. "It didn't take long for his shyness to go away." Johnny shifted his feet as his new shoes began to dig into his ankle. "Once Donny became one of us, he would always push each of us to treat each one another better … especially if someone was being bullied." Johnny smiled. "Donny always took the side of the underdog." Everyone in the room agreed. "No one else did or cared to do so, for the most part, but it mattered to him." Johnny's focus switched from Nurse Joan to the coffin where Donny lay. "Many times you kept us in line. You were our conscience." Johnny fell silent for a few seconds. He did not want to fall apart now. After thinking of Angela's soft touch from the night before, Johnny regained control. "No matter what pain you went through, you never complained." Johnny took a deep breath. "Maybe you thought we had our own private nightmares and wouldn't care about yours … but that would be wrong." Johnny's thumb and forefinger pressed gently to his inner eyelids. "I wished you would've trusted us more." Johnny looked back at his dead friend. "You let us believe in you, but that wasn't good enough." Johnny ran his finger across the coffin's edge. "I'm sorry I couldn't have made you believe in me. I will miss you … It will never be the same here again."

Hesitant and unsure what to do when he finished his eulogy, Johnny tried not to gape too long at the saddened stares of his friends. Shifting his eyes from one side of the room to the other, Johnny noticed a young lady in a dark-green coat sitting alone to the left of Porky. *Was she there … er, here all the time?* Johnny was beginning to wonder who the mourner was when Nanci tapped the empty seat beside her.

"That was beautiful. Stay up here with us." Johnny obediently sat, quietly forgetting the mystery mourner sporting a dark-green coat.

As Bain and Shanty stood in front and echoed the eulogies of Donny's other friends, Johnny's mind began to ponder. *People always say the one lying in the coffin does not look dead at all but asleep. That's bullshit. He looks pretty dead to me. He does look so young with this new haircut, new suit, and ... does he even have pants on below the bottom half of the casket? Na, that chubby fellow looks pretty legit.* Johnny listened to Shanty speak of a time all of them snuck down to the box seats at a Mets game. *Easy, Shanty. I think Nurse Joan's hubby is a cop or something.*

Johnny stopped listening to Shanty's ramblings and stared at the mural behind the staged coffin. He thought the painting's details were off the mark. The illustration, which depicted a desert with a stone fortress in its rear, seemed a bit odd. *What kind of background is this for the dearly departed?* Disturbing Johnny the most was what was happening on the sands of the artwork. In the mural's center were three empty wooden crosses. Johnny didn't know where the two thieves on the side crosses had disappeared to, but he knew the location of the portrait's main attraction. *Why have the butchering of Christ mixed with Donny's or anyone else's?* Johnny observed three men dressed in shepherd's clothing, along with two ladies in blue gowns, carefully handling the body of Christ. Sticking out of His white robe, Jesus's bloodied arm dangled toward the sand. *Where's the details? Blood? What about the two empty crosses? The sands below should be brown, nearly black, from the fallen blood, not bright yellow, as it is now.* Johnny doubted its authenticity. *The sky is bright. Didn't God get pissed and shake the skies with thunder, lightening, and rain?* Shanty stopped reminiscing, to the delight of Johnny's ears. *The wall should be of Christ's resurrection, not of the aftereffects of a slaying.* Johnny kept an ear open to listen to the chubby fellow's instruction about tomorrow's funeral mass and burial. Johnny's attention drifted back to the mural. *Maybe I'm wrong and the chubby fellow has it right with the image on the wall. What do the deaths of Donny and anyone else laid out here all have in common? Is it life, death, the carrying off of the body, the burial, and then resurrection? Why then the carrying off of the body?* Johnny sat back in his chair, vexed with the details. *What is it all about? Should we really fear death ... or life itself?*

Chapter 20

1978

...I may be lonely but I'm never alone,
and the night may pass me by,
but I'll never cry.
—"I Never Cry" performed by Alice Cooper

What happens to Rudolph next year when there is no snowstorm on Christmas Eve? Johnny stood at the rim of the bowl-shaped landscape formed by the incline of the hill and the ice-covered lake. *Did Santa use the reindeer and his red nose only when needed and discard poor Rudy when he no longer needed his oddness?* Walking on the cusp of the slippery high ground, Johnny took notice of a sloping maple tree. It was no different from other trees surrounding the pond, but this one had the boulder directly below it. Johnny was sure the snow-covered rock was the one where they had once battled to be king of the hill, ending with Donny shirtless, displaying the teeth marks from a monster.

Johnny turned to the frozen pond. *When we were kids, the water seemed so much further away than tonight.* Johnny's foot slipped slightly before he walked to the fateful monolith. With his ungloved right hand, Johnny inadequately wiped off a meager portion of snow from the king-of-the-hill stone. *That will do.* Johnny faced the water and then planted his ass cheeks on the remaining white flakes. *Yep, the pond was further back ... back then.* Johnny reached into his inner coat pocket and was relieved to feel the surprisingly warm but rough memento. He pulled it out and held it in both hands, slowly rotating the keepsake. *Funny, I've barely touched this thing since I placed it up on my shelf. I haven't really held it until tonight.* Johnny closed his eyes, heedless of his frozen environment. Tears formed inside his eyelids, and he protected the water droplets from the howling wind. *What's next? Donny's Christ-head is the church's property now. I had it long enough. I cannot carry the past around my neck forever.* Johnny stared down at his stone, the stone taken from this very shoreline. *And you, my soon-to-be ex-roommate, the days of carrying the guilt of not protecting Donny, or anyone else for that matter, are officially over.* Johnny stood up and reared back his once prized quarterback's arm. With an exaggerated arch, the thrown stone cut through the shadowy sky, stopping at its height before falling directly downward. Johnny witnessed the stone piercing the snow-covered pond and guessed it had settled somewhere on its icy surface. *Good, my stone will sink to the bottom of the pond sometime this spring ... a new start for all. Besides, better the rock than me.* Johnny closed his eyes again and for the first time listened to his surroundings—the sounds of a horse-drawn carriage, people laughing, and "Oh, Holy Night" being played on a trumpet in the distance. The cold air began to make Johnny shiver, which infused life into Johnny's psyche. *The football games, the fights, Angela, the guilt, hanging out, the beatings, laughing, loneliness, building models, the abortion, friendship, hardships. Most important ... life will go on for all. Here's to staring at the future as I leave the good, bad, and everything else in between behind. Yes, my future, introducing all new unknowns, unchained from my miserable past.* Johnny wiped both his eyes once more. This time the tears came not from the outside elements but from what was inside his soul.

Johnny slowly walked to the pond's edge, wondering if the tossed stone had made it through the ice into the water. *Should I try to get it?* Johnny again pondered suicide. *That's what tonight was all about, wasn't it? Sink or swim ... that is the choice ... right?* Sister Benedict's voice echoed Johnny's skull. *What type a person will you be? One accepting defeat, a loser ... or a fighter?* Johnny slammed his foot through the snow to hit the ice below. When it didn't crack, he took a less reckless step forward. *I'll never get Angela back, or our unborn baby. Nor will I get a second chance to run away with everyone to save Donny. With no do-overs, life kinda sucks. But what can I do now?* Johnny took a deep breath. The chilled air froze his lungs making him cough slightly. *Just let go. My tomorrow starts now, at this moment.* Johnny let the night wind cool his tear-covered cheeks. *Self-pity is not who I am. Everyone has their own sob story. Some are worse than others, but it makes no difference here.* Johnny coughed two additional times. *It's how you get up and what you do next ...* Johnny heard his name yelled above the music of "A Child This Day is Born" in the background. Johnny jerked around quickly, slipping awkwardly, thanks to his drunkenness and the ice below his feet. He lost balance, falling backward and landing headfirst on the solid ice.

~~~~~~~

Suddenly, Johnny found himself sitting alone in an office waiting room. He rubbed his forehead, not understanding how he'd arrived at this familiar location or where he'd traveled from. The lighting was faint but was bright enough for Johnny to spy upon what was hidden behind the murky shadows. Everything seemed to be in the same place as before. The receptionist's desk stood at the center of the waiting area; a phone and sign-in pad were its lone squatters. On either side of the desk were a pair of wooden doors, bookends to the empty receptionist's chair. The rest of the area was empty. There were no other chairs or windows, no diplomas or pictures hanging on the walls. Had they been there before? The markings on one of the two doors were different from before. The door to the right, with its white, stenciled lettering reading *EXIT*, Johnny remembered, but the words on the door to the left were mostly unclear. The letters were written freehand in chalk ... as if scribbled by a child. Johnny turned his head sideways, similar to a dog trying to understand his owner's command. Yes, the first letter was a *c*. The second one was definitely an *l*. Now, was that another *l* or a ...

"Well, well, well ... look who has finally made it here!" A young man's voice jolted Johnny from his translation stupor. "What, did I surprise you ... Johnny-boy?"

"Uh …?" Had Johnny not been seated, he would have fallen to the carpet-less floor. He gripped the armrest of his chair as if experiencing the drop of a roller-coaster ride.

"Oh, Johnny-boy … you don't remember me, but you sure know me." The young man smiled, showcasing his straight, white teeth. "You see, I waited a long, long time for us to meet, although I wasn't sure when or how it would happen." The young man wore a solid-green army coat, blue jeans, and black construction boots, similar to Johnny's daily attire. The unannounced guest walked to the receptionist desk and began to flip through the sign-in pad. Without looking up, the young man asked and answered his own question. "You do know me, right? Of course you do." He continued to fan through the gray book, and at its center, the young man slammed his forefinger onto the paper. Smitten with his find, he yelled out. "I got it! Right where you wrote it … Johnny-boy!" The young man fell silent while he pressed down on the vellum. His smile of achievement vanished. He began to cry. "Why did you? … I never had a chance …"

The moment Johnny set eyes on the intruder, he knew the puzzling man's identity. Was it his blonde hair, his blue eyes, his lean, powerful built, and his straight, white teeth, all identical to Johnny's characteristics? Or was it the shape of his eyes, the slightly turned-up nose, and his darkened, Mediterranean skin tone, matching Angela's trademarks. To an outsider, all of the above would have been proof enough, but Johnny did not require any evidence. It was his gut and heart bringing forth the identity of the mysterious man. "Yes, I wrote it." Johnny acknowledged.

The young man brightened and began to clap his hands together as he walked from the desk to Johnny's chair. Crouching before Johnny, the young man asked. "What about the bitch? When do I get to meet the baby killer?" Johnny leaned back, unable to mutter a response. "You know, my mother is no different from Donny's. How does that make you feel?" Not waiting for an answer, the young man continued in his taunts. "Life has a way of evening the score, Johnny-boy. Destiny not details. You'll see someday."

Johnny shifted his body to the right side of his chair for comfort while the room became icy with the bone-chilling words of the young man. He waited for the young man to quiet before expressing himself. Johnny blew warmth into his hands and then rubbed the back of his skull to ease its pain before speaking.

"I don't have the right to tell you why I did things back then ... or how you should feel now." Johnny was rudely interrupted by the loud clapping and laughter of the young man. "But I can tell you my feelings today."

The young man took a few steps backward to lean against the receptionist's desk. He went silent.

"The second I wrote my name in the pad beside you, I knew I would burn in hell forever for what I had done ... to you. There is no excuse, period."

The young man glanced at the pad he'd previously pointed to and stared at Johnny's name.

"I can say that I wish I hadn't written it. I should never have come here. I should have been supportive from the get-go, and so on. But that doesn't do you any good now."

The young man turned away from the desk to stare down Johnny. "You didn't give me a chance ... everyone else in your life you have, but not me." The young questioner threw his blonde hair back from his forehead, an all too familiar move for Johnny. "Why is that, Johnny-boy? Why the hell is that?"

Johnny gazed into the young man's eyes. "I have no answer ..." Johnny reached for his son's shoulder. The young man did not pull away. "I think of you every day … and of how badly I cheated you of everything." He slightly squeezed through the young man's shirt. Johnny was pleasantly surprised to feel warmth. "You will always be with me. I always felt you by my side … being part of my life." Johnny touched his son's cheek with his forefinger, drying a fallen tear. "I can't undo what I did, but know that you will be alive in my soul forever … if you'll have me."

The young man put his hand on Johnny's, removing it from his cheek before rising up from a squatting position. He pointed to the doorway on the left with the child's handwriting. "The third letter on that door is an *i*. Then it's *nic*. It was where I was officially murdered." The young man grimaced. "I never wanted to die and be alone. I wanted brothers and sisters … a mom and a dad …" The young man began to walk backward to the clinic door, not taking his eyes off his father's. "I am alone now …"

"Wait … you can't go!" Johnny felt the numbness escape his legs in a flash. He was able to stand for the first time since entering the waiting room. "Son, I won't lose you again … I promise!"

The young man smiled and stopped backpedaling momentarily. "Shhhh … you hear that?" He motioned to the exit door. "That's your two buddies trying to revive you. There is so little time now." He took another step away from Johnny.

Johnny stumbled forward. His son grabbed hold of his falling dad. "Please let me go with you now through the door. I won't lose you again …"

The young man grinned and then became serious. "Sorry, it doesn't work like that." He took another step back to the clinic door and reached for its handle.

It was Johnny's turn to cry. "But wait … I need to be with you. I always have … I wronged you so bad. You don't have to be by yourself anymore ... I'll do whatever I have to to make things right ... I'm so sorry. Let me make it right. Let me be your dad, please."

The noise from behind the exit door became louder and clearer. Johnny did not notice, but the young man did. "Listen, you'll have other chances. Then we could be together. Someday you will have sons, and I can only ask you this."

Johnny wrapped his arms around the young man's shoulders, not willingly to let him go. He spoke into his prisoner's chest. "What? Anything. But don't let go ..."

"Promise me that when you bandage your sons' knees, when you teach your sons how to throw a baseball, ride a bike, fight off a bully, do arithmetic, treat a girl, or become a man ... think of me. I will be there. I will always be with you ... I have nothing else."

Johnny mumbled in agreement. Then he felt his son gently push him away. "Wait, before you go ... I don't even know your name."

"You know it, Dad. I am your son."

〰〰〰〰

"Johnny! Wow, I thought you were dead or something." Shanty's Cuban-toned skin was camouflaged in the darkness of the trees, but his bright-white smile disclosed his presence. "Johnny ... we were looking for you all night, and we were here twice." Shanty's knee slipped on the snow, knocking Johnny's head.

Bain's scared frown quickly dissipated. "What the hell, Shant? You trying to kill the guy or what?"

"Where did Johnny go? I have to go with ..." Johnny realized he had awoken from a realistic dream before finishing his last sentence. Witnessing the concern and shock on Shanty's face, Johnny had to lighten the mood for his rescuers. "You were always arms and legs; now we can add in *knees* too," Johnny joked. Then he rubbed his head, feeling the bump from his fall growing. "But it's so good, so good to see you guys ..."

Bain trailed Shanty by a few inches. He greeted Johnny with a smile. "I knew you were here. I knew it. But why all the play tonight?" Bain bent forward and grabbed Johnny's forearm, helping his friend from the wet snow. "What were you just saying about finding Johnny or something?"

Shanty analyzed Johnny's bewildered words. "He must have heard me say 'I found Johnny.'"

"Yeah, something like that." Slightly dizzy, Johnny balanced himself on Shanty's shoulder for a second, not wanting any part of the frozen pond. "How long was I knocked out for?"

"About three seconds. That's how long it took Shanty to race down here when he saw you fall."

Johnny shook his head in disbelief. His vision of his dead son had seemed to last at least an hour. He changed the subject and focused on the here and now. "How did you find me? It's amazing you did."

Bain glanced at Johnny's tight grip on Shanty's arm before speaking. "You gotta thank a lot more people than me—Terry, Tommy, Joey, Kev, the girls ..."

"Me too," Shanty finished Bain's thought.

"Terry ... what did she have to do with anything?" After a second, Johnny continued, "Where is everybody else? Are they here too?"

"Nope, no one else is here in Manhattan. They're all looking all over Brooklyn for your sorry ass." Bain proceeded to fill in most of the blanks of the night. When Shanty would try to inject a portion of the story, Bain would give him the stink eye to shut him down. When Bain finished, he handed the left-behind Christ-head to Johnny. He was a bit mystified that Tommy and the girls cared he was missing, but a more concerning question remained: *How the hell did Bain find Donny's chain?*

Bain spoke before Johnny could ask. "The priest from Saint Stan's found it outside his church." Bain rubbed his hands together. "Let's find a phone and call the girls. You better call your sister, too."

"But wait ... where did the priest find you? In the schoolyard?" Johnny demanded. There was a falseness in Bain's voice. *He's not telling me the whole truth.* "Shanty, how did you guys get this?" Johnny raised Donny's Christ-head till it was three-inches from Shanty's nose.

Shanty shrugged his shoulders as his grin faded. "We all heard the cops and firetrucks go by and—"

"Yeah, same here. That's when I left the schoolyard and—"

"It was Paulie ... you know, Porky. He was run over by a bus." Bain interrupted. With no bullshit, he described the scene to the deadly climax. "Something to do with the Madd Tuffs, I'm sure of it." Bain went on about Brodie and Hogan being in the vicinity and how scared the two appeared to Nicole's little brother Billy. "The priest was in the park looking for you in the middle of all this shit. Instead, he got Porky's crushed skull." Bain finished with the priest passing Donny's medal off to him, since he had bigger, more urgent needs to address. *Porky's mother.*

"Shit. I feel like shit." Shanty turned away and heaved up a lungy. In his sickened state, Shanty's normally childlike demeanor skewed to rage. Bent over, waiting for additional spit to arise, Shanty shouted out. "It's Tommy's fault. He chased Porky away ... to those scumbags!" A second and third hack echoed around the frozen grounds.

Before Bain could reason with him that the Tommy and Porky thing had happened a long time ago, Johnny broke in. "You are so wrong Shant. You are. It doesn't work that way."

Shanty stood straight up as his coughing ended. To Johnny, the scowling Shanty appeared old, way too old for seventeen. Wiping spit from his frozen chin, Shanty questioned Johnny. "Whaddaya mean 'it don't work that way'?"

"Just that … Porky coulda, shoulda done things differently when it came to Tommy." The newly defiant Shanty was cutting-edge to Johnny. *Seems like everyone has moved up and on from our past.* "For sure, when it came to following those guys. Only God knows what Porky was thinkin' or doin' tonight. But it was on Porky and his decision to hang with—"

"Enough of this shit. I'm cold and thirsty." Bain broke in. "Let's get to a phone and call everybody before getting back to Brooklyn."

The three walked silently out of the park until Bain placed a coin into the phone and talked to Tori. Detailing the events of the night in answer to Tori's interrogation, Bain did his best to bring an end to the conversation. "Yeah, that's about it. Johnny will meet us tomorrow. Tonight he's good, but he's shot. Yeah, we all are. I'll see you later … and call Terry. Bye." Bain slammed the phone on the receiver. "Damn, she never shuts the hell up."

Johnny tried one last time to convince Shanty of Porky's personal responsibility for the situation. "Saying he has none or little fault in this is like saying that Tommy or anyone else has the muscle over Porky." Shanty said nothing. "It's all up to us to decide our fates … Family, friends, and breaks along the way are great, but it still ends with yourself being a winner or a loser."

Shanty put in his last two words. "Or dead."

"Okay, enough of this philosophy baloney. I need a beer for the train."
Bain reached into his pocket, pulled out a five-dollar bill, and slapped
it into Johnny's hand. "We can't go into that bodega, but you can. Get
us a beer." Bain smiled. "After you get the beer, ask if you can use the
bathroom."

~~~~~~~

"Vito's Pizza … We Deliver." Below the neon lights flashing red, green,
and then red again, a banner hung, which Tommy read out loud.
"Grand Opening." Uninterested in the pizza place or its advertising,
Kevin and Joey remained silent. Tommy surmised their tired, hungry,
and a bit beaten state, so he devised a pick-me-up plan. "Guys, how
much do you have?"

Joey, without looking into his pocket, spoke first. "Two and change."

Kevin stayed silent behind his grinning paper-bag head, shrugging his
shoulders.

"You know, you suck. When the hell do you ever have money?" Tommy
joked.

"Hey, I don't need your pizza." A heated Kevin defended his lack of
cash.

Tommy disregarded Kevin's anger. "Joey, give me what you got. I'll take
care of the rest." Joey handed Tommy two crumpled one-dollar bills,
a quarter, and two nickels. "Good, two nickels," Tommy mumbled to
himself. "You two go inside and order us a pie … to go … delivered."
Before Joey could question Tommy's logic, he was waved off. "Don't
worry, I'll take care of it, but first let me call Tori's."

"Come on, Kev, let's order the pie." Joey grabbed a hold of Kevin's
forearm to lead him into Vito's Pizza. *There's no reason to start anything
up here, big fellow. It will be all over soon enough.* Kevin was about to

protest Joey's grip, but because of the tightness around his arm, he relented. *That's right, Kev, no more fighting.* Joey with his left hand opened the glass door and released Kevin with his right. *Good boy. Let's get some pizza. By tomorrow afternoon, I got this feeling it will be the beginning of the end for all of us, or maybe just the end.*

Joey and Kevin walked to the service counter and ordered the pie as Tommy had instructed. Joey watched Tommy through the store's front window. He was bouncing on his feet inside the glass phone booth.

Carefully placing Joey's two nickels into the pay phone, Tommy wondered if anyone from Vito's Pizza had observed the ridiculous exchange he'd just had with Kevin's impersonation of the Unknown Comic. *What's it matter? Maybe they'll give us a break if they were watching that idiot with the paper bag over his head.* With his frozen fingers, Tommy slowly dialed up Tori's apartment.

"Why is he so pissed off all the time?" Kevin wondered out loud. "He's got a hot girl. He's gonna go to college. He's …"

"I'll tell you," Joey said, still watching Tommy speak on the phone. "Tommy's the type of guy who always needs to have the best." Then in a hushed voice, Joey resumed. "You're right, he's got the best with Angela, but he wasn't her first or only." Joey shrugged. "Not that it matters. But it eats Tommy alive."

A laugh echoed out from Kevin's paper bag. "Yeah, I could see how that would always piss him off. Poor Tommy."

His chuckling ended when Joey saw Tommy drop to one knee, massaging his temple. The fallen phone bounced off Tommy's bowed head, bumping into his left temple. Tommy's kneeling posture reminded Joey of a Catholic's blessing themselves before entering the church pews. *Tommy's not in Saint Stan's, or blessing himself, for that matter.* "Shit, what the …" Joey hobbled by Kevin and through the eatery's front door to the frozen sidewalk, unintentionally skidding slightly into Tommy's shoulder.

With no words of complaint about the sudden bull rush by Joey, Tommy went on massaging his closed eyes. "Tommy, what is it? What's the matter?" Joey demanded.

Tommy mumbled Johnny's name.

Kevin reached Joey's side in a sprint. Without saying a word, he picked up the dangling phone hidden between the phone's cash box and Tommy's head. "Hello?" Kevin yelled through his paper bag to a dial tone. "Must've hung up."

"Come on. Let's get him inside." Kevin placed his hand under Tommy's right armpit. Joey did the same to the left. "We'll get change and call Tori's again."

"No, no, no ... Johnny's okay." Tommy stood himself upright. "I'm good. Let go." Both Joey and Kevin simultaneously released Tommy. "Bain and Shanty found Johnny in Manhattan. He's all right." Tommy rubbed both his eyes. "Johnny's okay."

Stunned, Joey could only ask, "They found him? He's all right?" Joey let out a sarcastic laugh. He couldn't help himself. "I thought you hated him; you're always angry at Johnny."

Kevin added, "It was clear you only came with us tonight because of Angela." Kevin rubbed his nose from the outside of his bag.

"Stop it ... Johnny and I are best friends. He's not the same anymore. You know that. You both say it all the time." With his inner wrist, Tommy wiped moisture from his eye. "The last thing I ever wanted was for something to happen to him ... even if we aren't that close anymore." Tommy wanted to continue, but he could not—would not—speak of Angela or the way Johnny had mistreated her. It was none of their business; it was just between him, Angela, and Johnny. "Come on, Johnny's fine ... no more of this shit, okay?" Tommy's voice screeched in a desperate plea, halting the inquiries.

Joey nodded and changed the subject. "I knew it. I knew he was there all along."

Tommy recovered quickly from his despair, answering with sarcasm, "Why the hell didn't you say something earlier?" With a playful slap to Joey's head, Tommy finished. "I guess we would've missed all this fun together."

"Shit, tonight was crazy." Kevin's characterization of the evening rang true to all three friends.

"What else did they say?" Joey asked, returning to the subject of the phone call as he limped up the step of Vito's.

Tommy shrugged his shoulders as all three reentered the pizza store. "I couldn't hear what she was saying; my head went black."

"Let's call them back." From underneath his paper-bagged head, Kevin scratched his cheek.

The young man behind the counter flipped the oven's door down to turn the pizza around. "Two minutes, guys." He then asked for payment. "That's five bucks ... and you want it delivered?"

"Yeah." Tommy counted five singles and then added a sixth. "Here, this is for you."

"A tip for me? This is a first." The pizza man rang up the five dollars and placed the single into his rear pocket.

Tommy smiled and turned around to Joey and Kevin before addressing the pizza man. "Yeah, we want the pizza delivered to Guernsey Street, right over the bridge."

Kevin began to say something, but Joey quickly hushed his friend.

"What? Dirty Guernsey in Brooklyn," the pizza man began to protest.

"Come on, it's less than a mile away. The Pulaski Bridge is right around the corner, and Guernsey is like three blocks from there." Tommy decided keep talking to persuade the pizza man. "If Guernsey is so far from here, how did you know to call it Dirty Guernsey?"

The pizza man slid his wooden paddle under the pizza and took it out of the oven, placing it perfectly into its white box. "All right, you got me. It's not far, but my guy hates that street. People throw chicken bones out the windows, and rats the size of dogs eat them up."

Joey remained quiet until the pizza man's reasoning began to break down. "How many times could he have gone that way if this is a grand opening?"

Kevin and Tommy laughed as the pizza man began to turn red. "Look, no deliveries there. That's it."

Perfect, now Tommy's plan may have a chance, making Dirty Guernsey part of the solution for all. "How about this ... You deliver us and the pizza to Noble Street. It's a nice block now, and Noble Street is right around the corner."

"So we deliver yous and the pizza together?" The pizza man smiled at the balls of these three wise guys.

Tommy could hear Kevin rustle and Joey sniffle as the pizza man pondered the proposal. As the silence hung in the air, Tommy knew he had won. "Thanks, my friend, and Merry Christmas ..."

⌁⌁⌁⌁⌁

"Come on … go make." Gina tugged lightly on Bella's dog chain. "Tori said she makes right away. Probably her insides are frozen or something." Gina sounds out a kissing call for Bella to follow her to the curb. "Thanks for coming outside with me, I should have known Tori would bail." Gina giggled. "It is cold."

"Don't rush going back upstairs. The cold air feels good." Taking in a breath of the nightly wind, Angela went on. "I never drank so much in my life." She adjusted her wool hat and leaned on the rear of a parked car. Facing the brownstone buildings on Noble Street, Angela relished the novel sensation of tipsiness. "Look at the lights flashing." She waved her arms across five or six buildings. "They're all in the Christmas spirit." Angela's twinkle faded, and she began to cry.

Gina let Bella finish pissing before comforting her friend. "Come on, pooch." Bella hopped onto the sidewalk and pulled toward Tori's stoop. "No, no, sweetie, you stay out here and freeze with us for a minute." Gina tugged on the dog's leash, guiding Bella toward Angela.

"It's okay." Angela tried to stop the tears from flowing but could not. "Did you know?"

Gina stroked circles around Angela's back with her gloved hand. "About what happened with you and Johnny?" Gina did not wait for Angela's response. "No … at least *I* didn't. As for the two upstairs, their reaction was shock too. So, I guess your secret was a secret. Unless you told Tommy or someone else."

"I never told anyone. I don't know why I said anything at all tonight." Angela sniffled before recouping her self-control. "I never said anything to anyone. I was—am—ashamed of what we did. Johnny and I will have to live with this. We are, in a sicko way, attached together forever." Angela wiped her nose with the back of her glove to keep it from dripping. "We're a couple that could never have been one, until it's our time to be together in hell. Oh, Gina, it wasn't supposed to end this way."

Gina's wrist began to freeze as the wind turned up her jacket's arm. She stopped massaging Angela's back to shake warmth into her own limb. "Stop it now. You're being so freaking dramatic. What you did, well, it happens every day. Please don't think you're special." Gina bent down to rub a shivering Bella's chest. "Hang in there, pooch." She then turned her attention back to Angela. "What does Tommy think?"

"He loves me and will do anything I ask him. As for my past with Johnny, Tommy's no different from any other guy." Angela wiped her freezing cheek. "He's jealous of my past with Johnny. Tommy doesn't understand how Johnny could have left me."

Gina laughed for a moment. "You know, Angie, you do sound so conceited sometimes, but I do understand what you're saying."

Angela gave her a half smile and then corrected herself. "I didn't mean it that way. It's just how close Johnny and I were and how it all ended so quickly ..." She could no longer talk to Gina's eyes, so Angela gazed at the corner of the street. "You ever think back to a time in your life when everything was so perfect? School was great, your parents were healthy and happy, your friends were all in the same place, and you had a boyfriend that made you feel so special? It was perfect for such a short time ... I dream about it always, that perfect window of time." Angela gazed into Gina's eyes. "When we split, it was so final. We never had a relapse, never got back together on a rebound, didn't have a chance meeting. There were no phone calls, nothing. Once my bruised face healed, I had nothing left from Johnny."

Gina reasoned, "You gotta get over this shit with Johnny. It's not fair to you or Tommy or any other guy you'll be with." Angela let Gina continue to lecture. "Not once did I hear you say you love Tommy."

Angela began to speak when she noticed a car with what looked like a tire on its roof driving toward them. As the car neared the two girls and Bella, Angela had to reassess what she had seen. *That's not a tire on the roof but a … pizza pie?*

The car slowed and then stopped adjacent to the two surprised girls and the barking dog. A pizza box exited the car first, followed by Joey's arm and the rest of his body. "Hey! Anybody wanna slice?" Joey slipped on the slush-covered street but was snatched by Tommy from falling. "Shit … thanks."

Kevin leapt from the passenger side of the pizza car onto the opposite end of the street. The Unknown Comic look remained. He yelled from behind the three-foot pizza display, "What a night!"

Gina nearly lost Bella's chain as the two rushed into the street to greet Kevin. "You idiot!" She pointed to the paper bag. "Get rid of that stupid thing already." Laughing, she kissed his mouth through the bag's crescent slit. "This better be Kev underneath." Gina teased.

"Shit, Joey, what happened to your eye?" Angela cried out.

Joey stumbled up the stoop with the box of pizza tilting sideways. Without turning around, he yelled, "I'm freezin'. I'm goin' up … a long story." Not getting an answer, Joey hobbled up the stoop and disappeared into the hallway.

"Yeah, I'm right behind you." Tommy touched Angela's arm and whispered. "Joey's good. Things didn't work out as planned tonight, but we're here now."

Angela stood her ground for a moment to look Tommy in the eyes and stopped him from going upstairs. "Wait … I'm so happy you made it back safely. We were all worried."

"Yeah, yeah, no big deal." Tommy stared off toward the street. "We went through a lot, not only with the Madd Tuffs but with the shit we all went through together …"

Angela nodded, understanding Tommy completely.

"Come on, Angie," Tommy called. "I'm frozen now. We can talk later." He motioned for Angela to move on.

"But I want to tell you something else." Angela looked into the street where Gina and Kevin continued their make-out session. "I was scared something bad was gonna happen to you, with what happened to Porky. I just had such a bad feeling tonight." Tommy began to talk, but Angela put her gloved hand onto his mouth. "I love you … and I don't want to lose you."

Tommy had heard those words from Angela in the past, and he'd repeated them back to her. But her voice tonight carried a desperate tone. "Is everything all right?"

Before she could answer, Kevin, Gina, and Bella approached the two. Gina interrupted. "We're going up. I'm getting a slice before Nicky has two." Gina playfully poked at Kevin's head before ending her advice to Angela. "It doesn't matter what anyone voices or suggests … just follow your heart."

Chapter 21

1973

I didn't mean to hurt you.
I'm sorry I made you cry.
Oh no, I didn't want to hurt you.
I'm just a jealous guy.
—"Jealous Guy" performed by John Lennon

"That wasn't too bad, but tomorrow could be worse." Talking to no one in particular, Nicole referenced Donny's wake. His funeral would follow the next morning. She then peeked at her watch. "I have to watch Billy tonight. Mom has last-minute shopping to do." Putting it out there, Nicole sought company but had no volunteers. "Tori? Angie? … Gina?"

"You ain't picking me last and expectin' me to come over." Gina laughed and was joined by Tori and Angela. Gina spilt a small amount of hot chocolate on her exposed wrist. "Whoa, almost got it on my jacket." On second look, she did see a splatter on her jacket's arm. "Shit!"

It was time for Nicole to join in the giggling. "What's the matter, G, you making a mess over there?"

Angela grasped the situation. "It's so good hearing laughter … nothing to laugh at lately."

Holding back her smirk, Tori added, "Did you see Shanty up there today? He's talkin' shit about sneakin' down at the Mets game, sneakin' on the subway, sneakin' in the movies. Did those guys ever pay for

271

anything?" All four girls laughed so hard that Gina had to wipe a tear from her eye.

When the laughing quieted down, Angela broke the silence with a white lie. "Nic, I would hang out over your house tonight, but I'm shot and need a good night sleep before tomorrow." Tori and Gina bailed out with similar reasoning as Angela piggybacked the excuse. "I'm getting another hot chocolate, then a hotter bath, and then a warm bed."

"Suit yourself." Nicole responded to Angela, then she focused on Tori and Gina. "You all leaving then?"

"Yeah…" Gina answered, knowing the three girls would split after two blocks to go to their respective homes. "Angela, we'll meet you at the church before nine."

Angela waved good-bye to the three departing friends, and then she walked over to the candy-store counter and bought a pack of Chicklets, knowing they would work better than another hot chocolate. She brushed her two lips together, feeling the sleek surface of the red lip gloss. *Not too much, not too little … Don't want to look like a clown before stepping on stage.*

Two boys about ten years old frolicked by the comic books until one bumped into the display rack. They were immediately told to withdraw from the premises, leaving Angela alone with her thoughts. *Johnny, where are you? I'm dying to see you again … alone. Well, I shouldn't say "dying."* Angela scouted the store's front window. People went by in both directions, but there was no Johnny. *Poor Donny. I cannot believe he's dead …* Angela became hot. With her hat and gloves already lying on the table, she wiggled her unbuttoned coat to the backside of her chair. *It's everything hitting at one time. Kissing Johnny, but Donny's death; Christmas time, but Donny's burial. When do things die down? There I go with the "die" word again … but when will I feel normal again? I don't want my pull toward Johnny to end, of course not. It's the other bull that has to come to an end ... that's all ... after tomorrow everything will return to normal, except for my feelings for Johnny. They could only grow. Nothing will ever change that.* Angela spied through the glass window once more. *Johnny-boy, where the hell are you?*

~~~~~~~

"How did he look?" Terry sat on the floor rearranging the Three Kings. "Sister Benedict said the Three Kings did not hail Jesus until He was a year old." Terry moved the Kings and camel to the opposite end of the cotton-covered table. "If I really want this to be right, they should be walking in from the Bronx to get here for next year," Terry logically thought.

"Do you have to be so ... exact?" Johnny grinned but could not laugh.

"Well?" Terry asked.

Johnny tossed his tie on the couch and answered Terry honestly. "He had a waxy look. Sorta made up ... fake appearance." Johnny picked up a shepherd and rubbed its rubber-coated body. "This guy's face is more realistic than Donny's was."

Johnny parted ways with his sister once he'd recounted to her the happenings inside the funeral home. What saddened Terry most was that Donny had no family there. "No relatives? What about his father? Didn't Donny have an older sister? You were his only friends and family? No one else cared?"

"Yes, Terry, no family ... only us with Nurse Joan and her family and candy striper Nanci. That's it, Sis. Johnny ran out of his house with an open coat, despite the evening's near-freezing temperature. *The air feels good. Please, Terry, no more questions about Donny. I'm done. I need to talk about living, no more death ... I just need to see Angela.*

Johnny's house was three blocks, or a bout a five-minute walk, away from the candy store, where Angela waited impatiently. Johnny, wanting to arrive on time, gave himself a ten-minute head start. When he'd spoken to Angela on the sly outside the funeral home earlier, Johnny had suggested a secret rendezvous sooner rather than later. To Johnny's surprise, Angela had agreed. With a wink, Angela had murmured three words: "Seven ... candy store." It was now ten till the whispered hour. Johnny, with only two blocks to go, heard a female voice call out.

"Johnny?" In a quieter tone, the young lady with the dark-green coat asked. "You are Johnny ... right?" Walking between two parked cars, the unknown lady from the funeral home approached Johnny.

"Uh, yeah... I saw you at Donny's wake. And who are you?" Johnny's suspicion dissipated when she smiled. Her coat was now buttoned to her chin, and she wore a white mink hat. The colors she wore made him think of the New York Jets. *She could be a Broadway Joe girl.*

"I didn't mean to surprise you, but you seemed like you were in a rush, and I wanted to talk to you for a moment." She put forward her right hand to greet Johnny. Her white gloves matched her hat. "My rental car is right across the street. We can sit in it and talk." She saw the worry on Johnny's face. "If you must get somewhere, I would gladly drive you. We can talk then."

"No ... I'm just goin' around the block." Johnny spoke cautiously. He knew this young lady, but from where? *Her frown—she looks just like ...*

The young lady cheered up when she caught herself being too imperious. "I am so sorry, young man. I stalk you outside your home, ask to talk with you, and offer you a ride in my car ... and you don't know my name or who the hell I am." Her smile widened.

It's Donny's smile, like when he scored the winning touchdown.

"I'm Lorna, Donny's sister." She motioned for Johnny, wanting him to follow her to the parked car across the street.

Johnny checked for any oncoming vehicles before trotting out to catch up with Lorna. She walked to the side of her car nearest the curb and unlocked the passenger side door for Johnny to enter. Lorna went around to the driver side and let herself in the car.

"I … I forgot he had a … You two look alike." Johnny suddenly became tongue tied as he searched for words. "How did you know where I live?"

"The register book at the funeral home, of course." Lorna smiled. "Being clever is more important than anything you'll read in a book. Remember that."

Johnny nodded. *She's been through plenty. How did she get to this point? Being clever? You must be to escape hell.*

"You're wondering where I went, why I left my younger brother to a monster, why I came back now when it's all too damn late, and so on."

Johnny nodded a second time, a bit embarrassed the young lady was correct.

"We could be here all night with my story and the guilt I'll carry forever." Lorna went into her pocketbook and pulled out an open pack of cigarettes. Johnny refused her offer of one, so Lorna, with a shaking hand, put her own back in the pack. "Our mother had me when she was only fifteen. Donny came nine years later. I'm sure there were plenty of abortions and miscarriages in between." Lorna grinned. "I'm sure that was Ma's way of birth control." Lorna fell silent.

Johnny needed to fill the awkward silence with something. "Donny said he had an older sister but that she went to California for schooling." Johnny's mind raced. Was it California or Florida? He'd only heard the story once and remembered it being a warm state.

"No, not California … but yes, schooling. I went to a foster family down in Florida." Lorna squeezed her hands inside her white gloves. "I'm not used to this cold."

Johnny began to feel comfortable with Donny's sister. *She's vulnerable, at least to the cold outside.* "No one's really used to the New York winters."

"I guess not." Lorna went the end of her story, skipping the gory chapters. "I could go into detail about what I went through at home, but that doesn't make much of a difference now. Believe it or not, after I was taken away, my mother slowed down some … until she chose not to or couldn't control the beast inside."

Johnny sat silently and began to think of Angela. *I'm late. It's surely past seven now. I gotta get out of here. Lorna, please, I gotta go!*

Lorna saw the angst on her spectator's face. "Only another minute, please."

"It's okay," Johnny politely lied.

"When I heard about Donny's situation back in October, I selfishly stayed in school. What could I have done? She had done it … not me." Lorna went into her pocketbook a second time for a cigarette, this time lighting it up. "I wanted nothing to do with my past. I'd just gotten into a good college, and I had begun to heal from my past, or at least I thought I had … too many damn demons." Lorna blew smoke out toward the car's roof. "I lied to myself saying Donny would be all right. I'd get him during Christmas break when school was out. Mom would also be out of the picture one way or another by then." Lorna took one last drag and then tossed the butt out of her driver side window. "So I stayed away … I flew in yesterday morning and went straight to the hospital. It was there I found out about my brother's death …" Lorna's eyes began to swell, but no tears fell south.

Johnny did not know if he should hug her or say something, anything, to comfort her. Johnny instead remained silent and motionless.

"The nurses were so sweet and caring. One candy striper was so devastated that she couldn't speak but could only hug me. Three patients were wheeled out of their rooms to give me their condolences. Everyone was distressed … although no one knew my brother, had never met him …" This time Lorna was able to produce eye drops, they spilled down her cheeks. "All in the hospital only knew the life he'd lived through his friends … and Johnny, your name came up the most."

"I … I wasn't the only one. There was everyone else too."

Lorna went back into her pocketbook, to the dismay of Johnny. *Please, not another cigarette.* Johnny watched her push the cigarette box and a second item to the side.

"Ah … here you are." Lorna pulled out a clean, white handkerchief. For the moment, her tears stopped as her spirit rose. "I asked if my brother had had any personal items. I figured the answer would be no, but I was pleasantly surprised." Lorna motioned behind to the back seat. "I don't think Donny actually owned this, but the candy striper swore it was his. I think she wanted me to have something from my brother." Lorna displayed a soft-cover copy of *The Adventures of Tom Sawyer*. "The candy striper said the nurses would take turns reading it to my brother late at night … Funny, in a sad way, it must have been the only time he'd ever heard a bedtime story." Lorna stopped short of crying. She composed herself for a moment and then continued. "Inside Tom Sawyer, there's a picture of all you kids together on this stoop. My brother, like everyone else in the photo, looked so happy … so, so happy." Lorna sighed while the hand holding the snapshot shook. After a few seconds of silence, Lorna finished. "The second object Donny owned, which I believe was the only item, was this." Lorna produced a folded handkerchief from her coat and handed it to a stunned Johnny.

~~~~~~~

Angela mindlessly flipped through the pages of *Tiger Beat Magazine.* She tilted her wrist, peaking at her wristwatch. *Seven thirty exactly. Come on … I gotta be home by eight.* Angela closed the teen mag. She was not thrilled with The Osmonds or The Jackson Five any longer; she only wanted Johnny to show the hell up. *Did he forget me? Or is this how guys are? No … Johnny's different from the others. He has to be.* Angela, in a crumpled posture, moseyed along to the magazine racks at the back end of the candy store, returning pretty-boy David Cassidy to the other bubble gum teen idols. *You all have some life, always smiling, all the fame and women … I bet none of you have ever been stood up …*

"Angela … Angie, baby. Where have you been, sugar?" a male voice bellowed aloud.

Angela awoke from her daydream about the fortunate idols when her name was howled. *Johnny, it's about time. You're lucky I like you so much.* As she moved from the racks, disappointment and then disgust crossed her brow.

"Angie, were you hiding from me back there?" Fagan wiped running snot from his upper lip with his dungaree jacket's torn sleeve. "I was surprised to see anyone here tonight, especially someone as special as you, sugar."

Angela stomped swiftly to the table where she was sitting, retrieving her winter gear. Once she put her hat on, she shoved her gloves inside her coat pocket and went for the front door, slightly knocking into Fagan. "I was leavin' anyway."

With comical exaggeration, Fagan fell back toward the candy counter. "Whoa … baby, why such a hurry?"

"Hey, take your shenanigans outside, mister," the storekeeper demanded. "There will be no roughhousing here."

Fagan put on a charming smile and adopted an agreeable tone. "You're right, no roughhousing. She's a little emotional tonight—and physical as always—that's all." Fagan took two steps toward Angela, blocking her exit path. "Angie, you gotta come back to me. It's not the same without ya, sugar."

Angela zipped her jacket and then positioned her hand on Fagan's chest. "Move ... asshole." With a small nudge, she pushed Fagan toward the lockset of the door.

"Shit ... what the ...!" Just as Fagan's momentum forced him backward, the door began to open, and the metal doorknob vaulted forward, striking Fagan in the kidney. "What's your problem!" Fagan didn't know which person to confront first, Angela on her way out or the shit head on his way in.

The shit head made Fagan's decision an easy one. "Get away from her!" Johnny placed his left hand on Fagan's throat while storing his handkerchief and the treasure it concealed in his pocket with his right hand. Fagan began to hack.

"That's it ... everyone out, or I'm calling the cops." The storekeeper bent behind the register to obtain a weapon of some sort. Angela would not wait to see the defending device.

"Johnny, come on." She grabbed Johnny's left elbow, tugging his hand away from Fagan's neck. "Let go ... let's go."

Johnny slowly released his vice grip of Fagan's neck. "Don't you ever, *ever* go near her." Angela quickly put her hand into Johnny's pocket, touching the folded handkerchief. She forcefully escorted him to the frigid sidewalk.

Fagan coughed twice before barking out to the two retreating foes, "Don't be pissed, Johnny-boy." Fagan walked outside into the cold, wanting Johnny to hear clearly. "Don't be pissed at me 'cause I had sugar first!"

~~~~~~~

Candy striper Nanci sat quietly with Mr. Baden while he ate his chocolate pudding dessert. Ordinarily, Nanci would coddle Mr. Baden with a wealth of attention to the point of annoyance. Not tonight. She was oblivious to all the hospital's activities as well as to its patients. Even the annoying sound of the slapping of Mr. Baden's lips or the plummeting globs of pudding could bring neat freak candy striper Nanci back to reality.

"Nanci ... Nanci with an *i*. Earth to Nanci." Nurse Joan stood beside Nanci's chair. She was still wearing her black mourning dress. "I only came back here tonight to see you ... I may not be back for a while."

"Uh ... oh yeah. You get Christmas off too." Nanci stared forward. She was too numb to focus on her supervisor, although she was curious as to why Nurse Joan needed to see her.

Nurse Joan let the sarcasm go. *We're all hurting here, Nanci dear. Could you give me a break once in a while?* "Please, Nanci, let's have a minute alone."

Candy striper Nanci took a tissue from Mr. Baden's dinner tray and patted his chin clean. "I'll take that." She took his plastic spoon and the empty pudding cup and then tossed both in the plastic garbage can in the corner of the room. "No more smacking of the lips or drooling tonight." Nanci smiled and then added, "I'll be back in a few minutes to beat you in Hearts."

"You're so blunt with me. I might not let you win later." Mr. Baden waved Nanci to move on with Nurse Joan. "I'll be waiting for you."

One minute later, candy striper Nanci and Nurse Joan sat silently in the nurse's locker-room. Nurse Joan decided that it would be best to take a direct approach with her candy striper. "Nanci, you're not suited for this place. You have the heart and the spirit, but working in a hospital anywhere will wear you out. I don't believe it fits your personality to the fullest extent."

What the ...? What did I do now? Why is she always picking on me? Now my personality is in question. You bitch! Candy striper Nanci's jaw tightened. No words could escape. Whatever trance Nanci had been in earlier dissipated and mutated to rage. *Who is she to tell me what I can and cannot do? Bitch!*

"Nanci, why are you getting upset?" Nurse Joan put a hand to Nanci's knee. "Before you talk, before you get pissed, before anything, take a deep breath and listen." Nurse Joan let her pupil have a moment to recoup. *Maybe the direct approach wasn't the best idea after all.* Seeing the redness in Nanci's face diminish, she proceeded. "You have a special gift." Nurse Joan watched Nanci's brow soften. *If I hit a nerve before, I've soothed an ache now.* "I see it ... everyone here see's it in you." Nurse Joan pinched her hair behind her ears; normally her nurse's cap would guide her curls. "When I put you in charge of arranging Donny's room, you did an outstanding job ... and I'm not talking about the Christmas decorations." Nurse Joan reached over the small table and tapped Nanci's arm. "It was the kids. You were there for them when they needed someone. You listened to them, laughed along with them, and most of all, you helped ease their worries. You are a role model for the girls and are well-respected by the boys." Nurse Joan smiled. "I was jealous you had that with them, but I was happy you did too."

Nanci listened while her skin returned to its natural complexion. Once she realized Nurse Joan was done talking for the moment, Nanci asked, "What could I do then? If I did such an outstanding job here, why shouldn't I be a nurse?"

It was the first time Nurse Joan had laughed in almost a week. "Nanci ... Nanci, you could become a nurse if you wanted to. You would be a wonderful RN. I am pointing out that there are other options for someone with your passion. You're a difference maker. You're also a very lovely young lady, and I don't want you to wither working in a hospital." Nurse Joan rubbed her chin before speaking. "Being a caring nurse is golden, and there are many who are. But you ..." Nurse Joan took a deep breath. "I think you would be a wonderful school teacher. You're a natural around those kids. They relate to you because you genuinely care. Please don't take this or anything I have said to you the wrong way. You carry yourself with the authority of an adult but with the spirit of a child." Nurse Joan finished lecturing her student with some final reflections. "Think about it. As those kids believed in you, so do I. You're a difference maker. Whether it's in healthcare or education, you will forever touch lives."

Nurse Joan stood up from her chair and motioned for Nanci to do the same. "If you're not here when I come back from my leave, I'll understand, and if you are, then I'll make you the best nurse this hospital or any other hospital has ever had." As the two hugged Nanci cried into her dear friend's shoulder for the second time in the nurse's retreat.

~~~~~~

"What? ... What's he talkin' about?" Johnny demanded, and he turned about to confront Fagan for a second time.

Angela still clutched the handkerchief inside Johnny's coat pocket, and she yanked him hard enough to pull her defender off balance. "Come on, let's go. I'll explain on the way home."

Johnny wanted nothing more than to be with Angela. As for Fagan and his wise-ass mouth, that would have to wait. After a few curse words slung toward his tormentor, Johnny's focus was on Angela alone.

"I'm sorry I was late." Johnny enjoyed having Angela's hand inside his coat pocket, more so now than the first time three nights before. It was not only the arrival of his third leg, which was always welcome, but the sense of being wanted. *The past few days, she's been by my side—at the hospital, the funeral home, tonight waiting for me to show up. She cares for me, and I missed her. I could no longer be away from ... the scent of her hair, the softness of her touch, the concern in her eyes ... the way my heart pounds when I'm near her ...*

"Johnny, I said, what happened? Why were you late?" The two jaywalked across the street before any oncoming crossing traffic. Once safely on the sidewalk, Angela repeated her last question.

Johnny halted and then turned Angela to face him. Reaching into his unoccupied pocket, Johnny discovered his handkerchief and its encased treasure were missing. Before Johnny could react to the missing Christ-head, Angela put her finger to his lips.

"Shhhh ... easy, Johnny." Angela pulled her warm fist from Johnny's second pocket. "You looking for this?" Angela grinned and then handed the misplaced parcel to Johnny.

"Oh shit ... I thought I lost it. That faggot Fagan threw me off." Johnny grabbed the white cloth a little too aggressively from Angela's palm. "Sorry ... I thought it ..."

"Johnny, it's okay. What's in it?" Angela asked, not having a clue what was hidden inside.

Johnny lightly picked the handkerchief up and let its content fall to his open hand. "Donny's chain. She gave it to me ..."

An eerie feeling swept through Angela. The displaying of Donny's charm reminded her of Nicole and Gina showcasing it to the boys for the first time on Humboldt Street. Angela very lightly dabbed her temple, managing the oncoming dizziness she suddenly experienced.

"Uh … who gave it to you? Candy-Nandy? I mean, Nanci? Or Nurse Joan?" Angela continued to watch the charm dangle in the wind as Johnny held it.

"No, neither one." Johnny rewrapped the chain and charm in its cloth and placed it safely inside his front pants pocket for safer keeping. "Donny's sister Lorna. Candy striper Nanci gave it to her …"

"What are you going to do with it? Will you wear it?" Angela placed her hand back inside Johnny's coat pocket as the two pushed onward to her house. After a minute of walking in silence, she said, "I bet Donny would want you to have it too … and of course wear it."

As the two turned the corner onto Angela's block, Johnny broke his silence. "I wasn't thinking about what to do with it."

Angela gave Johnny a little poke. "Well, were you thinking about making out with me in my hallway, then?" She giggled but spoke sincerely.

Johnny did not answer her question but had one of his own. "What did Fagan mean, he had you first, and why was he calling you *sugar*? And you were gonna explain it to me on the way home."

Angela took a deep breath. She had been hoping to avoid this conversation, if not forever, then at least for tonight. "I made out with him last summer; it was one time only. It was before I started hanging out with Gina and all of the girls and way, way before I knew or had even heard of you." *That's right, Angie-baby, spit it all out at once … Johnny-boy wants the truth. Well, here it is. Don't choke on my vomit!*

Angela's mini confession transpired four stoops away from her own. It was here that Johnny stopped walking and began yelling. "You made out with that piece of shit? I can't believe it. What the hell's the matter with you? You that much of a slut?"

284

Tears welled in Angela's eyes, but her anger took command. "Don't call me a slut!" Angela shrieked. She shook her finger in Johnny's stunned face. "I didn't know you, any of you." Angela put both of her hands inside her own coat pockets, and then said in a lower tone, "I knew it back then and more so now; it was stupid. That was part of the reason I stopped hanging out with Kimba and the others on Sutton Street." She waited for Johnny to respond. When he didn't, Angela finished. "Johnny, I like you a lot. Please don't let this screw things up … please, Johnny." Angela's eyes welled up a second time, and she was unable to control the onslaught of tears.

Johnny stood there and watched the girl he was crazy about beg for him. It felt good, really good, to have power over her or anyone or anything, as his last few days had been filled with a sense of helplessness. Wanting to remain in the position of control, Johnny could only continue the onslaught of similar insults. "Did you enjoy it? If he's so great, go back to him. You're a slut. What else did you do? Who are the other guys?"

When he concluded, Angela could only wipe her red nose and ask, "Are you done?" Angela turned away from Johnny to walk the last few feet to her house alone. Feeling his eyes on her back, Angela walked up her stoop with her head looking ahead. She would be damned if he saw her cry again.

Chapter 22

1978

I am no better, and neither are you.
We are the same, whatever we do.
You love me, you hate me, you know me, and then
You can't figure out the bag I'm in.
—"Everyday People"
performed by Sly and the Family Stone

Everything will be all right. The two are together again. Everything and everyone will fall into place now. From across the railcar, Shanty watched his two closest friends quietly chat. *Johnny's smiling. Bain is laughing. Everything goes to shit when the top starts to crumble.* Shanty braced himself as the train bucked to a halt. It had arrived in its last Manhattan subway station. *Next stop will be in Brooklyn. Then we're only two stops from home.* Shanty smiled and closed his bloodshot eyes for temporary relief. *Johnny, no more recklessness. We've already lost Donny ... tonight Porky. Man if something ever happened to you ...* Shanty, for the first time all night, began to relax as the heat of the subway car seat soothed his worn bones. A sudden jolt from the train's engines thrust Shanty to the side bar of his bench. Adjusting his hip, Shanty let sleep momentarily take him over. *No need to be on guard all the time. Bain and Johnny are right here, some three feet away ...*

Bump!

"I want to fight you man." Standing in front of an awakening Shanty was an apparently homeless man. The vagrant bent forward to place the shopping bags he held in both hands on the tile floor. The two bags contained some clothing, a dirty blanket, and a rusty, red plumber's wrench. The vagrant took a step closer to Shanty, crowding any escape attempt.

Looking straight up, Shanty guessed the thug must be at least six five and over three hundred pounds, and he had eyes of desperation. The vagrant's blank demeanor was his most threatening attribute. "I ... I." Shanty's throat became dry. He tried to swallow, but no phlegm could be produced, so he began to cough.

Bain watched the calamity progress and calmly waited to strike the invader. He would stay in the shadows for now. Before Johnny could pounce on the vagrant, Bain whispered. "Wait ..." Bain knew he could take the vagrant with a surprise attack. He was fortunate enough. Having Johnny along as well as a skittish Shanty could only help. It was the tight arena inside the subway car and the uncertainties about what exactly was in those two damned bags that bothered Bain.

"Me?" Shanty had to stretch from his seat to peek around the vagrant's large waist. He searched for Bain, Johnny, or anyone else for help. *Why does this guy want to fight me? He's crazy.* Shanty was able to stake out Bain.

"Look at me when I talk," demanded the vagrant. He then kicked Shanty's shin.

"Whoa ..." The stinging sensation quickly traveled upward from Shanty's leg and embedded itself inside his right temple. *It's sorta like acupuncture. Put pressure on one part of the body for relief somewhere else ... except somehow I'm missing the relief part.* With or without his two allies, Shanty was no longer going to take this shit sitting down.

"Let's go!" Shanty shot upright from his seat, staring upward into the vagrant's nostrils. *He smells of piss ... no, no, a blend of piss and shit.* The vagrant pushed Shanty's chest with his own, daring his intended victim to take the first shot.

"Hey, guys … how 'bout you two take it off the train," Bain shouted out before any punches were thrown. He reasoned that the first Brooklyn station, Bedford Avenue, had a spacious and open platform, so he would have time to maneuver without surprises.

The vagrant turned around to protest as the train jammed on its breaks. The usual screeching echoed throughout the subway car, and the train jolted to a stop. Shanty seized the opportunity when he followed Bain's eyes. He hollered for the vagrant to follow him out the exit doors.

"Don't you yell at me, spic." The vagrant hastily lifted his two bags and steered behind his intended target.

Shanty let the slur hang in the air as he stopped adjacent to Johnny.

To the vagrant, Bain and Johnny were just bystanders. *Most likely two faggots going to a fag Christmas party.* He didn't figure they were coconspirators of "the spic."

"There you go …" Shanty politely put his hand out the doorway, allowing the vagrant first access to the Bedford Avenue platform. "I thought you'd never leave." Shanty's attempt at a joke did not impress the growling vagrant. About to accompany the vagrant out to the arena, Shanty's elbow was lightly pulled backward by Johnny. Bain stepped in front, and he and Johnny grinned. Shanty asked, "You guys are coming … right?"

"No, but you ain't neither," Johnny whispered.

With an aggressive tug, Johnny yanked Shanty by his collar away from the doorway and to the center of the subway car. "You even have to ask if we got your back?" Shanty stumbled and fell into his original seat. He bounced back up quickly to join his liberators by the doorway.

The vagrant dropped his two bags on the concrete platform and then reached inside one for his rusty, red plumbers wrench. *This needs some spic blood on it.* He handled the cold wrench, twisting the tool inside his palm. *Come on, I'm ready.* "What the ...!" When the vagrant looked up, the electronic subway doors were closing. The spic was nowhere to be found, and the two faggots stood in the doorway together, laughing. *The spic is still in the train. He tricked me!* "Get out here! I'll kill you all!" The train began its slow exit from Bedford Avenue to the next station. The vagrant charged the doors but could do little else to keep pace with the increasing speed of the train. He did hit the moving metal, leaving a few dents, but he could not reach the glass of the closed doors in time. His fury only grew with the last image he carried into the dark and freezing streets of Brooklyn: *the two fags flipping me the bird!*

~~~~~~

Oh shit, my poor puppies. Kimba kicked off her red boots into the pile of shoes and children's sneakers outside her apartment door. *Damn it! I hope I didn't wake anyone up.* Kimba unlocked the front door and tiptoed her frozen and blistered feet on the linoleum kitchen floor. The nightlight between the two back windows glowed with a yellowish-gray light, casting mystifying shadows around the kitchen table and its five chairs, which Kimba presumed empty.

Kimba softly strolled across the room to the refrigerator for a glass of milk when a ghostly presence shook the young girl's confidence. "Ma? Shit, you scared the hell outta me." As her sight adjusted to the darkness of the room, Kimba could easily see the silhouette of her mother sitting at the darkest corner of the kitchen table. "What are you still doin' up?"

"Get what you want from the fridge and sit down. I want to talk to you." Her mother rose to turn the kitchen light on. "Be quiet. The twins are asleep. They had a long day, but you never know what would wake them." Mother sat back in her chair and waited for Kimba to pour off a few ounces of milk.

Kimba sat across from her mother and asked. "Where's daddy?" Kimba was told her dad had remained at the club cleaning up after the children's Christmas party and should be home shortly.

"I know we haven't been too close this past year ..." Before Kimba could protest, her mother put her hand up to quiet her daughter. "Please ... I'm to blame too. Once you lied to me and your father, we had—I should say, I had—a very difficult time believing you on any subject." Kimba brushed her long blonde hair off her cheeks, tying it into a sloppy bun. "It was never that way when you were younger. Somewhere along the line, not too long ago, our relationship deteriorated." Her mother rubbed her forehead and continued. "I have been meaning to say this for a while now. How 'bout we both try."

"Mom, there's no excuse for me lying to you or Dad, but I mostly did it because I didn't want you two to be disappointed in me. I wouldn't say I was protecting you two, but ... I didn't want you to be ashamed of where I was at in my life."

Her mother smiled. "See, my Kimmie, this is the first time we are actually talking." Kimba agreed. "I think we should try it this way." Kimba listened to her mother's proposition. "Always tell us the truth, always. But if it is not our business or if you feel uncomfortable with the subject at a given moment, then say so." Her mother wiped her eye. Kimba was unsure if it was a tear forming. "I miss my daughter ... I want us to grow old as friends."

Kimba nearly knocked over her glass of milk as she bolted around the table to hug her mother. "Oh, Mom ... it was so bad tonight. Everything felt wrong, was wrong. I finally realized Junior and his crowd just ain't for me." Kimba sobbed into the nape of her mother's neck and went on. "They are all so miserable. There's nothing good, and I sank to their level too many times ..."

"Baby, baby, you are only a child." She let go of her daughter, pointing for Kimba to sit back in her seat and drink additional milk. "If you're telling me you and Junior are broken up, I say good. I won't bash him; there's no need to. You know now what kind of guy he is." Kimba finished her milk, leaving a white mustache below her red nose. "You'll know when the right man comes along, I know it's a cliché, but it is true."

Kimba relaxed. It was a great relief to open up to her mom. *It's so easy when speaking the truth!* "How did you know Daddy was the one?"

Her mother laughed and then explained, "Your father was and still is so handsome, but he thought he was king shit back then. All the girls wanted him, and his friends all looked up to him. But he was a nice guy. He had a swagger about himself."

Kimba leaned over the table to gossip along with Mom. "He was full of himself?"

Her mother grinned. "Yeah, something like that." The two girls laughed together.

When the laughing ended, Kimba had more questions. "How did you get him?" Kimba corrected herself. "Not that you weren't a catch."

Mother waved her off as if it were no big deal. "I was myself. I wouldn't chase after him. In time, I became intriguing, a puzzle to him, and most importantly, something special. He knew that if we were going to be together, he'd have to treat me a certain way, and of course, he'd receive the same from me. I took care of myself and never let any outside dirt invade my brand."

"Wow, your brand ... I like that. Sorta like McDonald's."

"Yeah, I should have McDonald's stock." Kimba's mother smiled. "But don't think everything goes as planned, because life in general doesn't work that way."

Kimba agreed. "But what was—is—your secret?"

"Once you find your man and the two of you are surely in love, you'll know, because you'll find each other attractive like no other. You will do for him first, and he will treat you the same way. You'll cover each other's backs. He'll have a great sense of humor, and you'll want to be with him always. His feelings, good and bad, will guide your own. But most the most important thing for a lasting relationship, one that ends up in a happy marriage"—her mother reached over the table and held her daughter's wrist—"compromise. It's a two-way street. Don't be stubborn just to win. Winning a football game is great, but in beating your partner in life, well, there is no winner."

Kimba waited for her mother to go on, but she kept silent. "Ma, what was your biggest compromise?"

Her mother expected the question, and she was ready with her reply. "I can't go into details now; daddy will be home any minute, and tomorrow's Christmas Eve. But remember this: any relationship has its tug of war. The guy wants his girl to stay the same as when he met her, and the girl wants to change her man into something that he's not."

"Wow, Ma, I guess you won with Daddy?"

Her mother had a twinkle in her eyes. "We compromised. I stayed true to myself as best as I could. I had to grow up." She grinned. "As for Daddy, he hit his potential with my help." The two laughed one last time. "Now, come on. You better get to bed. Your brothers got a foam basketball with a netted basket, which is now hanging in the living room. They played with it tonight for a bit and protested when they were sent to bed, so I'm sure a ball game between the two will start very early in the morning."

Kimba agreed. "Mom, thanks. Thanks for everything."

"Thanks? Thanks for what?" Her mother knew the answer but wanted to hear it from her daughter's mouth.

Kimba hugged her mother one last time before retreating to her bedroom. "For being my friend." Without another word, Kimba let go of her mother and walked to bed with her second thought of him tonight. *I got your back. One more chance, please ... I'll compromise.*

～～～～～～～

"Terry?" Johnny adjusted the covers so his sister could stay warm for the night. Johnny went to his window and lowered the sash closer to the sill without closing it completely. *She loves the cold and the fresh smell of snow.* Johnny quietly sauntered out of his room to observe Terry's self-portrait. The charcoal markings appeared complete. *Terry figured out how to depict her smile.* Johnny put a hand on either side of the canvas, starring into his sister's sketched eyes. *They have a slight squint ... yes, she softened them a bit.* Johnny cocked his head slightly but kept his focus on the drawing. *Her lips have a modest grin. Very modest ... matching her eyes ...*

"Johnny ... you home?" Terry stood in Johnny's doorway with her arms folded over one another. "What happened tonight? I was so afraid something had happened to you."

Johnny would tell Terry about his mini breakdown, but first he had to remark on her self-portrait. For the next few minutes, Terry explained how she'd figured the panorama of her smile and eyes. *They go together as one.* She was proud of her likeness but for the moment needed information on her brother's well-being.

"When I got up this morning, I felt nothing. It's happened to me before but never as bad. Today I only saw blackness." Johnny rested on the foot of his bed as Terry lay horizontally across the uncovered mattress, relaxing her head on his pillow. "It seemed like everything in my life meant nothing."

"I know what tomorrow is for you all, but is that it?" Terry questioned her brother's despair. "Is it Angela too? You're not over her?"

"There's more to it than being over her." Johnny wanted to tell Terry the painful secret he shared with Angela but couldn't. Johnny never wanted his sister to think less of him, so he held back the one detail that had led to their separation. "We thought we'd always be together, but ... it didn't work out that way." Johnny switched the subject away from Angela. "It wasn't only Angie or tomorrow or any one thing. I guess I was screwed up from everything. Terry, it's been in me for a long time."

Terry watched the lights cast on Johnny's walls by the Christmas lights in the window. From where she lay, her brother's childhood plastic models were out of view, but she was conscious of their watchful eyes. "What do you mean 'was'?"

Johnny sat on his bed beside Terry's curled body and leaned back onto his elbows. "When I went out tonight, I needed to clear my head. I couldn't see anything. So, like a dumb ass, I got a bottle of liquor and started to drink before going to the church. I needed something to get me into a confessional booth. When that didn't do it for me, I got pissed and left Donny's chain in the manger outside the church."

"You just threw it there?" Terry wondered.

"No, I placed the Christ-head around the Baby's neck." Johnny took a moment to gather his thoughts on the next sequence of the night. "For some reason, I took the skipping stone with me. I must've known all night I would end up there."

"Central Park?"

Johnny grunted yes.

"But what's the stone have to do with anything?"

"Nothing really. It was a reminder … of when we were all together. I remember that morning so clearly—the leaves twirling on the sidewalk, the football game, the girls bringing the charm to Tommy's stoop, going to Manhattan, Central Park, Donny taking off his shirt and showing us his purple bite marks … We were kids for the last time that afternoon."

"So the rock was your hold on the past?"

Johnny inhaled. "I wanted to sink it to the bottom of the pond. I wanted to, needed to go with it, or so I foolishly thought." Johnny could feel Terry shudder. He understood it was not from the cold. "Something as small as the rock helped me realize it was not always going to be about me."

"How so?"

"When I got to the pond, I thought of the river rocks we'd all thrown into it that day. I thought of myself as being the same as a rock, hitting the water. The splash would be me and my end, but the never-ending circular ripples throughout the pond would define my reaction. Did I want to be cried for, felt sorry for, thought of as one who could not adjust? Many of those ripples would be of tears, but many others would be of disappointment and people wondering why I gave up. 'What? Johnny has no fight in him? He did at one time. He's a quitter now, always was.' And so on. I decided that in the end, it takes more balls to live at times than not to."

Terry waited for Johnny's silence. "How do you feel right now?"

"That not knowing what's going to happen tomorrow and the next is more important than all of my screw-ups in the past. I had to let go."

"Are you sure?"

Johnny laughed. "The rock will be on the bottom of that pond this spring, once the ice melts. But the Christ-head I'll keep forever."

"You got it back tonight?" a sleepy Terry marveled.

Johnny pulled his collar down four inches, exposing the charm. "Bain got it back. Actually, I have to thank all my friends—and you—for everything."

"I'm glad. You should have never have given it up." Terry paused for a few seconds. "Johnny, I'm so tired. I'm gonna close my eyes for just two minutes, and then I'll go to my room. Oh, one last thing …"

"Yeah."

"If you're giving up on God or life itself, please give the medal to me. I'll know you're lost, and I'll surely help you back home …" Terry began to snore lightly.

Johnny responded in a painful moan. "Yes, Terry, destiny not details." Then he thought of his son's earlier warning. *Life has a way of equaling the score, Johnny-boy.*

Johnny eased himself off his bed quietly, not wanting to wake his sleeping sister. He elbowed Terry to the center of the mattress and then, with great care, covered her with two blankets. He spun around to his dresser's bottom drawer and removed his sleeping bag. *My floor will do. Don't want or need to pass through Dad and Mom's room to get to Terry's. It's after midnight. Let everybody sleep in peace.*

When Johnny returned from the bathroom, he checked on Terry one last time before hitting the ground. He looked at his little sister's sleeping face. *Her lips don't smile or frown … They rarely do.* Johnny thought of Terry's portrait. *She really nailed it, those details. Someday Terry will surely be a difference maker.* Johnny bent over to kiss his sister's forehead goodnight, a rare but recurrent happening. When Johnny backed off of Terry's brow, a morbid feeling that he was kissing his sister good-bye struck. *Life has a way of equaling the score … Johnny-boy.*

Johnny lay down on his sleeping bag and closed his eyes, thinking of Terry's brow. Sleep arrives suddenly as Terry's future is featured by the devil himself. *Was this just a nightmarish premonition?* Johnny shivered where he lay, for he must survive the upcoming grief beyond imagination. There would be no chance to guard against the carnage of "equaling the score … Johnny-boy," as his son had warned, for if he could …

~~~~~~~~~

Johnny inspected the mural. *Nothing had changed in twelve years.* The yellow sands of Jerusalem were still clear of blood, and the body was still wrapped in white sheets. *Oh, the details … now my destiny.*

Johnny peered down. *Not a smile or a frown.* "It's all in the eyes, big brother." *Yes, Sis, they go together. Those details again, just like The Wolfman's muddy boot or the sheep drinking from the water … the mirror, that is.*

I experienced this somewhere in my past, your end. I already know the details. It was way back when, the night I came home late on Christmas from Central Park. No, it wasn't Christmas yet, but it was a day or two away … It don't matter now, but I did see your end. I felt it that night. You were sleeping in my bed, not a smile or a frown …

Terry, how did we get here? I know we are here, but how? The night I held you until you fell off to sleep … I slept on the floor in my sleeping bag. Then I … I reconnected with an old girlfriend with your help. Terry, you graduated grammar school that spring. I fought alongside you against Dad and Mom when you were determined to attend the High School of Arts and Design. Yes, that was a big battle, but we won together. I knew it was the academy for you, Sis.

You traveled to Manhattan every day by subway to get to school. You had to commute alone, but you weren't afraid. You followed my directions— always travel in the conductor's car; be aware of your surroundings; and never stand near the edge of the platform.

Four years later, Terry, you graduated Cum Laude but were upset at missing Summa. Immediately after tossing your cap and gown, you were hired by a fashion design firm located three blocks from your old high school. You still must be careful, Terry. I warned you, the rules never change underground … You loved your job and were promoted after one year to be assistant to the assistant lead designer. You laughed out loud at how silly corporate America was, but you remained driven with desire.

You dated a few losers. Hey, no one's as good as me. Ha-ha, only teasing. They had no passion, you told me … no passion.

You volunteered at the hospital, teaching art to AIDS children. So few touch them, you said, and fewer love them. You taught the dying children the wonders of art while they taught you the art of love. You were never happier until …

On your twentieth birthday, borrowing my wife's car, you took my three-year-old son, Johnny-boy, to Coney Island Beach. Johnny-boy marveled at the gigantic hole in the sand you two dug and delighted in jumping waves with his aunt all afternoon. You treated him to a Nathan's hot dog and fries and spoiled him with ice cream. Afterward, you two squeezed into the single-seat bumper car and did a lot of damage to other joy riders, as your competitive nature had been released. When my son called out to you for a second ride, a previous bumper car victim of yours approached you for mercy this time around. A second round of smashing cars led to additional ice cream, but this time with the mercy-seeking victim. Three years later, your bumper car boyfriend, before asking our Dad, wanted my blessing to marry you. I would never have guessed, Terry, you marrying a grease monkey, but he made you happy. He was a hard worker and promised to save enough money to buy his own garage. He would take care of my sister, he promised. I believed in him.

At this time, Terry, you were a couple of months into your twenty-third year. Time was flying by. You'd ask me, "When will my man ask me to marry him?" And I'd reply, "Soon enough, Sis. I'm sure he wants to get his plans together." Terry, if you'd had time to complain, you would have, but there was so much to do—with so little time left …

Johnny felt a soft hand gently rub his damp back. "Baby, I'm here for you."

"Yes … I know."

The number twenty-three will forever have a sentimental meaning, and July 7 will be a day removed from all others.

Following work on that hot evening, Terry, you ran to your art students in the hospital. You put those children ahead of everyone else. You'd say they were your babies. Terry, you were sweaty from the jog, and the ninety-plus-degree heat and high humidity gave you a major headache too. When you finally settled in, the air conditioning inside the hospital relieved your migraine for the time being. After illustrating a reflection pool and reading Go Dog Go, you took your four babies to the night supervisor inside the nursery. You were all set to go home when you noticed a newly posted request tacked to the bulletin board: "Blood Shortage. Donate Today and Save a Life Tomorrow."

Fifty minutes later, minus a pint of blood, you were swamped by the city's nighttime humidity as you exited the hospital's cool lobby. Your headache returned with a vengeance, leaving you nauseated. Midway through your five-block walk to the subway, you heaved up orange juice and two cookies. The nourishments provided for donating blood were splattered between two parked cars now. Once you entered the subway station, to your delight and surprise, your train was sitting with its doors open. It was almost nine, but you no longer cared. The train's air conditioning blasted a cold, steady breeze into your face. You always liked the cold ... You would always sleep with your bedroom window open, even on the coldest nights. Terry, you then closed your eyes and let the headache evaporate. My voice spoke somewhere deep inside your head the three safeguards of riding the subway. "One, don't let your guard down; two, make sure you sit in the conductor's car; and ..."

A crackling voice aired on the loud speaker, waking you from a short doze. "Everyone off. This train is outta service. Another train will arrive shortly." You opened your eyes and let out a rare curse. It had been a long night. Stepping back onto the sweltering platform, you used one of the many metal beams at the edge of the platform for support. "The next train will be here any second. No need to walk too far away. Besides it's way too hot," you reasoned.

The screeching sound of the oncoming train was no different from the screeching sounds you hear from inside of one. You wrongly thought you were sitting, resting, and then sleeping on the train. Terry ... wakeup! Wakeup ... please, fall backward. It's okay, but you gotta fall back, not forward ... Terry!

Your blue eyes rolled vertically, reaching your brow, or at least it felt like they did. Your last thoughts were of playing with and teaching my two sons, reading Dr. Seuss to your babies in the hospital, your man's smiling face, your upcoming wedding, having your own children, your self-portrait, the sheep drinking from the mirror, me teaching you, and those damn details, Terry, always the details. Oh yeah, number three, Sis. You remember number three, right? Don't stand at the end of the platform. Terry, life has a way of equaling the score, ya know?

"Johnny, please …" his wife pleaded with him through her tears.

Johnny wondered why God spared Terry's face. *Surely she was twisted in many different directions as the sound metal on bone screeched throughout her crumbled body. But why not a scratch on her face? Did He deliberately want me to reminisce about the night long ago? Was this God's way of mercy?* Having no answers, Johnny removed Donny's Christ-head from around his neck and gently placed it on the silk blanket covering Terry's mangled body. "Here, you once said to let you have it if I was ever lost. You'd find me and bring me back home. Here, Terry, I am lost."

"Daddy, I'm scared … you're crying." Johnny's eldest son placed his small hand inside of his father's. "Mommy's not talkin'. Please, Daddy, we need you …"

"Yes, son, I'm right here … I always will be." Johnny's face was full of sorrow, but he was able to give his distressed son an encouraging smile. Johnny held Donny's medal inside his warm palm while he stared down at Terry. She was not frowning or smiling. He bent down and kissed his beloved sister's cold forehead. "Here Terry …I am lost, I need your help…" Johnny found his way back to his wife and infant son while he held his oldest son's hand, leaving the Christ-head with his dead sister.

~~~~~~~

The instant Johnny was struck by his frightful premonition, Tommy was drinking a beer in Tori's apartment while disputing Shanty's claim of courage. "So, you're telling us that you, you were gonna fight this giant mugger?" Shanty nodded yes and smiled. "Bain … come on, Bain. What really happened?"

Bain, a bit drunk and extremely tired, mumbled yes to Shanty's story. Lying on Tori's thin living room carpet, Bain had had enough to get cozy, but Tommy's ball-breaking inquisition of Shanty fueled his discomfort. "Tommy, it happened just like he said. You can ask Johnny tomorrow. Now leave me be." Bain turned to his side as he tried to tune out the senseless conversation.

"See, I told ya." Shanty proudly sat back in the cushioned chair and then asked Joey what the heck had happened to his blackened eye.

Kevin rested his cheek across Gina's lap while she twirled her polished finger nails through his matted hair. He quickly stopped the massage therapy to sit up, interrupting any response from Joey. "Faggy Fagan sucker-punched me. Joey jumped in and took the second jap shot."

Angela sat beside Tommy with her leg dangling over his thigh. "What's that?" She pulled at his collar, exposing a long contusion toward his shoulder.

Nicole and Tori were chilling at the adjoining kitchen table. Nicole spoke out, "What happened?"

Bain remained on the rug and listened to Kevin, Joey, and mostly Tommy recount their footsteps in search of Johnny: Kev having that bag on his head all night, getting beer, climbing the frozen picketed fence, Dylan tossing the hammer and all shit breaking out, cops and dogs chasing them over the fence, Madd Tuffs helping, Tommy pissing them off afterward, the walk, the bar, the bartender, Joey's bad limb and purple eye socket, Kevin's ribs, the cold, the phone call saying Johnny was okay, the pizza delivery, and then home.

"And I thought *we* had a long night," Shanty wondered out loud.

Bain rolled away from the couch, nearly crushing Bella. A scared cry screeched through the room as Bella ran over to Tori. Bain laughed but apologized to Tori and her mutt. Bain then corrected Shanty, and reflected on their own journey: the Christmas crowds of Manhattan, the search of Central Park two different times, the refugee not letting

Shanty use the bathroom, plucking the bastard with an exploding beer can, finding Johnny … the doubt they actually would, the train ride home with the crazy homeless man, watching the vagrant charge the moving train, and finally parting ways with Johnny.

"So you really think he'll show up tomorrow?" doubted Nicole, adding her two cents. "What the hell was his problem anyway? He made everybody crazy tonight, and that was after Porky got his head crushed …"

Bain sat up to lean against the couch. "He's coming tomorrow. His problem … it's worked out now. He'd reached into the past … hopefully for the last time."

Nicole had her suspicions. "I don't know what that means, but we ain't doin' this again for him." Tori agreed.

Before Bain could respond, Tommy barged in. "Nic, Tori, what did you do all night? Answer the damn phones? We did it all … and none of us are complaining." Tommy felt Angela's reassuring hand squeeze his own.

"Nobody's saying you guys didn't do it all tonight. Only, Johnny better grow up quick, because time moves on with or without him." Nicole remained defiant and kept the blame on Johnny.

Gina was tired of the whole conversation. It was late, and they all needed to move on from Johnny. She patted her lap for Kevin to station his head there. An exhausted Kevin, without saying a word, obliged. "One thing is for sure," Gina shifted gears, "Donny and Porky are together for Christmas."

"They were the closest," interjected Joey.

Tori dimmed the lights in both rooms. Everyone was tired; it would be best to ease all into the night's sleep. The only brilliance came from the

Christmas tree in the kitchen corner. "Is everybody good?" she asked all. "Gina, Nic, and Angie, you can sleep in my room whenever you're ready. You guys can crash wherever." Everyone agreed.

Then Nicole questioned Gina's previous statement. "How do you know they are together … Donny and Porky? You don't."

"Why wouldn't they be?" Gina tried to explain but had no words for the defiant Nicole, although Bain did.

"Shanty … all of the guys were there. Remember the summer camp? We went away for that week." The boys all nodded or muttered yes. "We snuck out the one night and took the row boats out into the middle of the lake to watch the stars … and get high." The guys laughed as Bain continued. "Johnny, me, and Shanty had one boat to ourselves. You guys were in two different ones. Right before the sun came up, you could see the outlines of the trees and the mountain tops. It was awesome." Bain was quiet for a second as the others reflected. "Shant, you were sleeping, and the other two boats drifted toward the shoreline. That's when Johnny told me about the dream he'd had the night Donny died."

Johnny was crying when I woke him, Angela thought. *He was lost way back then. What did he tell Bain? I never told anybody I was there. Did Johnny?* She saw Bain glimpse her way, and Angela was relieved to realize that her visiting and saving Johnny would remain private.

"Johnny dreamed he was in heaven. All of the guys were there. He described for me as best he could what was in it. Johnny said he saw colors there that were unknown to him, but that wasn't the only crazy thing going on."

"Sounds like he was on pretty good shit," a skeptical Nicole shot out.

Bain gave her the stink eye before continuing with his story. "Joey, you didn't have your limp anymore. You could run with ease and speed.

Donny was tanned. Johnny was sure underneath his clothing there would be no black and blue or teeth marks neither."

"Man, I can't hardly remember anything with my dreams," Shanty added.

"That's just it, Johnny went on about his in great detail." Bain grinned. "The scent in the air, the landscape, which was so defined …"

"What were we all doing in the dream?" Joey demanded.

"We were playing ball, of course … but Johnny was worried about our time running out. Not the time left in the game but of us all being there together. One by one we vanished until he was left alone with Donny."

Tori chimed in, "Where was Johnny when he dreamed this again?" When she was told of Johnny's bedside snooze in Donny's hospital room, Tori agreed. "I believe it. I really do believe Johnny was someplace—heaven, hell, purgatory—with Donny."

Bain bummed a cigarette off of Tommy and ended with "It doesn't matter if Johnny was anyplace with Donny. It only matters that Johnny believed he was … and all this whole while, he's reckoned he'd be with him again."

Chapter 23

1973

And his mama cries, 'cause if there's one thing that
she don't need is another hungry,
mouth to feed, in the ghetto…
—"In the Ghetto" performed by Elvis Presley

"Mommy, your belly … they are going at it big time." Kimba wondered if those two would kill each other in there.

Mom closed her coat over the small mountain forming from her midsection. "Shhhhh, it's about to start." Mom tapped her daughter's thigh, reassuring Kimba all would be well. "The two can't wait to get out and be with their big sister, that's all, dear."

"Yes, Mommy." Kimba sat back in the pew and waited for her first funeral to begin. Sitting in the rear of the church, Kimba spied on all of Donny's friends up front. The girls knelt alongside what appeared to be a married couple and three other ladies. The boys placed themselves on the opposite side of the altar, closest to the organ. No adult accompanied them.

Kimba wondered why the boys and girls just didn't sit altogether. *If I had the best seats in the house, I would have made sure to be situated next to Johnny or at least Bain.* Kimba pulled a few tissues out of her white pocketbook and wiped the moisture snowballing in the corners of her eyes. *It's hot in here, and that incense stinks.* She placed the damp tissues inside her coat pocket for easier access if needed again. *No reason for me to cry; I didn't know the kid.*

Kimba studied the group her best friend had run off to. *Angie … why did you leave our block and start hanging out with Gina and them? Spooky Tori? Big-mouth Nicole? I'm a better best friend than that fat ass Gina … I surely am. What about the guys? Bain and Johnny are okay I guess, but what about that Cuban? Or Bain's crazy brother? Or the limply boy with a hooker mom? What about Tommy? He's the biggest big mouth out of anyone. Last but not least, you were there a week, and Donny gets beaten to death … Angela, it's not the same without you. We miss you. I miss you.* Kimba's mother nudged her to stand up; the mass was about to begin. The short casket was carried by four pallbearers. They gently placed the coffin onto a long, wheeled table. *What's so good about them?*

Johnny insisted the boys situate themselves on the opposite side from where the girls grieved. "It'll make the church look more crowded," he'd fibbed to Bain when they entered the church. The white lie meant very little to Johnny on this morning. For the moment, it was all about Donny. *Later … is for Angela.*

Throughout the thirty-minute mass, Johnny's memories of Donny revolved about Central Park. *How could that perfect day end so badly? What and when was the turning point? Because I didn't want to run away with all of them? Donny's new red sweatshirt? How 'bout Donny getting home late? The girls kept him out even longer to say good-byes. They couldn't know not too, but we did. What about Lorna? She left him with that monster of a mom.* Father Jerry drew Johnny's attention back to the service when he spoke of Donny's favorite things to do, like playing ball with his friends in the park. *Stop right now, Father. There is nothing else.* Father Jerry went on about Donny being a good pupil and how he loved to read. *Bullshit, Jerry. You don't know shit about him. You almost had me believing you for a sec.* Father Jerry went into the mysteries of God and how tragedies cannot always be explained. *On and on. Thanks for nothing.*

Johnny peeked across the aisle when the mourners united together to stand. *There she is. I see the twinkle in her gaze. She's hurting too—for Donny, yes, but there's more. Angela ... look my way! I'm sorry! Just look here for a second.* With no luck catching the eye of his wounded ex, Johnny started to peer forward. He sensed a separate pair of eyes welcoming him. As he looked all around for the first time, Johnny actually saw how empty the church as a whole was. Johnny surveyed the other pews, all deserted with one exception. In the lone, inhabited pew sat a pregnant lady with what appeared to be her daughter. The mother and daughter both had red coats, long blonde hair, and smooth, white faces. *Must be Polish ... The girl looks so familiar. Who is she? And why is she leering at me?*

Once the coffin was placed in the hearse, Nicole and the other girls joined the boy crowd. They were all standing adjacent to the wooden outdoor nativity display. Noticing the wear on the timber, Johnny guessed all was not well in Bethlehem.

Candy striper Nanci separated from Nurse Joan and her husband to walk over to the group of anxious children. She carefully stepped down the church's stone stairway in her newly purchased high-heeled shoes. Nanci's complexion had a rosy color to it. Her eyes were AWOL, thanks to facial swelling, but her smile had survived. "Everyone in the police ... truck." Nanci didn't know the correct name for the 1960s wagon, only the stereotypical tag.

Kevin immediately cried out, "The paddy wagon is here!" His impersonation of an Irish police officer followed. "Okay, Clancey, take the boys and surround the house. All wight, wabbit, where's Rocky. Where is he hiding." Kevin went into his Bugs Bunny voice. "Not in the stove ..."

With a slight giggle, Bain grabbed his brother's neck and pushed him forward into the waiting van with a word of advice. "Enough."

The boys rowdily followed Kevin into the vehicle, leaving the girls and Nanci like second-class citizens out in the cold. Nicole protested loudly about their rudeness. "Where are the gentlemen? What happened to ladies first?"

"What ladies?" Tommy heckled to the laughter of his friends.

"STP. STP, everyone," Gina yelled before sitting between Angela and Tori.

Nanci had heard those three letters in the hospital before, usually when one of the boys got out of hand with his mouth. *The guys have no clue what that stands for. Shut, the ... P. What does that stand for? Shun the person? Yeah, that's sounds about right ... but I'm sure it's not. Nothing in life is figured out so easily ...*

The two wooden benches were placed along the sides facing one another. The boys sat on one side opposite the girls, and Nurse Joan sat shotgun besides her husband, who drove the paddy wagon. Porky guessed many drunks, hippies, rioters, and protesters had filled this van over the years. *Is this the first time one of these is going to a graveyard?* Porky sat at the end of his sex's bench, absorbing the brunt of any bumps from potholes or street snowcaps. He studied the slush on the metal flooring. *Who gets to clean that up? Or is it left for the next group of drunks?*

The ride to the cemetery took a mere five minutes, but the wait inside the wagon continued on. The grave needed to be prepared for the priest's last prayer for the departed. Porky closed his eyes, shutting out the quiet conversation of the girls and the somewhat boisterous sounds of his friends. *Friends? Not really, not anymore. Not without Donny here. Nothing will ever be the same here.* Porky folded his arms, waiting for the damn door to open. *Donny was like me, and not because we didn't have a dad or even know who he could be. Donny didn't need to be loud to be heard. He was who he was. He wasn't fake like Tommy or any of the others.* He wiped the sweat off his brow. The bouncing in the rear along with the tailpipe fumes began to nauseate Porky. *I'm a stranger here. The only attention I get is for being a clown. It's time to move on. Dylan and Hogan live on my block …*

When the engine of the paddy wagon stalled for a moment, Joey took notice of the rear of the vehicle, where Porky was dreaming. "Yo, Pork, you're drooling down your chin. What gives?"

"Nothing. I can't believe where we are," Porky answered. *Or where we are going.*

Angela bit her inner lip. The habit had started when her nail biting days concluded. Painting fingernail stumps was never going to be an option when puberty struck. Angela felt Gina's left hip nudge her to the end of the paddy wagon's bench. *Easy, there's room for everyone!* Angela wiggled her ass a few inches over before standing—or rather, sitting—her ground.

Angela, unlike Porky, was not impressed with the vehicle they all sat in. *It's a car, truck, whatever, that gets you from point A to point B.* Angela wanted—needed—to sneak a peek at Johnny. *He's at the far end of the boy's bench, near the driver. Is he looking at me?* Angela fixed her hair with her gloved hand before wiping her nostrils with her wrist. *No need for boogies … that'd look great. Hi, Johnny, how you been since yesterday? Last I saw you, you were yelling at me and calling me a slut. You know, I cried all night for you. I thought you were different … I'd never felt this way before. I thought you were special … Is this puppy love? First love? Love?* Angela unconsciously rubbed her nose. *Oh, Angie baby, I thought of you all night too. You want me to say I cried too? How could you make out with that dirt bag and expect me to put my tongue in your mouth without thinking of him having been there first? Besides, Angie … you got a big snot hanging from your nose!* Angela took a used tissue from her coat pocket and blew into it. *Nobody's gonna talk down to me, especially you, Johnny-boy! And that's what you are—a boy!* Angela removed her gloves and placed them and the snotty tissue inside her coat pocket.

Bain laughed out loud when Gina barked out the secret meaning of *STP*. *Whatever, G.* Bain wondered how everything would shake out after today. *Donny has really been dead since October. We all knew this day was coming.* Bain wanted to feel sad or at least a bit upset today but could not dig up his misery. *No one here is crying, nor was anyone at the church. And I bet we won't be at the cemetery, either.* Bain unbuttoned his coat, not because of the warmth inside the paddy wagon but because he wanted to feel something—anything—different. He tried to push back the negative thoughts surrounding the death of his friend but was unable. The teasing terrors snickered as they wormed their way throughout his head. *Donny's better off dead. He had no future. Oh yeah, you don't neither, Bain. What are you gonna do, kid? Move furniture for a bottle of booze? Be an unemployed drunk at thirty, like your daddy? Does Kevin have a chance? He's worse than you. What about the other losers in here today? Yeah, Donny's better off dead. Both the beatings and the game are finally over for him … what about you?* Bain hustled his conscience to the limbo zone where it was safe from reality. Silently he waited for the back doors of the paddy wagon to open. *Where's that shovel? I need to find that treasure chest of pain.*

Johnny took a deep breath when the wagon hit a third pothole. *Well, this is it. Sorry, Donny. I can't believe this is it.* Johnny wanted to mourn his friend properly but kept thinking of Angela. *She was crying last night. I made her cry. It doesn't really matter whether she kissed anyone before me; she's with me now—or was with me. I'm just a jealous baby.* Johnny wanted—no, needed—to spy down the paddy wagon's bench at Angela. *I can't. She may be looking at me. Then what? Smile like nothing happened? Something always seems to happen to me. I was a fool last night. She won't forgive me now … maybe in time.* Johnny kicked off the remaining ice from his now ruined Hush Puppies suede shoes and then reconsidered his self-pity. *Stop feeling sorry for yourself. You screwed up last night; you can fix it.*

Scratching beneath his coat, faking an itch, Johnny was able to steal a quick peek at Angela as she stared across at Porky. *She's biting her nail.*

I've never seen her do that before ... Her hair is a mess, there's a dribble leaking from her nose, and her eyes are swollen. She's torn up. Damn, she's beautiful, though ... even now. Johnny leaned forward, looking out the windshield through the metal gate that separated them from the front of the vehicle. He watched them approach the Greenpoint Avenue Bridge. *Two more minutes to the cemetery, and then what? This is the end for Donny, but what about us? Life goes on, but nothing stays the same. What other tragedies are in store for any of us? Is this life, preparing for each damn hurdle on our way to the finish line that delivers death? We all have to race, and we all must finish! What about Angela and me? Is she a hurdle or just the sprint in between each barrier? I shouldn't have been so stubborn with her ... Shit, talk about stubborn, it's my stubbornness about not running off to Bain's uncle's cabin with everyone else that's the reason we are here today in this truck following Donny in his chilled box.* Johnny closed his eyes and reflected on happy days when everyone was together. He was abruptly awoken from a soft nap when Tommy yelled at Porky about releasing the wagon's back doors.

<center>~~~~~~~</center>

Lorna pulled her rental car behind the hearse where her murdered brother lay. She lit a cigarette, her second since leaving the church. *Mother ... your image is now a bottomless, stained well, deepening on forever.* Lorna's hand shook when she pulled down the car's visor. She stared at her face through the visor mirror. *Baggy eyes from never sleeping, my skin can barely cover my bones, I'm losing my hair, and I smoke too much. But mother, I am alert ... you have made me alert. Oh, I'm so much more alert of my surroundings now, and I have only you to thank.* Lorna sat and waited in her car for the priest's vehicle to arrive. *There's no reason to wait outside by my brother's trench and shake some more, is there?* Feeling the relief of the nicotine calming her nervous system, Lorna's subconscious permitted her to momentarily brave the betrayal of her mother. *A drunk soldier is a dead soldier.*

Nothing more than that simple saying stoked the horrors of her lost childhood—not the thought of her mother, or her mother's boyfriend, or the scent of his cologne, or the three shower's a day where she scrubbed her body with a bar of soap until the soap would be no more, or the sudden temper tantrums, or the fear and paranoia, or the lack of sleep accompanied by the usual nightmare players. *None of them would or ever beat me.* Lorna could sidestep any or all of the above, but the one artifact of her past that would crumble her physique at a moment's notice was an uncomplicated quote from her always denying mother: *a drunk soldier is a dead soldier.*

Lorna cracked open her driver side window and shakily flicked her cigarette butt to the snow-covered lawn of the cemetery. *The priest is late. Great, he's late not for his own funeral but for my brother's.* Lorna folded her arms to shield herself and then leaned back into her seat and closed her eyes.

Lorna, sweetheart, RJ's upset because he's out of work now, so that's why all the drinking. And you know dear, if a guy gets drunk enough, he can't walk. He loses his legs. First to go is the middle one. Lorna squeezed herself tighter before going further back into the account to where it started, and it all still hurt just the same. *You know, baby, a drunk soldier is a dead soldier.*

⸏⸏⸏⸏⸏⸏⸏

Ten-year-old Lorna reclined on her bed, coloring inside the black lines of a smiling clown. Lorna did not know why joker's generally spooked little children. Jesters were fun entertainers. The clown grinned, displaying three balloons for any child to take. There's nothing scary about a performer offering a gift. Lorna tossed the magenta crayon to the side of her bed and dug in her box for the orange-red marker. She wanted the clown's lips and remaining hair to be different from his round nose. The balloons would have to be anything but a red hue; Lorna did not want any color, chiefly red, to dominate this picture.

Before continuing on her artwork, Lorna gazed out of her bedroom window. The autumn wind blew rain pellets against the glass, rattling it inside the wooden frame. The grayness outside rivaled her own inner sorrow.

Lorna missed her mother terribly on every other Saturday. Her mom acted a divider between Lorna and mommy's new boyfriend, that creepy RJ. *If he got a job, or at least searched for one while Mom was out, maybe things wouldn't be so disturbing, but he stays home ... alone with me. He stares at me too long, and he has that eerie smile when he drinks. He's so loving to Mom when I'm nearby, but when I'm not ... I hear them fight while in bed. Mom cries. Mom could get better; he's not a good man. He's two-faced, and I don't trust him.*

I keep my distance. I stay in my room. I color clowns as I wait for Mom's security. She's the wall between me and him. That's what Mom's do— protect their young ... from predators.

~~~~~~~

The nicotine snapped Lorna out of her unspeakable flashback. She reached over to the passenger seat where her pack of smokes lay. To her surprise, her hand was steady while she lit her cigarette. She stared forward at the parked limo that carried her half-brother, R J's son. *Donny, thankfully you didn't know your dear old dad, but I did ... and they were the worst two years of my life!*

Lorna glanced up at the gray sky. *It's too cold for rain, but the grayness up above does look like that Saturday morning with RJ.* She took one last drag before squeezing the butt out the almost shut window. *It's not the gray sky or the remains of his dead son ... It's Mommy's denial that did me in. A drunk soldier is a dead soldier.*

Lorna sat back in her car seat and let the nicotine race throughout her body. She was never able or willing to recall the first time. The second, third … all the way to the twentieth were visible and jumbled into one lifetime scar. The initial venture was thankfully a misplaced memory, but the aftershock was as clear as the gray sky above today's funeral.

⸺⸺⸺

Lorna stood over the toilet spattering the morning's Quisp Cereal around the white porcelain. When her stomach held no more breakfast, air with drops of spit followed. She wanted to kneel to lessen the splashing of the toilet water, but her hips and inner thighs refused to participate in her nightmare. A simultaneous jolt of sharp pain electrified Lorna's lower back and both her temples. When she mistook a bloody cocktail of a secretion for diarrhea, Lorna wondered how matters could become worse. And, not to disappoint, it surely did.

Lorna's jaunt to hell became a reality when the devil himself welcomed her to the abyss. "You better clean up, sweetie, before your mother comes home."

⸺⸺⸺

Flurries began to twirl outside of Lorna's car window, reviving her from the tortured past. She wanted another cigarette but decided on a piece of gum instead. *These cancer sticks will surely kill me someday … if my memories don't do it first.* Lorna leaned forward and saw a black limo enter the cemetery and head up the hill toward her brother's loitering funeral party. *About time, Father. My brother would like to be six feet under before Santa comes …* Lorna let the gum refresh her mouth while she closed her eyes to once again pick at the scab of denial and, most hurtful, betrayal.

⸺⸺⸺

Lorna stood in the shower. Although the water's temperature was hot, nearly scalding, she could only cross her naked chest with her bare arms and tremble with chills. Not satisfied with this cleansing method,

Lorna gingerly reached into the soap dish and carefully removed the half-used soap bar. If the bar were to slip from her hand onto the tub's floor, there would be no way she could bend to retrieve it, or worse, survey the remnants of ...

Lorna began with her neck. The smell of him had to go. She washed around her mouth, under her nose, each armpit, her chest, and lower back. She took the soap and lathered it further inside her hands before tenderly disinfecting her two thighs and her sore ass cheeks. That would be as far as she could go; there would be no way to actually cleanse the torn and trampled area—not now, not yet. Lorna repeated her purging at each site. She only stopped when the soap bar disappeared from use.

Lorna used the only towel in the bathroom to wrap herself up and race to her once secure bedroom. RJ yelled out for her to quiet down before he resumed his drinking. Lorna paid him no mind as she put on fresh pajamas and hid beneath her blankets beside her clown coloring book. *Mom will be home soon. Mom will be home soon. Mom will be home soon ...*

⌐⌐⌐⌐⌐⌐

When the limousine transporting the priest pulled behind the funeral director's vehicle, Lorna knew this was the last chapter for her younger brother. *Sad ... so sad, Donny. You never had a chance with that monster. Once the shit hit the fan, neither did I.* Before joining the mourners exiting the paddy wagon, Lorna was hit with the devastating tribute from dear ole Mom.

⌐⌐⌐⌐⌐⌐

"Baby ... it's your period, that's all. I should have explained things better to you ..."

Lorna wanted to cry but had no energy or desire to express emotion. She was beyond fear. *Is this what it means to be screwed with nowhere to go and no one to go to? But I'm telling my mommy. She's my protector. There's no one after her, just me and mom … and now RJ.*

"Ma, he did this to me." Lorna spread her hands out across her blood-stained bedding. "Why don't you believe me?"

"Look, baby, I'm sorry I had work this morning and I wasn't here for you … but I'm here now." Mother Marian went to hug her daughter, but Lorna pulled away. Feeling rejection, Marian became aggressive, grabbing and then shaking Lorna's shoulders.

"RJ is drunk, that's all." Mother Marian nodded her head toward Lorna's doorway. "He's sleeping on the couch now. He's drunk, that's all."

Lorna could not believe her mother's denial of the evidence that was smeared on her once white sheets. "Ma … he rammed—"

Mother Marian let go of her daughter's shoulder and pointed her finger in Lorna's face. "You remember this, and don't ever forget: A drunk RJ, or any other man for that matter, can't do what you're saying he did." Marian put her hand down and smiled awkwardly. "A drunk soldier is a dead soldier."

~~~~~~

Nanci carefully stepped onto the snow-covered grass. She concluded that wearing two-inch heals today was not a smart decision. Nevertheless, the black-leather Mary Janes looked and felt fabulous. Hopefully she wouldn't slip onto the coffin and into its eternal resting place.

"Nanci … Uh, Nanci?"

Nanci stepped away from Nurse Joan's side when she heard her name being called out. She thought shouting out was a bit unusual at this particular moment. The surprise on Nanci's face pressed the barker to quiet down.

"Oops … sorry, I didn't mean to be so loud."

Nanci's grimace softened when she recognized the barker. "It's all right. My head was somewhere else." She knew the person, but her name … *Lorna, Lori, Lou-Anne—no, no, Lorna. Go with your first guess.*

"Would it be okay if we stayed together through this?" Lorna asked.

Without a word, Nanci put her arms around the disheveled mourner. The wind may have blown Nanci's hair about, but from her polished shoes to her perfectly applied makeup, all was well kept. As for Lorna, a pressing at the cleaners would be a good start. Any makeup would do, as well as a good hair brushing. *And no cigs. They don't work well for your skin. You look older, too old for twenty something.*

Experiencing genuine warmth from Nanci's embrace, Lorna spoke softly. "Thanks … for being there with Donny. I'm sure he felt you and everyone else." Lorna peered over Nanci's shoulder to watch the mourners surrounding Donny's casket, which was momentarily stationed above his grave. "Thank you." It was difficult, nearly impossible, for Lorna to be intimate with a stranger, or anyone else for that matter, but Nanci had been there for her brother. *And she's here for me now.*

Nanci felt the awkwardness of Lorna's tenderhearted gratitude. *What was her childhood like? She survived her mother, unlike Donny, but at what price?* "Come on, we'll stay together." Nanci grabbed Lorna's wrinkled coat sleeve, then the two locked arms.

Johnny had seen this before when his grandmother died. He was only seven years old then, but he'd become curious and then disappointed with how one could not watch the grave diggers dig or fill a plot. "Son, it would be too upsetting for family members watching a coffin being covered with earth," his father had told him. *Earth … Why did Dad say earth? It's dirt. That's all it is. Gravediggers all over the freaking world use "dirt" not "earth."* Johnny placed himself between his two sizable friends, Bain and Shanty, wishing they could both protect him from Angela's sight. It's not that she cared to see him, but if by chance Angela looked his way, Johnny would be invisible. *When you are hidden, you are invisible, unseen, nothing … I let Donny down first, Angela second. Who's batting third?* Johnny unconsciously touched his newly acquired Christ-head from underneath his shirt. The silver metal was toasty from his chest, and the warmth made Johnny feel like he had a link or a bond. *But to what?*

Before the priest began the sermon to the mourners, Bain whispered into Johnny's ear. "She's hot … look at her long hair blowing in the wind." Bain panted a bit. "I bet she's wild in bed."

Johnny wanted to punch Bain's face in. *I'm not with Angela for one day, and he's already drooling over her?* Trying to keep his cool, Johnny responded to Bain's sexual evaluation. "Angela always looks good, with her hair tied back or let down."

Bain did not appreciate his tone and roughly shook Johnny's shoulder. "What the hell you mean? I was talkin' about candy striper Nanci." Bain pulled Johnny closer. "That's the second time in two days you've brought Angela up. What, you and her …?"

"Quiet. He's starting." Johnny sidestepped Bain's investigation for the moment and referred to the priest.

Bain snickered. "I thought you and fat-ass Gina …"

Johnny let Bain have the last word and laugh—*otherwise he'll keep digging on me*—and listened to the priest speak. *Donny, God's child, Christmas in heaven, the mysteries of the Holy Trinity … and in peace. All sounds good, but it's the same old shit.* Johnny turned his attention away from the priest beside Donny's coffin to survey the encircling mourners. Directly across from Johnny stood candy striper Nanci and Lorna. The two held on to one another. Both had long coats, and their hair tossed in the cold wind, but that was about all they held in common. Johnny guessed Lorna could not be more than five or six years older than Nanci, but she could have belonged to a previous generation. *Her skin is pale. There's no blood flow, no color. Her hair has no body—flat and lifeless. Under that coat … no soft skin, just rawhide grasping at bones.* Johnny tried to remove Lorna's naked image from his mind and focused on Tori, Nicole, and Porky.

Tori's appearance now could match her normal demeanor on any other cold winter morning. *There's something about her that expresses gloom. What's the matter, Tori? Your daily dress rehearsal has finally arrived. You're on the big stage now.* Johnny distanced himself from his last wit to gaze at Porky and his sullen brow.

Porky was freezing, but it was not from the cold like everyone else. His heart had been taken and tossed somewhere deep in a dirty grave. Porky had lost a friend, his best friend, and had come to realize that nothing would ever be the same again. Mourning Donny, Porky wondered what the future held. *"Time stands still for no one," says Grandma. Life continues, everybody moves up, moves on, or moves no more.* Porky thought of the security of his mother and his grandparents. *I can play it safe, stay home and outta trouble, someday be far enough from here. Then this could be remembered as a misunderstood dream … nightmare.* An unexpected, brisk breeze whipped past his neck, giving him a sinister idea. *It's the devil's touch. He's here scratching—no, digging—out his next victim.* Porky tightened his scarf for warmth and some needed protection and heard a slight tear. *Ma's gonna have to knit me a new one soon.* Porky turned away from the coffin and stared across the open grave to see Tommy rudely stick out his tongue. *He's still a shit head who will never move up or on, Grandma. Tommy will unfortunately stay the same …*

Johnny was the only person in the cemetery to grasp or even consider the predicament Porky might be in. *All along everyone here was there for Donny. Most of us knew him; some, like Nanci, knew of him. But no one will be as lost without him as Porky will be. The two were the youngest, not that that mattered much. Both had issues, Donny at home and Porky in the street. They trusted each other in a silent way. I've never seen that before.* The devil's grazing wind that chilled Porky was only a nuisance to Johnny as he continued reflecting. *We are all hurting, lost, and guilty here … no one more than me. Why is it I get the feeling, Porky, that you will be the most screwed?*

Johnny could not concern himself much longer with Porky's hopeless future. He closed his eyes and, for the second time in two days, blocked out the priest and his lost words. Johnny wished he could take back last night with Angela. *She was pissed. She was upset and hurt, but she wouldn't cry … at least not in front of me.*

While the gloominess of the gray clouds sank to the hillside where he stood, its engulfing phantom reminded Johnny of the original Wolfman movie. *The old gypsy woman tried to help the bitten guy in the foggy forest, but she couldn't. The man was already cursed. The fog's grayness was only a reminder of his looming darkened end.* Johnny wiggled his soon-to-be frostbitten toes. *Shoes are for warm, indoor funeral parlors, not for winter cemeteries.* He balanced himself on his right foot and then did the same to the left, successfully sending blood to each frozen extremity. *Was the Wolfman searching the mist for a cure or a victim? Donny's not searching for anything now; there's no cure where he lies, only victims down there …* Johnny looked around to where Angela stood. She was staring at the ground below. *What difference does any of this shit make anyway? We'll all go our separate ways, if not today, then soon enough. And what does that do for Donny? He'll be searching through the dark forest fog for answers but will only find more victims.* For the second time in two days, Johnny began to cry. The first was the night before, for his mistreatment of Angela, and now he cried at the realization that no one there or any place else in this shitty world would really give a shit about Donny once he was buried, when the gravediggers finished doing their job digging into the earth.

"Amen." Bain snapped Johnny from his daze. "Finally, he shut the hell up. My balls are freezin' off." Bain elbowed Johnny when he did not receive a response. "Hey, you good or what?"

Johnny mumbled a reply. Bain did not understand the words but did see his despair. With the good sense of a friend, Bain dealt with Johnny. "What's up? You not feeling this?" Bain did not wait for an answer. "Same here." Johnny could only nod yes.

The two friends followed Nurse Joan's husband to the unshielded coffin. Kevin stood behind Johnny as the rest of the mourners followed procedure. Removing a white rose from the "Beloved Friend" flower arrangement, every funeral attendee carefully placed or lightly tossed a bloom onto Donny's eternal shelter.

Bain pulled Johnny away from the procession as the two watched the flowers drop. "It's like, toss a rose on the coffin, clap your hands clean of dirt, and then move on." Bain shook his head. "I know what you are thinkin' ... after today we'll surely forget."

Bingo! Johnny thought. But before he could thank Bain for his insight, Nanci intervened.

"Nurse Joan and her husband are organizing a luncheon for Donny at Peter Delli's. Everyone is invited." Nanci wiped any leftover dirt that had been attached to the rose's stem from her gloved hand. She then shook from the icy air before pointing to the paddy wagon. "I'll meet you guys inside the restaurant. Gina, Angela, and everyone are going." Bain and Johnny observed the girls, and Porky headed for the wagon. Nanci stumbled slightly on the snow but kept her footing as she rushed for the warmth of Lorna's rental car.

Kevin, Shanty, Tommy, and Joey circled Johnny and Bain and asked what the plans were. "We're going, but I'm not ready to leave just yet," Johnny said. He was unsure what to do next. He could only blow air into his ungloved hands. It would not be easy commanding any of them, especially Angela, but this couldn't end here and now. "Girls! Come back here for a sec …" After a few complaints, the girls followed Gina's lead. Once everyone was huddled around him, Johnny decided, he would wing it and speak from his heart.

"This sucks. The past few days—the past few months—haven't gone too well." Johnny sneaked a peek at Angela. *Please know I'm so sorry!* "Leaving here without Donny … doesn't feel so right." Everyone murmured or nodded in agreement, but all fell silent until Tori raised her hand.

"I know!" Tori exclaimed. "We can come back every Christmas Eve morning and spend it at the cemetery with Donny."

"Now, how's that gonna work out?" Nicole doubted. "You think we'll be friends forever, or better yet, have time to do this every Christmas?" She began to walk over to the paddy wagon, but to her surprise, no one followed. Nicole stopped when she realized she was the only mutinous person. "Okay, next year and the year after, but then what?"

Nicole's eyes began to tear, Johnny wondered if it was from the cold or not. "I don't think any of us want to leave Donny alone all of the time. Tori and Nicky are both right. At least in the beginning and for Christmas, let's do our best to be here." Johnny tried to be reasonable. "For as long as any of us can, Donny should not be alone."

Angela added, "It would mean as much to us as to Donny." She gave a slight grin to Johnny in support of his idea.

Everyone but Tori was in agreement with this concept. She offered a Christmas. Tori devised an end game resulting in a morbid conclusion everyone would somberly agree to. The Christmas Eve ritual of toasting Donny at his gravesite would end, only when another from the gang would die. All agreed, Donny would never be alone.

Bain, Johnny, Joey, Tommy, Nicole, Gina, and Angela shared similar thoughts about Tori's proposition: *You are one ghoulish and morbid being.*

~~~~~~~

"Thanks for the ride back. The back of that truck is brutal. Every bump is literally a pain in the ass." Nanci laughed at her own unrehearsed joke. After sitting in the passenger seat of Lorna's rental car, Nanci carefully placed *Tom Sawyer* and the snapshot inside on her lap.

"I stared at my brother all night. He was happy when with his friends." Lorna referenced the book Nanci held dearly. "Thank you, Nanci, and please introduce me to everyone at Peter Delli's again. There are so many to thank." Nanci nodded. "You are sweet for all you have done." Before Nanci could speak, Lorna went on. "The kids look like they don't want to leave just yet. I'm going to pull up to the office for a minute. If by chance the van pulls up before I get out, just honk the horn."

Nanci sat back and let the heat from the vehicle warm her thighs. "Sure … is everything all right?"

"Yes, Nanci … it will be." Lorna exited the running car and walked into the stone building near the exit gate.

Twenty minutes later, Lorna returned holding a closed envelope. She placed it in the back seat of her car. "I'm sorry I took so long. Have they left yet?"

"Only a few minutes ago. I didn't honk … I know where Peter Delli's is at."

Lorna put the car in drive while Nanci straightened herself up in the passenger seat. "Easy, they only left a minute ago." Nanci gave Lorna a reassuring tap on her knee. "Why were you in there so long? How many people you tip?"

Lorna said nothing but drove to Peter Delli's. What could she say to Nanci or anyone else? *Well, Nanci this is the shakedown, my friend. I bought the plot next to my brother. No reason for him to spend eternity alone, eh … is there? I know, I know, I was never there for him in this world, but I'll make it up to him in the next. Donny can finally count on his big sis.*

Lorna's intentions were sincere. Her life itself would be lived by "Lorna controls." No one, man or woman would ever have control over her. The following day, Lorna experienced her first Christmas as an only child and her first and last Christmas alone. The day after the celebration of Christ's birth, Lorna flew back home. She joined a local church on New Year's Eve. It was there that she started a women's club with no other intention than to discuss women issues. Quickly she discovered that the same theme came up over and over again with few variations: abuse, starting as a child, moving to teen years, and then graduating into adulthood. Alcohol and drugs joined in the ritual. The path of worthlessness, hopelessness, and self-destruction was the only road the women understood.

Lorna was never one for pity, for herself or anyone else. She would tell the women, "It's time to shit or get off the pot. Only you have the power to change. Giving anyone else the ability to control you is giving up your power. God gave everyone freedom; don't give up yours!" Lorna believed everyone had the ability to change and to control his or her own destiny. *Strength comes from within, while strength will be aided by us all.* Some of the women struggled and others succeeded in life. For those who couldn't succeed, they knew they at least had sanctuary, and all had, if they so desired, a caring sisterhood.

Lorna never married. She had male friends but could never fathom being intimate with any of them. For all the women she helped in her twenty-seven years at the church, Lorna never sought treatment or therapy for herself. *In time. I'll get it in time.*

Lorna couldn't stand the smell or taste of alcohol. It reminded her of RJ and mother Marian, and of course Mom's famous motto. *A drunk soldier is a dead soldier … Thanks, Mommy, for your words of wisdom and your total abandonment.*

Lorna did have a vice, though; it was those damn cigarettes. Smoking was something to do after a feat, more or less—after waking up, after a cup of coffee, after breakfast, after a meeting, after taking a break, after thinking of the past, after, after, after … Ironically it was before her morning shower when Lorna noticed a small rash under her armpit. *A rash from laundry detergent, that's all. Change back to liquid.* When the rash continued to spread and Lorna experience pain in her nipple, she knew it was something serious. The invading tumor cells continued producing the rash, doubling its size within a week.

Three months later, Lorna lay in her bed, exhausted. Swallowing became more difficult by the day because of the swelling of her throat. So Lorna crushed as many hemlock sleeping pills her pained hand could handle before sprinkling them into a glass of warm water. She took a generous sip of the homemade brew. Lorna was pleasantly surprised with tranquil sensation of the descending poison. Before her second swig, Lorna reached over her nightstand and picked up two sealed envelopes and a worn picture sitting on top. The first envelope bore the words *Calvary Cemetery—Queens, New York*, and inside was the deed for a plot and the receipt for a tombstone, along with its inscription. Lorna recalled the patient and worrisome Nanci warming herself in her rental car during the transaction. *Nanci was there for those poor kids while those children were there for my dying brother.*

The second envelope was her will. The money in her 401(k) and bank account would all go to the woman's group at the church. Lorna wrote a letter to her friends, not to explain her demise but to thank them for letting her realize that life could be wonderful alongside such people.

Lorna sensed her throat would cooperate one last time tonight, and with a tired but steady hand, she raised the glass and toasted life. With one long chug, she drained the deadly cocktail. Lorna gently placed the glass on a coaster on the nightstand. Her eyes were weighted down as the pain of the cancer suddenly pulled up. *Take that! I'm letting you know it's over!* Below the deed for the cemetery plot were the words written for her own tombstone: *My beloved brother, your sister will never leave your side again.*

Lorna dropped the contract at the left side of her bed. To her right was the worn picture of twenty-seven years before. *Nanci said a small boy named Billy snapped it with Tori's camera. I thanked them all at Peter Delli's for a lasting memory of Donny. The picture was taken the day ... the day life was beaten out of him.* Lorna's hand holding the picture began to shake, so she propped her elbow up, using the mattress and part of the sheet for support. Lorna knew all of their names in it, having looked at it a million times, over and over again, while she laughed, cried, wished, cursed, and dreamed of that morning. *The boys were dirty. There was plenty of torn clothing and messed up hair. Gina, Nicole, Angela, Tori, Shanty, Joey, Tommy, Kevin holding the ragged football, and Porky. And Johnny and Bain squeezing in on both sides of my beaming brother.* Lorna traced her finger across the snapshot one last time before dropping the photo onto her dying heart. *Beware, anyone trying to find a way between myself and Donny. Little brother, your sister is finally coming home.*

Chapter 24

1978

Oh, take your time; don't live too fast.
Troubles will come, and they will pass.
Go find a woman, and you'll find love.
And don't forget, Son, there is someone up above.
—"Simple Man" performed by Lynyrd Skynyrd

It's hard to resist a bad boy who's a good man.
—Nora Roberts

Johnny sipped a chocolate egg cream while sitting on a torn plastic seat inside of one of six booths. The Greeks diner where Johnny waited for Bain had been established after World War II and had not changed since—an operating time capsule. The tan-colored tin ceiling, the greenish walls with pictures scattered throughout, the mirror behind the counter, the horseshoe-shaped soda fountain dispensers, the chrome bar stools, and the storefront window were all covered with thirty years of grease. *But the bacon-and-egg roll is so good ... although the grease-filled burger with onions and a crunchy pickle for lunch is a close second.*

Johnny stared out the murky store window, watching the school children head for Christmas Eve morning mass. He noted how carefree and happy everyone outside the grime of The Greeks appeared to be. Johnny was envious of the lack of skeletons hidden inside their closets. Johnny smiled to himself. He knew life changed suddenly, for better or worse, in the time between yesterday, today, and tomorrow.

Johnny sucked down half of his soda mix, last night's drinking had left an unpicked cotton field in his mouth. As he contorted his tongue to feel alongside his gums, Johnny was snapped out of his boredom by the Greek man behind the counter.

"There's no blood!" the Greek complained. He took the slab of meat on the counter and flipped it over. "Nothing is there neither." The Greek took his half-smoked cigarette from the ashtray and held it. Before taking a drag, he put his nose against the slab of beef. "Shit … no good!" He inhaled and blew the smoke straight up. "Sonnabitch."

Johnny was no longer looking forward to the bacon-and-egg sandwich with Bain. He needed to get outside. He needed to … *There's no blood … there is no blood …* Johnny awoke this morning with Terry buried under his blankets. She was snoring lightly when Johnny rose off his bedroom floor. *There's no blood … The dream. It was in my dream.* A feeling of queasiness passed through Johnny's stomach. He downed the remainder of the egg cream. *Terry … I dreamed about her last night, but … the blood on the desert sand?* Johnny shook his head, not understanding what any of that had to do with his sister, but somehow she had been harmed.

"Johnny! Man, you missed all the shit last night." Kevin stumbled into The Greeks followed by Joey and Bain. "The shit hit the fan. Porky got killed, and then we got into a fight with the Madd Tuffs."

Joey limped behind Kevin to the booth where Johnny sat. "Johnny, we looked all over for you. We had no idea what the problem was."

Johnny slid over closer to the wall to let one of the three share his bench. "Shit, Joey, that from the Madd Tuffs?" Johnny asked, referring to Joey's swollen eye. Joey gave him a half-grin, making Johnny feel worse. "I know 'bout Porky. Bain told me about him on the way home. What an ass he is for trying to get in with those scumbags."

"But Johnny-boy, what about you? What's the problem?" Kevin wanted and deserved an answer.

Johnny stirred and stared into his egg cream. "No problem. I'm an ass ... but how bad was it last night?" he asked as Kevin and Joey sat across the table. Bain dropped beside Johnny.

Kevin answered proudly, "It was spooky, actually, fighting in the freaking cemetery."

Bain, in a serious tone, said, "We're gonna have to do something about those guys." Johnny went quiet and nodded. "We're running late now, but we got home late from crashing at Tori's." Johnny waved off their tardiness, and Bain lightened up. "You shoulda seen these two stumbling around together, something out of *Night of the Living Dead*."

"What happened?" Joey repeated Kevin's earlier question.

"Last night? I feel like such a schmuck for making such a mess for everyone," Johnny conceded. "I fought with myself over a lot of things." Johnny saw the sympathy in Joey's and Kevin's eyes, so he continued. "I guess I went back in time to where everything was so much clearer ... and brighter. I wished for it all back, but that ain't gonna happen. My footprints in my past will always be there. I realized that when I step forward, I'll be creating new prints, and so on." Johnny reached inside his pocket to feel the warmth and comfort of Donny's Christ-head. "I'm okay, but I still feel like a schmuck ..."

Bain elbowed Johnny off the end of the bench, landing Johnny on his ass. "Come on schmuck we'll fill you in on the walk about our night following your footsteps." While Bain laughed, Kevin put his hand out for Johnny to grab ahold.

⌐⌐⌐⌐⌐⌐

"Pistol Pete! Yes ... and it counts!"

"No, no ... watch this, Josh," Jacob yelled back. After the sound of a slight struggle, Jacob pressed. "The Doctor J ... yes, and it counts!" There was a clap of hands, and then the skirmish proceeded.

The church bells of Saint Stanislaus Kostka began to ring for the early-morning Christmas Eve mass, drowning out the rivalry in the adjacent room. Kimba rolled over in her bed and listen quietly to the chaotic harmony she had, for some time now, failed to appreciate. *No more Junior. I don't need or want any of that.* Kimba tossed over on her back and stared at her ceiling. *It feels so good waking up home, being clean and not having a hangover! And talking to mom last night—no, not to mom but with her. How did she put up with my shit for so long?* Kimba shook with personal disgust. *Never again, Mom. I'll make you and Daddy proud.* The church bells went silent when Kimba squinted a tear from her eye. *I remember the day the twins were born. From your hospital bed, you said I'd always be your treasure ...*

Kimba got out of bed and saw it was 8:15 a.m. There was plenty of time to be revived. *Things are gonna be different around here.* Kimba slipped her orange sweat pants on and put her hair in a loose, bungled bun. *And out there, too!*

Secretly tiptoeing through her doorway, Kimba's first stop was her parents' closed bedroom door. Hearing her father's snoring and assuming her mom was still asleep, Kimba hurriedly made her way down the hallway to the living room and the ruckus generated from her twin four-year-old brothers.

"Pistol Pete! Yeah, and it counts!" Joshua slammed the ball through the netting of the three-foot-tall basketball hoop.

When Jacob went to retrieve the rolling ball, he noticed Kimba watching from the side of the family Christmas tree. "I ... I told Josh not to wake you up," a nervous Jacob swore. "Mommy said we could play if we were quiet." Jacob was on the verge of tearing.

Kimba walked to the front of the tree and motioned for the sponge basketball. Jacob awkwardly tossed it toward Kimba. The ball ricocheted off of Kimba's shoulder and hit a Christmas ornament. Jacob went pale, and Joshua ran to the ball and handed it carefully to his big sister.

"Where did you get this from, the ball and the basket?" Kimba demanded.

Jacob could not speak, so Joshua explained the best he could. "Dad got it last night at Knights of Columbus. Santa gave it to us."

"So it's Christmas already?"

Jacob nodded yes while Joshua shook his head no.

Kimba could no longer tease these two angels. "Oh yeah?" Kimba got to her knees with the ball in her hand. "Watch this one. Earl the Pearl Monroe!" With two hands, she slammed the ball through the rim. "Yes … and he's fouled!" She grabbed the ball off the floor and playfully tapped Jacob's nose with it before taking a second shot, missing the basket completely. Kimba crawled quickly to the ball. "Rebound Reed! Willis out-muscles Pistol Pete and The Doctor for a second shot!"

The boys quickly lost any fear of waking anyone up as their competitive nature and playful spirit took over. Joshua wrapped his arms around Kimba's neck while Jacob buried his head in her shoulder. All three landed on the area rug together, the three laughed until Kimba cried. Rolling on the floor, Kimba realized how foolish she had been and how fortunate she was now to have a second shot at getting it right.

Thirty minutes later, Kimba, Joshua, and Jacob crossed the intersection on their way to the children's Christmas mass. The church bells began ringing again, alerting the parishioners that the ceremony would begin in five minutes. Letting her parents sleep in was part the reason why Kimba decided to leave with her brothers. The other was that *it feels real good getting it right!* The two boys held her hands. Once on the sidewalk,

Kimba put her mittens together with the boys still attached. "Everything will be better between us. I love you guys. Merry Christmas!" Kimba gave them both a hug before walking into the church. *There's plenty more wrongs I must right—against one person in particular—but today is about my family. Oh God, I am so grateful for them.*

~~~~~~~

Johnny endured the story of the night before as he listened to Kevin's, and partially Joey's, version of where they had gone and what happened along the way. When Kevin finished the tale with all them crashing at Tori's Mom's apartment, they stopped to let Bain continue.

"See, you thought me and Shanty had it hard." Johnny had no answer. He could only grimace. "Come on, nobody's pissed at you … Get over it." Bain put Johnny in a headlock and began knocking his head playfully with noggins.

"All right, I give, I give!" Bain let go, and Johnny stumbled backward. With both hands, Johnny pushed back his mused hair. Changing the subject, Johnny spoke. "I guess today is it, then … What we all agreed on way back then, right?"

All three agreed in unison as they walked silently over the Greenpoint Avenue bridge on the last leg of their journey to Calvary Cemetery's entrance.

~~~~~~~

"I'm so cold … you'd think they would open this up even five minutes early today," Nicole complained as she took a nonchalant swipe at the lock on the iron gate.

Tommy held Angela's hand with one hand and a cigarette with the other. "It don't matter. We ain't goin' in until everybody is here."

Nicole bounced on her toes for circulation. "Where are they? What did Johnny do now?" Getting no response, Nicole finished, "Thank God this is it."

Gina bit her tongue, not wanting to set off her friend, but Tommy could not. "Listen, bitch, Johnny's always been there for all of us, especially when we need him, so stop your shit!" Tommy felt Angela's hand squeeze his own, so he fell silent.

Angela guided Tommy away from prying ears. "I want to thank you. You're right, she is a bitch, but more importantly"—Angela tapped Tommy's chin—"he's your friend. He always was, and he always will be."

Shanty was standing thirty feet away from the previous quarreling couple beside the iron picket fence of Calvary Cemetery. He began to shout, "Holy cow … this is where it happened." Shanty pointed through the fence to where an indent in the snow was surrounded by footprints and dog paw prints. Shanty looked at the ground outside of the cemetery where he now stood. "Look all around me; the snow is trampled."

Tommy and Angela were the first two to inspect. "It was dark. I didn't realize it happened right here. Everything was so fast." Tommy put his head partially through the metal spikes. "Look up there on the road. There's the hammer Dylan threw … and there's a broken bottle and another one."

Gina, Tori, and Nicole joined the investigation. "So you guys climbed out right here, with cops and dogs chasing you?" Gina was impressed. "That's at least ten feet high. I can't see where the snow starts and the spikes end."

Tommy finished, "Plus the Madd Tuffs … I didn't know whose side they were on when the cops and dogs were coming." Tommy heard his name being yelled. He scanned the bridge. It was Joey, with his usual limp, Kevin leading the way, and Johnny and Bain bringing up the rear. "They're here, just in time. Everybody made it!"

When the four completed the trip over the bridge and joined the circle outside the now open front gate, Johnny decided to squeeze in between his strongest allies of each sex, Bain and Gina. "Lately I've been walking around with my head up my ass, and last night was no different." Johnny glanced at Tommy holding Angela. "Tommy, I know what you guys did here, and"—Johnny looked over at Bain and Shanty—"of course you two in Manhattan, and all you girls, too, on the phone and staying in touch with Terry and each other. I … Thank you all for being there for me when I was going to hell …" Johnny rubbed his nose. All were unsure whether he would cry. "Yes, I was emotional jerk, and sorry for being such trouble." Johnny stared into the cemetery, not making any eye contact with his audience. "Anybody could be a friend when times are fun. But last night was not fun, so thanks for being a friend."

Johnny did not want his friends to see him cry, so he kept staring up at the snow-covered cemetery hills until Tommy grasped Johnny's dilemma. Tommy let go of Angela and put his arm upon Johnny's right shoulder. Shanty copied him on the left. Then Gina and Tori rubbed their palms in circles on Johnny's back expressing their support. Everyone ultimately made their way to Johnny, showing unity and expressing their gratitude that he was okay.

Ten minutes later, the group had staggered through the snow to Donny's grave. Joey unzipped his coat and pulled out a bottle of Bacardi. "Good, the light stuff. Last year you brought out the dark shit," Nicole commented.

Gina playfully waved her hand. "That's why I haven't had a drink all year. I was so sick from that dark shit."

Tori corrected her. "Last night you weren't drinking milk."

Kevin grabbed Gina tightly and pulled her close to him, causing his sore ribs to call out in pain. "Oh, shit …" He bent over for a second but went on with his dig. "So you drink once a year, and it's not with me?" he teased.

"Hey … don't pull on me so tight. I'm still a little tipsy." Gina laughed but was serious.

"Good, this is the best thing for a hangover." Joey raised the bag holding the Bacardi.

After a few chuckles, the group formed a semicircle facing Donny's tombstone. Joey cracked the Bacardi bottle open, took a slug, splashed a shot onto the ground before him, and then passed the bottle to Kevin. Once the bottle made it to the last person, Shanty, anyone or everyone could and would speak. The Bacardi was then passed to only the drinkers who now wanted a second, third, and fourth shot.

It's all about Donny this morning, Merry Christmas! The singular thought of all.

"Remember the time when the Polack threw the bucket of water from the top of his stoop on us … and the bucket slipped and hit Donny in the back?" Joey asked. He was interrupted by Bain.

"We were so pissed!" Bain drank a shot and then splashed an ounce onto the snowy gravesite. "Me and Johnny chased the Pole into the hallway." Bain laughed and passed the booze to Nicole. "Before he could close the door—"

"You and Johnny had him. I wasn't sure what to do with the dirty bucket except place it on his dumb-ass head." Tommy laughed, and everyone else joined in. "But the best was when Gina hit the damn bucket with that big hairbrush she had. Shit, that can was ringing his head off!" The laughter grew.

"Wait, wait … what about when that old bag came out and starting yelling at Shanty about us playing ball outside her house." Kevin went on. "She said, 'Who's the boss around here, you?' Shanty shakes his head no and says, 'No not me. He is.' And Shanty points to the smallest guy … Donny." Everyone joined in Kevin's hysterics except Shanty.

"But the best part was Donny saying. 'I'm the boss of you?'" Joey finished. Now Shanty could no longer stay stone-faced and united in the mania.

Gina motioned for the half-filled booze bottle from Kevin. She toasted the ground above Donny and then spoke. "Donny's smile … he didn't smile much, but that smile went ear to ear …"

Gina rubbed her nose, while Angela gently rubbed her friend's shoulders. For the next hour, as the morning sun became gray with clouds and snow flurries began to swirl, the group of mourners camped out. Everyone had their own memories involving Donny. The bottle continued to make its way around to the chorus of laughter, a few moans, tears, joshing, and all the feelings shared between good friends.

Unfortunately, everyone now knew the clock had run out on them. It was Tori who had ghoulishly prophesied this five years ago to the day on the ground where they all now stood. Tori's pledge, which they had agreed to five years earlier, was simply that every Christmas Eve, they would all come back here until one of them died and joined Donny. Then they could stop. Donny would no longer be alone.

"I never thought it would actually happen like this. I figured we would grow apart." Tori shook her head no, refusing the joint Nicole offered. "But it did, and now we can move on … if we want to or can."

"Of course, Porky." Bain took a drag of the joint before speaking again. "You know, Tori, I thought you were a creepy broad—and you are—but you were right. Donny's not alone anymore."

"I never thought it would happen so fast—another one of us dying, that is." Tommy shook off Angela's hold. "Porky always got me. Even though we hadn't hung out in forever, he'll be missed." Tommy motioned for the bottle from Johnny. "Here you go, Pork. Say hello to Donny." With the bottle raised, Tommy ended, "To the good and bad times we've all had."

Johnny unconsciously gaped at Angela. She stood alone while Tommy shielded his back to light a cigarette. *Angela ... I am so sorry that I hurt you. I should've protected you. It's something I gotta live with every day. You and I suffer alone. Can we try again? Please ... I saw him last night, our boy, our son. Please, there can be hope for us. I believe in you, in me, in us.* Johnny felt a kidney shot, shocking him into reality. "Hey ... what the ...?" Johnny's haze disappeared.

"Johnny-boy, you are bad boy." Gina smiled. Then she spoke in a very low tone. "Don't go there; it's over. She's moved on, and so should you."

Red-faced, Johnny nodded in agreement. "I didn't realize ... I ..." Tommy and his lit cigarette reappeared to the circle of friends, snapping Johnny's focus back to the reason all were present. "Like Tori said, this is the end." Johnny was unsure what should be said next until he heard Terry's voice. *Don't talk about details, Johnny. They want to know all is good with you and with them. Talk from your soul. Once you open your heart, there is no more hiding ...*

Johnny touched Donny's cold tombstone. The ice sitting on its top did not, for some unknown reason, freeze his fingertip. *It's warm ... Donny is here. I feel him.* "Tori's mostly right, except for one thing." Johnny brushed his cheek with the index finger that had touched the stone. *Warm.* "I think—no, I know—Donny is in a better place today. Maybe he was all along." Johnny turned away from his audience to focus on the tombstone. "Last night I struggled with myself for the mistakes I have made. Funny thing is, all of my mistakes trampled others. I guess that's how it works." Johnny now leaned onto Donny's headstone to face his listeners. Johnny took a quick peek at Angela. She returned a reassuring grin. "As for me and everyone here … I figure today we have 100 percent of whatever life we have left."

"Wait, say that again." Nicole was lost.

Bain jumped in. "He's saying there's plenty of life in everyone."

"Johnny's saying today, him, all of us are starting with a clean slate," Angela explained, correcting Bain's assumption.

Nicole puffed. "Then just say that."

Johnny returned his attention to the stone monolith for the last time. "Donny, it's time for me to move on. For the short time I knew you, it was the happiest time in my life. Unfortunately I didn't know it then or much appreciate our time. Merry Christmas. Who's better than us?"

Johnny stood back to allow everyone else to say their Christmas wishes and their farewells. Joey, Shanty, Kevin, and Angela swore they'd be back someday; the others made no such promises.

Bain put his hand on Johnny's shoulder and asked if he was all right. Johnny nodded yes. "All is good, then." Bain coughed up a lungy and spat it toward Dylan's tossed hammer. Missing the weapon by three feet, Bain cursed while the two followed the somber group of Nicole, Tori, and Shanty to the cemetery's gate. "I never wanted this to end, but in a way, I'm glad it has."

"Johnny … Johnny." Johnny peered over his shoulder and saw Angela standing by herself. Tommy stayed back at Donny's grave with Joey, Kevin, the rum, and the soon-to-be-lit fireworks.

Bain spoke next. "Those guys ain't killing that Bacardi off without me." He tapped Johnny's left shoulder and hustled back to the gravesite, intentionally leaving Johnny alone with Angela.

When Bain was out of earshot, Angela whimpered, "Johnny this is the end … right? I want to be sure." Angela frowned. She knew the answer but wanted it to come from her ex-lover. "I see how you look at me … Tommy knows." Angela's eyes began to tear, but she managed not to let them flow … not yet. "I'm sorry I came between you two, but I was scared and hurting. I was alone. Tommy loved me, but I really needed you. I only wanted you." Angela wiped her nose with the back of her glove. *Real ladylike, sister.* "We can never undo our past Johnny, but we gotta move on."

Pop, pop, pop.

Johnny snooped over Angela's shoulder and watched Bain, Tommy and Kevin begin to light Captain Jack's firecrackers. All seemed in good spirits. *What a cheap bottle of booze and gunpowder can do at a gravesite of a murdered friend.* "I have," Johnny lied. Seeing the doubt on Angela's face, Johnny corrected his statement. "I will …" Johnny spoke in a low voice, and Angela had to strain to hear as the firework show increased. "It's over Angie … but it wasn't supposed to end like this." *Don't say you love her, don't say you love her, don't …* "I was crazy about you."

Angela looked away. She could no longer look Johnny in the eyes, for her own began to seep. Angela shook her head up and down as if she understood where both stood today and forever. Knowing Tommy could return any second, Angela had to reveal her parting feelings for Johnny. "You are a good guy." Angela had to say it one last time. "I will always love you."

Johnny wanted to feel her, hold her, smell her and fantasize of happier times before parting forever. "Come here." Johnny opened his arms as if imitating Christ on one of the crosses in the graveyard. Without hesitation, Angela ran into Johnny's embrace.

Angela repeated her emotions. "I love you, Johnny. I always did and always will …"

341

"Shhhh ... I know. I feel the same." *Good, don't say you love her, don't say you love her, don't ...* "Now we both gotta start over." Johnny thought of the first time he kissed Angela outside the hospital in between two Christmas trees. Only five years had passed, but it may as well have been an eternity, for he couldn't believe how everything had perished. *If I say I love you today, we could only hate one another tomorrow.*

"Together?" Angela wished. Before Johnny could agree or not, Angela saw both of Johnny's eyes tear. "Please, Johnny ... is it really over?" Angela recognized Johnny's boyish smile of a long time ago, giving her a moment of false hope.

"Angie baby ..." Johnny shook his head.

Angela placed her index and middle finger on Johnny's lips. "No more, my love ..."

Gina and Kevin crashed the ex-lovers' powwow. "It's so surreal out," Kevin said, catching a snow flurry in his mouth as he watched the gray clouds above glide past. "I really don't know what that word surreal means, but ..." He caught a second flake before Bain slapped the back of his brother's head. "Hey!"

"Stop fooling around. We ain't even outta the gates yet." Bain then spoke to Johnny. "What you wanna do this afternoon? Go to the bowling alley? Shoot some pool?"

Johnny watched Angela walk back toward Donny's gravesite where Tommy and Joey continued to shoot off firecrackers. Unable to answer Bain, Gina grabbed Johnny's elbow. "No, we got him. Kev and I are taking him out now. He can catch up with you later." Gina put one hand into Kevin's palm, held Johnny's bicep with the other, and led the small posse outside the cemetery's stone-and-metal barrier.

Johnny shrugged his shoulders, letting Gina control the moment. He watched Angela kiss Tommy as the two held each other on the way out of the cemetery. Johnny was partially relieved not to walk home with Angela, Tommy, and the others. *Enough is enough, already. Clean slate starting now!* "Kev, where's she taking us?"

Kevin smiled. "It's no big deal, but you'll like it." Kevin teased. "Gina has half a bag on; I'm not sure how long she'll last."

All said their good-byes at the iron gate of the graveyard. Kevin, Johnny, and Gina hiked away from the Greenpoint Avenue Bridge and their departing friends. Johnny was down for something, anything, fun now. Leave it to Kevin not to disappoint. Like he had the night before, once he was fifty feet or so away from Junior and the Madd Tuffs, Kevin crafted a snowball. With his strong arm, Kevin whipped the missile into the parting crowd, striking Nicole's right shoulder. "Kevin! You shit!"

"Sorry, I was aiming for Joey!" Kevin lied. Hitting any one of them would have worked. Kevin stumbled a bit after his toss and then caught up with Gina and Johnny.

"I didn't realize I was gawking at her," Johnny answered as Kevin joined the conversation. Not wanting to spill out his guts with another guy present, Johnny had to finish the talk of Angela … for now and forever. "I was caught up in the moment, that was all … you know, our last time here and all." Johnny nodded toward the cemetery. "It's over. We talked. Like I said, time to move on."

Gina did not believe Johnny. Listening to Angela's story from the night before, she realized there was plenty of heartbreak and pain between the two, as well as plenty of unfinished business. *But why push him for an answer now? If Johnny believes or is trying to believe he's done with Angela, then leave it. Not that it's my business anyway.* "How far is this place?" Gina asked Kevin. "My feet are cold, and they're already killing me. Now my head is starting to hurt too."

Kevin insisted that Gina be patient and that in the long run, it would be better this way. Kevin then quietly reminded Gina that it was her idea to separate Johnny from the others. *Let's end all this right; no need for dramatics.*

Thirty minutes later, Gina sat on a barstool with her coat unbuttoned while drinking a warm glass of milk. She kicked off her left boot to rub a sore pinky toe. Johnny drank his beer from a bottle; the glass was too grimy. Kevin put a quarter in the jukebox, searching for a disco song his girl would like. "Hey, Gina, I got a good one. You'll like this … but no dancing in your seat."

~~~~~~~

At the same moment Kevin selected "Don't Leave Me This Way," Joshua was crying out for a hot chocolate.

"Please, Kimba …"

"Of course, but you two have to sit at the table and drink it here, not on or by the pinball machine." After church, Kimba thought it would be a good idea to treat the boys to a comic book and a hot drink, giving Mom and Dad an additional break from Pistol Peter and The Doctor hacking it out in the parlor.

Kimba gazed out the storefront window, watching the energy of people zoom by. The seniors all carried grocery bags of some specialty food from the old country, moms went by with their babies in tow, dads carried the bulky stuff, like a shit load of booze, and grammar school children ran past excited and carefree. *Life is good. How did I miss all of this?*

"Can we have a quarter? Kimba, pleeeease." Jacob put his hand out. "Me and Josh want to play. We put the box there; we can see now." Jacob pointed to a blue milk crate the two had placed in front of the pinball machine.

"Whose idea was that?" Kimba asked. The boys did not recognize the new and improved Kimba yet, so they stayed quiet. "Well, that was very clever to use the milk crate that way. Sometimes it's better to be clever than smart."

Joshua loosened up, but Jacob spoke first. "I told Josh to move it … I did."

"Here's your quarter. No pushing each other."

"Better to be clever than smart? You sound like my brother," a soft and sweet voice from behind surprised Kimba.

Even before she turned around, she already knew the voice, but seeing the person speak it shocked her. The little girl was no longer little … or a girl. Her blonde hair was as blonde as ever but was no longer in pigtails. Her hair was brushed to shoulder length with upright curls. The braces that had once hidden her teeth had been removed, revealing pearly whites. She had a slight coloring of eye makeup with tint of blush on each cheek. The slender child of a year before now had the curves of a young woman.

"Terry, I … Merry Christmas!" Shocked, Kimba did not know what else to say. With no words coming forward, Kimba put her hand out to greet the young lady.

Terry smiled broadly and would have none of the courtly handshake. "Merry Christmas!" She hugged Kimba. "It's good to see you." When Terry let go, she knowingly asked who the two pinball wizards were. Kimba spoke proudly of her little brothers as they continued trying to hit the metal ball for points and a free game. Kimba then inquired about Johnny and what he was up to.

"It being Christmas and with the whole ritual they have about Donny"— Terry frowned—"he's a bit down but doing well." Terry did not want to put out negative vibes about her brother to his old girlfriend, or anyone else for that matter. She slyly changed the subject. "What have you been up to, besides running around with these two pinball wizards?"

Kimba shrugged, until last night, she had not been up to anything positive. Now life had changed and for the better. "I broke up with that jerk Junior, if that's anything new ... nothing else." *Why did I say that? I sound like a fool. I'm such an idiot!* Kimba smiled awkwardly before telling her brothers, to their protests, that they all had to go home in a few minutes.

If Terry had noticed Kimba's awkwardness, she kept it to herself. Instead, she appeared to have been struck by an idea. "Why don't you come by tonight? My parents will be across the street. I was going to go, but I'd rather stay home ..." Terry saw the smile spread across Kimba's face. "I'm sure Johnny would stay home if he knew you were coming." Terry playfully tugged on Kimba's elbow and then gave her a reassuring grin. "He's lost for the moment ... but when he finally snaps out of his funk, he'll be his old self." Terry let go of Kimba's arm and placed her hands inside her coat pockets. "He was always happy with you. Maybe it wasn't the right time back then, but now could be."

"Really?" Kimba couldn't believe what she was hearing from Terry. *She's so right. I was so immature and jealous of Angela back then. Johnny trusted in me, telling me they'd made out after Donny's wake, so I made his life miserable. I cheated to hurt him. I asked Johnny to open up and share things with me, and when he did ... I was jealous with no compromise.* Kimba giggled insanely to herself when her second thought arrived. *I now know Johnny and Angela did a lot more than swap spit back then, and you know what? I don't give a shit.*

"Earth to Kimba." Terry was now laughing. "So is that a yes?"

Kimba teared up uncontrollably. *Kicking that loser Junior out of my life, Mom and I talking honestly last night around the kitchen table, my brothers this morning playing basketball with me, Terry now, and a second chance with Johnny tonight!* It was Kimba's turn to initiate the hug. Her squeeze around Terry provided the younger with the answer.

~~~~~~

Johnny shook his head no and then waved his hand, nearly socking Gina's nose. "Oops, sorry. You know, I'll have one more."

"Easy, Johnny-boy ... this shit is good though." Gina was euphoric. Her feet had gotten the break they truly needed, and her belly was full. Drinking rum on an empty stomach and going on two long walks this morning was plenty after a late night. *But Kevin was right about this. I cannot believe my man was right!* Gina squeezed Kevin's thigh and whispered thank you. Gina giggled.

"Gina, you're stone drunk already?" Kevin teased. Gina's only response was to squeeze her boyfriend's thigh harder. "Ouch ... you are a nut job." Gina silently bent over and kissed Kevin's neck. "Oh, you're drunk." Kevin turned away to peer up the street and saw what he was searching for. Excited, he began to bark out orders. "There they are ... slow down. Yo, slow down a little more." Kevin rolled down the rear window and tossed the box of half-eaten pizza onto Gina's lap.

"Baby, it's greasy ..." Gina snickered.

With his head sticking out of the car, Kevin yelled. "Hey, asshole! Yo, assholes!"

Tommy, Shanty, Tori, Angela, and Nicole turned around immediately. Bain and Joey followed but were already laughing, understanding the joshing. Once Tommy realized he'd fallen for the oldest joke of them all, he searched for an ice ball to toss.

"Okay, you can speed up a little now, but let me do this first before we pass 'em." Kevin reached into Gina's lap where the pizza box rested. Taking one of the leftover pizza slices, he returned to the window and pushed half of his body out the window of the moving car, waving the slice for all on the sidewalk to see. "Hey, who's better than us!"

Tommy found the perfect-sized ice ball and fortunately had the car near his sights. He saw Kevin waving something out of the car. *A slice of pizza? Don't matter … eat this!* Tommy flung his bomb at Kevin.

Kevin had no chance to do anything but to cover his face with a forearm. The ice ball struck the lower part of his coat and then landed in the backseat between Gina and Johnny. Gina screamed and knocked the greasy pizza box and the remaining three slices onto Johnny's stomach. A second throw from the sidewalk hit the letter *V* on the top of the car's sign advertising "Vito's Pizza—Free Delivery."

The teenage driver had had enough of this nonsense, so he hit the gas pedal to flee the onslaught of snowballs. An ice patch caused the car to slide a bit to the right before righting itself straight. The motion and sudden burst of speed of the delivery car was enough for Gina. She bent over and let out the rum, the warm milk from the dirty glass, and the slice and a half of greasy pepperoni pizza with extra cheese she'd recently swallowed onto Johnny's lap.

Johnny sat stunned. *Is she kidding me? How come she didn't throw up on her boyfriend? He started this shit … Kevin gets away with everything!* Johnny began to laugh. It felt good to wholeheartedly laugh. *Life is how you live it today—Not yesterday's regrets or tomorrow's worries.* Kevin rolled up his window and began to boast about how he'd blocked Tommy's shot, not knowing about Gina's puking episode. Johnny listened to his unsoiled friend brag. *I'll take the happy memories of this world,* Johnny decided as the warmness of vomit seeped its way through his jeans. Johnny's thighs were no longer cold. He relaxed into the car's cushioned seat and ate his pizza. *Kevin, you are spot on. Who's better than us?* Johnny grinned. *Nobody!*

Epilogue

Time flies over us
But leaves its shadows behind.
—Nathaniel Hawthorne

At the same time Kimba was gratefully hugging her future sister-in-law, a young school teacher was Christmas shopping thirty miles north in a suburban mall. The last-minute bargain hunter was extremely proud of herself for driving alone from Brooklyn across the George Washington Bridge and along the Palisades Parkway to the gigantic shopping center. *I didn't get lost!* She smiled and decided that Macy's would be her first stop. *I know I have a Macy's in Manhattan, but I like this store. Hey, I drove all the way out here all by myself. I can shop wherever I want!* She read the mall map and saw that the Macy's was right around the next corner. *Wonderful, I can start spoiling my man.* Across the corridor from her first destination, she spotted two teenage girls wearing Rockland High School Swim Team jackets. She experienced lightheadedness but brushed it off as a spat of déjà vu. *Hmmm, funny. Seems like I've been here before ... with those two girls in tow.*

An hour later, with two full bags of dress shirts, jeans, a pair of white sneakers, and pajamas for herself, the young teacher decided it was time for a break. She bought a coffee—"light with no sugar"—and searched for a mall bench to relax on. After five minutes, with no luck, she strolled over to where young children sat on Santa Claus's lap for a picture and a wrapped toy. The blue boxes were for the boys, the pink for girls. She took her own newly purchased presents and placed them between her and the metal railing surrounding Santa and his elves. She leaned on the three-foot-high guardrail and watched the children's expressions as they sat with Santa. The boys greeting Saint Nicholas had their hair wet or greased back or to the side. Most wore a red shirt or vest. The young girls had their hair done professionally or at least combed about with great care, and their dress colors were mainly green. A few children cried, more of them young boys than girls. The teacher giggled to herself. *Boys take forever to grow up ... and some never do.* She focused on the Santa and his beard. *Those whiskers are real, and that belly is too. There are no pillows inside that suite. I've never seen such a sincere Santa Claus.*

She sipped her coffee and was pleasantly surprised how good it tasted. *Nobody makes it this good. This mall is something else.* Her attention was drawn away from the children and Santa to the people outside the metal gate. She noticed how well everyone was dressed. Although she liked her man a bit more rugged, that didn't hinder her admiration for the people in this affluent community.

She was about to toss her empty coffee cup into the nearby trashcan when she noticed the two girls from the Rockland High School swim team for the second time. Each held multiple plastic shopping bags. One pointed into a teen clothing store window and ran inside. The other was right on her tail. *Hmmmm ... I know them, but from where?* She left the railing and pushed open the lid of the waste basket with the bottom of her cup, not wanting to catch germs from inside. *They might be rich and proper out here, but germs are germs.*

She looked at her watch and saw it was almost three. It was time to leave if she wanted to be in Brooklyn before dark. *Most importantly, Frankie will be over later tonight, and I gotta look my best!*

"Nanci! Oh, candy striper Nanci!"

Nanci struggled not to drop her store-bought gifts when she heard her name being called out twice. *Who the hell knows me way out here?*

"Oh my God, Nanci … I can't believe it's you!" A well-dressed, middle-aged, attractive lady with long, dark hair approached Nanci smiling broadly, her arms wide open for a hug.

Thunderstruck, Nanci dropped her presents on the mall floor. "Holy shit … Nurse Joan?" The two cried and laughed while they hugged one another. Nanci was the first to speak. "I'm so sorry. I didn't recognize you with long hair … and I've never seen you smile before."

Nurse Joan wiped her eyes of joyful tears. "Oh, Nanci, that mouth always goes before that head." Nurse Joan took a step back and checked out Nanci. "You have grown into such a beautiful young woman. I wasn't sure it was you at first, but then I saw how you placed the cup in the trash. It had to be my neat freak candy striper." The two laughed and hugged a second time.

They chatted about trivial things—hair styles, clothes, the mall, and how late it was getting. Before parting, though, Nanci could not stop herself from bringing up the past. Nurse Joan was grateful her long ago pupil did.

Nanci rubbed her lip before speaking. "A couple days after the funeral, I gave the hospital my two weeks' notice. You were right; I am better in a school. I decided to become a teacher, and I really love it." Nanci's smile disappeared. "I had wanted to thank you personally before I left for everything, but the only information I got from the fat nurse … I forget her name. She's sorta ugly too. But anyway, she said you were on leave. You'd told me you were going on leave, but I thought you were just on another vacation and would be back before I left. You didn't come back. When I asked what was wrong, no one would tell me. When my two weeks were up, I still hadn't gotten to say thank you and good-bye." Nanci rambled on as her face saddened. "I called numerous times afterward but received no information, so I gave up on you. I figured …"

Nurse Joan's smile remained while she took a peek at the line of children leading to Santa Claus. "Nanci … you're right."

"I am?" a stunned Nanci asked.

"I should have spoken with you, I wanted you to be as far removed from the hospital as possible. Believe me, I would have loved being a mentor to you, but I couldn't at the time. It was a very difficult time for me too, mentally and physically."

Nanci's face lightened, and her tight jaw relaxed. "I get it. With a husband and your daughters and …"

Nurse Joan's expression became sincere. "Nanci with an *i*, you didn't know. How could you? By law, the hospital could not have told you." Nurse Joan frowned. "How foolish I was."

Nanci shook her head no.

"I, unlike you, missed the next two weeks of work after Donny's funeral, but it was not for another vacation or by choice, dear." Nurse Joan waved over the two girls with the Rockland High School varsity jackets who were involved in a deep conversation with two teenage boys. "Shoot, they didn't see me. You remember them; they were at Donny's wake."

Nanci nodded.

"The oldest graduates this year. She's going to Villanova. Her sister is in her second year of high school, unsure where she will go."

Nanci was impressed with the growth of her daughters but wanted Nurse Joan to finish her side of the events following the burial. "You never came back to the hospital that January or ever, but why? I thought we would stay friends."

Nurse Joan watched one of Santa's elves give a smiling, dark-haired boy about four years old a wrapped blue gift. She then turned her attention back to Nanci. "I had placental abruption. I needed rest. I was so stressed, and … well, things were very iffy …"

"Placental … what? I'm lost …" Nanci was interrupted by the voice of a young boy calling out to his mother.

"Mommy, look! I didn't cry! I didn't cry … so Santa gave me this." The young child presented his blue gift box to Nurse Joan. "Ma, I told you I wouldn't cry this time …"

It took Nanci a second to identify what the heck was going on. *That kid is Nurse Joan's. She had a difficult time during her pregnancy, but here he is.* The boy's hair was combed to the side. He wore blue trousers, a white button-down shirt, a red bow tie, and red Santa suspenders. His smile and hair coloring matched his mother's, but that was all Nanci could immediately tell. "Oh my God, oh my God … Joan, he's so beautiful—I mean, so handsome. He's so adorable." Nanci gave her friend a third hug. The two stood there holding one another and sobbing. "It was just a horrible time back then, but look what you got out of it … a beautiful son."

"Mommy. Ma, can I open the gift now?" the little boy questioned his mother.

Nurse Joan nodded yes and then let go of Nanci to stare into her eyes. "It was a very difficult time for everyone. Those poor kids went through hell. I know you were with them all the way, especially the girls … Gina … and Tori, Angela, and Nicky. I'll never forget them." She laughed then added. "Remember S.T.P.?"

In unison both ladies cried out. "Silent Treatment Please!"

Nanci sighed. "The boys … were a handful, but they truly were friends." "I think of them all the time." Nanci's eyes began to swell up with tears.

353

"I teach young ones now, and I love them. I try my best to be passionate and considerate of them all. Bain, Tommy, and of course Johnny and the rest never got any of that. I am trying to make a difference."

Nurse Joan handed Nanci a tissue from inside her coat pocket. "You are."

Nanci did not want any credit. Her teaching came naturally and from her heart, but she wanted to tell Nurse Joan one last thing. "You were hard on me. I was a bit spoiled when I came to you, and you correctly rode me. But most importantly, I wanted to earn your respect." Nanci blew her nose and then finished. "Nurse Joan you believed in me."

The young child cried out with frustration when he opened his blue box. "Oh, this is no good."

The two ladies looked down at the action figure the boy held. Mother Joan spoke. "What's the matter with the toy?"

The boy held it up for both to view. "It's The Flash. He can't be real." the defiant young boy replied. "If he could run so fast, he'd starve to death." The boy huffed heavily in frustration.

Nanci began to laugh before speaking to an embarrassed Nurse Joan. "It's okay. I guess we all took something from those kids back then."

Nurse Joan lightened. "More than you know, Nanci."

Nanci wiped her face clear of any moisture with the backside of the donated tissue. She knelt to have eye contact with the little boy. Nanci smiled. The boy smiled in return but looked up to his mother for approval.

"Yes, she is a friend of ours. Miss Nanci is a school teacher. I told her you will be going to school next year."

Nanci put her hand out to greet the little boy. "Hello, young man. My name is Miss Nanci. What's yours?" Nanci's head began to spin, because she knew what the boy's answer would be. Everything became crystal clear, and why not? *Those three months together, the children, the laughter, and the pain, will be a part of our lives forever.* Nanci was unsure whether to giggle or cry, so she did neither. *Nanci, we all took something from those kids. Yes, more than you know, Nanci ... more than you know.*

The boy took The Flash action figure from his right palm and placed it into his left. Displaying good manners, he smiled, putting forward his right hand to shake Miss Nanci's. "Hello ... my name is Donny."

Printed in the United States
By Bookmasters